BOMBING THE MOON

BOMBING THE MOON

A Novel

NANCY CHISLETT

| N₁ | O₂ | N₁
CANADA

Copyright © 2022 by Nancy Chislett

All rights reserved. No part of this book may be used or reproduced in any manner whatsoever without the prior written permission of the publisher, except in the case of brief quotations embodied in reviews.

Publisher's note: This book is a work of fiction. Names, characters, places and incidents are either the product of the author's imagination or are used fictitiously, and any resemblance to actual persons living or dead is entirely coincidental.

Library and Archives Canada Cataloguing in Publication

Title: Bombing the moon : a novel / Nancy Chislett.

Names: Chislett, Nancy, author.

Identifiers: Canadiana 20210366001 | ISBN 9781989689318 (softcover)

Classification: LCC PS8605.H586 B66 2022 | DDC C813/.6—dc23

Printed and bound in Canada on 100% recycled paper.

Now Or Never Publishing
901, 163 Street
Surrey, British Columbia
Canada V4A 9T8

nonpublishing.com
Fighting Words.

We gratefully acknowledge the support of the Canada Council for the Arts and the British Columbia Arts Council for our publishing program.

For dad

The shadow of a fat man in the moonlight
Precedes me on the road down which I go;
And should I turn and run, he would pursue me:
This is the man whom I must get to know.

—James Reeves, *Collected Poems, 1929–1974*

Chapter One

Devin

Gramps jams the gas pedal and we ramp to Departures. I'd like to ask if he's going somewhere, but safe to assume I don't get that lucky. A taxi breaks free of the line, leaving a gap between parked cars. He swings in and pops the curb. His Chevy Bel Air rocks. A heat haze smoulders off the hood and he kills the ignition. I feel him wearing the expression I know best—disapproval. As though he can't comprehend how such a life ends up on a man.

He gets out of the car, opens the back door and snatches a shopping bag from the seat, before strolling to the rotating doors. Then, he stares back, as if I'd missed something. International flags balloon overhead. I get out and we stand together, dwelling in an underworld of things unsaid. Finally, he takes a half-step closer and cuffs me on the shoulder.

"It's time, Devin," he says. "I had such hope for my first grandchild." He squints towards the sky for so long that I follow his gaze. "I thought your Dad was ready for children." His bloated nose sniffs the air and then drags in a lungful. "Did you know he used to smoke, your Dad? The day you were born he drove me to the hospital. On the way, he flicked his last-ever cigarette out the window. Said he wanted to be around to watch you grow up. Your Granny? You never got to meet her. Just as well. 'Cuz looky what's happened? You've turned into a gutless shit." His finger drills my forehead. "Twenty-four, and no job, no schooling, no respect for your parents. You want food and shelter, while you do *what*?"

"I wanna write music."

His chest puffs out, but he's not laughing. "You'll be piss-poor living on poetry."

He puts his hands on his hips, giving himself a six-foot wingspan. "As I remember it," he says, "you were given a choice—get back to school, get a job. Or move."

★

They tag-teamed me on the deck, Gramps and Dad. Defending the succession of Rush men.

Gramps said to Dad, "You can't pay the kid's meal ticket forever," and then passed him a sheet of paper. Dad looked ruined, like an old warehouse. Without perusing it, he then passed it to me.

Notice to Devin Rush
September 2015
Nearly six months ago, your father and I met with you to discuss your future. You were informed that you had to finish your high school credits and get a job. Since that time, you have done nothing to improve yourself, and you deserted your schoolwork. This, then, is written notification that things must change immediately.

We insist on a signed declaration from you concerning what you are prepared to do. You must decide and report to your father within one week on whether or not you will complete your high school credits or find a full-time job. If you need new clothes or transportation, we will pay all costs.

If you want to remain as you are, and decline to accept and abide by rule #1, then you must find a new place to live. If this is your choice, we will do everything possible to help you find a place and help you get settled.

The current situation cannot continue any longer. You are an adult and must choose one of the options below.

__ I will make the requested changes and will make a total effort toward school or finding a full-time job.
(sign)
__ I will not follow the above request and will look for another home.
(sign)
From Granddad

I didn't unleash a hit parade of swear words. Instead, I asked for a pen and drew out the moment, starring at the page like my answer shouldn't have been obvious. Then I signed my name.

Dad's stress vanished into relief. He might've even had a tear in his eye. He took the paper from me and shook my hand before looking down at what I'd written.

___ *I vow not to be pathetic like you. Devin Rush.*

*

A car alarm sounds. Gramps faces the hotel across from the airport. It gives me an idea for a song. Don't know if there's heaven or hell. But I'll bet they're both about twenty-six degrees. The only difference, the second one's got family.

"It's a betrayal," Gramps continues. "Of your parents. Of me. Of everything decent." His voice drops to a whisper. "The way you're going, you'll end up a slab on my table."

I'm thinking, You're not the Chief Forensic Pathologist in Manitoba anymore. Dad called him a stickler for quality. So what if he's carved up his share of runaways, gangsters, drug addicts? "You know what a kid with a bullet in his stomach looks like?" he once asked me.

"The world's teeming with spoiled brats with no work ethic," he continues. "No respect. No sense, period. Well, I'm on a mission. It's my job to see what needs done, gets done. And guess who's twenty-four now?" He points a knobby finger between my eyes. "Bingo." Gramps puts his hand on my shoulder. We're walking. "Time away will show you the real world. Where people hafta make something out of nothing, instead of having everything and doing nothing. Where they hafta fight to survive every goddamned day."

Passersby reroute their eyes. Their steps quicken.

I wish for once we could dispense with the obvious. The whole "hard work equals success" line is a stunt. Think we haven't heard the shock talk of the year, "downward mobility"? School counsellors said, "Expect to have up to seven jobs in your lifetime." More like 7-11 jobs.

"Here," Gramps says, and hands me the shopping bag. "It's everything a smart guy like you needs off the top."

Lines around Gramps's eyes deepen as he watches my wheels turning. The bag's light. I reach in, feel something and lift. A wad of cash—shillings? I flip through them. There's thousands. I'm confused, yet my heart leaps. I can't remember the last time he gave me anything.

He nods at the bag. "Keep goin'."

I pull out the passport Mom insisted I get last fall, even though we were just going shopping in Fargo. I reach in again and touch something soft. I pull out a roll of toilet paper. "One more thing," he says. "Your itinerary." He holds a crisp, white paper steady, cupping it from the sun's glare. It reads, "Winnipeg to Toronto. Toronto to Frankfurt. Frankfurt to Nairobi."

"What's this?"

He levels his eyes with mine for what must be the first time today. "It's Kenya, pop tart! A-fri-ca." He's whooping it up.

It's nothing but lyrics this afternoon. How about a song about a kidnapper and hostage? The hostage is torn. He loves his captor yet he'd love to get away. Too bad it doesn't matter. It's not like he has a choice about leaving.

"You could've got her killed," he says. I drop the plastic bag. "Didn't think I knew, did you?"

"If it's the party you're talking about, Lily wasn't gonna die."

"How do you know? Could you read the minds of those punks?" He hacks into his sleeve-Kleenex.

I pick up the bag and hope that's the end of it.

"Well," Gramps gestures toward the stream of people going inside. "Go on."

"You've had your stroke or whatever," I say. "Mom and Dad are waiting." Smug amusement spreads over his face. "You're supposed to take me home," I continue. "I haven't had dinner." His face is a bag of puffed wheat that I'd like to plow with a shovel. "What's your problem? It's not like you care about what I do."

"You're not gonna change, are ya?" His voice goes song-like. "Don't tell me you're scared?"

Of course he's the same as the other boomers, expecting millennials to live as though the world's been rigged in our favour. Automation. Environmental disasters. Wall Street. North Korea's nukes. Like I should have all these dreams. Like I can trust my life will be of my making. Scared? We've inherited an uninhabitable planet. Folks my age can imagine how the world ends. Honestly, it's like anyone over forty lives in a soundproof cage.

Gramps's jaw has gone soggy-teabag. Now I'm nervous. Is he weeping? People are gonna think I did something. My face splits into a yawn so wide you could stick in an apple. Gramps marches back to his car.

"Hey," I say, before having any idea what to say. "What about Mom?"

He pretend-searches as if she might be hiding in a bush. "You see her?" He pulls the driver's side door. It shrieks. "They're not gonna catch you this time."

The old man laughs.

"Don't think I'm not goin'," I say.

"Don't forget the toilet paper when you get the shits."

The door slams, and he drives off.

The airport's rotating doors send a cool draft into humidity. A young female voice announces a flight number to Vancouver. Another to Mexico.

I could let things cool off and then go home. Or I could refund the ticket and hang out at a friend's house. No. There's a reason Gramps did this. The family agrees. They think that they're better off without me. It's three generations of Rush family jeering me off the stage. Maybe they're right. Maybe the only way to control something is to throw it away.

If I go, it's like I'm following the old man's wishes. I can't do that.

But he doesn't expect me to go. Let's dispense with the obvious, he doesn't think I can do it. If I go home, I give him the satisfaction of being right.

Besides, how hard is it to go to, *where*? Right. I wanna be gone. It doesn't matter that it was Gramps' idea. This is a load of cash and I'm not a baby.

I've been passed over for the absence of me.

Or maybe I'm throwing them away.

Outrage carries me through to the back of the Air Canada line. Kids run around, and a father calls after them. New song idea. Lyrics re dinner table where strangers call themselves family.

The attendant at the counter has a sad smile, yet her voice gives my twist of courage a pull.

★

"Been to Nairobi before?" my neighbour asks. The overhead bins shake. "You're not gonna chunder, are ya?"

"I'm alright. Just a bit sick."

"You're a real battler. Tuck into these." I squint. My neighbour is thin, with hair like beige shag carpet and a jawline you could cut cheese on. He offers a bubble pack of Gravol and a barf bag. "By the time you get to your hotel, you'll be bliss." He looks more closely. "Unless I'm too late. If we're lucky, it'll come out of your mouth and not your clacker. Think good thoughts."

I lean back and remember the time I found my sister in my bedroom. Lily had my songbook in her lap and some of my vinyl collection lying in a semicircle around her. I didn't mind the invasion. Gut-wise, she was my twin.

I held out a mandarin orange I swiped from the kitchen.

"Want half?"

A smile bent her cheek.

I peeled the skin, and a mist sprung between us. Lily. The walking strawberry. She handed me my songbook.

I put on my headphones and shut my eyes. Meanwhile, the five-and-a-half-foot thief must've got busy. Then, she cut the volume to my headphones.

I opened my eyes. She'd crawled on the bed and had her face almost pressed against mine. A gangsta scowl twisted her chin. She backed up off the bed and pulled back into an arms-crossed, heavy-on-one-hip, rapper pose, and started bobbing and wagging a finger. "Aaand, don't ya be pinchin my cred. O, I'ma be bustin's yo head." Then a slew of karate chops. "Ninja style."

She collapsed on the floor laughing.

With his usual MO, Gramps saw an open door to a private space and walked in. He scanned my domain, scowled at my Bernie Sanders poster and shuddered at the sight of Slick the rat. It was like he'd slipped into a shaman's trance, and foresaw hell and the special circus cooked up for me. No wonder he was terrified for Lily. Under my influence, Lily's corruption would soon be complete.

"You're not alright," my neighbour says. "Can I do something? Maybe fetch your carry-on while the stewardess is busy."

"No thanks."

"No worries, mate. I'm bored shitless." He pops his seatbelt and gets up. The compartment clicks open. "Which one's yours?"

"I don't have one."

He glances down at the plastic bag at my feet. "A no-fuss kind of guy." He drops into his seat with his backpack.

"Where'ya staying at?"

"The Mercury. By the train station."

His lips form a silent O.

"What? I saw it online at the Toronto airport."

"Just," he says, "I'm hopeful you won't be robbed before dinner, that's all. Up and out and suddenly ya can't pay. Some bastard's got your wallet." His seatbelt snaps together. "Welcome to Nairobi."

TV screens lining the cabin show our plane on top of my destination. A voice talks of descent. I finger-comb my hair. It's dank at the roots. The stewardess gives me water. I retch. Nothing comes out, yet my neighbour has bounced into the aisle.

"No offence," he says, "I don't wanna wear your brekkie."

I hold the barf bag open a crack with my thumb. The plane soars over the tarmac. I press my forehead against the seat ahead as my guts threaten to explode from the north and the south.

"Listen. You seem like an okay bloke, right? So you'll taxi with me, yeah? And we'll forget your hotel and head to River Road."

"Sounds like you know your way around."

"I know Nairobi, if that's what you're wondering. I'm Paul by the way."

Gears bounce on the tarmac. I burp-retch as the cabin tosses us in our seats. Then we settle in for the glide. When the plane stops, buckles pop. Passengers cram the aisle. The cabin begins to smell like diesel. I start the journey's only soothing part: following the passenger stream out of the plane, down the stairs to the shuttle and through sliding doors to immigration.

"What's this?" I ask.

"Hell's half-acre."

People—enough to pack a theatre. The line to the immigration officials is a bloated, dead snake.

Paul returns from a side table handing something to me. Declaration. Words and lines and boxes. I can't catch the meaning of any of it.

"Bend over," he says.

I must've given him a queer look.

"So I can write on your back," he explains. He shoulders off his pack as I stoop. I'm facing a baby, blowing spit bubbles, in one of those harnesses strapped on a man's chest.

"Here," Paul says. "Take mine and do one of your own." With his paper beside mine, I can fill it out.

The line shuffles ahead every few minutes. There's a girl with short, dark hair and a clingy purple dress. Her guy has a beard and a bag slung across his waist. They speak French. I overhear another guy say, "Canada." He's with some girls from the States who are here to do volunteer work.

When we get to the immigration desk, I push my passport under the partition to a woman of tight braids and short sentences. She says, "Visa."

My head torques toward Paul.

"No worries," he says. "You can buy it here."

After fingerprints on an electric doohickey and handing over shillings, we are free to scram to the toilet. I get some relief, but the sour feeling in my gut remains. Paul grins as I meet him at the baggage turnstile. He retrieves a massive backpack with wheels, and I scan for the exit. He catches my shoulder. "You don't have luggage, at all?" He looks down at my Dollarama bag again and a new look crosses his face, as if he's seen something from faraway and wants to zoom in.

"Tell me you have money."

I nod. He slaps my back. "Here," he foists his carry-on into my arms. "Take that for me, wont'cha mate?"

We approach the exit: a set of sliding doors skimming the surface of another world. It should be exciting. But it's too unreal to be adventurous. Too foreign to be fun. I can't stop thinking about the black globe in Dad's den. If I were to put my thumb on Winnipeg and my index finger on Nairobi, how many time zones would there be in between? It doesn't matter. I might as well be in space.

The doors glide open and I brace for trouble with hyper-fine-tuned senses. Funny how particulars spike when you're treading new turf. Cab drivers slouch in taxis, black as quartz. Twenty-something degrees. A breeze, so light.

The line up to the cabs is quiet, except for a few young people, all high-pitched giggles and romance. Soon a taxi toggles up, and someone opens the door for us. Inside, Paul slaps my knee. "Made it," he says. My heart explodes with gratitude for cabs and windows and Aussies. "About thirty minutes 'til you're home sweet home."

A dozen hallelujahs later, and our cab stops at a toll booth. Paul gets out, and the cabdriver says, "You to be going in dere." He points at a small building on the side of the road. Inside, it's airport security all over again. A uniform signals the French couple to put their bag on rollers leading through a scanner. I put my plastic bag down. The man demands my documents. I hand my passport over wondering if I'll see it again. "Proceed," is all the uniform says, and I find the exit at the opposite end. Our cab rides up to meet us.

Paul says, "Poorly policed areas are the most reassuring."

I hear Paul tell the driver to head toward the CBD. "Central Business District," he explains to me. The sign says we're driving Mombasa Road. Paul chats, but I'm too exhausted to listen.

Instead, I watch electrical wires rise and fall between poles. Two odd-looking white birds with black wings sit at the top of a large tree. Their nests are prehistoric-sized conglomerates of sticks and plastic. I catch sight of another one landing. Its big wings flap, and its long legs reach for a branch. Its tube-like beak points down.

"Storks," Paul says. "They eat carrion. You know, dead animals on the road." I watch the storks and wonder who's inspecting whom.

As we near skyscrapers, traffic slows until it clogs, yet no one honks. Between cars, motorbikes weave through traffic, some with women and children on the back. One rider has a goat lying across his lap while he talks on a cell.

"*Boda bodas*," Paul calls the bikes.

Exhaust fumes rise and images blur. There aren't enough windows in the car to open. The cabbie's radio crackles. A raspy voice, in English, announces that a lion has been spotted on a highway. Our cabbie tells the voice about a vehicle pile-up at such-and-such roundabout. Then the conversation switches to plans for the weekend. Food. Music. And family.

We arrive at a small hotel. It fits in with the rundown businesses beside it. Paul pays the cabbie, and talks about how I owe him a drink. People are everywhere. Even the middle of the street is a stream of people between two lanes. Van after van, blaring techno music, they honk in repetitive bursts. On the back flap of one reads, "*marat tormenta*," and on another, "kill me plz."

The air is thick with the unknown. Still, the brain picks up details. Not everyone is African. Some are Indian. Two Muslim women pass, their clothes flowing curtains of black. There are Chinese business signs, but no Chinese people to be seen. And no other whites. As soon as the cabbie drives off, I feel exposed, seeing myself as these people must see me. White. Rich compared to them. Only I'm not rich. It's all been peeled back. I'm a baby in this world.

We check in. I give the ham-fisted man behind the desk my address and passport number. "How many nights?" he asks. I take the wad of bills out of the plastic bag and gaze at the currency, having no idea what it means. "How about two?" He takes the wad out of my hand, wets his finger and leafs through it, taking what's his. I get the wad back along with a key. "Your room is at the top. Three, zero, one."

Paul and I mount the stairs. He pauses at the second floor where his room must be.

"Oi," he says. "Can't be two nights. How long are you really stayin'?"

"Don't know."

"Well, guess we'll get that drink later."

I put one foot in front of the other until I break out into a jog up the steps. I reach the door. It's a tiny room. Single bed and window. I'm greeted by cigar stench, grey water-stained paint, and a sinking feeling. The mechanics in my throat leap. I have three seconds to empty the Dollarama bag on the bed and then hurl. I hear myself—the brutal yodelling. Another refrain later, I shut my eyes, but the stench of vomit is too vicious to ignore. There's no garbage bin. Or closet. I'm in no mood to go back downstairs, so I tie a knot in the bag and open the window.

Below, the crowd boils. How many floors would a hotel need to be to escape the racket? The people keep coming. Clustering on street corners. Walking over crumbling curbs. Hustling. The grind. The effort. A world that doesn't know me, and would go on just as well without.

River Road. It looks like a wrong turn could be someone's last. And this is probably just the tip of the cahoonah. I bet there's another horde on the next street. Then another. And another. A whole other planet. Everything's got to be learned from zero.

Along the sidewalk a man pisses into a grove of trees. Near my window frame, jutting out from the brick wall, there's a nail. I hang my vomit bag there and shut the window.

COLE

I first saw Julia in a little bar in the Italian district. Her right wrist was bandaged, and she was trying to pull on a sweater with the other hand. When her head finally popped through the neck hole, her raven hair was a static halo. One of her friends jeered, saying, "A person willing to break her wrist to save tomatoes deserves one hand." Out came the story. Julia fell, and with fanatical devotion, blocked her fall to avoid smashing stems. I stood behind her just before she said to the barman, "Who do I have to sleep with to get a margarita?"

Julia was ballerina-esque. But what I was drawn to was what felt like a racy, yet tamable mix. When her margarita landed, she licked salt from the rim and asked what I did for a living. I told her I worked in the university's admissions department. I wouldn't have gone into detail, but then she said with a purr, "When you were a kid, did you always dream of becoming an admissions—what did you call it?"

I might not have been hooked, if it weren't for the way her irises waned whenever I used "me" as the first word in a sentence. Me and this person. Me and that person. At which time a sliding door of judgment would pass behind her eyes. It told me she was discerning. Lust was instant. The kickoff to a ping-ponging one-upmanship that keeps me charged. She, on the other hand, hasn't been charged since the spring of last year. For example, Thelonious Monk is on the stereo, and she hasn't complained once, although subtle spasms suggest the brink of derangement. Chess? The last time we played was eighty-two days ago. The board, placed on the coffee table, is still open, my rook forever ready to nail her queen.

A cooling-off of our marriage, one could call it. It's a pity and a basis for genuine distress. I come home, and everything seems normal, that is, until I touch her, which sets off a frenzy of avoidance: cooking, gardening, all of which benefits me, except in the way I hunger for most.

She blames me for the communication breakdown with Devin and has furled herself into a thorny prophylactic of indifference. Whatever ideas hatched and unchecked lay inside her head, I don't know. She's brewing, even now, as she luxuriates in the nesting chair, legs sheltered in silk, with a glass of Cabernet held against her cheek, where the muscles at her jaw ripple like embers of birch.

There are three steady knocks at the door, and then Dad calls out, "Hal-lo! Anybody home?" Julia, so apropos, rolls her eyes. I can't let it bother me. Dad took Devin out for a talk. Now they're back. The family will work itself out. And I will get Julia back on that chessboard.

"Meets his father at the door," Dad says. "See what a little training will do?"

I slide Dad's windbreaker on a hanger, and he gives me his customary pat on the shoulder. Admittedly, it's one of the few things to feel good about, this love between father and son, something I haven't been able to teach Devin: that kindness is suspended upon reciprocity.

"Don't look so glad to see me," he says.

"I trust everything went well today?" I say.

"Twenty-eight in the shade, but you know, as you age, you get colder? But let's not think about it. By any account a beautiful day."

"Julia's in the living room."

He leaves a clot of leaves on the mat and totters forward. It's the beginning of that forward curl that hooks elderly bodies. His head hangs, and his chin juts out, like he's blind and given to sniffing his way around. Which is not to say that his competence has lessened. He's still got guts and vision, and that's what I've tried to learn from him by heart. Because some people are more than the skin they inhabit. Some are what they symbolize. What they contribute. What they overcome. Tissue and bone with a meaning. A source against which others are defined.

"Ah!" Dad says, reaching the living room. "There she is."

"Bill."

"Nobody get up on *my* account. Just kidding, Julia. Relax. The recliner is available. Don't mind if I do. Wha-do-yah-say, Julia? Time to stretch the ol' legs? Ahhh."

Julia's eyes flicker with belligerence. "Bill," she says.

"Yes, dear?"

"Where's Devin?"

Dad pushes the recliner into a coffin-like position.

"Isn't this something?" he says, ignoring her. "Home safe and sound. With you two. What a treat. Just in time too before the sun goes down. I hate driving in the dark." He cranes toward the window. "Is that rain?"

Julia's head tacks towards him like a mechanized assault weapon. "I'm sorry," she says. "Did I not just pose a perfectly clear—"

"I hate to interrupt, Julia, but is it possible to have some tea? Some of that citrus stuff you serve at Christmas? I don't have those nice things at home. Please. For an old man. That would be... Oh, thank you. That's a good girl." Beyond the reach of Dad's sightline, Julia waves a balled fist.

I've got two thoughts about what's coming next. One: I'm hoping beyond hope Julia doesn't make a scene. Even now, she's staring at me as the kettle boils. Doesn't she understand I'm stuck piloting this mess from the middle? That this man is my father? The one who was there when the columns were carved? Two: That's about right. Her hostility toward him is a passive act of treason against me. One jab kills two men. Could she be more pragmatic? It's such a scant territory of imagination she treads. Like a snatch of classical music that doesn't change key. God. Listen to me. Pull back, Cole. See? She's making Dad tea. She's beautiful. You're just sleep-deprived.

Dad slaps the side of the recliner. "Wood frame?"

I nod.

"Not that cardboard foolishness people buy now." He glances toward the kitchen. "Hey, son. Have a seat. You're making me nervous. Never mind the kitchen. Julia's fine. Tell me, have you been to Ikea?"

"Can't say that I have, Dad."

"Can't beat the meatball special on Tuesdays. But don't go into the back part. I'm tellin' ya. Not unless you like swearing in circles."

"You're pretty fit," I say. "For an old guy."

"Heh, heh. You'd better be smiling."

"You're one of the strongest men I know."

Out of the corner of my eye I see Julia spit in the garbage.

"I still remember the time you helped move the old furniture into the cottage after Julia's dad died. You practically unloaded the rental by yourself. All I had to do was push things in place."

"Yup. 'Strong like a bull,' heh heh. That's growing up on a farm, right there. Always lots to do and not enough people to do it. Not enough money to go around neither. Makes you appreciate an opportunity to make things nice for your family. Ah, but we age, son. Blood pressure. Cholesterol."

Julia arrives with a tray. "Here's your tea."

"Ah. Thank you, dear. It warms up my chest."

"And here's some of those mixed nuts you like." Julia smiles sweetly.

"Oh boy. You can bring me these every time. Yes, yes, yes. I like this restaurant. Good service. Heh. Heh."

"And a couple of Kleenex should you need to blow your nose."

A flash of suspicion enters Dad's eyes, but quickly evaporates. "We're lucky," he says. "Lots of folks out there don't have this kind of comfort. They're fighting, thieving, begging, fleeing, starving and drowning right now. And we don't have to listen. What a world. No stop, drop and roll for your kids. Just what flavour of ice cream." He takes a long sip of tea. "That's some nice music, Julia. What program do you have on?"

"Bill," she says. "I think it's time we talked about your afternoon. I'm wondering if you and Devin had a nice time together?"

"Sure. Took him for lunch and a walk. Talked about the old days on the farm."

Julia touches her throat. "Oh, no."

"Oh, *yes*. Devin's just the kid to hear those stories. Acute poverty is what it's called. Inspires people to work. Make money washing the neighbour's clothes if necessary."

"We know, Dad," I say. "Mom washed the neighbour's clothes because your Dad left. We've heard it many times."

"Okay, smart guy. But do you understand it yet? Can you just imagine what it must have been like? Collecting bottles outta the ditch and choking on apple cores? Of course not. And that's just what your mother and I intended—for you to never know that kind of existence. People today don't appreciate what they have because they don't know what it's like to suffer for it. And the old, invisible ones like me have to watch you screw up your kids with iPhones, video games, takeout, when all they do is complain about being bored. Then there's the tedious negotiations about what time they'll go to bed or if they'll mow the grass. How about, 'we're not asking how you feel, sonny. Do it because we said so?' How else will they grow into functioning humans? Or be happy? Honestly. Life's harder now 'cuz it's too easy."

Somewhere in the middle of Dad's ramblings, Julia stood up.

"Bill." Her voice is harp-strung. "Where's my son?" A canonnball could've been shot over Hudson Bay by the time Dad responds.

"I gave him a free trip." Julia's face is a slipknot. "Something had to be done," he says. "The kid's lost."

"What?" Julia asks. "Where?"

"I'm an old man, Julia. Please. One question at a time."

I know Julia. She'll want to contact the Emergency Broadcast System, have them send out a red-felt message and get our son home. But there's no Amber Alert for the skies.

"Dad," I say, "before we get too upset. Is our son on a plane somewhere right now?"

"I believe the plane took off forty minutes ago."

Julia's eyes clamp and burst back open. "How," she says, "in that warped brain of yours, did you go from 'rebuild your relationship with Devin' to sending him away?"

"Julia, let's get the facts," I say.

Julia whisks herself back to the nesting chair and sinks. The kid is on a plane, not plummeting into a lava pit. Could we not say, for argument's sake, that he's an adult, and as such, could make some decisions? But I get it. It's exhausting, her relationship with Dad. For the sake of family, she's maintained a bitter alliance.

"Julia's understandably upset," I say. Julia scoffs. "But surely you see you've overstepped here. At least we know Devin's safe," I say to Julia. "It's better than when he disappears for days, and we've got no clue where."

"I sent him to Africa," Dad says. "One way."

Please. Oh, if ever I needed you to give me a lifeline, Dad, it's now. Say anything, but don't accelerate Julia's wrath one more notch.

Dad begins to chuckle.

"What are you laughing at?" Julia screams.

He pulls out his handkerchief. Tears fall from his eyes. "You two should see your traps hangin'," he says. "You know, this is it. Right here. Where the road of infancy leads smack into maturity. It's all you can do to hang on. Your son is going to grow up now, Julia. Isn't that what you want? For him to become the man he needs to be? Because I assure you, he's gonna have to. That country is no Margaritaville. He's about to swim or sink."

Light on her feet when she wants to be, Julia crosses the carpet like a rogue rocket and strikes Dad's face. "You're going to tell me everything I need to know," she says, "and you're gonna stop playing cute. And then you're gonna get the hell out of here."

"Julia!" I shout.

She turns on me. "He doesn't know what it means to be a child. He doesn't understand people. He worked with corpses for Christ's sake!"

Dad has a hand on his cheek. He's perplexed, I assume, not at Julia's violence, but about what happened to the days when the head of the household peed standing up.

"Let's calm down. Dad. What is it? An exchange program?"

"No, son. There's no program. No momma. No cheat sheet."

"Cole," Julia says in a sedate tone. "Your Dad just sent our son, alone, to a shithole country."

"Julia, my dear." Dad's voice shakes. "Stop crying. Please." Dad wipes his eyes, as he tends to tear up when others cry. "Not all of Africa is a 'shithole,' as you call it. That's racist. Where I've sent him is like that, true, but you shouldn't think all of it is."

Julia sobs.

"Dad. I think you can understand that we're eager to track Devin down. And you're gonna hafta go soon, right? And I'll talk to you later, okay? But listen, this won't stick. Okay? That's my message to you. So, please, give me a copy of his itinerary."

"I gave it to Devin. He's an adult. Why-oh-why would I have a copy?"

The faintest creak off the basement steps.

"Mom?"

Three heads turn at once to a riot of auburn curls. Lily wanders in and stops at Dad's chair. "What's goin' on?"

"Uh, hey, Lily," I say. "I didn't hear you come upstairs."

"I'm hungry."

"Why don't you go in the kitchen and make us some of those buns? You know those things Mom puts on a cookie sheet? Put it in the oven at... 450 for ten minutes? Make your own toppings if you like. Surprise your Gramps with something creative."

"Okay," Lily says. She takes a few steps toward the kitchen and stops. "Where's Devin?"

"He's gone, honey," I say. "And this time we're not sure where yet."

"But you're never sure where," Lily says.

"It's not like when he normally disappears. This time might be different."

"Is he in prison?" she asks.

"No," I say. "He may have gone somewhere else." Julia and I exchange looks. "We're not sure. That's why Mom, everyone, is a little upset. So, if you could help…"

"Why would he do that?"

Dad shifts.

"Well?" Julia says to me.

"We don't know everything," I say. "Devin didn't tell us."

"But how do you know…"

"Your parents," Dad cuts in, "have as many unanswered questions as you do. Now, if you would go into the kitchen and do as your Dad asked…"

Lily stares off in contemplation. "He left without saying anything to anyone?" she asks. Dad clucks his teeth. "He didn't leave anything for me?" Her expression is a puzzle missing a piece at the centre. She tears up, and then fixes herself. "That sounds about right." She saunters out of the room.

The door to the kitchen swings shut. There's a sliding of pans. Through the bullhorn Julia's made with her hands, she stage-whispers, "I've got to leave. Or I'm gonna die. You, old man, have lost your mind."

Dad says. "I'm sorry you feel that way."

"Here's the thing. You don't get to pull this off. I'm gonna find Devin, and I don't care if I've got to fly to... Oh my God. Where exactly is Devin going?"

"Nairobi."

She lurches at Dad.

This time my arm instinctively blocks her.

"What in the hell were you thinking?"

She shoves me once more, and we freeze, afraid the noise could coax Lily back.

Julia exits. The air conditioner kicks in and blows away her perfume. Dad looks at me like I've only just been shown life and the vastness of work involved.

"Dad, I don't know what to say."

"Julia's said plenty."

"All we've got is a city. Does he at least have a hotel we can reach him at?"

"The last thing in the world he needs is for you lot to reach him."

"She's furious."

"You know, you two could get unlucky, and he didn't get on that plane. Maybe he walked out of the airport and caught a cab. Maybe he's doing what he always does—nothing specific."

"Let's hope for that," I say. Dad tosses his hands in the air. "You're right. He's at a friend's house doing God-knows-what, but at least he's here. God, Dad. You're gonna explode my marriage. Can't you see what you're doing?"

"You know what, son?" says Dad. "I did what had to be done. Period. If my kids don't hate me once in a while, I'm not doing my job."

Chapter Two

Julia

As soon as Bill left, I called Devin. "Come home," I said to his answering machine. "We'll explain." The minutes chugged by. I called again. "You don't have to do this. We'll fix it." An hour later, "I know you're mad, but this is ridiculous." At four AM, I called again. The automated voice said Devin couldn't be left any more messages. Then I remembered when Bill and Devin left the house together. Devin was giving me his 'please, no mom' eyes and Bill thought he was being funny and I screamed something about them mending their relationship and "Just go! GAWD!" Bill pulled Devin out the door, saying, "See Julia? We're leaving. Bye. Bye-bye." I threw off my duvet and went downstairs where, in the gloom, I found Devin's cell.

Cole was up because of his restless legs syndrome, rubbing his jumpy calves. Using his laptop, I searched contact information for the Canadian High Commission in Nairobi. "I'm calling from Canada... I'm panicked," I said. "Let me apologize in advance. I don't even know how to tell you what's happened."

I stumbled through the set of facts. How I knew he was flying to Nairobi. How I came to the notion that Devin might be in danger. How it could be that, at twenty-four, I still considered him a boy.

"He'll arrive at Jomo Kenyatta International," she said. "I understand that you are concerned. However, even if I could identify your son, it is unlawful to report the whereabouts of individuals." Devin was not missing in the way authorities understand that word. As for tracking him, any information they found out would be private. When she asked, "Would it make you feel better if I take your contact information?" I knew I'd taken enough of her time.

I rang the police. "I need to report a missing person," I said. A battery of questions ensued.

"I didn't catch that," the sergeant said. "So, what you're telling me is, Devin Rush had a ticket to Africa—and he went?" I heard liquid pouring and a spoon clicking the side of a cup.

"It was a mistake," I said. The sergeant put me on hold.

"I told you," Cole said. "No one buys that Devin's in danger. There are risks when anyone travels. It's no time to send the army."

"The sergeant's talking to his supervisor, probably. Then we'll get somewhere." I heard a click, and then the sergeant said, "Sorry, I needed to change phones."

"What if he didn't go?" I said.

"Didn't go? Why did he get a ticket for a trip if he wasn't going to go?"

My brain ached. The story kept caving in on itself. I apologized and hung up.

"Get some rest," Cole said. His eyelids hovered over bloodshot eyes. "Devin's gonna have to figure it out."

"What if he doesn't?"

"If he's scared, he'll come home. Then maybe we could talk some sense into him."

I rifled through the nightstand drawer and found notepaper. I scribbled down all the things I'd do come morning. Names unspooled down the page after the word "Call," along with the few places I could think of that were connected to Devin. I wrote down where I planned to search: Devin's room, the basement and his phone, if Lily knew the password. "I want an accounting," I said. "You can check each of these off as you do them. That way we know where we are."

"This isn't going to change anything!" He cupped his mouth. Lily. She could have heard through the sunken insulation. We listened. The house creaked.

I turned my attention back to my list. Something told me to remember the events of the day. What happened before Bill and Devin left? How was Devin dressed? I closed my eyes and put myself in the past.

The next time I saw Cole, there was a bluish glow around the curve of the earth.

"Are you alive?" he asked.

"No."

"I'll let you sleep then."

His steps faded down the hall. I yearned for something explosive to happen. I wanted a fight. Then, almost inaudibly, from Cole's den, I heard Chopin's Concerto no. 1. I slammed my eyes shut. The next thing I remember was having a nightmare. I saw Devin, in his runners, walking over a desert. Swirls of sand weaved by his feet. His backpack fell from his shoulder, but his runners kept plodding, leaving the bag behind. The water bottle strapped in an outer pocket was empty. Beside the bag an awful insect with a black armoured shell crawled out of a hole.

Devin's face was dirty except around the eye sockets. He came across a village. African women with babies sat outside huts. He walked toward a teenaged mother and her suckling baby. Her eyes turned hopeful. The young mother held the infant up. Devin took the baby, and then walked away with the baby's feet grasped in his right hand. The baby was upside down. The child wailed. The mother screamed. She gathered her skirt and ran with it in her hands.

I woke to groaning and Cole shaking me, and I blathered on about "my baby is dead." He patted my forehead, and when my crying didn't stop, he got half into bed and put his arm under my neck. "That hurts," I said. Then, he lay beside me stroking my face. I can't explain what happened next. When I still didn't stop crying, he lay on top of me, with his forehead resting on my pillow. I thought about him crushing me. It felt wonderful.

When my breathing returned to normal, Cole rolled off me, and I turned to the alarm clock and let him watch me wait for my son. I had no intention of staring at time for eternity. Though later, I'd buy two more clocks, the ones with metal earmuffs that jangle, and put one on the dining room table and the other in the bathroom.

Worry had hatched a ball of rage. It spurred me into Devin's room, in case there were clues. What can posters of sweaty musicians tell me? Bernie Sanders, what's your take? Devin's clothes. I stuffed my nose in a ball of them and craved more mess. I lifted Slick's cage to the bed. I poured pellets in his dish and replenished his water. Then I cried over the thought that a rat and I would miss the same person.

I found Devin's earphones and tried to click on his stereo. His music didn't play. The live earphones had an empty buzz that muted the world. We'd yelled about Devin wearing these things. I should've seen the appeal.

I found a shoebox in his closet. It contained old class pictures of boys and girls with their thin, alien-like arms dangling. Old crayons. Mother's Day cards. Devin drew me in pink. My body is a triangle with two catcher's mitts for hands. My shoes, probably supposed to be heels, look like golfer shoes with spikes stuck in the grass. Lily is a botched cradle. The lines have been drawn over in swirls of frustration. Cole is blue. He's twice as tall as me and wears a balloon for a head.

I found Lily's homemade valentines. Red hearts with messages like, "To my bro, Devin. Much love, Lily." And "Dear Dee, what'cha doing tonight?" And "Devin. This valentine is lonely."

I heard Cole breathing in the hall and realized I was sitting in Devin's closet. An indescribable feeling swelled. Full sentences were a luxury. "Out!" I yelled.

A nothing breeze twisted a few leaves; their shadows appeared on the carpet like spinning toys on an infant's mobile. I dipped a hand in a drawer and touched Devin's notebook. He never let me see his work. I laid it open in my lap. There were poems and lyrics to songs with some words and phrases crossed out, underlined or erased. There were enough songs to make an album. I swore to read them, dole them out to myself, slowly over time.

Lily's bedroom door was shut. In the bathroom, I heard suctioning feet on tile. A hole opened inside me with the questions Lily would have. I thought long and hard about that. I'd been thinking Cole and Gramps did this great injury to me. Explaining it to Lily, it won't seem that way. I left Devin's bedroom, descended, and stepped off the stairs. Lily and Cole were in the kitchen. They were unusually quiet.

"Lily's looking for something to eat," Cole said. He stood at the sink with a cup tipped toward his lips. I saw in the window's reflection that my hair was a bird's nest.

"What do you want?" I asked her.

"To sleep forever."

"How 'bout eggs?"

Cole ruffled Lily's hair. He peered inside the fridge, handed me the egg carton, and a message passed between us that seemed to say, we're on the same side.

"So Dee's really gone?" Lily asked. My hot eyes dared Cole to speak.

"He'll probably come home when he's ready," Cole said to her. "Right, dear?" I ignored the attempt at tacit understanding. His eyes fell to Lily. "Are you okay?" he asked her.

I thought I saw her chin quiver, and she said, "He listens to anti-folk. Maybe he's anti-me."

Two yolks bubbled in my pan. I scraped them onto Lily's plate and said, "Where did I go wrong?" But Lily had slid back into thought.

I began to see how things might have happened. I say things, and people do what they want anyway. Personal campaigns and managing rifts was what passed for conversation. We were passengers on a Siberian train rounding the curves of a snow-packed mountain. We were coming off the tracks, headed toward a rock shelf. It glistened with ice. Part invitation. Part promise. I thought I heard the brake's high-pitched squeal.

A plate rattled near the sink. "I'm done," Lily said.

I waved my hand towel. Lily left, and then finally, the wonky machinery of silence whirred around Cole and I.

"How does life look to you?" I asked. Cole sighed. "'Cuz here's what I see. A missing child and…" my voice trailed off before adding, "a Cole."

"I'm worried, okay?" he said. "Just not like you."

"You say Devin's a child. You complain he can't do anything. Then you say he'll manage in a foreign country. Which is it?"

"You know, parents are supposed to provide a scaffold." His hands lifted as if I didn't know what scaffold meant. "We support them to go higher."

Cole takes a perverse delight in telling me what I already know. "Enough with that," I said. "Tell it to the police when Devin's dead."

I saw Devin, alone and unwanted. I ached. I wanted to sit with him. Better yet, I wanted to be inside his skin. Surely he was afraid. He had to be. I needed to feel what he was feeling and see for myself the layout of a country where he didn't belong. Send comforting thoughts when he saw how alone and small he was. And how things are hardly ever what they appear to be. Even the most well-meaning, semi-intelligent person can bring you down, because you don't know who you are until it's too late.

Devin didn't know about money or security or what people are capable of. I wished I could be there when confusion kicked in. When the culture didn't respond the way he hoped. To fend off the disorientation that comes when you see yourself outside your bubble, and you have that long, harsh look at yourself and find that you're not special, just one among billions of beating hearts. I wanted to shield him from strangers who'd like to hurt him. Or at least walk beside him whispering when someone approaches. You can trust this. Or, don't make eye contact. Or, keep walking away from this one. Or, there's a pay phone. Call your mother.

He was gonna learn how cold the world can be, and how the sun keeps getting up and the music keeps playing. Or he was gonna wind up dead in a ditch somewhere.

The grandfather clock bonged eight times. Cole stood in the doorframe of the garage. He was looking up, and I sensed he could use a wave or a smile. After I gave neither, he came in and descended to the basement.

I knew almost nothing about Kenya. I couldn't have drawn it on a map. African images I had were dominated by the 1980s, when cameras focused on Ethiopia. I watched those African children with their swollen tummies and gummed up eyes.

I cradled my cup and thought I could track Devin myself. But going to Nairobi was far-fetched. I saw myself spying in music shops and hiring a detective. Cole stopped at the mouth of the living room and lit into a string of concerns. Was I okay? Hungry? Did I need a walk? I didn't understand why it wasn't obvious what I needed.

"I'm flying to Nairobi," I said.

"No, you're not."

"I'm looking for our son, which you should be doing too."

"There's as many people in Nairobi as there are in Mongolia. Are you gonna find him in all that?" He squinted like I was at the far edge of a pier.

He left the room and returned with a myriad of multivitamins. He took a handful for himself and dropped another pile on the couch, near my head. "Betty Ford Clinic," I said. From the opposite end of the couch, he pinched my toes. "I haven't had an aneurysm." Cole reviewed his points, but I couldn't hear it without my temperature rising. "I'm gonna lose it if you don't stop."

"What do you want me to say?" he said. "You're all lizard brain."

I stormed upstairs. Ran the shower and, in the mirror, saw a lit fuse of a neck.

Devin

I hear muffled laughter through the wall. A dream dissolves in a puff of smoke. I roll over, willing myself back to fix it.

I'd dreamt I was in the woods behind the cottage. In the way dreams make no sense, I was terrified, even though there was no threat. Shafts of moonlight silvered tree branches. I walked toward the back road. Twigs snapped. I crouched behind a shelf of rock. Loons called back and forth. The scene seemed still, so I walked back toward the cottage, careful not to make noise. It's when I saw him. On the ground, brightened by the full moon, fat legs kicking. A baby. He started to cry, and the sound was horrible. I thought, What kind of psychopath leaves a baby like this? Into the darkness, I said, "Hello?" I repeated it, careful not to yell, since the night has ears. The baby went on screaming. Tears dripped sideways, the face tight and pink. From across the lake, the moon put down a yellow highway, and I thought of all the predators the baby would attract.

Wolves.

I didn't know what to do. I couldn't just take him, could I? It's trouble either way.

One of the windows in the neighbour's cottage went on and shadows appeared. It dawned on me that they'd think it was me who'd put the baby there because I'm thoughtless and sad and bored and just airheaded enough to think that would be funny. So I booked it back to the house. Inside, I was panting. Mom tapped my shoulder. She asked, "What have you done?"

That's when I woke up, thinking, Pick up the baby.

A door shuts. Men yap in another language. I cover my head. It all comes back like a river running backwards. My neighbour on the plane, me carrying the Dollarama bag. Why didn't I ditch the shit tickets and put the rest in my pocket? Street noises riff below. I look outside. Glowing street lamps filter through the grit of night. Batches of black guys float by in leather loafers. Underneath the groan of traffic, I recognize a dull pulse. American Top 40.

The wind's strong, as if it's grown as it passed over deserts and oceans to get here. Across the street, rubber tree leaves sway over a pot like cobra heads. I find my clothes hanging on the back of a chair. I flick on the light in the bathroom. I blink beneath a fluorescent bulb and my watch reads 10:15 PM. I'd been asleep for ten hours. Green veins at my inner elbows give me an alien tone. My stomach howls, and I think of Mom. Up mornings before everyone else, even weekends, making bacon and pancakes. I see the bottle of syrup and the goo drizzling around a high stack, but I won't let myself miss it. Besides, we never had the togetherness that goes with pancakes. The whole orange juice commercial, cheerful family veneer, didn't work for us. Not for me, the thumb that threatened to pop their bubble wrap.

Dozens of vans are parked quietly in rows. Roofs on storefronts look like garage doors made of bars that roll down. The street is less intimidating without the day mobs. Maybe if I break Gramps's cash into piles I'll feel braver. I hide a few hundred shillings under the mattress. Hide another few hundred behind a picture. And the last couple thousand in the bathroom drawer. I'll keep another thousand on me 'cuz who knows what this currency's worth?

There are pickpockets, though. Paul said so. As I pull on my jeans, I remember that tiny square pocket, the one no one knows what it's for. I fold notes over and over, until I have a stamp-sized cash accordion and jam it in. Feeling prepared, I pull on my t-shirt and hoodie and go downstairs for a look.

The deskman hands me a card with the hotel name and address, and I watch outside as people pass. Crowds begin thickening until everyone's out. Dressed in collared shirts and fine dresses. I walk into the street and use the Top 40 to guide me. It comes from across the street, about three blocks down.

River Road is a party street. There are kiosks of candy and pubs. Suckers bulge the cheeks of guys dressed like the magazine covers of *GQ*. When they have something to say, the suckers are removed, waved around and slipped back in. At the pubs, customers talk to the bartender, while a DJ shouts into a microphone.

A black guy steps into my path. "You no want to go dere, boss," he says. "Too local." He walks with me to the next corner and points at a place with white faces. "Here be more suitable."

I test a smile and keep walking. Two black guys under a street light look me over as they flick their cigarettes. People cluster in front of a pub. Forget personal space, I think, and ooze my way through, moving quickly, as though someone is expecting me.

How am I doing this? Maybe there's been another person inside who suddenly wants to make decisions. Or maybe Gramps was wrong. Nairobi's a city with streets and cars and people. Not exactly a horror show. It reminds me of another dream I had where I'm deep in water and sinking. I know I'll drown, and it will be awful. As I sink further, though, I'm waiting to run out of air, but I don't. I get deeper, and I can still breathe.

A man, mid to late twenties, has his eye on me. He breaks away from a group and speeds up to match my stride. There's an amused glint in his eye.

"Hi," he says. The tone is warm and gooey.

"Hi."

He looks at my feet. "I like your runners."

"Okay."

"You're always wearing runners. Where are you running to?"

He veers down a side road. When I peer back, Johnny Runners is gone.

I pass a few boarded-up shacks and a store. The wood frame may have been pounded together by a twelve-year-old. Inventory is crammed, and all I see are junk food and drinks. I buy a Fanta and two bags of chips, devour them and get to the steps of the club with surprisingly few stares.

Outside the club, women are dressed well enough for church. Except some girls. Over their heads I see the inside is lit by red lights. The rest is shadows against pale blue walls. Dance music pumps. A DJ barks into a microphone about music, and how we *must dance*. I tell myself, Do one thing. Have a drink. Safe to assume I can do *that* much.

The bar has a bomb shelter–sized cage surrounding the bartender. Strobe lights come from boxes in all corners. A few heads swivel in my direction. I make my way to where money and liquor pass back and forth. The crowd is mesh. I have to squeeze through like a foreign body penetrating a membrane. Little by little, I'm at the bar and spot Heineken and Guinness high on the shelves and feel safer. The bartender, a woman, says, "What?" I shout my order. She slides a Heineken over, and it's warmish cool in my hand. I pull the origami bills from that square pocket. They spring out like a mechanical claw and fall on the floor.

Idiot. I've shown my money. A grin forms at the edges of the bartender's mouth. I pick it up, and she reaches for a bill from the wad.

I just want to observe. I spot a stool and take a step. Out of the corner of my eye, I see two dresses. Then there's a hand on my crotch.

"You go marry me," one of two black women says. Her hair is divided into braids running down her back, plus braids spun on the crown of her head. The back of her dress is a V.

"Such soft skin," the other says. Her dress is hemmed below the knee, like what girls in middle school wear to graduation.

"Can I help you?" I say. Their heads toss back in laughter. My privates are released.

"Where dey drink?" Ms. Prom Dress says. She presents her hand to show that it is without a glass. Magically, I'm handing over shillings. I see myself doing it. Handing over money like a rock star. They saunter to the bar, arm in arm.

Forget money.

Don't stare.

They rock together in time with the music. Shiny black curls bounce. When they glance back, their faces almost touch.

With drinks, they are complete. Ice catches light as they wheel back. They each take an arm. I let this happen, even though I know what they are, because it feels good. I'm led to a table. Then they stand on either side, hands on hips.

"Where dey you come from?" Prom Dress says.

"Iowa."

Her head cocks, then swivels slowly back and forth.

"Me I no believe it."

"Why not?"

Her finger touches my hand. "I can't reckon you that accent."

"You know everybody's accent?"

The one with the v-back leans in. "We know a lot, boyo." A group of guys glance over. "When we done say it, we know dey truth. So?"

"You wore me down," I say. "It's North Dakota."

"Nooo," the girls say in unison. They laugh in the way that makes a guy feel lucky. I bob with the music. Just a person on the planet having a good time. I reach for a second drink. A new song shakes from the speakers. The under beat has the same thumping hammer.

"What's your names?" I say.

"Mercy," Prom Dress says.

"Samirah."

Samirah takes my hand and pulls me to a clearing on the dance floor. I shake my head, mouthing "no." She grabs my waist.

"Really," I say. "I don't dance."

But stubbornness doesn't work if girls have dimples. Samirah twirls. Her dress makes a narrow bell. As the strobes hit, I see that it's sheer. She lifts her arms one at a time. I'm dancing a hole into the floor. Mercy joins us, and it's three.

Trance.

Joy.

I close my eyes and sway like I'm loved. The girls are strutting. They touch my arms, my chest. Their arms are streamers. I turn in the opposite direction. We are a carousel.

The song ends, and I rest while they get more drinks. Soon we're swimming in them. My haze is pleasant, until I notice a black guy with marble shoulders staring. It's like he's seen me before and remembers not liking me the first time.

The girls go to the bathroom and there's pressure in the room. Like something's mobilizing against me. Men whisper. A new black guy comes in the door. He's introduced to whatever violation I've committed.

Suddenly, the bar is a boxing ring. I sigh in relief when the girls come back chattering in Swahili. As they come up, their eyes dart to the side.

"Sorry, handsome," Mercy says. Her eyes flit toward the guys. "Dey not appreciate dis. You no dance." She puts her hands on my shoulders, turns me, and gives a light push from behind. "You get, boy." I sit and they use their bodies as a blockade. "No come out, *mon ami*."

"Okay," I say. "But isn't this your job?"

"Them Somali no like *musungu* tourist wid de women. We no touch you."

The light changes. Music slows into an anthem for broken hearts. Bodies crowd the floor. A barrage of interlooping lines crosses faces until the lights brighten into a head-splitting glare.

"When does this place close?" I say.

"Didn't never close," Mercy says.

"I need sleep."

"So we go," Samirah says.

The hostile men no longer pay attention. The girl's smiles are thin, but relaxed. They see me searching. Mercy points as if to say, "the bathroom is over there." A wall curves into a dim hall.

The bathroom door hangs on one hinge. My knees are like jelly. Still, I nudge on and am attacked by a horrific stench. Liquid two inches deep covers the floor. I back up with my hand to my mouth. In the hall, men and women smile. I can't let people think I'm weak. Or superior. More folks crowd into the bar, and I gulp in the sweet air before stepping into what feels like a tropical pool. I unzip. Aim. Let the world listen to this rush.

After that, I stagger through the swinging board. Eyes roll down to my squishing runners. On the dance floor, Samirah contorts frantically. "It's back there," I say. She grabs my hand and leads me through the crowd to outside. She's searching again. "You're prostitutes," I say. Deliciously sleepy, I follow her. Warmth has given way to cool. I can already see myself in bed with the sheet up to my chin. I shiver and thank the universe with a yawn.

Samirah trembles. She points toward a police car. Cops dressed in army fatigues push Mercy into the back seat. Their sides bulge with weapons. Samirah hoofs it towards her. A cop starts the car. Mercy moans through her tears. They speak in Swahili.

"She hit on a cop?" I ask.

The cop's shadow flies away from the headlights.

Samirah gives me a glare. I jog towards the car, hot with remorse.

"It's my fault. I was dancing."

"Who would you be?" the cop asks.

"Devin."

"Do you have papers, Devin?"

"Papers? I left them at home."

"Where is this home?"

"That's a good question," I say.

"Do you possess the required documents, yes or no?" The cop has a special feeling for intimidation. His finger is the muzzle of a gun. "We'll be watching you." He joins the other cop inside the cruiser, and the interior light shines on a welt fruiting on one of Mercy's cheeks.

A voice comes over the radio. It's weak and electrical. Mercy slumps in her seat. The car wheels away.

"Let us go," Samirah says.

"Guess that happens to you girls a lot," I say. Samirah's eyes are resigned, and I sense it's because I should shut up. "You two should be more careful," I say.

"It no good," Samirah says.

"She'll be back, right?"

Samirah stares.

"I mean, aren't girls like you used to it? Prison, I mean? You're kinda in and out?"

"They be done eat her alive. She no arrive dey prison." Samirah shivers. I put my hand on her shoulder, and she wraps herself around me.

Seconds later I pull away and feel for the lump in my jeans where my money should be. I yank. The bills are tucked away tight as ball bearings. Samirah is watching. Her frame is small like faith is draining. Frustrated, I tug. The bills fall and uncurl at the edge of a puddle.

★

I'm mesmorized by the flow. Every one of them with somewhere to go, especially the guy in the truck with what appears to be his life strapped down. Mattress, chairs, table and blankets piled high under a see-through tarp. Seems so sad, his small life about to restart somewhere else.

Below my window, a girl wears a little white dress with a red belt. She's in the road, and cars are coming. She's alone. I jerk on the window, but the day's heat has vacuumed it shut. The barf bag I left outside is missing. In the meantime, a woman joins the girl and crosses with her.

Why am I so afraid?

I remember that day. The kitchen was like a funeral home. Mom and Dad held the charge that fills a room when fury and panic combine. I remember how Dad robotically flipped hamburger patties and made puns and later pasted himself in the rocking chair on the patio, stoner-staring into space.

Mom was coaxing Lily to eat, which is rare enough to alarm a person. Later, wrapped around a pillow, Lily seemed crumpled within herself. Like someone had blown out her fire.

When they filled me in about the party, I wanted to help Lily, but "sorry those assholes tried to rape you" didn't seem the right thing to say. I didn't protect my favourite person.

Traffic drones in response.

I go downstairs.

"Don't act so glad to see me." It's Paul in the lobby with a large bag at his feet. "Do anything yesterday?"

"Went to the Green Room."

He wolf-whistles. "First day and you pull an all-night rager. And up early and talking to me. What're you doin' today?"

"Shopping." It's a stupid thing to say. Like I've got the world by the tail. "Just walking around."

"Tell you what," he says. "Lemme take you to the CBD. It's more fun than it sounds. Street markets got almost everything. You can load up, whatever you need."

"I can get there myself."

"Well, if you go by yourself, it'll probably be alright." His head ticks back and forth. "Probably won't get fleeced by the first guy to size you up. If I go, you'll get a fair hour. After that you can come along to Kibera."

"Which is?"

"The Nairobi they don't want you to see." He gets up and turns his back toward the street's river of people. "You won't be bored. Bored doesn't exist in Nairobi. C'mon." He glances back. "You're not going to pass on a tour guide?"

"You're gonna do that for nothing?"

A smile spreads. "Nah. I'll have company too."

"Why?" The question comes out like an accusation.

Paul is Sherlock Holmes rubbing his chin. "Why do I want you to come with? That's a great question, Devin." He reads my face. "Surprised I remember your name? Who can any of us trust in this world? To answer your question, I guess I don't know *why*. Maybe why-the-fuck-*not*, mate, is more to my way of thinking. What were you gonna do? See the sights? Okay, remember the storks?" I nod. "You're the road kill. Then, there are other travellers. They're fine. The difference? Proper introductions. So, are we alright to push off?"

"Why not?"

He takes the bag, and we step into the street. Walking on the crowded sidewalks, I'm grateful for his presence. Everyone in Nairobi is going to work. Paul breaks the wall of people in half.

He stops at a fruit seller. "Hungry?"

"Is there a word hungrier than starving?"

He hands the old woman cash and gives me a bag of sliced mango. He pulls a water bottle out of a pocket in his cargo pants.

"Eat on the way."

Paul is unfazed, like a guy visiting the neighbourhood he grew up in. I wonder what it must be like, to know you'll be all right.

A man in front of a graffitied van shouts from the curb.

"He's hustling," says Paul. "That *matatu* won't move 'til he gets as many passengers as possible."

I trip on a curb at an intersection. Muslim women peek and a pierced nose glints in the sun. After we cross the next intersection, Paul yells over the blaring vans, "Notice the people? Diverse, right? Local blacks, yes. Blacks from South Africa and Somalia and other African nations. Lots of others too. The 'London of Africa' is what they call Nairobi." Paul pauses for effect. "Descendants from India, Persia. Chinese contractors. Revved development. Company headquarters. Tech giants, for example. Expats from Britain and Europe. Nairobi's bursting with innovation and creativity and waiting to be noticed."

We wait for a light change. "I don't see any white people," I say.

He leans his head back. "Up there."

I follow his gaze where glass towers compete for their quota of sun. We walk for a bit. Then he says, "Did you expect this?" I have no answer. Not everyone has time to expect something. He puts his hand on my shoulder. "Nairobi's great 'cuz the Africans here get it. It's not this antiquated notion of 'we don't have anything, so neither can you.' Here, everyone wants in and they're willing to work for it."

"What do you do again?"

"Buy low, sell high." Paul gestures to say the Central Business District is close. I know from the red tents. "I wanna duck in," he says. He signals to an electronics shop.

"I'll come with." People behind are tripping over me.

"Nah," Paul says. "Go on. It'll take a sec. I'll catch up."

Banks are on every corner. Guards are rigid on the steps. The market is just ahead. I see blankets spread, separating one seller's goods from the next, and people milling between.

I wait for an opening in traffic to cross the road. A young woman stands beside me. She steps out. I follow, optimistic that if cars come too close, they'll brake. A motorcycle swerves between us, almost nicking the woman. She's undaunted and reaches the other side. I freeze. Another motorcycle swerves on one side. Another bike swerves on the other. I feel surrounded. The woman glances back in horror. Vans honk, and a man somewhere is screaming. It's Paul. A car squawks to a halt inches from my hip.

"You can't hesitate!" Paul shouts. "You'll get killed. You'll get someone else killed." He's out of breath. The bag has begun to weigh on him. "They'll go around. Or they'll slow down or speed up."

"It sounds like no one knows what they're doing."

"It's a dance, kid. So DANCE." Paul stands back, inviting me to go it alone.

I wait. Minutes go by.

"Fuck me dead," Paul says.

I take my first step. A man on a motorcycle has two children clinging behind him. He swerves in time with my pace. Good. Like bandmates, we're playing the same tempo. Keep going. Steady. Traffic responds like rapids parting around a protruding rock. I reach the other side and wave at Paul, who skips across.

He aims me towards the market. "You can find everything within 200 metres," he says. "Wholesale." He leans towards me. "A smart person can get by on very little in Nairobi. The exception, rent. Only the rich can afford it. CBD is the worst. You got a cheap place, luckily."

In the market, wooden tables are coated with sunglasses, underwear, sports jerseys, children's toys, cleaning supplies, jewellery and plastic gadgets. Black women and men slump dead-eyed, waiting for a sale. Paul gestures to a table of shirts. "Thirty shillings. That's about twenty-five-cents American." I pick up a few. Paul smiles. "Do yah feel rich yet?"

I'm gawking at the loot. But Paul is taking me away.

"I thought I could shop?"

"Next one." We walk forever and reach a parking lot arched by a strip mall. Dodgy looking men in worn threads gather near the mouth of a lane. "This way to the Toi Market," he says. "Spelled T-O-I." We're in a tight corridor between vendors occupying rickety cubbies.

"This leads to Kibera Road," Paul says. "See there?" I'd seen people selling fruits and vegetables before. What I've never seen is charcoal sold a few coals at a time.

"Now I know where the bars get their strobe lights," I say.

"When was the last time you saw a machete?" Paul picks one up from a box. "Need a suit? There's heaps." Something rumbles in the distance. I tilt my head to discover where it's coming from. "Southern Bypass," Paul says. "My ride will take it home so you can get an overview." The thought of overview stocks a fresh need for orientation.

There's a line of ancient trees with bark so rough they seem prehistoric. The top branches reach sideways, giving it an umbrella effect. Stuck in there are large nests.

"I need everything," I say. "Everything."

Tables hold piles of t-shirts and jeans thrown into mounds. I browse and find two sweaters, a rain jacket, underwear and three pairs of jeans I can live with. I hold them to my waist one at a time.

"Give us a twirl, lovey," Paul says. A stork takes off. Confused, Paul follows my gaze up.

"Always with the death storks."

We come to an old vendor whose face has long gone blank. Paul crouches so he's looking her in the eye. I feel sorry for her. This big guy giving her the gears, and her, a frail ole thing. Then she meets him there in the shrinking space between them with the steely eyes of a bulldog. Even the scarf tied around her head gives her a don't-try-to-fool-me flare.

Paul puts a finger on a pair of jeans. "How much?"

The old woman sucks in her bottom lip. "Best price for *mon ami*? 200 shillings."

Paul chuckles like it's the most adorable thing he's heard. He speaks to me. "That's the opening bid. Don't panic. I'll get you a mate's discount." He turns back to her and jerks a thumb at me. "He's the foreigner." He turns the thumb on himself. "I'm a local. Darlin'. It's not worth fifty shillings. I'll do you a favour and give you twenty-five."

The woman laughs a sturdy "Hoo! I kid," she says. "I will discount you guy." She holds out a plastic bag, and while I put in the jeans, Paul hands over some money.

"I'll get you back," I say.

"Yeah, you will."

"Does anything here have a price?" I ask.

"Only if you invest yourself." His face brightens. "That's gotta be two drinks you owe me." We pick our way down the lane. We comment on gadgets and the quality of men's ties until we come up to what must be a mirage.

Life never lives up to the dream. So, I don't believe it's here, parked beside goat meat—a Lionel Richie poster half-buried behind vinyl records stacked from ground to roof.

My eyes shoot around. There's no labelling. No categories. The LPs are crammed so tight; plastic sleeves send a tedious message.

On my knees, I thumb through titles. After a while, the man stands beside me.

"English?" he says.

"Vinyl."

"Santeria," he says, mimicking my tone of voice. He has a badly repressed smile. "You speak santuri? Tell me what you are looking for?"

I search the walls for a quick answer. "I don't know. Something that's me."

"For many," he says, "vinyl speaks of the past. Kenya wants only to do with the future. Even as independent record labels make their headquarters here." His finger curls around the inner lining of his vest. "People come to my stall from around the world."

Paul paces in front of the small shop. "You will want to give it lots of time. If," he raises a finger, "you want the right music to find you."

The vendor sees Paul waiting. "Or perhaps, another time."

"Nairobi just got a lot more interesting," I say.

The man bows and I join Paul. We walk together with sun on our faces.

"This is it," Paul says. "At the end of the Toi Market is Kibera. Like we're crossing a border. My first time, I couldn't believe I was in the same city. What I didn't tell you is it's a slum."

"The projects. Like on TV?"

He turns me towards him. "Not as sweet as. Be ready to have your eyes opened."

We pass through a partition, and I remember reading somewhere that the brain protects itself when the truth is too hard. What I can comprehend are the parts. The street is mud. Streams of milky brown water run down the middle. Holes caked in garbage where you don't dare step. Children. Small and beautiful. Hovels made of wood and mud and corrugated steel for roofs. Strips of steel hammered haphazardly over holes. Electrical wires, handcrafted twists jacked to the main line. Shanty shops, dark inside, where light splinters. Women bent over plastic tubs, hand scrubbing clothes. Their expressions are stone, as they watch me watching them.

"Second largest slum in Africa," Paul says, as if narrating a documentary. "Almost three kilometres." We pass a sign on a shop that reads, "Hotel Butchery." "Permanent 'squatation' is what I call it." He checks me. "Don't worry. I know these people." We walk in bonfire scent and, at a stunted peak with an overview, we stop. I see hundreds, maybe thousands of dwellings. The last depot of post-apocalyptic survivors. Shoeboxes. Spread out for miles. Splayed as if a giant dropped a pile of rusty razor blades.

"Why are they here?"

"Landlords make a mint stuffing them in. It's chockers."

We come across a chain of stores. "It's like a small town," I say. The men and woman have movements so smooth and quick it looks like they have been rehearsed a thousand times. Awnings, held up by posts lashed together, give rare shade. Women stop by the open windows of the shops, their clothes too clean for this living. An elderly man drags a cart of fruit. Muscles in his arms are ropes pulling against the braking effect of muck.

"Where's he going?"

"Probably to work in the city."

Boys dressed in green vests run at us from behind, quick and cheerful. Their smiles make me wanna hit the reset button on life. "How are you?" they ask. Fearlessness. I want to understand the mechanics beneath that. Instead, I look at Paul.

"Big entertainment," he says, "talking to foreigners." He raises his eyebrows at the boys. "*Musungu*," he says. The group peels in laughter. "Means, 'white foreigner.'" Paul slaps me on the back. "Expect to hear it a lot."

"They can't be that happy," I say.

"No."

We walk in the middle of the street. There are no cars. No street signs. Just hovel and mud from ditch to track. The sun sends its sticky fingers down my back, bringing an unpleasant smell.

It's official. I've been kicked in the gut. I'm nauseous. The heat's full on and cruel. I need to sit. Paul seems to sense my drag. He's checking my face. I don't want to admit I'm sick.

"You could've warned me," I say. "What kind of person takes a tourist to a place like this?"

Paul mouths a silent "wow." "First off," he says, "you're welcome. Second, a person warned is a person with the privilege of being warned. Are these people warned before they step outside for the five-minute piss hike? I can take you back, if you want. I'll even take you to a clubhouse built colonial-style, where people can afford to be aloof. The world's not obliged to buffer you, I reckon. If you want reality, there's one way. Headfirst."

I'm staring at laundry blowing on a line.

"I wasn't saying I wasn't better than nobody," I say.

We walk in silence, down what might be Kibera's main street, and veer down a path that takes us between dwellings. The path is the width of a man, and a shallow sewage gutter carves a vicious backwater reek.

"Have to catch my breath." I say.

"Want me to hold your bags?"

I shake my head and lean against a wooden wall.

"It's not Marrakesh rancid, but that's not the problem with you, mate. It's the bag of bricks been dropped on your head called culture shock." I nod with eyes shut. "When they tire of Spain, the British pay big money for that sensation. You should see the old ladies around Marrakesh's Djemaa El Fna. They hide in the tea shops and revive with pincushion pastries."

We troop forward. The path fills with people. Their faces pass and looks are exchanged and some are indifferent and others seem sore. Mostly, I'm keeping my eye on Paul. I don't know how he knows where to go in this labyrinth. But then, he knows so much. Like how Africa is a continent, not a country. That the population in Nairobi rises by as much as a million per year. That terrorist attacks and terrorist threats explain the extra security everywhere. That businesses sell goods in single-use plastic and that's the garbage everywhere. And some people wash away during heavy rains, when the floodwall collapses along the shore of a river.

We come across a door. It's fabric that reminds me of what Indian women wear. An elderly man parts it and lets me pass before stepping out. For a split second, I glimpse his existence—a mattress stowed in the corner. The fabric door drops. I step past a group of serious young men bent over a chess game. Their eyes lift as Paul approaches, fall on me, and return to the board.

A woman with two small children tucks one under each arm and scurries down the path. When I turn to see where we've been, I see I am being watched. A boy, maybe five years old, wears a grey suit stained with mud. Clasped in his hands is a handful of plastic bags. He doesn't speak. Just holds the bunch out to me. Paul is getting further ahead. I turn away.

Finally, a clearing. Sparks from a fire zip through the air. Paul looks past me and pans right. The alleys are tight again, and I can't see past him until we are free. Another slope, and soon we're standing on a mound speckled with grass. Somewhere, a woman screams. Paul moves toward one of the hovels with a pallet-like door. There's crying coming from inside. Something in his face changes. I glance around. No one is doing anything. The door bursts open. A young black woman flees with something in her arms. The crying inside continues. It's coming from a young woman lying in the shadows. The taste of iron is in the air. The lower half of her dress is wet with blood. Her eyes find mine. An older woman wipes the woman's forehead with a dripping cloth. I hear moaning. It's weak and guttural. I realize it's me. Mooing like a sick calf.

"Sorry, mate," Paul says. "There's a doctor's strike."

He takes me by the elbow and leads me out. I totter sideways. Paul takes me to a quiet spot and claps my cheeks. "This is it, isn't it?" His voice goes high on "it," as in, "beautiful, isn't it?" He releases me and shakes his fist at the sky. "This is the real shit. When's the last time you didn't worry about a bunch of soul-deadening minutiae? Rent. Bills. Here, all that recedes."

I drag a sleeve across my eyes. "It's nuts that people live like this," I say.

"It's perfect sanity. When corrupt politicians are done with you, it's the only sane response." His finger wags at the bypass. "Out *there* is nuts. I knew when we met, I said to myself, 'Now here's someone who can roll.' You're not hung up on the details." If this is Paul's idea of a pep talk, I'm not sure it's really about me. His eyes are two burning suns. "I mean, most well-to-do Kenyans wouldn't come here. Now look at us. Anyone could kill us. We're living on 100 percent trust. Have you ever felt so awake?" His enthusiasm is hard to resist. I find myself watching his body, his face. The constant hum of his mind. Can he see me in him?

"Welcome to the watering hole, son."

Paul moves on, and I lumber along behind him, holding sickness close under the skin. We make maybe 100 hard-won metres, and I shrink to a stop, making way for a handful of elderly women. I have a smouldering headache. I can't keep the sick in. Things slide. I'm down. Panting and trying not to breathe in the smell. Something stirs behind a tarp. An arm jets out and flings a plastic bag in the mud two feet away. My nose points at a bag brimming with piss and shit.

Acid reflex licks the back of my throat. I scramble into some shade and look for Paul. What I see is a thousand ways to get lost. Put myself somewhere else. What I want is clean air and a fountain to look at. Grass. With people walking past with dogs. The duck pond in Assiniboine Park. I can hear the sloshing sound of the fountain and breathe the clear, blue sky.

Sweet Jesus. I'm alone and all turned around in this maze. A man in a checkered shirt walks toward me. I turn and run smack into a rooster. It squawks and bashes the air with its wings in a violent scramble. I hightail it toward a row of hovels, and then cross another row, back to the business street, where everyone can see me. I swear. If I get out. I'm gonna do something. I don't know what it is, but I'm going to do something productive. I promise.

I've stepped close to someone's home. A low-toned humming is interrupted by the voices of children. The hum resumes and makes the tragedy of the slum seem distant. I can't place the tune, but I see an elderly man sitting with his arms spread apart. He wears a kind of skirt. An arc of children clings to his torso, and he bundles them in his arms. His eyebrows rise with the unhurried melody, like the pace of a story you like to tell. It's Dad's music he's been humming. Bach.

A child holds her hand to her mouth and whispers in the old man's ear. The child has surprised him with her words, and he couldn't be happier. Before he responds, his eyes dart over and the smile vanishes. The children turn from the old man's face. I ease away.

"That's a first," Paul says. I jump.

Three black guys are with him, all hyper-groomed like they could lay the beats to a person without breaking a seam. They don't mind staring, either. Except one. He gazes off to the side. He has a mystery he'd really love to solve.

Paul gives no indication of what's next as he scrolls on his cell. "Wait here, okay?" The men follow him as he walks several yards away and stops near a ditch. Bach Man walks near. The group pulls together. The men shift on their feet like boxers before re-entering the ring. Paul shoulders the bag off and bats his fist in rhythm with his words.

"How long's this gonna take?" I ask.

I'm ignored and with nothing to do but wait, I feel something in my back pocket. My lucky lighter.

★

Dad was ecstatic. Gramps gave him his big house in River Heights, even though he wasn't dead. He said the rest would go to my uncle who lives in Ottawa. We needed the space more than him, Gramps said, after he found an apartment in Tuxedo, where a few widows from his curling club lived.

Dad had picked me up from a friend's house, which was weird, because Dad always wanted me to find my own way around. Dozens of times I'd call Mom for a ride and hear Dad in the background saying to her, "Why's it *your* problem?"

When Gramps let us in, we were offered old lady biscuits from a cellophane pack. Dad followed Gramps around, saying how terrific everything was. It wasn't terrific. The foyer was all tiny white tile and dirty grout. The hallway carpets were a stomach-turning pattern, and the air smelled like ripe fruit and peppermint.

After they rushed to save a boiling kettle, I found the lighter on top of the bedroom bureau. It hadn't been tossed with keys or a wallet. It was in a special silver dish. Beside it was a sleeve of matches from a New York club. I'd heard the story before. Back in the day, Gramps and Grandma had enough money for a five-night honeymoon. Grandma loved movies, and so they went to different restaurants and street corners that appeared in her favourite films. I remember seeing about twenty Hollywood-like photos of Grandma with a cigarette, laughing and tossing back her wavy hair. After she died, Gramps put those pictures away.

I stole the lighter knowing what it meant to him.

★

Hands clap. Paul gives a couple of low fives and finally the circle breaks. The guys stride by me and thread down a narrow alley with Paul's bag.

"Not a place you want to get lost in," he says. We walk. The pressure is somehow lighter. Paul dips his hand into his pocket and pulls out a Coke. My heart skips.

"Why didn't you bring that out earlier?"

He hands it to me. "Give it to the driver," he says. "He's been waiting in the sun."

"Are you an aid worker?" I ask.

"Nuh. I'm not that mean. I don't suffer from the white saviour industrial complex. There's plenty of those types. Hell, we would've passed the World Health Organization if we rode up here. Besides," he gestures to the slum, "these folks don't need saving. Sure, there's a toilet situation. Water situation. Safety situation. Other than that, though, I think they're doing all right. What do you think?"

I can't believe I'm hearing this. Nothing about what we saw was "all right."

"When you were lost," Paul says, "who was the one needing saving?" I look back over Kibera. Around it, a halo of grass grows. I feel oddly stung. I'm not as happy about leaving as I thought I'd be.

"Our rides are here. *Jambo*," he calls to two leather-clad punks on motorbikes. "*Habari gani?*"

I walk up to one and hand over the Coke. "They'll wait," Paul says about the drivers. "You pay these gentlemen and they're your friend for the day." He smacks one on the shoulder. "Give him your bags." The driver stows them in a compartment behind his seat. "So, whad-ya think?"

"How do you do it?"

Paul adjusts his crotch. "I've gotten lost many times. But as you probably noticed, Kibera has a way of finding you."

Paul scrapes his boot on a rock. Muck comes off in sheaths. "So you didn't answer me. Whad-ya think?"

"Interesting."

"Bullshit."

"I don't know how to talk about it. It's too much."

"I know what you mean, mate. Takes time to process. It's just so unjust, eh? It's the end of the road of the rich get richer and the poor get poorer. But you survived. You didn't squirm too much. That tells me something." He looks out over the sprawl. "Some people jump bikes off a ramp. Others throw themselves out of a plane. This is my version of extreme sports." He throws a few fake jabs my way.

Paul sounds crazy, but he's right about one thing. It's as though I've hatched and just kicked off my shell.

The *boda boda* drivers hoof the engines in gear. Paul hoists his leg over one of the bikes. "Hop on." I jump on the second. The bike is trembling. I barely have time to tuck my feet in before the wheels begin to spin. We catapult down the highway.

We veer and weave. I can't look away. Finally, a stoplight. Safe to assume I'll be able to breathe, but then the driver jumps the curb. I scream. We're riffling down the sidewalk and then plunk back into the road. Soon we're surfing the edge of the median. Pedestrians shout at us. By the time we stop at a spot off the highway, dust sticks to my skin. I am a donut.

Paul's bike jerks to a stop beside us.

"National park," Paul says. I see a row of trees and brush and a fence. Paul dismounts and walks up to it.

"All I can see is a buzzard in that tree," I say.

"Vulture."

Something rustles in some nearby bushes. "A hyena is coming, Devin."

Low branches jiggle. Out comes a wiry, tusked pig. The drivers laugh at my disgust.

"Don't get yourself into a lather," Paul says. "Just a harmless warthog." We share a laugh.

"Hell," he says. "Why end it here? Let's head to Carnivore. It's a restaurant." I nod. The drivers restart their engines.

As we blast along, trees in the park stagger, and the interior opens. Under big trees, grey desert ripples at their feet. I see zebra. As many as ten.

Nairobi might have almost brought me to my knees. Now, it's bought itself some time. I'd give my new underwear for a set of binoculars.

★

The restaurant, fortressed in stone, sits at the end of a gravel road flanked by brown-green fields. The *boda bodas* stop yards short of the drop zone. A gritty, pink glow looms behind a white tent. As we walk the rest of the way, black servers set up table linens. At the doors, two guards. Since the Mercy incident, I've been nervous around guards and cops. Paul is cool, though, as if he's mulling over a larger question.

A waiter leads an all-white group to a table, where napkin crowns sit. The flash of a camera goes off. Servers circle tables with two-foot skewers of meat and machete-like knives ready to lob off a cut. They lay the skewer end down on an old woman's plate, and as she claps, flesh is sheared away in edible chunks.

"It's not the animals we saw in the park?" I ask.

"Nah. They don't serve those anymore."

A waitress leads us to our table. A stout man saunters up. He has a strap around his neck that supports a tray of drinks. "*Dawa*," Paul says. The man sets two glasses down. It tastes like lemonade and candy canes. Paul also orders Tusker beer and tells the waiter to keep them coming, then he analyzes the crowd.

"Look at 'em white-haired ravers. Where do you suppose they're from?"

"Don't know."

"Guess."

"I don't know. New Guinea?"

"Look at the bastard talking. The one who combs his hair with a balloon."

"English. I can hear the accent."

"That's pretty good," Paul says. "Lots of people can't differentiate."

"My grandmother was a Scottish immigrant."

"Where from?"

"Scotland."

"Jesus, Devin. *Where* in Scotland?"

"Dunno."

I watch the table and wonder what's so fascinating. "Oh, the English," Paul says in a lovestruck tone. "They really know how to bugger things up."

"What do you mean?"

"I'm not gonna get into centuries worth of carnage. Read on the imperial tongue yourself." He scopes the menu written on a chalkboard: Chicken. Lamb. Beef. Ostrich balls. Crocodile. Suddenly there's thunder, and rain begins to fall by the gallons.

"I'm not eating balls," I say.

"Man," he says. "Grow up and *try* things." A man comes with a skewer of lamb. Paul tears into it like it was the centre of a hard grievance. His fork is a shovel, returning again and again. It's disgustingly impressive what he can pack away. A server comes by with ostrich balls. I shake my head. Paul is fuming. "You're a guest. God. Your parents must've had a great time with you."

Tears run down the side of my nose.

"Blimey. What's with you?"

"Nothing." I press a napkin to my face, "Forget about it."

He sucks juice from his fingers. "Out with it," he says. I shake my head. "They abuse you." When he gets no reaction,

"They love the other siblings more than you." He signals a server. "Girlfriend dumped you. Oi, I'm not gonna stop 'til you tell me. You know you want to."

"It's just, the worst things ever said to me were said by my parents."

"That's it, isn't it?" he says. "Life is learning to ditch all the right people." A server reloads his plate.

"They kicked me out and took me back only because the shelters were full."

Paul sets his fork down. Mops up his chin. He seems to understand more about me than what I'm saying. "I'm not sure you realize what you accomplished today. Still. It was tiring. And I came along and struck a nerve. Every man has limitations."

"Yeah."

"On the other hand, I don't wanna say, 'who cares,' but suffering is a choice."

★

"Are we gonna have dumplings?" Lily asked. "I had shrimp dumplings at Jemma's house last week."

"Lily, you know you can't have shrimp," Dad said. "Mom's allergic." Mom carried a casserole from the kitchen. When she put the dish down, Lily looked at it suspiciously. "What's going on in that head of yours?" Dad asked.

"If food can kill Mom, then maybe she *should* die."

"Lily!" Mom said.

"I'm just saying. If a person can't eat, how are they supposed to live? It's a message from nature maybe that they're supposed to die."

Dad could barely speak for laughing. "It's a kind of logic, Julia. She doesn't mean it."

"I know what she means, Cole."

Lily dragged her fork on her empty plate. "Like the kid in my class with impulse control."

"*Lack* of impulse control, honey," Mom said.

"Is this the kid with the chew toy?" Dad asked.

"It's not a toy," Mom said. "It's a self-control device. He bites. He can't help it."

Dad snort-laughed. Lily laughed so hard she started to wheeze. Dad regrouped, then let off a fresh round of hilarity. He was pretending to have a bone in his mouth. Lily reached for it. He wouldn't let go.

"Okay," Mom said. "Enough already."

As Lily spooned coleslaw onto her plate, Dad said to Mom, "He bit the teacher. Please. Tell me it happened."

"He should be a *dog*," Lily shouted.

Tears leaked down Dad's cheeks.

Mom pulled the lid off her famous shepherd's pie. The recipe was from one of her posh cooking magazines. She always cooked and baked like it was her own portrait she was creating. Lily bounced in her chair. "I won't die today," Mom said. "Is that okay with everyone?"

Dad gave thumbs-up and gestured for me to remove my headphones.

"It's turned way down," I said.

When I didn't take them off, he held his hand out.

"We know you're allergic to people. But please," he said.

He hung the headphones on the back of his chair. Mom passed serving plates to the right. I passed the salad beside me to the left. And anything else that came my way. The family didn't register this until Lily passed a dish to me, and without even looking at it, I passed it back to her.

"We pass to the right," Mom said, as if sixteen years of rehearsal wasn't enough.

"Just to tell you," Lily said, "you're gonna get in trouble."

I put the pie beside me, swept the mash potatoes off the top, and plopped them on my plate. A minute later, serving plates piled up at my elbow. Dad had the last dish, a hefty cast iron skillet still hot from the stove. His arm began to quake.

"Take the damn thing," he said.

Lily knelt in her chair and reached, trying to steady the pan. She knocked over her milk.

Dad ticked his head at me and then towards the spill. "Just for once, could you make yourself useful?"

Let's dispense with the obvious; Dad didn't care about me, my music, or what I wanted or who I was. I'd spent enough time in my bedroom fiddling with guitar chords to learn Cantonese. Humming melodies. Strumming. Clicking record. Stopping. Rewinding. He was pushing me into becoming someone else. I've always said the answer to every problem is stay away from those with something to sell. That's why, when the dishes piled up, I took another swipe of potatoes and chewed slow and cow-like.

Dad took his napkin and, with a jerk of his wrist, snapped it open. "How 'bout a fresh glass?" he said, referring to Lily's spilt milk. I sauntered like an invalid, poked around in the fridge and took out the carton. "Can't you figure this much out?" he said. "Pour her some." I poured Lily's milk.

"That wasn't so bad, was it?" Dad asked.

"Terrific."

I sat, and Dad pointed his knife at me. "Be careful. You wouldn't want to get good at anything you don't want to do." Then, he wouldn't back off. "You think you're smart," Dad said. "Smarter than everyone else at this table. But we're on to you." He sawed into his green beans and was struck by another thought. "You know what you are. You're one of those can't-see-the-forest-for-the-trees people."

"Huh?"

"The trees are the obvious things. You can't see the forest *and* the trees." He wiped his lips. "Mom thinks you'll grow out of it. Maybe you'll never know the difference. Lemme spell it out for you. It's not just what you do and don't do, it's what every act *implies*, about your respect for us, about you as a *person*. You don't care about anything that's good or worth doing, even if it's for the sake of your family. Family who supports you, by the way, and your expensive tastes."

I stared out the window at the snow's sheen. What is it about brightness through a window that makes you want to float away? Mom, as if reading my mind, said, "We care about you." Her signal for when a talk is about to happen. "You know that, right?"

I considered my answer.

Dad slid to the tip of his chair in a forward leaning position.

"So anyway," she said. "We care about what you're doing right now, and not doing." Dad nodded. "We're worried. For one, you leaving the house whenever you want and we don't know to where. It's a safety thing. It might be better if we knew you had a job or were in school. Which is the main concern. You're smart enough to do university, let's say that. But no, obviously being out all night is more fun. What we mean is, we could… take a little, I don't know the right word, misbehaviour, if you were making some progress. But it's like you're floating."

I mock-slapped my face. "Not floating!"

"You're twenty-four years old," Dad said. "Aren't you even a little embarrassed? Your mother is saying in a nice way that you're a sponge."

Mom's eyes became dinner plates. "That's NOT… Look. We have the money and we want to support you. But support you in what? It's not easy, you know, going to the grocery store, the gas station, seeing your friends' parents. Your old friends are working this summer. And graduated university for the most part. Everyone's going somewhere but you."

Dad's fingers interlaced into one large fist glued at his forehead. "At some point," he said, "You have to man up. Don't you want something for yourself? Be someone? Stake some territory? Get a girlfriend?"

Same images. Same words. Same word order.

"When I was his age, I couldn't wait to have my own place." He turned to me. "I can't understand why you're not motivated. Why we should even need this conversation."

"I'm not… not motivated," I said.

"You need heart to succeed in this world. Stick-to-it-iveness."

I laughed.

"What Cole is saying, dear, is that we're worried. There's stories of young men in their thirties living at home indefinitely. That's not healthy."

"I think what Dad's saying is I'm a loser," I said. "And you're saying it's embarrassing."

Mom buckled as if her lungs had been pierced. "That's not true! But your father has a point." Then her voice floated on a river of balm. "If you need something, we can help. Tuition, work clothes, anything. So long as you move in a direction. You can't honestly think your future is in music."

"And not just come and go as you please," Dad said. "This isn't a hotel."

"I never said that," I said.

"Really?" he asked. "Enlighten us. What would you say about your behaviour around here? 'Cuz I'll tell you what I think…"

"Cole…" A curtain had fallen behind Mom's eyes. "What we mean is, we're listening."

*

In the bathroom mirror, I'm a creature with crescent moons under the eyes. Though Paul is fun and likes buying drinks, it was naïve to think I could have one carefree night. The only option is to go home. I decide to book my return flight tomorrow morning.

I weave past two servers and see that Paul's got more *Dawa*. His Hollywood smile turns towards me. "Ah, here he is." I sit, and he elbows me. "I've been wondering," he says. "How did'ya get the idea of Nairobi?"

"I didn't. Someone else made the choice seem obvious."

"Ah, well. Whatever oracle did this, good on them." He looks up as an older black guy shakes hands with him and pulls up a chair. Paul introduces him as Mr. Mugbo. He has cheekbones of steel, and his hair's shaved close to the wood. He has a steady way as though he's tracking everything. The line of his shoulders could be used as a leveller. "Paul," Mr. Mugbo says. "I hope you have been well. I have not heard from you in some time. Friends are looking forward to your next visit."

"I'll see them soon, in part thanks to this guy," Paul says, gesturing towards me. "Devo here is gonna work for me." Paul aims his *Dawa* at me. "If those English drunks can be expats, so can you. Cheers." Mr. Mugbo looks back and forth between Paul and me.

"You serious?" I ask.

"I'll take care of your immigration papers, so don't get your back in a sweat. You don't fully appreciate what you accomplished today. Even survived the storks."

He pokes me again with his elbow. To Mr. Mugbo he says, "Devin came to Kibera today. He's flexible. Can think on his feet."

"I guess I did do pretty well today," I say.

Paul says to Mugbo, "You know what they say. 'Children are the bright moon.'"

Mugbo stares expressionless.

As Mugbo and Paul continue talking, Mugbo's voice reminds me of a singer in Dad's jazz collection. It has the etched sound of life experience. I imagine him being the eldest of a large family. Protecting a horde of siblings. It was what he was born to do, this clenched mass. Keep threats down.

Paul turns and jerks a thumb toward Mugbo. "This guy took me on my first trip to Kibera. I told you I puked? He saw it."

Mugbo's body shakes as he laughs. Paul goes on describing his first day, while the room fills with customers.

"How will he be successful if he is a stranger to Nairobi?" Mugbo asks.

"Let's see how he goes," Paul says.

"He soft like dey breast of a woman."

"Let me prove it. With my guidance..."

"You do not send a boy to collect no honey."

"I know what you're saying. He's got the right... situation. He's gonna mind his business."

"Doing what?" I ask.

"Driver," Paul says out of the side of his mouth. "Right?" Paul glares me into a response.

I can't believe what I'm hearing. Yet I'm different with Paul. He sees something in me. It's like he gives me permission to be better. Otherwise, why would he bother?

"What of thieves," Mugbo says. His glittering eyes settle on my reaction.

Paul drops a foot under my chair. "It used to be that way," he says. "I told you about 'Nairobbery.' There was, for a time, a phenomenon where people, not all people of course, would hijack cars or steal from drivers at gunpoint. Almost no one has been killed." Mugbo is grinning. "The government has cracked down on that. Hardly happens to tourists anymore." Paul slides back a notch. "You'll be in charge of transportation. Mr. Mugbo organizes the folks who receive the deliveries. Forgive him for being careful. He's paid to worry."

"People keep letting me down, and I'm getting older," Mugbo says. He brings his drink to his mouth, and as he sets the glass back down, I realize that when it comes to older folks, they just want things simple.

Paul raises his glass. "To *Dawa*."

"To *Dawa*," I shout. We drain our glasses and slam them down.

"To business," Paul says.

I say, "To life, liberty, and the pursuit of money."

If Gramps could see me with Paul, he'd be heartbroken that his experiment had failed. The rest of the family too. They don't know it yet, but they're gonna miss this new Devin.

Two more sugar drinks and the room tips. Paul play slaps me in the head. His expression dares me to strike back. I slap him lightly on the side of the head. Paul cuffs me in the ear, and I try the same and accidentally poke his eye. We're speed-balling insults. Laughing hard as hyenas and pushing each other away.

A waiter asks if we're okay. We straighten up and see that Mugbo's seat is tucked in. A marble sits at his place setting. I hold it up to the light. There's three levels of rainbow swirl. The centre looks like an invitation to slide down dark tunnels.

"*Kigogo*," Paul says. "Ancient game. Keep it as a souvenir."

I drop the marble in my pocket and see movement behind the glass wall. It's my reflection. The back of my seat is a circle of zebra print.

"If we're gonna do this," Paul says, "I reckon there's something I need to know." He inhales. "Tell me you're not a minor."

"Nope."

"Got a police record?"

"No, but..."

"What?"

"Cops here are giving me a hard time."

"You gotta be careful, mate. I'm told Interpol's got a new technology to track criminals. Connect I-ONE it's called. It links across Africa. Do they have your name?"

"I don't know."

"You got a driver's licence?"

"No."

"You can't *drive*?"

"I can drive. I just didn't take the test."

"Fuck me dead." He focuses on the corner of the room.

I don't know what to hope for. It's hard to understand how Paul's business works. But would I like to stay and play a game with the folks back home? Think how stupid they'd look if I actually did well. "It's not important," Paul says. "It's not like *every* driver in Nairobi has a licence."

"They don't?"

"Actually, they do. Listen. Take my advice, and you'll be fine."

"Why?"

I didn't mean it to sound ungrateful. Just, what's more intimidating? Believing you don't have a shot or finding out the only barrier's been you?

"You with the *why, why*. Because I like you, you silly bastard. Yah, you have a smart mouth, but that's how it is with smartasses. I'd even say you have an intelligent face. But just once I'd like it if you were one of the stupid people just smart enough to keep their mouths shut. And because you seem to need this. You need this, yeah?"

He asks it as though I've never had a life.

★

I didn't just dream of being in a band. I dreamt of writing music for movies. Epic stuff and all the scene-cue music in between. The ultimate challenge for a musician, I figured, was not getting locked into style. Movie music would make a musician spread their territory out. Course people hate watching movies with me, because for *me*, there's no such thing as background music. For example—our family trip to Vienna in 2011. After Gramps gave over the big house, Dad decided on a family splurge. Mom had been to Europe many times, but he hadn't. He took two weeks off in late April and let Mom pick the place.

The day after we arrived, the family walked around the central part with the big buildings and shopping streets. I didn't expect to like Vienna so much. But it reminded me of children's books, where everyone's outside and eating ice cream cones.

That evening we were in a grand mood. Dad took us to a jazz place called Porgy & Bess. It had red velvet seats and small, round tables. On the stage was a piano, a big bass, a drum kit and, on top of a stool, a horn. The musicians came on. The lead guy said he was from Cuba. He introduced the musicians and picked up the horn.

That guy could play. I found myself expanding a little as I sat there. I liked watching the piano player too. His fingers raced up and down and, more than once, I noticed the Cuban guy gawking at him. Full. Frontal. Appreciation. When the show ended, the musicians stood arm over arm. Mom strolled back to the hotel hugging herself, and all Dad could say was, "Excellent. Just beyond."

Mom asked why I hadn't said much, how did I like it? I didn't tell her the truth because the truth was I was depressed. I'd looked at my future and saw no opportunity to have the impact on anyone that band had had on me. That's when I knew what I wanted. I told the parents I wanted to study music.

The glow went out of Dad's cheeks.

"It's not like it's going to pay," Mom said, with a touch of bitterness. "Only the best make money. And many of those people, they sing and dance too. Do you sing and dance?"

"Look," Dad said. "It's nice that you play music and that you like to write. I'm sure some girl is going to find that irresistible. But that stuff doesn't make a life. A man needs to know when to prioritize. I know it sounds like I'm old and insensitive. Well... I'm sorry."

"What Dad is saying is, it's not like you can't keep up with your music."

"Right," he agreed. "But what's your Plan B?"

"You mean the B-side," I said.

"Plan B, not the B-side."

"Plan B *is* the B-side. Like on an album. It's filler."

Dad sighed. "Filler provided for this family," he said. "You don't think your Mom and I had dreams growing up? I wanted to be a doctor," he added. "I know. *Quelle surprise*. How disappointing was it not getting the marks? Can you just imagine a second? Wanting that and failing? What that would've meant to Gramps to say his son was a doctor? Dad taught me about expectations. Setting sights on what he called, 'achievable goals.' I didn't like it, but I reoriented.

"Your Mom, believe it or not, wanted to be an actress. Don't believe me? Look at Lily." Lily pirouetted on the curb. "She gets that from her mother." Mom smiled into the collar of her jacket.

Suddenly, everything about Mom seemed interesting. I realized she was actually pretty. I imagined her with a small theatre troupe, surrounded by creative people. Why didn't she follow through? She could have brought that into my life. That was probably the life I was supposed to have. Surrounded by similar minds and encouragement. If I'd had at least one creative parent, a community, I'd be so much further ahead.

"Did you really want to be an actress?" I said. At first, Mom seemed moved by the question. Then something changed under the surface.

"That's none of your business."

"Julia," Dad said. "It's your family's artsy-fartsy side. Talk to him." We walked in the cool air, and finally the vice grip in her jaw broke.

"Sorry," she said. Her eyes welled. "We spend so much time on the B-side of life." She looked at Dad. "Don't we?"

White buildings slept all around us. Their columns tucked in for the night. The cobblestones and red store awnings and music and the bust of Beethoven replayed in my head. But I could also see myself disappearing. I partly wanted that. To just end it there and poof, be gone.

"Devin," Dad said. "I'm sorry to tell you, but people spend the greater portion of their lives on the B-side. Haven't you ever looked at what people are doing and wondered if they know why they're doing it? There's a reason that zombie show is popular. People like looking in a mirror. None of us can afford to be totally authentic, adventurous, and pursuing our dreams. We need Plan B. Because we have to eat. And need roofs over our heads."

★

Paul's hair is sticking up, and the surge of alcohol has his face bright pink. "You'll have a vehicle," Paul slurs. "With GPS. And a cellphone. Make my deliveries without drama." An empty glass is cradled in his hands. "You think you can do that?"

"So what, exactly, is the job again?"

In another part of the restaurant, someone checks a live microphone. Check. Check. Bah. Bah. Bah. Someone on guitar plonks through an electric chord. Paul is losing patience.

I want success. Repeat, I want money. Besides, people can't expect to be full-out happy.

"I'll do it."

Finally, the world can relax.

"Now that we've bonded," Paul says, "we dance." He grips my wrist, and pulls me to my feet. Others stroll onto the dance floor. Problem is, I don't wanna dance. A spotlight roams the floor, and Paul raises his arms. The beam hits him, and it's like he's just slid down a tube. He twirls twice and grabs me by the waist. "You're gonna be the cowgirl," he says. He hoists me up, and the ceiling lights are a thousand red trails. I try to wriggle away. Now he's got me in a bear hug. I get my forearms between our chests and push. When that doesn't work, I buck. He's so strong he can angle it so I can't kick his legs.

Finally, he releases me. While I pull down my shirt, he steps back, palms out, as if to say he means no harm. Then he walks towards me and swings a fist. Dancing couples ripple away.

"Are you kidding?" I say. I'm confused and embarrassed and fighting back tears. And I'm starting to tire of his twisted amusements. I gather my wits and circle him like a cat. My feet and hands move without asking. He watches me come around, a cheeky smile crawling across his face. My fists land hard on his chest when I shove him. He staggers to the edge of the dance floor. A woman screams as he backs into the legs of her chair.

The lead guitarist zips off a slide. Paul straightens and pardons himself to the group, yet his death glare says he's not done with me. He charges, elbow raised. I throw a torso punch. He catches my fist and pulls me into another bear hug.

"I'm just pissin' in yer pocket," he says.

I winch away and see servers clustering in a corner. A man in a suit joins them. The music stops. The singer is standing back from the microphone. The crowd murmurs as we pull and push against one another. Paul's eyes are closed like he's re-enacting a private act of revenge.

I'm expecting an advance of club-carrying guards. But there isn't any great movement. Just the whole place whirling around and around. The guitarist strums the opening chords from a popular '80s dance song. The riff lands hard with the crowd. Paul tips me back and puts his other hand over my mouth and pretends to kiss me. Cheers rise up. People flood the dance floor.

"Enough!" I scream.

I stomp to the restaurant entrance for a cab. The rain has stopped. Under the bright lights, gentle laughter tells me someone had a pleasant night. Elegant people pile into a white Land Rover.

Paul comes out with his off-rhythm, lopsided step. "Devo," he calls. His skin is green. His eyes are slits. A guard signals a cab. Paul's knee slowly gives out, so I give him my arm. Seeing him like this gives me a new perspective. Tonight was a small price to pay for a new life. Maybe this is what it's like on this level. You deal with it and move on. That's how you get the big-boy marble.

"Seems you're the life of the party," I say.

"You don't know the half of it."

JULIA

"They're here," Cole said. I drew the curtain as two policemen strolled up. Cole greeted a Constable Barnett and a Constable Corbin at the door.

"You called about your son?" Barnett said. "He's trespassing, you said?"

Cole ticked his head toward the basement where the sound of screeching tires blared from the television. "He's not been cooperating for some time. As a result, he's not welcome anymore. We've explained that to no avail."

"Is there anything we should know? Drugs? History of violence?" Constable Corbin asked.

Cole shook his head.

"We'll have a chat. If all goes well, we'll walk him out."

The constables moved toward the basement. There was an air of finality, watching those men, and I struggled to keep resolve. Since when do children trespass in their own home?

Constable Barnett paused. "He has a place to go?"

Cole looked from me back to him.

"I see," Constable Barnett said.

The constables went down the stairs. Cole pulled me to his chest, but I pushed away.

"I can't listen to it," I said. "Can you?"

Cole shut the basement door, and we went into the dining room. When we heard the television stereo switch off, our eyes met. Though we couldn't make out words, we heard the cadence of Constable Barnett's voice. We heard Devin's murmur and suffered through several more minutes before he came up, with a face both malicious and serene.

Resolve, I thought.

★

Cole was home early from work. He had the newspaper open and was talking about the weekend. I'd been preparing lamb that would yield leftovers for two days. Lily was home from school and had just unpacked two textbooks when all the lights went out. Cole tried the light switches. Dead. He checked an element on the stove. No red light. He opened the fridge and closed it right away. No electricity, no television, no internet. By the time Lily put her backpack away, we'd got the gist: the power was out.

When Devin turned eighteen, we had converted the small room in the basement into a bedroom. Cole kept his files and a small safe down there. With a few valuables around, he bought a doorknob that locked. He added a futon and an old brass lamp from his parents' basement. We'd decided Devin would sleep there on nights when he watched movies into the wee hours. The thing we hadn't figured on was his stealing the key and barricading the door to the electrical box. With the flick of a switch he controlled our lives. Once, he shut us down for twenty-four hours. Everything in the freezer had to be replaced.

"Dee's got to get a life," Lily said.

Tendons on Cole's neck stood out. He usually lumbered outside to cool off. This time, he went outside to spy in basement windows. He came back clenched. "I couldn't see a damn thing." He poured water into a mug and absentmindedly placed it in the microwave. He pushed the buttons where numbers normally lit.

I said, "Why don't we go out for dinner?"

"You must be kidding. Pay good money for dinner when we have lamb rotting in the oven?" He paced with hands vice-gripped on his head. Then he barged at the basement door.

"What's going down going to accomplish?" I asked. "You can't get in the room."

As if rewarded for a brilliant revelation, the lights went on. A radio announcer barked softly from one of the bedrooms. Then it played an old fifties tune about young love. The fridge hummed, and the element light was on. I took a breath, and Cole straightened his shoulders.

"Well," he said. "Guess he's ended it early this time."

I considered the lamb. "Maybe curry this time," I said. Cole helped me search the spice cupboard. He found a bottle of Bordeaux above the fridge. I minced garlic while Lily flipped through a schoolbook. Burners inside the stove glowed red. Cole floated up from behind and groped me. "Soon that's going to smell delicious," he said in my ear. He winked at Lily. "Our resident troll will be up in no time." Cole handed me a glass when the lights went out.

"That punk has got to be kidding," Cole said.

"Please don't get excited."

"The sun's going down," Lily said. "I have homework that I was actually gonna do."

Cole stared at the oven like the lamb was turning green before his eyes. Paying no heed to what I'd said, he stomped downstairs.

"What're you going to do?" I said after him.

"Nothing," he called. "I don't know."

I crept over and listened at the basement door. "Devin!" Cole yelled from below. "Turn the power on." When Devin didn't talk back, I descended with Lily. Cole had steadied himself outside the bedroom door. He pounded on it for so long that I told him to stop. The silence froze us. Cole at the door. Me at the foot of the stairs. Lily at my back.

"Let's go out," I said. "I'm starving."

Even in the day's failing light, I saw Cole's lips turn white. He disappeared upstairs, and there was a hollow sound that rolled back, thick as smog. When Cole returned, face shimmering with rage, he was brandishing a cordless power drill.

Cole turned it on and worked the screws around the doorknob. The drill bit slid, and the sound of grating metal made me wince. Cole swore under his breath, but eventually got into a rhythm. A screw dropped. Then another. Then the doorknob was loose in the hole. Cole tried peeking through the gap. He then pulled the knob apparatus out and pushed his way in.

The basement window was open. Though it's not legal size for a bedroom, it's wide enough for a scrawny kid to pull himself through.

Another classic Devin nightmare was when he was still in high school. I was opening the sliding door to the deck. The wind bent trees, and leaves were flying about. Devin came in with another boy. "It's like *The Wizard of Oz* outside," I said.

The other boy was a skinny kid with plucked eyebrows and dyed-black hair. He had homemade tattoos carved into each finger. Together, they spelled "M.A.D.E." I gave Devin my *who-is-this* eyes. Devin didn't introduce the boy; instead, he opened the fridge, took out two pop bottles and opened them on the edge of the counter, causing the caps to zing off and settle into unseen places.

I looked at Devin's friend. "Who do we have here?"

Devin guzzled the soda, wiped his mouth on his jacket sleeve and then took the stranger to his room. I heard them murmuring and then the gate to Slick's cage swinging open. I checked the time on the microwave.

I went striding toward his bedroom thinking, It's my house. Everything that goes on here is my business.

"Don't you have class?" Both boys broke out into heaves of laughter. I heard my mother's words come out of my mouth. "What's so funny? Devin!" I shouted. "Tell me you didn't skip. You can't just bring strangers here."

"Ah," said the kid I hadn't met. "Go beat your meat."

I couldn't fathom how a person could speak to someone like that. It was like I'd been hit with the butt end of a cleaver. So I stood there, barraged by hiccups of laughter, feeling disoriented. Things around me held the grainy residue of an amateur film. Though I yearned to, I couldn't cry. Even back then, Devin had lost his capacity to surprise. As I stepped outside, the stranger tore through a fresh sleeve of machine-gun laughter.

I marched to the Subaru parked on the street. The same vehicle I'd used to chauffeur Devin. I put the key in, but didn't start it. I don't know how long I was like that, gazing at the front yard. But I remember the streetlights coming on. A puddle glowed like a white, moonlike ball. Day had passed into evening, and Bill's words about tough love began to make sense.

★

Memory gave me the will to let the constables take Devin out. I picked off a scab at my elbow and searched for what to say. See you later didn't occur to me. It'll be all right didn't either. I loved you, and what did I get in return? Those were sentiments I kept to myself.

"Let him take some things," Cole said.

The cops put their hands in their pockets. Sometime later, Devin emerged with a duffle bag. The constables parted, letting him pass, before folding in behind him. Once the worst was over, I was sorry and not sorry, to see him go. In an effort to cheer myself up, I tried seeing him as a donation to society. Like a kidney transplant.

Underneath an embankment of trees, Devin stopped for a few last words with the constables. Constable Corbin scrawled something on a piece of paper. Devin took it. Then, the constables took turns shaking Devin's hand.

Cole spoke into my ear, "Things are going okay."

They left Devin there and drifted back. "Something the matter?" Cole asked.

Constable Barnett rubbed the back of his neck. "That he has nowhere to go is a problem. We've suggested a shelter."

Devin strolled away, white soles flashing. Cole weaved his fingers through mine. He held me like that until Devin disappeared beyond the Jack pine seven houses down.

We stepped back inside the house. Cole pulled me to him and stroked my hair, as though such gestures pare away doubt. Then, I parked in the living room, as aftershocks from Devin's departure pulsed in my veins. Cole must've felt it too. He was careful not to leave the room for long. He talked about restaurants and movie reviews. Vacation deals and street closures. My husband and I, after making our son leave home, engaged in small talk.

It was a contrived simplicity, mastered only when a brain is distraught. Cole fetched masala chai, poured it in my favourite cup and brought a box of chocolate-dipped figs on my favourite plate. He rolled over a nesting table and laid a wool blanket on the sofa. A newspaper was put near my feet, with a Spanish fashion magazine.

We talked about gardening as sunlight poured through the drapes and shone in the shape of a sail on the wall. It took the afternoon for the sail's mast to fall across the chessboard where the pieces were still frozen in combat. "Do you care to end it?" Cole said. He ticked his head at the board. Outside, my dogwood bushes sagged. "Tell you what," he said. "Go out for a while. I'll get dinner and then come get you."

In the fresh air, I felt less wooden and remembered the feel of roses in my hand last May. That was my second try at the Explorer Series.

The previous spring I'd tried grafting. I also tried mounding earth with the selvage of oak leaves around the roots and fertilizing well into summer. The petals turned yellow. In autumn, so the wind wouldn't snap them, I cut the tender stems back. When the wind carried the promise of frost, I tucked the shrubs in burlap. Cole approved. He thought it prudent to protect perennials. He preferred a garden full of givens.

Since then, effort withered away. Broken stems and dry leaves were as prevalent as buds. It was an autumn cleanup in summer, the day Devin left. Gardening had prepared me for endings. I grabbed the stems and pulled.

The exertion seemed right. Sweat was relief. I thought about spreading the roses around, so they'd have more room to breathe. So I brought out my shovel and stuck the tang in dirt. I dug two large holes along the neighbour's fence and transplanted two bushes there. After I unravelled the hose, I soaked them in mist.

The fresh blood on my elbow had dried, and the stain on my sleeve hardened into a bottle cap. By then, what I wanted was a hot bath. Walking by the patio, I saw there was a staggered line of dark, crumbly bits a metre out from the house. When it hit me to look up, I saw that our shingles had curled. I held shattered bits of roof.

I got the rake to comb the grass. Once I had most of the bits piled on the patio, I pulled the huge garbage bin from the lane. I scooped the bits in and clapped my dirty gloves clean. On the way back, the cumbersome bin bounced over stones. I struggled again, trying to get it back on the platform. I managed to lift the bottom, using a foot to raise it from below. Once the lip settled on the platform, I shimmied it into place. That's when I felt something behind me. Something vascular.

Devin. The intensity in his face made me stagger, so much so, I slipped on the mud on my shoes. I didn't feel pain when I fell. I only saw Devin standing over me, with a mouth like a fist. I slid around trying to stand.

"You and all your McParenting manuals," he said. "And still so cold."

I got to my feet, and it was there that I could see, through Devin's suppressed glaze of tears, the field of my own suffering. Then he cut through a neighbour's property and was gone.

Chapter Three

Lily

It's like a pool. From the shallow end, you get a pretty good view. Men are predictable. Falling for the slightest encouragement. It's not my fault. Bars are the perfect hunting grounds. A shoebox with limited conditions and calculable results, where opportunity lives in intoxication and the transit of blinking stars. For men, a smile is a written invitation. What they'll initiate with just one. That's not to say there's no challenge involved. Sometimes I run into a rare breed—the hesitant ones. These please me most. They tease out the actress in her fullest manifestation. The International Thespian Society motto is "Act well your part; there all the honour lies." Tonight, I've let my colleagues down—no prospects.

From childhood, as far back as kindergarten, I've had success with boys. Life was a lark. I sauntered into recess, and both boys and girls cleared a path. My hair was a hit. At story time, our class sat cross-legged on the floor. Girls behind me would touch my locks while the boys watched. In junior high, my body found me and became a thing to flaunt. Though, I never degraded myself. That's against policy, along with predators and perverts.

The tastiest treat is the philosophy major. You might think they don't go to bars. They do. And they like nothing more than talking about being philosophy majors. I've come to understand their stance on sex. They fall into one of two categories. The optimists, who don't have ethical issues with casual sex. And the pessimists, who see sex as immoral, meaning they try to rise above temptation, yet they are doomed to fail against it. Sanctimony is delightful to tear down. By two o'clock, they're bumping like the beasts they loathe. Love them. They don't stick around after.

I can't quite say what drives me. Society says girls should keep their number of partners down. Yet I can't relent to double standards. My current theory is that it's the power I crave. I mean, what's more powerful than letting someone else think they're in control?

It takes a long time to learn how to kiss like a virgin. Flirting, however, is almost nothing. It consists of touches, compliments. Separating myself from the pack. I sometimes doodle on napkins. And not stick figures. A guy comes over and says, "Whatcha got there?" I let the drinks and electro music do the rest. Men. How they hope. Has there ever been a more emotional animal?

I wait until just before last call. "Let's go," I'll say. Sometimes it's back to his place. Sometimes it's a park near the foot of a bridge. I can still add them up—Michael. Sasha. Greg. Carver. Beardy. Blinky. Ginger. Pancake House. I mop the floor with them. Because sex is just applause. Performance is the part I do, legs closed.

In the aftermath, I'm committedly monosyllabic. "Well... here's... yup... bye." Not to say they want anything further to do with me. I'm just seeing to it their choice is taken.

Tonight, however, I'm decidedly off game. I have a theory about why. I didn't pay enough attention to my body. It warned me it wasn't drunk. I nursed coolers, which I hate. We arrived early, so I thought there was time. Yet, even as the muscled DJ played through sets, I felt I wasn't in it, or it was happening behind Plexiglass.

My friends, a small group I've infiltrated from university, have wanted to leave the bar for half an hour. Now, they're at the steps. As the bouncer chats one up, the rest look back. But I can't leave without a conquest. I ask myself what Camille Paglia would do, then lean over the counter and French kiss the bartender.

They greet me outside with laughter, which soon gets slapped from our faces by the wet cold. Snowbanks melt into rivers of broken ice. Knots of people gather on sidewalks. As we stand on the boulevard waiting for cabs, the euphoric buzz of the kiss turns sour.

Mindy is talking about next weekend. Born in the wrong decade, she has a reliable, low maintenance beauty. She's a year older and studies economics. We met because she volunteered as an "ambassador" for the university's orientation week. I said I knew nothing about economics. She said she didn't either. The most she says about it is when she imitates the way her Pakistani professor says java.

The girl to my left is Mindy's friend, Jade. When we're all out, she's never the one enjoying it the most. She extends the meaning of everything I say as though my ideas are chronically insufficient. If I said Freddie Mercury was a great musician, she'd say Mercury was the best. If I say a taxi driver hit on me, she says they're all like that. Once, I challenged her to a cream pie fight. Instead of laughing like Mindy, she crossed her arms, exhausted by my immaturity. Jade's a professional second fiddle to Mindy, who dresses sexier than she does. My guess is she's in love with Mindy and doesn't have the guts to come out.

And then there's Bianca, from one of the south end's cul-de-sac hatcheries. She's a touch screen, long blank from lack of input. If people were named based on the content of their minds, I'd have named her "Surface Content." The expert tagalong, that's Bianca. Good for laughing at antics and joining in without question. When she talks, which isn't often, she indicates recognition of happenings by saying, "Oh-my-gaah-*DUH*."

What I like best about them is none of them went to my high school.

I'm waving goodbye as a cab takes them to their part of the city. I'm alone with the Exchange District buildings and their spooky inner sanctums. Their entrances gape like mouths. Arched screams frozen in mortar. Up and down the street, people are beating me to cabs. Deep slush at the curb keeps my heeled feet back.

My coat is little barrier to this cold reaching under the skin. I make my way to the corner and cross back toward the bar. I get myself stationed at the curb and hold out my hand. I feel ridiculous. It's a rare state, me being alone. Suddenly, there's that Plexiglass feeling again. Beyond the security of the real, my mind hooks onto a shred of the dream I had last night, and I now have a new theory about me.

The dream started with a lamp in the corner of a living room with a t-shirt draped over it. There were two teenagers necking on the couch. Others were huddled at the foot of the stairs. I sat on one of those seat-and-a-half couches, watching as jeans and plastic cups passed my view. My head was an anvil. I leaned back and closed my eyes. When I woke, the lamp was uncovered. Kids were lined up and laughing. I felt filthy. I looked at myself. Hickeys ran down my arms and chest. I touched my face. The crowd shrieked.

That dream threw me off my game. Panic hung around and became like a premonition.

Men wrap their arms, puffed with Gore-Tex, around their girlfriends' slender bodies. A pock-faced man with a hot dog stand has his eye on me. He's ladling onion on a bun. My stomach growls one of its extraterrestrial howls.

God. I wish there was a morning-after pill for shame. Half memory, half fragments are what return at the least convenient times.

*

That morning, Devin had been on his cell talking about the party. Later, I went in his room, rifled through his pants pockets, got his cell and tapped in his code. There was the address. I called some friends. Everyone told their parents they were sleeping at someone else's house. It was exciting because the party was in our neighbourhood. Lots of older kids would be there.

The night started off with a sense of adventure. Flashback to doing our hair, shivering in skirts, working up the nerve to enter the house. Looking back, I think it was about more for me. I expected to see Devin there. Maybe he'd scold me. I think I wanted that. But Dee never showed.

The Remillard house was the biggest on the block—a two-storey with big trees out front. Someone offered me a drink the shade of cherries. After half an hour, my stomach went topsy-turvy, and my brain turned into pea soup. In a helpful tone, someone said, "C'mon." My legs followed them. I turned back and saw my friends until I couldn't anymore. From there, memory is all still lifes. Flashes of sight and sound. Coaxing stubbled lips. Eyelid piercing shafts of light. "That's it," a voice said. More flashes. Mouth sucking my pinky finger. "Lift your bum for me, baby." Thunderbolt of panic. The sensation of wanting to fly far away. Finger down my throat. A voice saying, "What the fuck?" Screaming. Shaking. Crying "Mom." Rag doll legs. Cool breeze on sweat. Metallic thuds.

I'm totally over it. My only complaint is I wasn't told the story sooner. Torture is waking up to a too quiet house. I lifted the sheets. I looked fine, but had an ominous feeling about my body, like walking into a room and sensing someone else had just been there.

The radio said it was eleven. That's when my mind really whirled to fill in the blanks until the lid came off a memory. The Remillard living room. Classmates, backing away. Why would they do that? I yearned for a quick grave on a sloping river shore. Let soil bulge in spring and spew me out.

Even Dee. How, on that morning after, did he not know I needed him? The only time I felt perfectly calm was with Dee. I relished the way he used to look at me—like I was his favourite person. When you think about it, that's a compliment and a half. I thought he'd come, as if pain conversed through space.

It wasn't easy skipping grade ten when Dee failed grade twelve. But he didn't seem to mind. He liked my books—Literature. History. Biographies. Yet it was around that time he started disappearing for days. Things between us, between everyone, changed. "Bottom line," as Gramps would say, Devin left me like I was nothing. And though I'm independent, he's the only anger I have left. Which is why I refuse to think of him.

The second worst feeling? Something you used to do without thought seems impossible. How was I supposed to wander into the kitchen, easy as Sunday morning? Reach into the cupboards for the Frosted Flakes, saying Hey, Mom, ever been so mortified you wanted to soak your head in acid?

Thankfully, there was a cheerful knock on the door. "I was looking for some milk," Dad said, "but all we have is that almond soy you like for smoothies? I thought you might make one for me?" A stream of hot tears burned my face. I'd been hit with kindness.

My door opened to knowing eyes. I followed Dad into the kitchen, where sunlight made my headache scream. Mom was at the island, motionless. She hadn't slept. When she strode toward me, her robe, a cavern opening with her arms, swallowed me whole. We stood like that for ages, until she whispered, "They didn't get you. They didn't get you."

And so the story of the party unravelled. I'd been drugged, partially stripped, and photographed. Basically, almost raped by rapist wannabes.

Not raped. Rape-interrupted.

Mom got me out. She'd been listening to Devin's call about the party too. She'd been scared and frustrated not knowing where he'd gone or with whom. So she ransacked Dee's bedroom.

I imagined her tiptoeing through the Remillard's bushes, peeking in the house windows. When she didn't see Devin, she must've checked the basement window. I shudder thinking about what she saw.

I guess the rape charges she pressed were some good news. All I could think was, who would wanna do that to me? I cried because she cried. Cried for what could have happened, how there are people who will hurt us, take things from us despite knowing the cost. Course what she didn't know was the pictures taken were thrown up on Snapchat.

★

A Yellow Cab pulls up. I get in and say my address, when a stranger slides in the opposite door. Slightly older guy. Wavy hair to the jawline tucked behind one ear. Black-rimmed glasses pushed up on his head. Tweed jacket that is somehow unstuffy. Silk scarf. Not the strictly winter kind.

"Sorry," I say. "This is me."

"Where you heading?"

"River Heights," I say. An interval passes, and he tries again.

"I get it. You don't know me. It's late." Then to the cabbie, "Driver. You'll make sure I behave?"

The cabbie leans toward the rear-view mirror. "Yes, sir. But it's up to the lady."

"If you're assuming I'm an asshole," he says, "I can be one. Would that be easier?"

I'd like to punch him. It's his tone. I'm not a child. It's not like I find reason overbearing.

The cabbie checks me in the rear-view. I nod. Our taxi glides away from the curb.

"I'm off Osborne," my guest says to the cabbie, then his eyes stray back to his window as we wait to turn on Main Street. The road is shiny black. In the intersection, our cab fishtails, and my guest sways towards me.

He's different, fascinating even, but I'll not make the mistake every woman makes. I'm not going to audition. Performance and audition are different. Performance is finite, and the performer can change the act in the middle. When women, hoping for marriage, audition for men, with cooking, cleaning, whatever subservience, sooner or later they land that role. And all those things they did in audition are now "their job." Never to be seen or appreciated. Look at Mom. We act like she was born to do it. I say, learn from their example.

Downtown Winnipeg endures. Main Street. My stomach growls like a man whispering from the bottom of a well. Portage Avenue. Christmas lights hang every 100 yards or so. Grand, familiar displays highlight empty streets. If people are out this late, they walk in groups.

My guest checks his watch. He's kept someone waiting. I assume it's a woman. I wonder what she's like. If she's young, beautiful, witty. Spontaneous.

"I guess the professions of people," I say. His expression reminds me, technically speaking, that smiles are a muscular pinch.

"And you pegged me as what?"

"Realtor." He laughs and looks down at his hands. We turn onto Memorial Boulevard. I twirl my ankle and am glad I straightened my hair.

Osborne Bridge is ahead. River ice spreads away from us on either side. A sign that the bitterest part of winter is still to come.

"Interesting you say that," he finally says with a chuckle. "I'm in the arts."

The cab stops at the edge of Osborne Village. Ahead, people unload from a punk rock bar. We hear their hollers over the cabbie's radio. Men smoke outside an English-style pub and watch women leave. A busker with a long, black ponytail holds a lighter up, and when he flicks it, blows fire, lighting up a semicircle of faces. It's a carnivalesque atmosphere. My guest is squinting a few blocks down.

"So," I say, "what do you do, exactly?"

"You first." His hand flies up to block my answer. "Wait. I've got it. Cop."

Suddenly, the cab's tires spin in slush. People, seeing our rear-end slide sideways, dart across the street. The cabbie lets up on the pedal. My guest offers to push. The car behind blares a horn. The cabbie tries the pedal again. This time, wheels kiss pavement and the car lunges.

All I see is a grey coat. I scream. The cab swerves. We miss the woman, yet the oncoming car turns, slides, and we bounce off another car's bumper. We're knocked sideways and glide into the wrong lane. Outside the pub, people stare. A woman lays in the street. A well-heeled crowd forms around her. A man holds a cell to his ear.

"The other car must've clipped her," my guest says.

Our cabbie is frantic. "Is it safe to back up?" he asks. "I can't see."

"Is she alright?" I say. I hear an ambulance siren from far off. I glance over and see that my guest is centred on me.

"Are *you* alright?" he asks. Cars on the bridge begin nudging to the sides. The cabbie, seeing traffic is about to be at a standstill, gets out. His leather jacket passes my window.

"I'm fine," I say.

"You sure?"

The door opens. The cabbie offers his arm and gently helps me out.

Flashing lights of an ambulance dot the intersection. My guest says, "Looks like she's sitting up. Hard to see." He gazes up the other side of the street. There it is. He's already thinking of walking the rest of the way.

"I'll call you another cab, okay lady?" the cabbie says and gets on his phone.

"Wait," I say. The cabbie pulls his phone from his ear.

"I mean, you," I say, gesturing to my guest. "Don't you want to make sure I'm okay?"

He stands, blinking.

"Shouldn't you buy me a drink? To make sure there's nothing's broken. Besides, that 'in the arts' comment was a real cliffhanger."

My guest looks up the street and then points a thumb at the tavern.

It's warm inside the pub. The lights are low. The din of music and chatter. The smell of polyester and barley is unmistakable. It's surprisingly full for the hour. I'm the only one dressed up and, for once, feel like dancing.

Two guys at a table turn as I walk. My guest, who walks ahead, doesn't notice. He's beelined it to the bar, where the bartender, a scruffy, red-haired man in an old harlequin t-shirt, appears to know him. They're laughing at something private as I stand in the shadows. After a few minutes, I slide onto a bar stool. When attention doesn't come my way, I pull my hair from my neck and stick a straw in my mouth.

I order, drop a five on the counter and twirl and face the room. Winnipeg-familiar faces are huddled across tables, row after row, with eyes on each other. University kids. Devouring cartons of French fries with winter jackets pooling at their hips.

We meander, searching for a table. On the way, I see one with two glasses—one empty, another half full. And an abandoned rose. Our waitress clears the mess. My guest is at the window trying to see what's happened to the woman. He takes out his cell and talks for a good five minutes. When he sits, "They're gone," is all he says about the accident.

We're stationed on an aisle, near a Pac-Man arcade game. I tick my head toward it and say with a honeyed voice, "Wanna play?"

"How old are you?" he says. I laugh to get the upper hand. He squares his eyes with mine and says, "Why are you laughing?"

I stop laughing.

I asked about the game as an icebreaker, a fun challenge. Can't a girl set up something she can handle?

"Old enough," I say.

"Don't be an ass," he says. "It's unbecoming."

I laugh again. It's like he hates me. I've never had to work so hard at the outset. If I sulk, I'm a child. If I speak, I have to analyze words before they come out. It's infuriating.

"So make this easy," I say. "Tell me what you'd like to discuss."

His eyes wander the room and fall somewhere near the bar. "See him?" he says. He nods. I follow the line off his nose. It's a homeless man.

"You mean the grubby?" I say. "His beard makes me wanna vacuum."

He glares at me as if I'd made a racial slur. "He's homeless," my guest says, as if I didn't just say the same thing. He lifts his beer to his lips, and I watch his throat work.

We're silent for a while. It's awkward amid the low roar.

"Isn't that his dog outside?" I ask. A large mutt with matted fur is tied to a rail. "If you're homeless, why have a dog?" For once, my guest doesn't have a hot comeback. Seems I have a brain. I can talk on many levels. If I can't talk, I can at least ask good questions.

Pleased with the acute observation I've made, I cross my arms. Behold. Queen of Animal Rights. Involved with more than her physical beauty. My guest watches the dog through the window.

"Has to be a terrible life." I shake my head. "Kind of selfish if you think about it."

"Have you heard of a two dog night?" Before I have time to formulate an answer, he butts in. "They keep you warm when you sleep. If a homeless person has two dogs, they're lucky."

Is this what it's like not being in charge? I ask myself. If it is, I should quit. Yet, it's like I'm rooted to this guy.

"Where do you live?" he asks.

I lie. "Corydon area. Apartment."

I've surprised him. Maybe my guest shouldn't judge a person so quickly. Just because my dress hugs my boobs doesn't mean I can't take care of myself.

He excuses himself and goes to the bathroom. When he's gone, I have a terrible urge to steal something of his. The waitress comes, and I ask for two beers, though ours are half full. Waiting, I think how foreign pubs are. I'm used to big entrances. A stage. Here, there are no jersey dresses. No Rihanna lip paint.

The waitress, wearing a helmet of Mom hair, returns with fresh beers and coasters. Her smile is shy, and when our eyes collide, it crumbles.

"Thanks," she says, when I empty my wallet. Afterwards, I stow the coasters in my purse.

Challenge makes me want sometimes. I hate that. I remember the first time I felt want. I was in grade four. Richard. He lived on the same street as me, one block down. He invited me in once. I don't remember talking to his mom or even if anyone was home, but I remember sitting on the lower mattress of his bunk bed. Before I left, he said, "I love you." On the walk home, a pressure formed between my legs. A deep-rooted awakening. Broader than having to pee. A budding consciousness with its own blood supply and pulse.

My guest comes back. Music shifts to something slow. "Do I get to know your name?" I ask.

"Ezra."

"Lily."

He shakes my hand.

"So, *'in the arts.'*"

Ezra tightens his lips for a second and then chuckles. He has a degree in fine arts and rents studio space in the Exchange where we met. He's experimenting with different genres and styles. It's a finicky business, he says, but he'd like to at least sell to corporate buyers. What he really hopes is to revolutionize the art scene. As he explains this, he doesn't seem pleased with himself, his shoes are tucked behind his chair legs.

"My thing is mixed materials, different textures. I'm presently exploring white."

"You paint… white?" He nods without a trace of self-consciousness. "And the canvas is…"

"It's white." I try to imagine the conversations amongst gallery walkers. "It's pretentiousness," he says. "For the cognoscenti. That's the point. It's a reproach to the clusterfuck that is today's art world." When I don't say anything, he continues. "Art is produced like factories produce cars. I refuse to make art for the age of the selfie. Of course, I change things up with different attachments: braces, hooks, etcetera."

"That works in Winnipeg?"

"Winnipeg is an eclectic city full of cults. So, yes."

"You're not from here."

"Vancouver."

"So why move here?"

"Why does anyone move to Winnipeg? It's either love or punishment."

If there's an Almighty Being, I pray that it's not love. I mean, he's hard to read. His tone was disparaging, which might suggest a breakup. It was also arrogant. Detached. Definitely not elated nor tragic. If it's punishment, I could have a shot.

I want to chip into this conversation. Whip it into a quick-witted tornado. I volley a question. "What is white, anyway?" The question lands softly in Ezra's lap.

"Not white," he says. "There's always a referent. Pink. Grey. Green. Always some tint. White against white you can see."

I want to keep the exchange going, but I'm no art critic. I'm good at two things—asking questions and sexual innuendo. Oh! And strategically conveying personal information.

"I see faces in everything," I say. "It's a disorder. I could be looking at a cloud or a puddle on the sidewalk. Shapes in tree branches or the front of a house. In almost anything, I see a face or a body. When I was a kid, I'd lie in bed at the cottage looking at the wood grain in my bedroom. I saw things in the colours and knots and vines. My Mom told me once that I came downstairs and was going on about a bullfighter's wedding. When I wouldn't stop, they dared me to show them. I dragged everyone up. They couldn't see the bullfighter, so I had to point. Like here's his cape, his shoulders. Here's his wife, her dress is faded like white. Mom said the bullfighter's head was deformed. I told her that was his hat. I said it was blurry because they're dancing, and his wife's veil is flying. They laughed harder when I said there was more than one image of the bullfighter and his wife. Because there were. Like slides on a plank. I pointed out four pictures. Here they are. And here. Scenes from a wedding. It's called par-ah, par-ee-dole-ee-ya."

"Why're you talking so fast?" he asks. "It's pronounced pareidolia."

Outside, tree branches reach and curl, layer on layer. There's a skeleton's skull in its light and shadows. Eyes and mouth open as it makes the sound behind a howling wind.

He should have punted me by now. I can't stand that feeling. Rejection.

★

They used to make me shudder—River Heights' drug dealers, those upper middle-class dudes who talk like they were born in Compton. Like Emery. He wore a fur coat to class. When teachers volunteered for the dunk tank during a fundraiser, he'd show up with a wad of money spread out like a Chinese fan.

Sometime after the party, Emery came up to me and said, "Yo, Lily. Surprised I know your name? Hear you're havin' a tough time. Yo, these kids can be mean. The trash they sayin' about you is all over. By kids I mean guys too." He leaned against another locker and looked at my jeans. "You know, you're lookin' nice today."

I turned to leave. "Hey now, give me a second. What's your rush? Sorry, didn't mean to grab you. Listen. I see what they do. Callin' you names. Ain't right. You're not gonna stand for that, are you? Because you don't have to. Oh. I know. Seems hopeless. This thing, high school? Welcome to the mill. Still, Remillard party? That's a little old for a skinny girl like you? Throw in a few assholes. Man, you had no chance. But, with me, that could all change. Seriously. I'm not such a bad friend to have." He twisted into a pose. "Sharp dresser. Who could say 'no' to my Jerry Springer t-shirt? That's authentic, man. It's my cousin's, but you won't tell anyone. Will ya look at me? I can protect you. I'll put the word out; no one's to screw with this little girl, or they answer to me. Wouldn't you like that? Shake them for a change? Just think. You come to school and do what you want. No one's got a harsh word. Maybe you even get a friend back. So what if you got hair on your arms. You got hair on your knuckles too, baby? Joking! Where you going? No, no. You wait up. No chance, puny girl. Sure you got a cute face but let me put this simple. I can make things better for you. I'm just gonna need you to be real sweet."

I ran. Ran out the front door, away from the lie that was my new reality. If everyone believes you're something, it gets into your head and rumour becomes the way you measure yourself. I figured it out, though. The way to reverse pathetic is to own it.

So Lily hunts. She avoids relationships. I mean, it's not as if love's free, as in unguarded. Can't imagine what that'd look like. People being their authentic selves, expressing true emotions, being compassionate and understanding. Would I know it even if I saw it? I'm the one who's free. This is me. Lily. I live entirely without contradiction. I expect I'll live a life of sordid affairs. Isn't that, deep down, what everyone wants? The adventure? The newness? I mean, why watch an adventure on TV, or read a romance novel, if you can live it yourself?

What I could do with Ezra if given the chance. Too bad it's gonna end. Any minute he's gonna say something polite, and in one polished motion, stand and tug on his coat.

"Anyway," I say, "I like the bullfighter story. Like long ago, before mass printing, there was this love, unnaturally natural, it had to be put on paper before there was paper. In the flesh of a tree." I laugh. "I'm in university, thanks for asking. Third-year psychology, minoring in theatre."

"Should have guessed," he said.

"There was this article I read once about art and therapy. How researchers get kids to draw their traumas before they talk. Later, I thought about those famous self-portraits, like Van Gogh. How they expressed their insides. Artists feel rather than see. Or feel first. Maybe that could be a motto, 'feel first.' It got me thinking, maybe, to artists, there's no such thing as a stranger."

A smile spreads. "Well," he says. My watchword. "I should get going."

I follow him to the door. Outside, there's a loud crack. Snow falls from the awning and explodes. Smokers have been half-buried. They laugh and toss their wet cigarettes away. We wait as a barman rushes out with a shovel. A cold draft blasts in. I pull my scarf up to my nose. Ezra reaches for my face. My hair is trapped inside the scarf. He takes a tress in his fingers. For a moment I think he's feeling it. Then he pulls it free.

Devin

Four weeks. That's the time Paul allowed before deliveries would begin. I spent the first week wandering Nairobi with a journal and a camera. I didn't know how else to learn my way around a city of four million. It was a cool, July morning, in what passes for winter here. But in the hub, human sprawl blows hot no matter the season. Downtown is a prison of noise and confusion, of jangling alarms and the constant grind of narrowly avoiding a sucker's web. I was swallowed by robes and veils and choked on the airborne dust of dry season.

I turned down Ronald Ngala Street, and it announced itself with a plastic bag stuck in a tree. A man with a large cross hanging on a chain spoke to me. When I said I was Canadian, he opened a black notebook and flipped through pages. He said, "I have made a note saying the Underground Railroad led to Canada. Is this true?" I said it was. He asked me more questions and assured me he wasn't begging, but could we buy some rice?

I ran into a bright child in the middle of a crosswalk. His face wrestled down the smile of knowing one's target. He pranced along beside me, asking questions. Street children are persistent.

"I don't have any money," I said.

"*Musungu*," he said, "You *is* money." Then a chorus of his friends joined in. "You *is* money!"

One drizzling day, I explored the CBD. Necessity made my radar burn through the details, recording everything. Kenyatta International Conference Centre, the University of Nairobi. It's a spaghetti western set, complete with railway and grid-like streets.

As the second week wore on, Kenyans stopped me midstride and asked if I was a writer. Others were interested because I was alone. Kenyans don't do alone. If I bought food on the street, the vendor would often chat, and sometimes join me for the meal, even if I was sitting on a curb. It wasn't long after "hello," I'd be interrogated about family. How many siblings, cousins, what they do for a living, what's their educational status? Obsessed with people, Kenyans talk and laugh easily, as if they come alive only when they're with someone. They're clasping shoulders and pressing cheeks. They say "hello," and the world halts. It's disarming. When I took a day off from roaming, a vendor asked if I'd been ill.

A glimmer of bravery began to shine. I meandered outside the centre one day, glad to see the view improve. I found myself in Westlands, in a bar called Havana's. A beer in, and about to call an Uber, a tall, fiftyish white guy came in with electric-looking hair and happy hour written all over his face. A thin, smartly-dressed Indian guy followed. The white guy put his unlooked-for focus on my accent. He asked if I was Canadian and then if they could join me. The music was loud, so I missed their names. But I got the gist. The white guy was born in Toronto and moved to Kenya, where he lives on an estate growing tea.

When the waitress came by, he pinched her stomach and asked for a kiss. After she fled, he sat with his head close, as if there was something about me he was trying to smell.

He asked if I liked hockey.

I said, "No."

He told me a story about an owner of the Toronto Maple Leafs. Guy named Ballard. "During the seventies," Mr. Canada said, "Ballard made so many bad deals the coach was fired. Fans went to games with bags on their heads." The Indian guy smirked. "But they couldn't replace him in time for the playoffs, so they had to ask him back. They couldn't admit fault. They asked him to be a mystery coach, meaning he'd wear a bag over his head."

"Talk about shaming a person," I said.

Mr. Canada placed the butt of his beer on top of his head and smiled like in a vacation photo. Had to admit the old drunk was funny. After he started the hockey story a second time, I turned to the Indian guy and asked him what he did for a living.

Over the music, he said, "I'm a documentary filmmaker."

Mr. Canada shouted, "He's got footage from Kenya's 2007 elections. Speeches. Protests. Might have more action this summer." He finished his drink. "Hey," Mr. Canada said. "What hockey team do you follow?"

"What's happening this summer?" I asked.

"Elections," the Documentarian said. "Kenyatta is the expected winner, but not because he's popular. They're talking election rigging and voter fraud. Fatalism is in the air. Nairobi is neck-deep in it. People seem resigned to the idea that violence will follow. As for what will happen, it's like playing cricket in the dark."

"What kind of violence are we talking about?" I asked them.

"Oh, you know," Mr. Canada said. "Protesters fire projectiles at the police. Rocks mostly. Whatever they can get their hands on." He smiled to himself. "Riot police specialize in force. Protests don't last long. They come in with army apparatus. People have been known to die. Protesters run over each other." He let the image come into focus.

"It's not like other African countries where armies loot for income," the Documentarian said. "The Kenyan government pays. The police have water cannons and tear gas. Last time, the police shot gangbangers in the slums. Some call the violence inevitable. I call it state-sponsored thuggery."

A nightmare ran through my imagination like digital effects projected on a screen.

"Do people like the president?" I asked.

"Depends where you ask," the Documentarian said. "The Luos, definitely not. Generations of special neglect. Kenyatta's tribe, the Kikuyu, they have done well. Here, people think, 'why should I vote for you, if you won't help me?' When you have scarcity, racial divides are felt. People betray their friends to fend off something worse."

"The Blacks," Mr. Canada said, "can pin facial characteristics to certain tribes."

"Most Kenyans," the Documentarian said, "want peace whatever politician that is."

It was as if I'd watched a nice family's house burn. The Documentarian put a lit cigarette to his lips. Mr. Canada weaved. Another waitress couldn't leave without another cutesy round of harassment. The Documentarian threw shillings on the table.

"We were just going to another pub. Want to join us?"

I told them I was tired.

Going home, storks soared with eyes focused on the street. I veered away from bright lights and stopped in a café to log on the internet and scroll through Nairobi news. The Documentarian wasn't exaggerating. Headlines featured claims of fraud. Vote rigging. Police killings.

By the third week of July, misery was my middle name. Mornings were spent working up the nerve to drive. Paul parked a Land Cruiser at our hotel. It was newish and white. He'd gotten it from a business deal gone sour. Problem was, its luxury emphasized how much I had to lose. The next day, I forced myself out of bed at 5:00 AM. My plan was that, by 5:30, I'd be on the road, driving British-style. When nerves took over, I ended up sitting on the bumper, going nowhere. I wished I could find where fear lived, so I could grind it to dust. All I've known is a hundred easy ways out. Who am I to live in a foreign city?

There. I'd admitted it. Out came Gramps. Floating from obscurity into view. Laugh lines smoothing into satisfaction. "Whad-I tell yah?" his apparition said. "This kid's lost in the clouds."

July spun into August. It was learn how to drive or go home. My imagination got a wide-angle shot on the family, as if they'd been telepathically transported to witness this—Mom fidgeting, worried I'd be stupid enough to try, and Dad too disappointed by history to get his hopes up.

I thought, Paul's right. I have to push pain under. Down and away. Forget those people.

*

A dark blue peak among the Ngong Hills sits in a void of black. From out my window, Nairobi is purple haze with a light yellow glow. When I get to the parking lot, fear has got my feet planted. I need to psych myself around it. Traffic's light, I say to myself. Maybe I'll just sit behind the wheel. I move for the truck, but don't get in. Gramps was right. I'm doomed for failure. Even when my life depends on it.

"She be Land Cruiser?" someone asks. I turn. An ancient black man with shining-saucer eyes gimps along the opposite side of the vehicle, dragging a finger along its curves. Against the dull glow, his bright, pleasant manner seems odd. He points with his elbow. "What year is she?"

"2014," I say, and his forehead creases. "New."

"Me uncle from Mogadishu had Land Cruiser when I boy. Even white as dis. A white blessing. A sign from God He smiling after us. Me believe I gone grow and be good man, eh! The rich reward! Me mother said I be crazy. Deh obsession wid deh Isuzu. Me and me uncle. Machine we thought legend. We part of de legend. Uncle done make me drive on me birthday. Me say, 'How me go drive?' He tell me stop foollich talk. Him laugh. No me kid you, guy. She go fast. That day me bones feel free." I struggle to find something to say. The old man continues. "Me uncle. In dose days he happy. Later, he skinny. No truck. And me my hand be empty-o. Still he visit me, boy. He lift me way up."

His body clears the length of the hood. For some reason, my heart is thumping. His hand is jammed into his pants pocket. The breeze has picked up one of his pant legs. I follow the seam where his left foot belongs. Nothing is there but a wooden knob. "You no believe in destiny?" he asks. "Meself believe dis car." He backs away to take it in.

"Is Mogadishu in the north?" I say.

"Somalia," he says. I try not to look at the stump. He follows my eyes and lifts his right hand from its pocket. Except there is no hand. No wood either. Just a limp sleeve with a butt of purple flesh curled in on itself. "Don't be de son of pain," he says. His eyes go soft. "Years ago me and me friends steal many things for life. Al-Shabaab, deh catch us." He gazes at the empty sleeve. "People done come watch. It govament way." Pieces of a broken picture come together. In it is a boy, and behind him, a country on fire.

"You mean the authorities did that to you?"

"One pole support no house," he says. As I look at him, I think, What he's seen and survived, he's nothing but strength. What's it like to live minute by minute? Living by your wits. Does a man like this worry about who he is? He gestures at a place across the street where two carts wait. "Me watch. I be dere."

"Watch?"

"You drive her, no? Me I warn't stop you." A smile reveals some teeth. "I bin go stand here." He hobbles across the road where he can behold the magic truck. An old woman bends over fruits and vegetables. I wonder if they're from Kibera. The old man, after rounding up the fruit, watches with mouth cracked in anticipation.

When I don't move, he says, with his voice gliding upwards, "Dis your car?" The three of us stand for a few tedious seconds, until he says, "*Nabadeey,*" with a wave. Now and then, the old woman gazes over his shoulder.

After six. Traffic is steadier now. The sun frees itself from the horizon and is about to climb into a cloudless sky. Five, on the other hand, is my favourite time. There's an aching glow. A planet about to come to life. I find myself wanting to freeze that time of day, when, no matter how unchangeable things seem, they crave light.

6:10. The old couple. Their eyes drift over. They think something's wrong. There is. I'm a machine with a thousand competing parts threatening to implode.

I'm tired of useless! I open the driver's side door. My heart knocks at my ribs as I remember what the old man said. "*Uncle let me drive it when I was eleven.*"

Inside is still the hint of new car smell. The beige leather is smooth and cool. The seatback inflates to fill the small of my back. I understand luxury now. It makes men feel like kids. I turn the key, and the engine roars to life. The old man whirls around. I let the floor vibrate beneath my runners. Then put it in drive. The Land Cruiser rears up. I touch the brake, and it stops. I gently let the truck glide into the street. Not too fast. I want to prowl past the old man. His eyes light up. With traffic at my back, I hit the pedal. When I look in the rear mirror, I swear the old man's just raised his stump.

The Land Cruiser is accepting. Gramps and the hecklers disappear into the fog they rode in on. The new anxiety is imagining what would have happened if I hadn't gotten into the truck. It's driving on the left side that rattles me. The world is moving too fast. Reaching for the turn signal, I set off the windshield wiper. Hyper-awake, I mimic vehicles ahead. Luckily, downtown hasn't hardened into rush hour. My mental map of the city lays down for me. Soon, the collapsed umbrellas of markets come and go. Slight push on the pedal, and three city blocks throttle by.

I circle around and thread through the CBD again. Market Street. Biashara Street. The city is no longer a cloak of steel and glass. I see a future with Paul. My mentor. I see the outlines of people I may come to know. A girl.

I decide I'm ready for the highway. Soon, I'm passing Uhuru Park and the Independence Monument a few hundred metres away.

Adventure isn't what happens. Adventure is what happens to *you*. To keep Gramps and them at bay, all I have to do is meet the challenge. Overlook any issues Paul might have. I'll do that for me and for maintaining this feeling. Need to protect it. Feed it. Not startle it with questions.

JULIA

I met Ervan at aerobics class. She'd emigrated from Istanbul. I appreciated her worldliness. After all, she'd left her husband.

In spring, she mentioned needing help moving. Cole and I had met a few times, though I wouldn't call it dating. The night before the move, he called and asked if I'd like company. The next day, at two o'clock, Ervan and I were at the curb when Cole showed up in a van.

At the new place, Ervan and I put her bed together. We saw Cole standing on the boulevard, looking at the canopy of trees.

"Is he helping or what?" Ervan asked.

When Cole returned, he hefted boxes until his hair stood on end. "He's strong," Ervan said. Her tone was suggestive. "In Turkey, you rarely find such a man."

"Maybe you'd like to date him?" I said.

"*Arkadas*, he's all about you."

Cole held doors open. Ate dinners with my friends. When I think of him in those days, he either had a flashlight in his teeth or a leaf blower on his back.

He asked me about myself.

Then, one day, I'd been listening to spa music from the television channel, and the phone rang. My Dad was calling from Regina to say he had liver cancer. When my mind comprehended, I sobbed. How was it possible that one minute I was fine, the next I wasn't? It was my first significant death. By that I mean the kind that spins you off the table of life.

I said to Cole, "It's a horrific death."

He said, "There's a solution to every problem."

I became busy with Dad's dying. He moved in. I came and went, running chores, and there he was when I got back, getting weaker. His neck and shoulders took on the shape of a question mark, as his head sunk toward his chest. I asked how he was feeling, eyeing the medicine bottles.

"Still dying," he said.

He shrank so quickly I couldn't cope with the downward slide. The progression sent me into night terrors. I woke clenching my chest. Cole was calling every night.

"Hey," he'd say, with that downward inflection reserved for funerals.

At first, the conversations were soothing, though we didn't say much. I felt he understood that words failed when things were difficult. Then, when I hadn't seen him for weeks, our conversations changed. He quizzed me about the prognosis, Dad's pills, his appetite and my state of mind. I had only so many mental resources. I grew resentful and said "Stop..." or something like that.

Cole was quiet, and the void reflected my rudeness back to me. Frustration gave way to an aerial point of view. There I was. A week's worth of spent dishes on the counter. My robe missing its belt. Why couldn't I accept help? Was I really so independent? I was in a relationship with a guy who called every day while my Dad was sick.

"Thought I'd ask." He chuckled self-consciously. "A guy can only try."

"I'm an idiot," I said.

The next day, leaves and crabapples fell and rotted into sludge under a tree. I pulled a lower branch down and felt a black clump near the tip. Most branches had similar clumps. I ran to the shed for my shears and chopped the clumps off. After an hour, branches were scattered at the base of the tree. A long month later, Dad shrivelled.

He died in the wee hours, at the end of a long weekend. I went to palliative care where nurses whispered in their cubbyhole behind a desk. One gave a taut smile as I passed on my way to see him. Cole called that night. I told him I could only think about tree clumps.

"Let me come over," he said. When he came, I let him guide me to the hand-me-down kitchenette, where, with a hand on my wrist, he watched as I stared into my tea. "You should eat," he said. He found tomato soup in a can. He heated it in the microwave and opened a sleeve of soda crackers. He placed the spread in front of me and said, "I like taking care of you."

When I put the spoon to my mouth, something was missing. "The bowl's warm," I said. "But the soup's cold."

The seasons changed. On an uncommonly warm winter afternoon, Cole leaned out a window he was cleaning. Then, all at once, his head dipped, and he pulled his body back in, bonking his head on the windowsill. I hurried over and put a hand to his head. He put his arms around me and planted a kiss.

The word that came to mind was "textbook." The kiss spoke in whispers of fear and compensation. I lead him to my bed where his traipsing tongue became a plug in my throat. Lovemaking by suffocation. He pulled off his clothes and draped them on the back of my chair. He did the same with my pants, after he gently slid them off. His neatness gave me a shiver.

To describe the sex, I'd have to say *Greatest Hits* album. Standard riffs delivered with vigour. Can't say it was bad. It was a proper romp. Like I'd been somewhere and spent money.

I wish I could say I was breathless afterwards, that I screamed, because he'd hit the nerve near the root. But it was more like pinball. Press the button to start her up. Rock machine with hips and try not to drain the ball too soon.

Who was I to complain? I still slept under my father's duvet. A girl with mouldy bread and filthy fingernails carrying an anvil-sized fatigue. Yet, she dreams of living. I told myself what any girl does when considering her future. How much scope can any one man have?

Cole's lips were parted. A fine layer of sweat coated him. "Maybe we should do a date," he'd said. I was thinking, we have. We hadn't. What we did was let Cole take care of me.

He sat up with his legs off the bed's edge. His hair pleasantly mussed into standing waves. He pecked me on the forehead and washed up in the bathroom. When he returned, he lay again, this time generously alongside me. Sumptuously close. I felt his eyelashes graze the end of my nose, before he sank into sleep.

Morning came, and feeling as though I'd rested better than I had in a while, I opened my eyes. The window was open, and the air was full and sweet. Beside me, Cole was splayed with his fingers cupping his scrotum.

I made him breakfast. I whipped cream. I cooked sausages in one pan and pancakes with blueberries in another. Cole was behind me, with arms around my waist. Then, when breakfast was served, he was hypnotized.

We spent that afternoon shopping an outdoor market. With a light arm around me, Cole talked about beets and Swiss chard, sharing my excitement for cooking, or at least eating.

Going home, we zoomed along Pembina Highway. I said, "I used to want to act." The median swept past his window. "That was my number one dream growing up."

"Mmm?"

"When I was acting, I never had an issue being myself, you know?"

"I thought acting was a put-on," he'd said.

"I think it's more of a filter," I said. "A part comes through a person." He seemed puzzled. "I tried some improv and community club acting. People said good things. But I thought something was holding me back. I couldn't get to the level of rawness I wanted."

"Guess we'll never know."

By dinner, an edge crept into my mood, like the chill in a late summer breeze, when leaves start to drop and float on lakes like shards of rust.

I remembered swimming at our cottage at Lac Lu. the second weekend of October. Mom was in a turtleneck. She stayed on the shore with a towel folded over her arm. Dad was on the dock ready with a camera. I did a jump off the end and then made a clenched climb back up the ladder.

I thought about those days at the lake often in my grief. Then, on a Saturday, Cole asked if I'd like to go to the beach. It was mid-June. He packed the van with beer, sandwiches, and

CDs. At the beach, there were eleven cars in the parking lot. The sun was high, the air was warm and my mood brightened. I took Cole's hand and we walked, passing young people. We lay the blanket and popped a beer. I pulled my skirt in tight around my thighs. Cole looked at me. "Care to swim?" Waves far out curled over a sandbar.

"I don't know," I said. "Might be cold."

He vaulted to his feet and jogged to the water's edge. His white skin glowed against steel blue as he poked the water with his toe. He turned back squinting. "You should come." I waved for him to go on without me. He bounded in. Water splashed around his ankles and thighs. Eventually, he dived. His heels disappeared under water, and three seconds later his head bobbed out. He waved and then swam deeper with a breaststroke. When I looked again, he was treading water. "Come on!"

"You go ahead," I said.

"What?"

"I said, that's okay!"

"You should." I could see his arms working. "If you don't, you'll regret it. Besides, you don't want to keep me hanging, right?"

"Alright," I'd said. It was a thumbs-up from Cole.

I pulled off my sundress. Water met my feet, and I flinched at the chill. "That's ridiculous," I said. Cole only smiled. I crept in further. Cold flew up my shins. The breeze off the lake made it worse. Muscles constricted. From kneecaps, to crotch, to waist. I hugged myself and stepped along the gentle descent of the sand below.

"I'm getting tired," he'd said. "Dive."

I started whispering to myself. "One. Two..."

"What's that?"

"I'm talking myself through it."

"Be with me," he'd said. Waves slapped around his jawline. "It's fine once you're in."

We married a year later. Honeymooned in Fiji in a hut built on stilts, surrounded by water. See the woman admiring the ultra-blue? She steps down into surf overlooking the future.

Even so, there was a chill. All I knew of love was that it was not evasion. Not getting in would've been harder.

DEVIN

Having brushed up my bargaining radar, I lived Nairobi-cheap. I ate street food and wore used clothes. Finding my room spruce-able, I washed away hard water stains from the faucet. Cleaned the washstand. Even gave the walls a new coat of paint. I bought dishes for soaps and razors, new sheets, a duvet, and a wool blanket for late August nights. I did it for me. I deserved it.

Three days later, I had a cold. When Paul called about my first delivery, I coughed in his ear. "You're gonna wanna get up early," he said. He gave me the address. I scribbled it down with the date and the name of the guy I'd meet. "How do you feel?" he asked. "You're doing this, right?" When I hesitated, he added, "If you could answer, that'd be superb."

"Hope so." I launched into a coughing fit and held the phone away.

"You *hope so*?"

For days, I'd had a bad feeling. "Tell me it's not drugs," I said.

"No, you silly bastard. It's not drugs. I'm hurt by the accusation. Now, are ya doing the delivery or not?"

The alarm goes off the next morning. 3:45. It takes a century for the hot water to come on. Pack a travel bag. Raincoat. Extra money. Cell. I creep past an empty registration desk to the chilly parking lot. It's Paul. I'm stunned to see him at this time of day.

"I know," he says. His hamster eyes are half-mast. "You got it together?" I nod. "I'm here for moral support. And this." He hands me 500 shillings. "For incidentals." The bills are cool and smooth. "Don't spend it unless you need to. The package is in the trunk."

"Is there a reason I'm not putting it in the trunk myself?"

"I'm the one they trust," he says. "My business. I pack it." I ask how I'll know when it's time to leave. He rubs grit from his eye. "The last thing you do is drop and run. There's such a thing as leisure. Let them look at it. Be rapt by it. They'll have a way of letting you know when they're done." We walk to the truck. "Relax. The money in your pocket's a little insurance. There's always a chance a customer won't be happy. You have that to sweeten the deal."

"If you think the customer won't be happy, shouldn't you be there?"

"The customer *will* be happy. I'm giving you the power to make an executive decision if need arises. If they're unhappy about the quality, give them that."

"Just... every time you talk about it, the story gets more complicated."

"Ever talked to a banker? Listen kid, I buy and sell."

Paul reaches into his pocket, and I think how easy it would be to ask, what's in the trunk? But then I might be out of a job, all of this would have been for nothing, and Gramps would be back, riding shotgun, blathering how I'm the only person who failed at a job dished on a silver platter. Besides, Paul is my friend.

I look at my watch. 4:40. If I don't get going I'm gonna have a late start. Paul is in no hurry. He rubs the back of his neck.

"You alright?" I ask.

"Just a bit taken aback, I reckon. You're not acting like the Devo I know. Devo is a guy who can roll with whatever comes. Take 'im to Nairobi. No suitcase. Take 'im to Kibera. No problem. 'Cuz he's got an open mind. That's how I saw you, prairie boy."

"What's prairie got to do with this?"

"I got an image of you. In a barn-shaped house with the shutters." I scoff. "The wind's blowing through, taking the dead air out. That's Devo. An open window."

"I am open."

"You seemed like an asset..."

Paul wears the snagged expression of complication. I shouldn't've asked the drug thing. He thinks I don't trust him. I had a good thing and now? I want money. I want the truck.

"You had me convinced I was an asset. Suddenly, I'm not?"

His eyes narrow. "You tell me."

"I'm game," I say.

His eyes dart around my face, and he exhales. "Then, here." He hands over a fat envelope. "Your earnings." I flip through the wad of shillings.

"I haven't done anything yet." There's at least 10,000 shillings, roughly $100 American. "Why're you paying me now?"

"You're a friend, and you need to know the job's important. How important?" He taps the envelope. "*This* important. Because you're carrying something valuable enough that you'll be accommodating and flexible. Your skill set."

It's been a while since someone talked about me having skills.

I get in the truck and roll down the window. "Cell phone," he says. He taps in the password, hits contacts and hands the phone to me. Paul is the only contact on the list. Under phone numbers, several are listed. As if reading my mind, Paul snickers, "I'm a lot of man."

Almost five o'clock. Paul holds me up another minute talking about windows. They shouldn't be rolled down more than two inches. If you stop with the wrong guy beside you, he'll take the phone out of your hand.

I punch the address into the GPS. I misspell Kirinyaga Road twice, even though it's a road I know. Finally, my route appears on the screen. Paul claps the roof.

Little shops with awnings line the street. Above them appear to be apartments. The feel in this part of town is raw, with poverty too vivid for disguise. I turn onto Kirinyaga Road. Passing a side street, I notice a sidewalk half-a-foot deep with garbage. A man picks his way through, leveraging himself with the help of a shop wall.

The arrow on the GPS closes in on its target. Ahead is "Sam's Motor Parts," a rundown garage with an office. A woman's electronic voice says "destination." I pull to the curb and glance at my watch. Paul gave me a ten-minute window for arrival. Between 5:20 and 5:30. I've beaten the window by five minutes. A black boy dressed in a sweater stands in grass, as if he's waiting for his bus to Princeton. He's a beefy bugger and he's looking at me like there's a connection between us.

I get out of the truck pulling the address out.

"You early," Little Beefcake says. I look around, scanning for an adult. He walks toward the office and stops just shy of the door. "Banana," he says. "Me I call you dat."

Mind. Imploded.

He cannot be the contact.

I stumble through the pronunciation of a name. "Mr. On-y-in-yechi?" Little Beefcake glares. Nothing's gonna happen until I move, so I follow him to the garage. When I get to the door, he doesn't let me pass like a regular person. He takes my arm and hustles me through. Fat fingers press into flesh. I'm being manhandled by a four-foot can of Spam.

I get that he's being rough to set the tone. But I'm the elder in the situation, so I give Little Beefcake a shove, a lesson in respect for future reference.

Somewhere within the building, keys jingle. There's the turn of a lock. Voices come from a back room. A door shuts. Booming laughter. Little Beefcake turns his attention to the door at the far wall. I peek in the office beside us. Yellow papers are strewn on a desk, as if workers broke for lunch and never returned. The garage is a void, except for a shard of light seeping past the edges of an ad taped to the window. Dust floats like mist over a canyon.

When Little Beefcake crosses his arms, flesh at his biceps dents like folds on a balloon animal. Apparently, there are bigger things on his mind than me. He pulls on a rope, and the large garage door opens. Light stretches in and lights up our shoes. I can make out his face, which has swivelled toward my truck.

"Get it inside."

I coast the truck into the garage, with Little Beefcake waving me in. He fades in the shadows. I stop. He pulls the rope and lowers the big door.

"Dah trunk," a voice says so suddenly I nearly choke.

Two men. The guy out front, fortyish, square body, appears to be Little Beefcake's father; they share double chins. The second man is skinny, with hip bones barely wider than his waist, and shoulders barely wider than his head.

"It's already open," I say. I show them the keyless remote, and they pass without greeting. The front man goes to the truck, while the skinny one reaches into the air, one arm helicoptering. I hear links in a chain. He's caught hold of something and pulls. A naked light bulb pops on.

A shadow appears beyond the ad at the window in the shape of two hands cupped around a face. Little Beefcake peers around the ad and opens the door. A third man enters. He keeps his eyes on me, even as he joins the other two.

Daddy Beefcake opens the trunk. The flank rises. Even though I'm not close, I back away, a signal to them that I respect their privacy. Daddy Beefcake's wearing a shit-eating grin. "Babies eat bananas," he says. Little Beefcake's told him my nickname.

There's the sound of lifting a large object wrapped in fabric. The men consider their loot and chat in French. Then, everything goes quiet.

Daddy Beefcake says, "*Excusez-moi, si'l vous plâit.*"

Everyone's looking. I'm supposed to do something. When I move toward the door, there are no complaints. Stares drop. I hear fabric falling on wood as I walk outside.

The morning heat has come to Nairobi. Men remove boxes from an idling truck outside an electronics store. Children walk to school. With each box lifting off the truck, with each child grabbing for another's hand, I feel the world turning. I stand off the sidewalk to make room for others.

A *matatu*'s tires are stuck against the curb. The driver is backing up and driving forward, trying to eke the thing free. A dozen faces in the windows are motionless, as if painted on playing cards. The *matatu* drives ahead. The rear wheel rolls over the curb, and the top of the *matatu* becomes a treetop, heavy with birds. Ca-chunk. The rear wheel hits road. The machine pulls out.

There's a bang. I whirl around. The men from the garage march towards a truck on the street. One lugs the canvassed-covered delivery and hoists it into the rear seat. The truck's sliding doors clap shut. As they pull away, Little Beefcake lingers at the garage door with a hand on the knob.

"No bad for day's work," he says.

"If you say so."

"Paul to be happy. If Paul happy, Banana happy."

There's nothing left to say. Like Paul said, I know when to leave.

My truck rumbles when I turn the key. The radio tuner scans and lands on a rock station. It plays a song I haven't heard before—

Lay down your burdens by the riverside
Take a deep breath and go for a ride
Welcome to the groove machine.

I roar a quarter mile before I hit gridlock. An emergency vehicle screams. I poke my head out, but I can't see the accident. Forty yards down, pedestrians have gathered into a human chain. "What's going on?" I call.

As police direct traffic, it seems to me this might be Kenya. Diverse people linked by hindered progress.

Twenty minutes pass. Then, vehicles break away and veer down side roads.

"Nice machine," a voice says. A black guy is on the meridian. His mouth smiles, but his eyebrows dip at the centre. My head floods with Paul's warnings. Robbery. Windows no lower than two inches. Hijacking. "Almost no tourists killed."

I relock my doors. Still, my mind whips off a scenario where this guy lobs a rock through my window. Then, relief, when I remember I tucked my bag under the passenger seat. Nothing to see. Nothing to steal. Except the wad of cash Paul gave me.

Meridian Man shouts. I search the crowd and balconies for his friend. I locate a man at the crosswalk. The man calls back. Meridian Man points and then walks in my direction.

I scan the truck for anything useful as a weapon. The glovebox holds maps, a few restaurant candies, my MP3 player, phone charger. As if I woke him, Gramps's smug puss appears. He's wearing a "not-so-fun-now, huh?" look on his face. I slam the back of my skull on the headrest.

In the rearview mirror, a woman is crying. Her hand balls under her nose. Meridian Man gestures as if desperate to calm her.

People are still scattered on the road. Someone limps with the help of a young woman. The smell of cooked wire drifts in the air. I'm able to pull ahead, then, when traffic really opens up, I see a *matatu* lying sideways. Men closest to the wreck stand with hands clasped behind their heads. Twenty or so people collect and lift one side, trying to push the *matatu* right-side-up. Metal groans. The machine lifts and sinks. More men come, and with one group heave the *matatu*'s roof rises. It rocks on its wheels. Men ripple back, cheering.

Near an ambulance, people with bandages carry bags back to the *matatu*. A girl lies prone on a stretcher, unnaturally still, eyes searching, and I think the toughest part won't be work. I'm going to have to know people. I have to become part of the puzzle, not try to figure it out from afar.

Julia

I was thirsty for hope, and the sun spilled a river of blood orange sangria.

Cole and I rounded a St. Vital street to look at a bungalow for sale. It was the early '90s, I was pregnant and our price range was modest. We were keen on that house. We could see ourselves growing there. But then, we had no idea our unborn child's first word would be "bees."

The house hit us with a faint scent of smoke. Before I could run, Cole shook his head as if to say, "Don't worry." We surveyed the bathroom and kitchen. We moved through the small bedrooms, past scuffed baseboards, over blush-coloured carpet.

Pregnancy had taken a toll. My youthful energy was sapped. Afterwards, in the car, I leaned on the door. "You look like a deflated airbag," Cole said. I checked my reflection. The whites of my eyes contained a network of tiny, red veins.

"Just thinking about the packing," I said. "And unpacking. The upheaval. All the starting and stopping and starting again."

"I know you'll help where you can," he said. "But don't worry. I'll do it."

The last snowfalls of spring melted as soon as they arrived. That's when Cole settled us in. He worked fourteen-hour days. I slit boxes with an X-acto knife, but did little else except snack and rub my ankles. Cole didn't complain, though his back did. I ran Epsom salt baths. My belly and I didn't fit in there, so I kissed his face instead. He said, "You only want me when I'm busy."

After our first winter in the new house, Cole prowled the outside perimeter. He wanted to know how the house's foundation had fared. I heard murmuring from outside. It came from the back corner of the house where Cole and the neighbour were on their knees. Cole was gesturing at the stucco and the angle of the yard. When he came in, he said, "Those trees are the culprits."

Cole thought the fir trees three metres from the back of the house would push roots into our weeping tile. He said we had to cut them down. But I loved those trees. Often when I woke early, I'd lie in bed and watch the way their branches waved on a hot day. I told Cole the neighbour didn't like branches hanging over his fence. But as Cole saw it, our child could eventually get to the roof and fall.

That weekend a man showed up with a chainsaw. He climbed the first tree and cut the top branches. The rest he cut two feet from the trunk and used them as a ladder. Down he descended, lobbing branches in quick succession, leaving behind the dank scent of wood chips. For years, Cole mowed circles around those stumps.

By late August, I'd had Devin. A seven-pound, six-ounce bundle of screams. House renovations had begun. They made my kitchen useless. I put Devin in a sling and took dirty dishes to the basement sink. Cole was upstairs, in the would-be nursery. I heard him through the ventilation grate. He was on the phone with his Dad.

"Julia? She's nursing. Of course she can't do much. She would if she could. Yes, she's an excellent cook. Makes things I'd never heard of. No, it's interesting. What about cleaning? There's blankets everywhere because of dust. No, because of the floor polisher. We're redoing the hardwood... it's usually fine. Not like Mom. Vacuuming is done when it needs to be."

I was still big from pregnancy, a semi-engorged tick. My hormones were a wreck, and what I heard was that I wasn't as good a Mom as Cole's Mom. I crept upstairs. My fight ignition was on and revving. I ate a plum, and when Cole came out of the bedroom I threw the pit at him.

Workers were in the dining room pulling up the carpet. "Excuse me," one said. "Floor's no good underneath."

"God, no," Cole said.

"I recommend a new subfloor too."

"If it can't be fixed, it's no good to anyone," Cole said.

By mid-September, with the work nearly done, I left doors open so the workers could quickly come and go. Things weren't clean, and I was testy, and Cole, aware of my sensitivity, didn't mention the dust.

That was when Devin was learning to crawl, and a mother can chase a kid for only so long. One day the tape on his diaper came off. He was bare-bummed and scooted along, leaving a filthy brown smear. Cole came rushing in. A fight ensued, this time about parenting.

"He can't do whatever he likes," Cole said.

"He's a baby. What do you suggest?"

"That's now. I'm talking generally. You're lax."

I took Devin, leaving Cole with the mess. I shut the door to the basement bathroom and replaced Devin's diaper. When I sat him up, he giggled, and I cried, thinking how everything has to be so difficult.

Then, I carried Devin upstairs to the bedroom where we both eventually dozed off. When I woke, I heard an unusual sound. It seemed to come from the hall. I zeroed in. It was coming from the baseboard. There was a hole, and in the opening I saw something fly by. Inside the skeleton of the house, a bee colony had moved in. From a stooping position, I saw where the teardrop-shaped wafer hung. I found Cole and led him to it.

"Bees," I said. "Inside the house." I wrapped my arms around Devin. "Get an exterminator."

"They're wasps, actually. I'll do it tomorrow."

I thought, great, I have to keep Devin away from bees. Of course, he became fascinated with them. Once loose, he scooted to the hole. It became a chore, steering Devin clear of the nest.

"We can't have it," I said to Cole the next night after dinner. "Do you want Devin to get stung?"

"There's maybe two there," he said. "I'll do it this weekend."

"Saturday," I said.

I announced that Saturday I was shopping, which meant I'd be walking up and down aisles of a box store with Devin in a cart. It was a perfect date for Devin and I. He was watchful. Women kept commenting on how well-behaved he was. One woman stroked his ball of hair and said, "He's so thoughtful. Hey, little one? You've got some theories?" After that, whenever someone came by, I introduced Devin as a philosopher.

When we got home, the house was dim. I padded around, gleaning from the tools on the kitchen table that Cole fixed the problem. The hole had been patched with what seemed like plastic. I wandered into the living room. We had a baby pen with a plush baby toy. I put Devin in, and ordered delivery from Cole's favourite Vietnamese place. When I thought I heard the buzzing, I was sure I was hearing things. I found Turner Classics, and Cole came back minutes later.

"Had to return some things," he said.

When the food arrived, Cole happily crunched on egg rolls and I leaned back, under a blanket, and sipped pho soup from a deep Asian spoon.

At two in the morning, I woke and couldn't sleep. I went to the kitchen and filled my water glass. On the way to bed, I swerved into the bathroom. The tub had a ring. I promised myself I'd clean it before Cole got up. I washed my face and then, almost inaudibly, a noise. My mind narrowed. I got down with my head not far from the baseboard. Nothing.

The next day, Cole, with his bill statement, said the renovations had run past the estimates. But he'd counted on some variance. We'd make a few sacrifices, but on the positive side renovations were complete. We had an extra bedroom, newly polished hardwoods and new cupboards in the kitchen. The place was airy and ready for a deep clean.

I swept, vacuumed, washed, and wiped, and I was just getting started. I stood on stools and disinfected cupboards. I even washed walls. It was a fast two weeks, my stomach was flattening, and Devin hadn't rubbed his bare ass on anything.

We spent evenings playing with Devin, who had begun to babble.

I said, "Mommy?"

Cole said, "Daddy?"

We sang little songs.

After Devin was down, I went to bed. I was just lying there, having a private moment of gratitude, feeling tired, when I heard it.

Buzzing.

I sat up. It went away.

In the hall, faint light from the television flickered. Cole slept on the couch. I shut off the TV and thought about waking him. The wee hour crying had put us both in a state of mild confusion. So I knocked off the lights and returned to bed.

The duvet was freshly washed and smelled of lemon. I had the window open a crack, and the nicest breath of evening air wisped in when I heard it again. I kicked off the covers and flew out of the bedroom. I lowered myself near the floor and heard them. Low-pitched and meandering. I screamed Cole's name.

"What?" I met him in the living room. "What could it possibly be?" he asked.

"I have to show you something."

"If you got a head start on the nursery, now's not the time."

"It's the big reveal."

I lead him down the hall.

"Listen," I said.

With eyes adjusted to the dark, I saw Cole looking back at me. Devin woke and shrieked. Cole took him, and when I returned with Devin's bottle, Cole was bouncing the boy in his arms.

"I guess it wasn't the best idea," Cole said. Devin sucked the bottle. "We were spending money we didn't have, Jules. You know how I feel about debt. I bought some duct tape. Found your drawer of plastic bags."

"What did you do?"

"Christ. I wrapped them, okay? You know," he pinched his nose, "snuffed."

"Bees," Devin said.

In the morning, Cole found a bullet-sized hole in stucco. He went to the store and bought goopy stuff that came in a can. Six days until the sound died.

Chapter Four

Cole

A divorce is coming on. Can feel the clap-click in my throat. Since Devin left, Julia's blamed Dad and I, and now her behaviour falls under a concept I've coined: divorce vocabulary. It's linguistics spelled in visuals. Postures. Ticks. When I approach, Julia's cheeks fill with blood, yet the surrounding skin is sallow. She's a graphic reminder of how disgust can mushroom against the tincture of disbelief.

As I step off the stairs, our eyes lock, yet Julia retreats and her private escape begins. I find her at the kitchen counter. Her back is to me, yet I see she has her cheese cutter out, the one with the handle and the wire. She fetches grapes from the fridge, crackers from the cupboard and jam she's put in her drooping sweater pocket. She's given to this style lately. Shirts with extra fabric at the underarm, like a vampire bat. I give a curt clearing of my throat so as not to startle her.

She doesn't turn, and there you have it. Divorce vocabulary includes "remove." Diverted eyes. Icy stare. How sophisticated we are to impart remove in such myriad ways! She unwraps the crinkly paper on the cheesy slab. I recognize the label: Chateau de Bourgogne. It costs eight dollars per 100 grams. I see its milk skin and think how unwilling she is to acknowledge I'm close. She pushes down on the skin with her finger. Twice. Now, with the wire, she cuts herself a thick wedge and lifts softness to her mouth.

Aghast by her resilience, I move in. My chest grazes her shoulder, a move that once elicited a curve in her waist, a flip of hair or the side view of a smile. Today, the psychic space around Julia is an electric fence. It makes me want to smash things.

As she cuts another wedge and pushes it in her mouth, she is surprisingly unencumbered by regret. Her stillness tells me she's transported. Where, I wonder, has she put herself? I think about where she'd rather be. Examples shouldn't come so easily.

Vienna.

Any village in the south of France.

The alley behind Giant Tiger.

I imagine her somewhere miles away. Transoceanic. Where the air is perfumed by the scents of entirely different trees. Far from this mess, where her shoulders would drop and she'd breathe roomy, yoga breaths.

In no time at all, a man would notice her. Though she's pushing fifty, she still possesses a fine body and handsome face. She could return the key for a gas station bathroom, and men would notice. Especially if she wears her black turtleneck and stovepipe slacks. Sitting, ankles tucked underneath a chair, reading a magazine or contemplating passersby, some sod would think how elegant she seems.

Hell, I'd like to meet this Julia. I've put in the work. It kills me that I get the worst of her, while someone else might get her best.

Julia's cellphone pings. Her face lights up. Text message. I see it's her friend Ervan. She taps a message. I wait, thinking, I shouldn't have to ask, who's that?

The kettle's whistle trills. I collect the tea bags and cups, and Julia tucks her phone away. Without a word, she pushes her cup at me, as in, "Fill, please." I pour in silence, hoping she'll say, "Thank you." Or, "What's the matter?" Instead, she pulls her full cup, and it strikes me. I've seen this before. We've been mercenary-style for months.

Silence is here to teach me a lesson. I'm meant to worry and reflect and find the error of my ways. A new word for the divorce vocabulary vault: stonewalling. That's the thing about a faltering marriage. Arguing is a duet. But what we have is all-out war, except we're practically inert, because the first layer of separation isn't fighting. It's stockpiling resentments.

I'd like to force a reaction. I could crack a champagne glass in the sink. Drop one of her plants so the dirt flips out at a forty-five-degree angle. I could cup her shoulder in my hand and run it down the length of her arm.

"Can you stop wheezing?" she says. The cheese returns to its den in the fridge.

"Can I have some?" I say. She retrieves the cheese. Crackers are pushed towards me. She sidesteps from the counter and moves to the cupboard over the stove, where we keep wine. Something in her posture, the looseness in her neck, is unapologetic. That wine is for her. "I've been thinking of moving the grandfather clock," I say.

There are two crevices between her brows. "Great. Move it out of the house."

"Actually"—I gaze over the expanse of our main floor—"I've been thinking of putting it along the wall, between the dining room and the living room."

"No way," she says.

"Why not?"

"It interrupts the natural flow."

"It's a clock."

"I hate that thing. It's your Dad's. It's like an all-seeing eye."

"I'm puzzled, Julia. Not sure of your meaning." She turns towards the living room as if it's a realm I dare not go. "Do you know where Camembert originates?" I call.

"Do you suppose I give a shit?"

I find her sitting sidesaddle on the couch with a fur throw over her legs, like a cat's tail.

"Does it ever occur to you," I say, "that everything you love is an accident? That if you hadn't married me, for instance, you would have had a very different life, one in which you wouldn't know Camembert or appellations. That the palette you've cultivated could have plateaued at, say, Olive Garden?"

It's a delicate operation, marital cruelty. Enmity in this house, it isn't expressed through combat. That would give cruelty shape, and shape would give it girth, and girth would include police and hell no. Cruelty is strategically withholding laughter.

A beard.

"Speaking of accidents," she says. "What's with the ZZ Top beard? When did that crawl onto your face? Honestly, what're you going for?"

A man never admits pain. To win at interaction, you can't give them that. So I stride over and kiss her mouth, mashing my beard into her chin.

"Get off," she says. She pulls away and rubs a pink after-ring. "It's like necking with a curling broom."

Exactly.

Divorce vocabulary amounts to sadism. I plunk on the couch opposite her, pretending to read the weather. Her cellphone pings again. She's tapping with a smirk.

"I've been thinking about burial arrangements," I say. She looks up. Gradually, the tautness of her mouth relaxes again into fatigue. "I think we should go the less conventional route. When I die, I think you should sprinkle my ashes."

"When you think of your place, let me know," she says.

"I've been thinking about you too."

A stifled laugh dances at her lips. "Really?"

"Your Mom loved casinos, right? So *I* thought, what more suitable remembrance than sprinkling you on the carpet at the Club Regent?"

"I think, my dear, you're on to something," she says. "I've been thinking about energy a lot lately, you know? And where I want to spend it. I think you should be buried along with me."

"Is that so?" I say.

"I was thinking I'll do half with Dad over at the MacGillivray Cemetery and half with my grandfather on the Fisher River reserve."

"You wouldn't dare."

Her fingers lace in deliverance.

I lunge for another kiss. "God," she says.

With a hand cupping her mouth, she hustles upstairs, footfalls pounding the hardwoods like hammers. The only thing left talking to me is the boiler. These old homes are basically wells. I'm at the bottom, looking up. And night is falling.

★

At the top of the stairs, through a slightly open bedroom door, I saw Julia under the covers, facing her tablet. She didn't move save for one foot, a mound under the sheets, ticking, as if counting the seconds till I left.

When Julia fights, her guns are kept hidden. That way catastrophe isn't her fault. And guilt is something she's had enough of. Since Devin left, she's borne a burden, and it has made her sensitive about mistakes of a conclusive nature. This furled vulnerability entitles her to roll eyes, twitch feet and leave rooms. Yet, it stops her from walking out on a peace offering. If I say something vulnerable, an almost step, she'll play.

"I don't know what to do," I said. I closed my eyes in monastic contemplation. "About this feeling I've been having. A reckoning." The ticking stopped. "Yeah," I said. "I think that's it." She shifted under the covers and propped herself on pillows.

"What are you reckoning, Cole?"

I hadn't properly formulated my idea. So I pulled the lens way back. "When I was a boy," I said, "my parents fought. Over money. Those early years, especially. Hard to imagine now, but Mom was so hard on him, you know? Just berated the guy over scrimping a few savings together. Maybe. Maybe that affected me."

"What does that *mean?*" she said. "That it made you and Bill go too far with Devin?"

The trick to vulnerability is to reverse blame. I said, "Are you saying I can't find fault with myself? You're always just around the corner from accusing me of self-denial." Craving a tally of my sins and having seen me once again deny their existence, she let her head sink in the pillow.

I sat at the end of the bed, looking longingly at her. She shot me her *you've-got-to-be-kidding-me* look. I put my hand on the duvet over her hip. "It's been a while," I said, letting my meaning sink in. She stared as one does at a television that's lost reception.

She withdrew to her tablet. The volume was down on one of those talent shows, where semi-talented misfits parade before a panel of yesterdays. She knows I hate these shows, with the fawn-talk and teenagers clapping like trained dolphins. She turned the volume up just in time for the star judge. He was talking to a young man who responded with a stutter. A stutterer! But he has a dream. Julia's eyes welled up.

"How 'bout we take off these clothes?" I said. I slid under the sheets on the opposite side, kicking out the tucked end with my feet. She ignored me as the screen split between the judges and the kid's mom. The interviewer pushed a microphone in the mother's face, and she talked about how proud she was of her son. His life has been one long fight. "C'mon," I said. I felt for her hand and took it. Miffed, she half-turned. Into her ear, I said, "All I've done is try my best. With you, with the kids, with Dad. And still."

There. I'd found it. In her eyes. The last horseman of the apocalypse. Contempt.

I went for my reward. I deserved it, the right to control. I could guilt Julia into a romp for the same reasons that peace offerings worked. If she argued, gave an excuse, I was ready to contradict, with ready-made angles, analogies and twists of logic. Sometimes she succumbed.

One might say it was a theft. I'd deliver a few licks of foreplay, enter and thrust until I tired. If sex were a hockey game, I'd score, and she'd barely have her skates tied.

Afterwards, I'd lie on her, like fallen deadwood, and roll off in a shattered heap. Her eyes would search the ceiling in endless loops, and I'd turn away and leave her with her bewilderment.

★

I pause at a picture of Julia in British Columbia's Gulf Islands. We'd taken up a friend's invitation to sail tidal waters. I remember taking that picture. Julia, the sea breeze in her face. Her hair blows long and curly. Sexy. She's wearing white shorts that cut approvingly on tanned thighs. What stands out is that her face is turned away from the camera. Every time I pass by it, I think, is it pictures Julia hates or me?

Julia is back in bed, under the covers. This time the shield is a magazine. The afternoon sun pours a deep yellow cast across the bedspread. She flips a page. I step in, sending a floorboard squeaking.

"All this going on with us," I say, "yet I want you."

Her magazine slides into the sheets. I undress, lavishly. Parachuting clothes in abandoned shapes. I slither under the covers and raise my arm, the signal for snuggling.

"Wait," she says.

She swings her legs and swerves to the bathroom. Ah, I think, taking in the fading coolness of the fitted sheet and the rising envelope of warmth. A toilet flush and a faucet stream later, the bathroom door opens, and Julia, still dressed, steps forward. From under her shirt, she picks off her bra straps. She stops, distracted by the movers in the street. "I thought they were selling," she says of our neighbours.

"Miscarriage." I pat the spot on the bed beside me.

She removes her socks. Off comes her t-shirt. Her jeans and underwear. Finally, she faces me, hands on hips, with previously unannounced Brazilian wax.

"Let's do this," she says.

She launches on me with a wallop. I gasp. She kicks the duvet back until it's a river frothing on the floor. "Maybe we should slow down," I say.

"I want you too, Cole." Her voice is breathless. "You're not gonna shut me down." She straddles me with her knees. Sagging skin folds under her chin. Her hair dangles shy of my eyes, tickling my nostrils. She licks my forehead.

"Okay," I say, not intending to sound haughty. She licks my earlobe and drills her tongue deep into the ear cavity. "Okay!"

"More?" Her knees peddle backwards until her head hovers over my stomach. She kisses me and continues to peck her way to a nipple. She bites down, and I jump.

"Okay already!" I shout. With her weight on me, my restless leg syndrome kicks in from the claustrophobic conditions. Convulsively, I bend a knee.

"Got it," Julia says. She bites the other nipple. My torso heave-hoes. I push her to the side. "Enough," I say.

Lying beside me, she says, "I'm bringing the heat." Her skin is white marble. She'd have made a magnificent chess piece.

For a moment, I think, *yes*. Her eyes are wet. Her hard-fought win with intimacy is finally here. Near silent sibilance shakes in her throat. I'm getting ready to embrace her. Her body convulses with laughter, and her face is about to split. Tears stream down her cheeks, and each time she looks at me, she says, "God no," and howls again. Her body is racked with gyrations. Minutes chug by while I listen to her vulgar cackle. Several efforts are made to pull herself together. Many hoots and sighs. Eight minutes it takes, for normal breathing to return.

As I calculate my next move, she flies around the bedroom, searching for clothes. She stops at the floor-length mirror leaning by the door. She turns her naked body this way and that, peering over her shoulders, relishing what she sees. She turns her back to the mirror, bends, and wrenches her neck round to see her rump. She gives me a devil look and then glimpses back to those folded pink lips. She moves a hand to a breast. Then both hands find a breast and give them a gentle lift, until they're warped torpedoes aimed at the neighbour's tree.

She does a side stance, and I'm looking at the curves of her bottom and the dimples in her back. She brushes her fingers through her hair and lets it fall down her neck until the mane rests above her shoulder blades. She's flaunted lesser things than her body. The question is... what is this bizarre silent film? Compellingly awful is what this is! She caresses her bum cheek, fingertips grazing her heavenly divide. And I get it. She's fucking herself. I catch sight of my face in the mirror. I'm raised up on elbows, blotch-faced.

She slides on sweatpants and a fleece shirt. Dressing elaborately. One shameless leg at a time, like a man. She finds her tablet and strides away. Soon, full volume on another talent show. Piercing screams from frantic audience members. She descends the stairs.

I feel loose. Like an untethered moon.

I dress quietly, listening to her movements in the house. The expanse of the living room and the hardwoods send sounds travelling. Humming. She clicks on CBC radio. The radio host and a history professor from Penn State discuss arms buildups. The program is ending. Or so I thought. The host introduces a film expert and, between bouts of chatter, plays excerpts from *Who's Afraid of Virginia Woolf?*

I'm on my feet but something stops me outside Devin's door. Julia thinks it's telling that I haven't visited his room since the airport. It's meaningful in a way she wouldn't understand. I've stayed out because she's taken over Devin. Taken over his role as chief critic. Taken over his memory as territory only she can occupy, making me an interloper in my own home.

I go in and am not the least bit surprised Julia hasn't cleaned it. It's as if Devin will return any minute. Blinds are closed. Air is poignant. Like Devin's here. The fug clinging to the duvet is definitely teenage boy. I'm overwhelmed by memories in this dusty room. They float through me like plankton. The time he bought a Mother's Day gift with his allowance. When they were in Osborne Village and he gave his windbreaker to a homeless guy. I lie down thinking this would be a good time to die. But people don't die when they need to.

Downstairs, Julia is whistling. I take a deep breath and detect a scent. I put my nose to the pillow. Lavender. And Devin's notebook under the pillow.

Julia laughs. Her and her damn friend. I have to find something that'll get her attention. Let her understand I'm not to be played with.

Then. A teensy squeak.

Fantasia! The rat. Julia's taken the cage off the desk and put it on the floor. Should've known by the clean spot. I slide the cage into the light. The nine-inch plague stands on its back feet, nose lifting upward.

*

"Get the door," Julia said. She carried a cage big enough for a twenty-pound dog. I held the screen door while she hoisted it through. "And clear a spot there," she eyed the kitchen counter where I'd been eating, "*Now* please. I'd like to take my shoes off."

The longer I'm alive, the more humbled I am by the unpredictability of my own house. Devin, hearing Julia's increasing incredulity toward me, had taken up the art. "Yeah, Dad," he'd said. "Clear the road." When Julia got the cage squared on the counter, we all had a look. Devin, who I'd hadn't seen cheerful in some time, was beaming. "Look at him, Dad," he'd said.

In any given scenario, my son's including me might've imparted a chance for connection. Then, Julia rubbed Devin's back as he leaned towards the cage, an act touching on a hundred different cravings, but most of all, it meant that moment was hers and his. Not mine. I saw it in the proximity of their bodies, and in the way their outline formed a larger work, like those Inuit bone carvings of an adult figure and child. Julia smiled at me, and I thought *great*. At least I'm a pleasant afterthought.

"So," I'd said. "A rat."

"I'm calling him Slick," Devin said. He poked his finger through the bars, and the rat sniffed.

"Call him whatever you like, honey," Julia said. "You look after him." Julia ended the back rub with a pat, and I realized that at the core of this rat decision was responsibility. The rat was going to teach Devin reliability under the guise of a crass addition to the family. Devin might've loved the rat. He may have wanted to test us. It's a touch of the absurd to register a vile animal at the Rush household. But the purchase was going to test Devin instead.

Clever.

"So, it's a rat," I'd said. They paid no heed. "Over the centuries, they've insinuated themselves onto ships, spread infectious diseases. Brought plague to cities."

"You should've seen Slick and Devin earlier. Back at the store. An instant bond."

"It's a rat," I said.

"For God's sake, Cole. Believe it or not, it's domesticated. No different than a guinea pig."

"According to whom? The pet shop owner?"

Devin opened the latch, and the rat climbed up his arm and perched on his shoulder.

"Awwww," Julia said. "Look, Cole. He's like a little Devin. Slick's really taken to him." The rat sniffed Devin's collar, and he laughed at a flute's pitch. The untold number of times I'd have killed to have an unforced moment of family intimacy, and it's brought on by a rat.

"Devin redux," I said. "What better spirit animal could the boy have?"

★

Oh, rich! Oh, luck!

The rat's body reacts to the darkening sky above. I open the latch and reach inside. It bolts to all corners of the cage, kicking up poop and then cowering at the edge of its estate. I plant my palm in the centre with sprinkled rat food in the middle.

"Come on, oh object of disgust." Tacky, webbed feet on skin. *"I should say sorry, son."* I hold it by the tail. In the pale light, he has one pink, one brown eye. Time to make an entrance.

As I sail into the hall, watching for Julia, I have to hand it to her. She's really decorated this place. It's best to hand that kind of thing to women. They know how to push disparate items into something reflecting unity.

Julia stands before the elements, working a saucepan. Seeing me, she resets her face to neutral. Then, something changes. I'm almost sure she's aware. I park on a stool and rest my arm on the counter with the fiend dangling from my fingers.

"What are you doing?" she says. Note the tinge of panic.

"Visiting."

"How would you like to be held like that? Put him down."

I like her like this. Tense. Cagey. A little on the run. A little incensed. "Him? *Him?* Him *who?*" She comes at me meaning to take the rat. I block her with the other hand. "I've got an idea," I say. "Our friend here has been locked in that stinky cage. So unfit for a Rush-calibre guest. It's time he took a bath."

"Don't be stupid." She swipes at my arm.

"Careful, Julia. You're going to hurt him." Divorce vocabulary is disassociation. I hold Slick high away from her reach and walk toward the sink. The radio show comes into focus. Elizabeth Taylor's and Richard Burton's voices fill the room: *"And I'm not gonna give a damn what I do, and I'm gonna make the biggest goddam explosion you've ever heard."*

"You try and I'll beat you at your own game."

I flip the faucet so hard the handle gongs. Water sluices into the sink until it's a half-foot deep.

"Stop it," she cries. "You're hurting him." I drop him in, and then there's the awkward moment of holding Julia back. Slick's chin edges up. He swims. His tail is an oil spill waving in his wake. He swims a length and stops at the steel, scratches it with his front feet and swims back. There are several more laps.

Julia swears in my ear. Not the customary cuss words. Swearing on her life what will happen if harm comes to the rat. I hear "car," "sledgehammer," "poison," "multivitamins," "shampoo," "hair remover," "Lily" and "truth."

I'm losing patience. Julia's body's gone slack, and I take my opportunity. I drop a litre-sized measuring cup into the water. A pint-sized tsunami strikes.

"Fuck off with this," Julia hisses.

"I'm sorry. Am I talking to Devin or his mother? Such language." She whirls toward the stove. The large drawer at the bottom opens, and she pulls out a barbecue scrub.

"Time to clean that ridiculous beard." She's wielding the brush over her head and screaming. "You can't clean everything with a napkin, Cole. If someone shat on you, would you wipe it with Kleenex?"

I catch bristles in the cheek. I run to a mirror. My eye is a twitching puddle. Julia's fishing the rat out. She lays it on an oven mitt and blots it with a tea towel.

If only there was a parallel universe, where Julia and I live as we did before kids. I still see her back then in those floppy summer hats. Despite everything, I'd like to think we're out there in the multiverse. Living however love intended.

Julia puts on a jacket and leaves. From the couch, I watch her trot down the street. She has the rat tucked in her pocket. Soon, she'll disappear from sight.

I'm the face across enemy lines. Bunkered by silence. Bracing for divorce.

Devin

Our all-night drinkathons had pinched to a slow drip with an offbeat. When Paul called back in October, it was a humid night in Westlands. A downpour sent the masses inside. I was drinking at an Irish pub. The phone connection was static, and I said, "I'm losing you a little bit."

Paul arrived and thanked me for all the drops I'd done. "Been zero complaints about Banana," he said. "You've got a proven track record."

Business was booming, he said. He was on his phone most hours. Meeting people. He paused to gnaw on a hangnail, and then said I shouldn't expect much company for a few months. He brought out a map and tabled a scheme in front of me. The map marked Kenya's larger veins. With his finger, Paul traced a highway all the way up north. He pressed down near a thick, black line. I had no experience travelling that far out.

"Use the GPS."

"It's an all-day event. Practically outside Kenya," I said.

"It's not outside."

I remembered the Somali vendor on River Road—the ropy-armed one who looks as though he spends nights wound in a ball. "It's basically Somalia. Scary shit goes on down there."

"Hoo. Look at YOU learning." His voice carried during a break between songs.

"Scary stuff's happening here too," I whispered.

Paul nodded as one who had seen this coming. He took a deep breath. "Back home, my pa took me fishing once. To Eildon, a good freshwater lake. Back then, he had an old tin-can boat. Hundred horses on the motor. A screamer. In two hours, we yanked thirteen fish between us. Until a storm came over the trees. The wind blew up. Rain lashed us in the face. Pa gunned the motor, and the bow slammed over white caps. And then the craziest thing happened. A curtain of bloody rain." He laid his forearm on the table. "On this side of the table is rain. On this side, bone dry. From where we were, it looked like a curtain of rain. Pa drove on the dry side. What I'm saying is, if things get rowdy, you're gonna keep your head on the dry side."

"What if I can't? What're you gonna do?"

"Did you hear something?"

"I mean if someone's unhappy, unhinged." I point just within the Kenyan border. "It's way the hell off."

"You know, Devo. You've met ferals before. But I see this is gonna prey on you, so here's what I'd do. I'd send in the cavalry. Knights on horses."

"It's putting me in a crappy position," I said.

"Devo you've been around now, how long?"

"About six months."

"Right. So you're wise enough to know that in Nairobi, planning is a sham." He shifted back in his chair. "What're you doing these days?"

"Redecorating, thanks to the Toi Market."

"You have any dough left?"

"There's the drop on Thursday."

"You might wanna hang on to some coin. I know it's all gravy now. Something can happen. And you'll want a little green on the side."

"What do you spend your money on?" I asked.

"None of your business."

"All advice. No give. You sound like family."

"Don't compare me to anybody. You have a choice, mate, to be, or not be, like this or that person. It's up to you. Blow all the dough you want."

A shank of sun drove across Paul's cheek. A waitress floated over to the window and dropped the blinds.

"I renegotiated the rate on my room," I said. "Started eating at the vendors more." Dark suds sank inside his beer. "Been surfing the net reading about Kenyan history." He put his tongue in his cheek and mimed whacking off. "What? Never thought about politics before."

The waitress gave Paul a beer, and he tipped the hole at me. "It's the machete that carves between tribes." He clinked my beer and fell into thought for a minute. "The other reason I'm here," he said. "I'll need you to make more deliveries."

*

The A3 to Garissa is mostly multi-lane tarmac. The ride starts with killer rain. Past Mount Kenya, where the cocoa-skinned Tana River snakes away from the highway, and the road collapses like soufflé. It's a muddy basin washed out by the second rainy season. If I drive with two wheels in the weeds, it's passable. An hour and a half in, the road becomes a million divots. A washboard. The truck shakes. A green safari vehicle whizzes by, seemingly untroubled by the quake.

I slow to twenty miles an hour and settle in for what will be a long day. Eventually, the washboard ends. Plains stretch on both sides. Acacia trees grow miles apart, pinning down a tidy sparseness. Further, past patches of thorn scrub, is the sunken rib cage of a half-eaten wildebeest.

Eucalyptus trees.

Further east, the forest erupts into lush, pregnant green. Roadside bus stops are few and far between. At one, a baboon holds her baby in tall grass. I pass by a school where children carry buckets hanging from wood beams propped on their shoulders. Some wave. Others yell, "No picture!" Past that, steam rises from a river.

GPS isn't much of a map. A line extends the length of the display, and an arrow indicates a lone dot. I'm inching through space. Might as well be going to the moon.

Side roads cut gravel paths toward unseen places. A nervousness gels in my veins when I think of the people living at the end of those roads. Their stories don't get stirred in with the grocery specials and beauty pageants of the morning paper. I bet that at the dead end of those roads is where pain happens. Where hard facts aren't shielded by the din of hub city hustle.

Above me, clouds, some nearly black, move at different speeds. My stomach begins to rumble, and I think it's as good a time as any to pull over. My wheels crunch over stone. Grass whips against fenders. I am nowhere and at the same time completely at home. Just me and the unfiltered real of the world. I bring out a drink and sandwich from my bag and push the back seats down.

There's a crack of lightning. Then, the sound of something stabbing dirt. A cattle herder, wearing a golf shirt and a red-checkered skirt, points his stick at the sky.

"I'm okay." I say. He treads on as his herd rivers along the highway's edge.

I begin to wonder if I should find somewhere to cocoon for the night. I'm afraid it might piss off Paul if I put the delivery off. I finish lunch keeping one eye out for shifts in the weather. It appears to be holding.

The highway is a parched tongue. I strike out, and after a while, I spot something in the ditch. It's the safari vehicle from miles back, leaning slantwise against brush. The tourists and driver are gone. Guess I was the smart one, respecting the road.

I remember a program I once watched. It was about brain doctors who worked with a woman who'd had a stroke. The doctors strapped her good arm to her waist, which forced the dead arm to work. In the final shot, the woman and one of the doctors were dancing. I think, maybe, that's what's happening to me. Strengths I didn't know I had are expanding around fear. I blast the horn in memory of all I hadn't tried and was now just making up for.

Garissa is short and bossy—a Nairobi without skyscrapers. Rain has passed through this part. The wind's knocked grass sideways. People dart along sidewalks, as if recently trapped inside. A commercial vehicle pulls up. Through the slats, a tail flicks. Cows. I've wondered about them during transport. Do they feel lonely? Cheated by their mothers? Do they feel their luck changed? I mean, all the signs of execution are there.

A gas station is the meeting place. I know it's in the centre, near a yellow hotel. I find it off the main road so easily that it seems to float into view. Paul mentioned there'd be a second stop. He even gave me an envelope of extra cash, in case I need to buy my way in. Everything about it is unfair. They know me, and I don't know them. I take the risk and get all the disadvantage.

While I fill the tank, a Muslim woman stands near the station, wrapped in layers of dark grey. Her hands are lost in its folds. A slit at her eyes is all that reveals her body. Those eyes go everywhere but on me, yet I know she's the one. I wait by the bumper, until a small, female voice says, "Devo." And that's it. The Muslim woman moves and doesn't even glimpse in my direction.

She starts her truck, then rounds it onto the main drag, with me tailing at twenty clicks. I listen to a CD I found in the market. By the third song, the woman has wheeled into the desert. We're driving over a trace of tire tracks whispering "road." Her truck gently rises over soft dunes. But the sand is deep. I'm plowing. We're way out, deep in copper sand country. It's flat desert and bush, and the view is wider than anything I've seen. The horizon is a one-eighty split between tufts of silvery grass and vicious purple sky.

Her truck is aimed at a clearing in the bush. She brakes to a crawl, easing past a jumble of rocks. I slow too, but misjudge the space. My left wheel rises sharply and scrapes, and now something on the truck clanks.

Ahead, dark mounds swell out of the sand. They are dome-shaped huts strapped with mud, steel and tarp. Just beyond the community, against a red sun, camels rest on folded legs. Zebra graze at the outskirts. Their rump muscles twitch and their tails swing.

The woman's truck slows to a stop. She gets out and so do I. She walks with a body bent forward. Around her feet, fabric dusts the sand. Old women mind orange embers of a cooking fire. Further out, boys run after warthogs that dart away. The woman's diverted eyes tell me I'm to be as silent as she is. So when she walks, I follow her to my trunk and unlock it.

Now we're going somewhere else. We pass by a number of domes. Men meet me only with their eyes. They are the most beautiful people, this tribe—with the most beautiful faces, heads and necks. Except for one towering man ahead who seems to be standing on a pillar of air.

The fading sun outlines a profile of perfect proportions. The line off his forehead falls into a gentle nose. His muscles are controlled curves. He's intimidating, but not like the dopes at the end of most deliveries, the ones who use intimidation as sport. This guy is original. When he turns, the only imperfection is his top-row teeth that are slightly bucked.

Towering One doesn't acknowledge the woman. He disappears inside a hut. I peek in, making sure to remain outside. Furniture is sparse. A proper mattress is covered in a tight, flowery bedsheet. A quilted blanket with pink buds folded at the end. There are four wooden stools and a small, round table. It's carved. The figures etched on it are at battle. Incense sweetens the cooling air. Towering One signals for me to come in.

We are a strange pair. I'm wearing counterfeit designer jeans, my Red Hot Chili Peppers t-shirt and Nike shoes that smell like glue. He wears fabric tossed like a cascade of authority. I wonder if the community has given his grace quasi-legendary status.

It's the most personal drop yet, being in what must be his home. I sit with my hands in my lap thinking I can see his life. It is simplicity directed at critical things. It comes off as restraint. The kind that allows one to live in life rather than dreams.

He's in the small kitchen area where there are basins, metal plates and a small burner for cooking. He pours himself a drink. Dips a spoon inside a pot and tastes. The light sounds of home. He leaves, and I remain by the carved table, taking in the significance of a few fine things. Listening to children and the wind. Wondering what it's like to live so exposed to the weather.

When the woman returns, I smile to show I'm harmless. She doesn't see my promise. She places a cup of tea on the table, along with a small iron pot. She pads to the other side of the room with her back towards me. Her fingers fall on objects lightly, as if she feels for me in this stillness. Those dainty, hidden feet. The effort she makes to be smaller than what she is.

The door flies open. Towering One, his body a machine with a single-minded occupation, says, "Dis be not what we agree!" with a voice from a cavity concealed under the earth's crust. "Me to talk to Paul. Must be to speak wid him."

Jesus. I'm in outer space and here it is. The unhappy customer.

Towering One shoves a cell in my face. Another man enters and gives off a scrambled energy; one pupil is a runny yoke. As he chews something, I reach slowly into my pocket. Johnny Wild Eyes makes a move toward me.

"I'm nobody," I say. "I have my cell, see? I can get Paul. Just pushing the buttons." Towering One holds Johnny Wild Eyes back. My hand trembles between taps. I hear ringing. So I smile to indicate progress. It rings several times and, with each ring, hope fades a little. "I have other numbers. Wait. Please." As a new number rings, I look over the men, wondering what their relationship is. Johnny Wild Eyes is riff-raff. He's the face of pain drawn outside the lines. A man willing to ride on life's least populated roads.

Towering One grows impatient. The strings have been pulled tight along his perfectly sculpted brow. In the distance, a cow moos.

I've never needed so badly for something to work. Where are you, Paul? The simple answering of a phone. This is what the world hangs on. I hang up and try the next number. After the eighth ring, Paul answers.

"It's me," I say. The connection is scratchy.

"Oi, Stevo."

"It's Devin. I'm in hell, remember? There's a problem." Towering One nods as if I've said the right thing.

Paul says, "You messed around in the trunk, didn't you?"

Towering One snatches the cell and puts it to his ear. "I say twenty," he says. "We agree dat der be fourteen. Me I count eight." I hear Paul's voice on the other end. "No wait no week." I can't make out the words of the story unfolding, but Towering One takes in every word, examining me, as if I'm the epicentre of fuck-ups.

★

"Are ya gonna finish that?" Gramps said to me.

"No."

"How hard is it to finish three bites?"

I gave him a catatonic stare. He turned to Mom. "What kind of person leaves three bites? It's salmon for Christ's sake."

"Leave him, Bill," said Mom.

I went to the sink. He gaped as if witnessing a car crash.

"You're not throwing it out?" he said.

I tipped the plate toward the trash.

"You better not be scraping it, kid."

I scraped.

"Julia! This kid of yours puts premium salmon in the garbage."

Lifting a piece of salmon with her fork, Lily said, "Why can't salmon swim in whisky and maple brine?"

"Get over it," I said.

Mom looked drugged. "We're gonna talk later about that comment, Devin." Her hands power-sweeping crumbs from the table. "Sorry, Bill. And Lily. We're not rude like Devin."

"Since when?" Lily said.

I grinned at her, but her eyes didn't meet mine.

"Let's try this again," Mom said. She went to the counter where she'd put the dessert.

"Know what my daddy did?" Gramps asked. He untwisted a napkin, mopped at his chin and continued, "If I didn't clear my plate, he'd remove his belt. Pull it out of the loops and carry it around."

I tried disappearing into the basement. "Hold on, Devin," Mom said. "Dessert."

"Is it pineapple squares?" Lily asked.

Gramps shook his fat head. "How is pineapple squares gonna solve this? Julia, your kid threw out perfectly good food despite being told to finish it."

"Bill. We know you grew up poor."

"Poor as a word doesn't cut it."

"No one is criticizing that. But times are different. Parenting is different."

His hand waved in my direction. "This kid is rude. You say times have changed. You mean you've left behind the wisdom of us old ones."

"Would you like dessert, yes or no?"

"I'd love some."

Mom pulled the dessert from the counter. Dad turned another page of his newspaper.

"Because," Gramps said, "I appreciate the work someone went through to prepare a nice meal start to finish."

Dad folded the paper and put it down.

"Cole's mother made dessert every week. Pies. Cakes. Made a lovely trifle for our anniversary. Gorgeous."

He blotted his eyes with his hanky. Blew his nose like a trumpet.

"I wish I'd met her," Mom said.

"Passionate woman. To her food was the way to loving people. When we first married, we had a place in the North End. Size of a hut. She made friends with the Ukrainian and Polish ladies at the Metropolitan Cathedral and learned to make perogies and cabbage rolls."

"Sounds like the perfect life for you, Bill."

Mom brought over the dessert platter. Dad pushed plates and glasses away from the centre of the table.

"Julia's an excellent cook too," Dad said.

"Oh, *my,*" Gramps said. "That looks just fine. Thank you."

Dad glanced at the grandfather clock. "Don't want to interrupt, but the news is coming on. You think we could take this into the living room?"

By the time I trailed in behind them, Lily had her crumb-coated plate beside her on the couch. Gramps was scraping his clean with a spoon. I sat in a recliner, slid back and cranked the footstool out. He glared at me for the longest time. Dad turned up the volume on the TV. The news was replaying a scene from a US debate where Hillary Clinton was talking about the Russians, and that guy was chanting, "You're the puppet. You're the puppet."

Then, in the middle of the living room, Gramps stood.

"I know you think I make too much of things. So, let me say, without sarcasm or otherwise beating around the bush, that I'm scared."

Dad tore his eyes from the tube.

"Not of illness. Or withering death. I'm scared that one day Devin will need something—money, shelter, without his parents there to provide." Mom's eyes lingered on the carpet close to my feet. "No employment opportunity will be there to greet him." His hands parted like evangelicals on TV. "But let's not speak of it. We wouldn't want to confront someone with the truth." He sat down.

"Why don't you relax, Bill," Mom said.

"Point a finger at everyone but the boy," Gramps said.

Mom's eyes rolled over to Dad.

"No one said that," Dad said.

"Sorry, Julia. What else are the old gonna do but worry? So before everyone stares listlessly at the TV, and I show myself out, I thought I could tell a story. Lily, you'd like to hear a story?"

Lily looks at Mom.

"The year is 2045. Quick," he pointed at me, "how many years is that from now?"

I sighed.

"Cole?"

"Just tell your story, Dad."

"Earth has become uninhabitable. Scientists have found a way to colonize Mars. The last passengers are aboard the rocket to outer space, but they leave the inconvenient behind. Elephants, rhinos, the big cats, a mixed bag of hefty predators and prey who roam the land."

"In Canada?" Lily said. One eyebrow was twitching.

"Yes," said Gramps. "Why not? Night and day, trampling fields of granola and wheat. If people still drove cars, they could watch from the highway as cheetahs raced in pursuit of caribou, tumbling together at the far edges of the tree line. Just imagine when the sun goes down and you can hear the lions roar in the distance. Or rustling leaves when impalas burst through bush."

Lily egged him on. "Do they get away?"

"Sometimes," Gramps said. "Sometimes the harsh reality is, no-sir-ee. So earth, goodbye. The people are blasted to Mars where houses and roads and schools are made of trim cement. The engineers brought the latest technologies, the doctors and nurses brought the best medicines and, as a result, the people prospered. They planted red vegetables, and soon green shoots sprouted. Everything was great."

"From cement?" Lily said.

"In a garden."

"What about the animals?"

"The earth animals prospered without humans. Trees and vegetation grew over roads and highways so there was always lots to eat."

"Super," Mom said.

"Then something in the ground awoke. A yawning little vermin, buried deep in a hole. Hunger sent him scratching to the surface. When the roots were shred away, he sniffed around his new world, where every living thing was bigger and faster than him. Many with sharp teeth."

"Was he a groundhog?" Lily asked.

"He was a rat." Dad's eyes flickered at me. "He tried to feed as he'd done before, but he was dull-witted from his long sleep, so he was stalked at every turn. He tried to run as he'd done before, but there were animals everywhere. They could taste how helpless he was."

Lily had her knees pulled up to her chest. "Did he die?"

"No," Mom said.

"While he lounged with his head in the sand the world built itself beyond him."

"Alright," Mom said.

"He could go back in his hole," Lily said.

"Bill. I think that's enough story," Mom said.

Gramps turned. "How 'bout you, Devin? Do you think the rat died?" Mom's mouth was a stitched line. "Do I really need to say it?" Gramps said. Mom rose. "You're a failure, Devin."

"Cole…"

"Okay." Dad rose and put his hands on Gramps's shoulders. "Let's get you home."

Mom followed them to the back door. Gramps nattered about a distinct lack of social graces in this day and age. The front door puffed shut. Newscasters on the television rambled on about the polls. I leaned my head back and wished for death.

★

Towering One's jaw softens. Quietly, the call ends. He places the cell in my open palm. Our eyes meet briefly before he pushes Johnny Wild Eyes out the door. The terrifying thing is hearing what you don't want to. What I hear is an "oomph." A muted percussion of hands against skin and a laboured suck of air. Now it's too quiet. My imagination's on fire. A whole wilderness out there and not a sound? I wait on the stool, a pixel in the universe, trying to see through the smallest of slits. Sound of an engine. Of a warthog shriek. You find out quickly that when you're scared, listening is about deciphering intentions. The clank of a bucket. What does that have to tell me? For once, I could go for some old-fashioned Nairobi traffic.

I peek through a crack. Beyond the huts are a few gazelles hiding a newborn fawn. Dogs and children and chickens are painted by the pale glow of dusk. I walk out. Walk past the cluster of huts, huffing as my feet sink in the sand. The only eyes that follow me are the children's. My truck comes into sharper view. Towering One snaps its trunk closed. Eight large bags sit at his feet. Young men glide over to carry them. They disappear behind a handful of huts, leaving children in their wake to kick a makeshift ball.

I push out. Tires cut against the grain, digging the truck in, before carving grudgingly forward. The sand is low peaks and shallow valleys. Finally, the truck planes. Rocks in the headlights become the nose and fingers of a giant, a buried man who's kicked his way to the surface. A man underestimated. One who won't let himself be left behind, even on this one spoor track.

Cole

"Dad? Everything all right?" I push open the bathroom door. Dad's down. Pants hang at his knees. He's had a bowel movement.

He says, "My chest. It's crushing."

I dial the emergency line and return to his side.

Stroking his forehead, I realize I've never had occasion to offer him a caregiver's touch. He's been the stronger one. Now, he's a newborn calf curled on the floor.

I ask him if he's still awake. He nods, and for a while, lies motionless, except for strenuous breathing.

I should be doing something. Why didn't I learn CPR?

Call someone.

Julia. What's there to say? You'll be happy to know Dad may die. She'd come back with some budget-emotion response. Still. I *should* call.

Julia doesn't answer. I've got to come up with a pithy message for her machine. "Dad," I say after the beep. "Going to the hospital." I hang up satisfied the message will hang there unfinished.

My watch says it's been twelve minutes. If it's a heart attack, how much shelf life does he have? My imagination flashes to some future point when I'm at the foot of an ocean. The skies are grey. Wind is up, and the tide is coming in. That's it for my future point except for the feeling of being utterly alone. I'm struck by the absurdity of it.

Finally, there's bedlam at the door. One of them is full of questions. "How long has he been in pain? What did he do today? Medications?" Don't they know you bastardize a man in the retelling of simple facts? My brain liquefies and spills in divergent directions.

IV needles go in. Someone's shaving Dad's chest. Between the paramedics, I see, for one shivering moment, Dad's eyes filled with terror. A towel covers his waist; the rest is sunspots and indignity. In a matter of minutes, I've watched the man I admire become sentient meat.

"What kind of man will he be?" I say. The question catches everyone off guard and I realize it's obscene. He's more than electric pulses. People shouldn't care about that. Will the man live, yes or no? That's the crucial variable. Not, meat or vegetable?

The crowd prepares to leave. "May I come?" I ask. The captain says I can ride with them.

We jog behind the twitchy wheels of Dad's gurney. Down the hallway, apartment doors open. Old people stand in those narrow spaces, as if death is here and recruiting. It's a long forty-seven seconds until the elevator doors open. We cram in.

"You're going to be okay," I say to Dad.

"I'm in good hands, son."

The fact that he's conscious must be good. I admire the commitment of the paramedics and firefighters. I sense their minds clicking three steps ahead. Every step, possible compromise or snag: they foresee it.

Ground level. The door reopens, and old people linger outside like bowling pins. The firefighters shout, and the old shuffle away. In the frigid air, the ambulance is a flashing beckon of humanity.

"Sorry," one of the paramedics says to me. "You ride in front."

Dad's hoisted into the back. His skin looks ashen. The crowd is at work. More IVs. Medicines. Dad's body parts nudge in time with each inquiry.

I put my face in my hands. So much to reconcile. So much to put away, as if we could, as if we aren't all marching a gauntlet of indignity toward the finish line.

A paramedic turns from the monitor. "Mr. Rush," he says to Dad. "You are very sick." He turns to me. "Might wanna contact family."

The thought sags at the centre and pulls at the edges. "We're really at that point?" The paramedics nod in unison.

I call Lily. When she answers, I hang up. "Can't tell her over the phone," I say. Talking back is the driver's blank stare.

"Christ," he says.

"She loves her Gramps, but has no way to get to the hospital."

"I don't mean that. Train."

The ambulance halts as a red-and-white arm comes down over the snow-cleared street. The window shield is a wash of graffiti. It's an apt countdown till my head explodes.

"Such a strain on the system," Dad says. "What does this chauffeur treatment cost?"

"Not important, sir," a firefighter says.

Dad's eyes are pinched and raw. "You're white as a sheet," I say. He lifts his hand into mine. "How do you feel?"

"What happened?" he says. "Did I fall from a bridge?"

"Don't talk, Mr. Rush," a paramedic says. Her ponytail punctuates a stiff tone.

"Taxpayers are going to like this," he says. The woman shoots me a look.

"Okay, Dad. We're gonna relax now."

The train's end is in sight. Snowflakes swirl in the air. I'm tired beyond measure, like I've been here for centuries and could chat in a lowered voice about the passage of eternity.

"Eyes rolling back!" a paramedic says. "Mr. Rush?" his voice rises. "Sir?"

"Yeah. Yeah," Dad says.

More jargon.

The ambulance roars into the drive and stops. The back doors fly open, and everyone but me is busy. The gurney lifts and lowers. Wheels warble on ice and cut through snow.

As soon as we ramp through the sliding doors, Dad's swarmed. Nurses. Doctors. One is a tall, sporty type with blond curls. He pulls me aside. He's talking through a tunnel.

Waiting rooms house worried faces. A nurse hits the elevator button to the second floor. Ding. The stretcher rotates, and I'm galloping out of the way. The doors open, but we don't go in.

"Don't do that, Mr. Rush," the doctor says. Dad is pulling out his IV.

"Don't fight them," I say. "They're the good guys."

Dad says, "You never knew which side to be on."

The IV is back in. While squirrelled in the corner of the elevator I see the backs of their heads as they work. Dad's mouth opens. He seems as though he might be sleeping.

"Mr. Rush," the curly-haired doctor says.

Dad's eyes are slits. "Someone should fix the roads," he says. His eyes are watering.

"Don't cry, Dad."

"It hurts."

"Your chest?"

"That too."

We get into the elevator and ascend to the next floor. The elevator door opens, and we're moving. Passing ceiling lights tap Dad's face. "Remember me to my grandchildren," he says.

"No, Dad."

His eyes open wide. "You will."

"But, Devin."

"He deserves to remember as much as anyone." Dad stares from his netherworld.

"Don't talk like that."

A sound comes out of me. A wail. Something fever-pitched and primordial. Julia would say it was a cry from the heart. But only the pancreas could dispatch a sound so repulsive.

Someone asks if I'm all right. "I'm with Dad on this one," I say. As they wait for the cath lab to be prepared, confused eyes stare back. "I'm with you, I mean."

It's embarrassing to cry in front of strangers. A nurse leads me to the waiting room, where I'm a blubbering child lost in the grocer's aisle. Is there any wonder why? These buildings inspire people to foam. Indigenous paintings show hunters and wide-eyed creatures strapped in an eternal death match.

"We're doing everything we can for your Dad," the nurse says. I weep knowing what she really means. The man's old. Did you think he'd save you forever?

A woman slumps against the shoulder of a man, while a child plays with interconnecting plastic blocks. The blocks are primary colours. The child doesn't care that she hasn't got them together right. Cross. Triangle. Square. When the circle is formed, she spins individual pieces. I stare at the blue one and wonder if it's genius. What are family if not an incoherent circle of charms?

There's a problem with the cath lab. Dad's calling. I sprint over. His mouth pans into a smile. "They speak a foreign language here," he says. A woman and teenage daughter pass by. Dad's brows lift. "She came with me to Scotland one summer," he says.

"Who?"

"Your mother." His voice rasps. "We were in Oban, by the Firth of Lorn. She stood in the sea breeze at the end of a long fisherman's dock. Did you know our people were fishermen? In those days, she wasn't so *rotund*." I glance at the doctor who pins a smile to his face. "It was the Highlands and Islands Music and Dance Festival. The sound of distant bagpipes still brings a tear to my eye."

"Me too, Dad."

A paramedic comes for the stretcher.

"One second," I say. I hold the gurney still.

"Dad. The Americans dropped the bomb on the Japanese. Remember?" The paramedic glares like I've lost my head. "To teach the Russians a lesson?"

Dad's lips purse in concentration. "Yes."

"With Devin, who was that lesson really for?"

His fingers give mine a squeeze and let go. The stretcher moves, and I want to yell, you can't do that! Doesn't family have some solidarity? Is it so impossible to love all of me?

"Whatever happens, Cole," he says. "Remember. It begins and ends with love."

The lab door shuts. Eyes from the waiting room are on me. Generous eyes, offering expressions of kinship. Take a breath, I say to myself. No bombs going off. No disaster so far. I settle in, surviving on threads of normality.

Of course nothing is normal. Nothing but ambivalence, a word commonly misunderstood as indifference. Indifference is not giving a shit. Ambivalence is life. You go about your days, things happen, most of it you have mixed feelings about. Someone makes a joke, it was funny, but goofy funny. Someone gives you a compliment, but they give the guy next to you a bigger one. Good lives with bad, making us neither happy nor sad.

The surface chatter at work. The surfacing that is long-time marriage. Most of what happens isn't worthy of examination. God, I'd do anything to return to that. Spend your day. Breathe a lungful of never mind.

A pile of magazines sit on a table. I grab one about cars. Flipping through the pages, I find nothing worth reading. I toss it back. Then, after a tinge of regret, I put it on my lap. I find a page with a Chevy: Dad's line of vehicle. I gingerly pull the page tight, until it tears along the binding. Trying to be quiet, I go slowly. Rip. Rip. My vandalism horrifies the child.

The ad is mostly the car. It's looming large at the top of the page. A family is below. A couple smiles at one another. The man has an arm over his wife's shoulders. There's a little girl looking up at him. She has pigtails and wears a baseball uniform. She cradles a baby pug, a sad-looking creature, with its downward mouth and eyes rimmed in ink. He's isolated in that saccharine world.

I fold the picture. First in half, separating the husband from the wife. What's left is the husband at the edge of the picture, laughing to himself. I fold it in half the other way. Heads are missing, but the girl and pug remain. I smooth the ad flat in my lap to start over. But getting the pug to the man seems impossible. The only thing to do is rip. Rip. A tear splits the page. I'm met by baffled glares. I put the page in my pocket.

None of the other people here appear to be scholars; yet, I'm grateful for the company. Our thoughts are directed at much the same things, I'd wager. The future as it was supposed to be, versus a future minus one.

Scratch that. No matter what happens, I'm gonna go on being Cole Rush. I may be crying, but whatever story comes out of that room, my dad is not the template for his son. I'm not gonna be wiped out if Bill Rush disappears. I'm gonna outlive him.

The child on the floor throws a block. It goes tumbling into the hall. The mother is mortified. She hustles to scoop up the toy, apologizing along the way. When she bends down, her

Slurpee spills: red cream soda. She tells the child she shouldn't throw things. The child, her fun cancelled, shrieks.

I can't take my eyes off the red slush on the white floor.

*

Bill Rush didn't mess around. The night before, friends from school had stopped by and brought beer. After they left, Dad, after returning from the basement, threw the bottle caps at me. I thought that was the end of my punishment, as I was a good kid and was deserving of extra legroom. But at five in the morning, he pounded on my bedroom door and kept pounding until I got up. The hall revealed a tall, black blob, Dad's photographic negative. "School's not for another couple hours," I said.

"Let's go," he said. I knew by that tone I wasn't going to pillow talk my way back to bed. The only way to appease him was to do as he said.

That was a thing of his. He never waited. I reached for my jeans and shirt in the dark. It was a hard winter morning with a scouring wind. Dad had already pulled into the lane. He seemed furious under his wool hat, with his garbage mitts gripping the wheel tight.

I asked him what was wrong, but he refused to talk. That was a thing too. Not talking to me had its desired effect. It made me fully aware of my unworthiness. Silence fell just short of a smack.

Dad drove down Henderson Highway and over the Chief Peguis Bridge. Soon we were passing big, out-of-city properties. A passing sign told me we were ten kilometres to Lockport. We crossed a bridge. Sunlight poured over the frozen river, stippled by animal tracks. On the other side of the bridge, Dad pulled in.

We got out and took the auger, fishing rods and tackle out of the trunk. I relaxed.

Powdery snow carpeted the ice. Dad stopped and said, "Here." We were twenty-five, thirty-five metres from shore, the only people on the ice. An eagle was my only witness. That's when the scene took on a weird, *coup de grâce* undercurrent.

My red jacket clashed with subtle, nuanced colours of winter. I didn't have a hat or mitts. The wind burned my ears, and my fingers ached. Dad gestured to the auger, meaning I was going to drill the hole. I asked if I could borrow his mitts. He asked if the pioneers had mitts. So I put the steel tip down and rotated the handle. The snow was easy to penetrate, but the ice, not so much. I cranked, and the handle gave way in timid spurts.

"It'll take all day," I said.

"What if it does?"

My fingertips were white with pressure, red with cold. I asked for Dad's mitts again. He gave them to me and sunk his hands in his pockets. When the auger dropped through the ice, I dragged it out.

Ice shards floated in the hole. Dad kicked off another chunk, and when it was bigger than a human head, he sat on the ice, cross-legged. I pulled my jacket low and sat with the rubber rims of my boots digging in my thighs. He baited the hook. I released the line. A shiny yellow lure swayed and sunk.

Heat from the sun was welcome relief. Its dome light flooded the shoreline. But I began to shiver. Ice is hard on the ass. Once cold seeps into the body, you're done. Dad was meditating. He was one with the baited hook. I told myself to wait it out. That the misery would end in due course.

Then, I had this great insight. *Why* did we have to sit on the ice? I got that he was teaching me a lesson but his constant demand for proof of conversion wasn't just extreme, it was cruel.

"Maybe the pioneers did this," I said, "but no one else has."

"You ever heard of Rooster Town?" What amazed me about Dad was that he had a trigger-ready story for every lesson. My head listed back in disbelief. "Grant Park Shopping Centre," he said, "before it was a mall, it was bush. Métis people lived there. In shacks."

"Think I would've read about that in school," I said.

"How do you figure they fed themselves?" He zipped his jacket up to his chin. "Okay, I don't know for sure they fished, but I think they must have. Point being, they had almost nothing those poor people. One of the police officers I knew from the lab, he was a refugee from the Congo. He escaped by pretending to be a woman. Quite a story. He was brave. Humble. Spoke English and a beautiful French. He told me about slums in Africa and metal and mud shanties. This morning, I knew you, man about town, could withstand a teensy dose of the Winnipeg version."

I thought about the broader lesson this had, when my fishing line grew taut. The rod curved and shook in my hands. "Pull it," he said. He screamed about reeling it in before the line broke. I went into panic mode and reefed on the reel. The fish shot out of the hole and flopped along the ice. Its gills opened, and its eyes seemed to bulge.

"Give me the club," I said. He patted his pocket to say he didn't have one. The fish spasmed on the ice. "I need the club," I said. "Let me hit it."

"Do it yourself," is all Dad said.

Its silver mouth gasped. I torqued around, looking for a new instrument. We didn't have anything heavy or strong enough for a head blow. A rock would have done, and like he'd read my mind, Dad took me by the elbow. "Lemme get a rock," I screamed. He held fast.

The fish twisted and flung about. There, at the height of the action, I froze in the crack between two minds. On the one hand, was the intoxicating notion of the kill. Might be invigorating to forget one's reservations and let ego take over. On the other hand, killing wasn't in my repertoire. Sooner or later, you have to ask what the sense of a notion is. Everyone understands it's better to shorten an animal's suffering, but I wasn't eager to be a monster just to please him.

I got hold of the fish and looked at Dad. "Mom wouldn't make me do it," I said.

"Mom doesn't have to think about where things come from. If we don't, we might as well learn to boil an egg. I don't do that. Do you?"

The fish leaked from my hand. Its rough gills cut a red line in my skin. I grabbed as it raised one final hell. It flopped and missed the hole, and I was sorry. I got it in my hands and whacked it headfirst on the ice. I raised it up again. For one timeless instant, I thought the fish looked as though a strange light flashed from behind a veil. I whacked it again. The blood on my hand was a curtain.

When it was done, I was physically sick.

Asking a son for the utmost isn't the lesson of Dad and me, but maybe it's the story of men. How we hold each other close and apart and squander opportunity.

*

The door to Dad's room bursts open. Inside it's a busted hive as people fly in and out. The words, "code blue," come over the PA system. Faces in the waiting room set on terror. A Chinese woman sitting beside me says in a confidential voice, "Crash cart. Now shocks." She has wrapped her fingers around my wrist. I take another breath and think of Julia, who's been cheerfully avoiding my calls. Who, at this moment, might be perusing a list of divorce lawyers or the caloric count on a bag of mixed vegetables.

Then, it's not so loud in the lab anymore. The doctors drift out. The Chinese woman says, "There," and the pressure around my ribs lifts.

Chapter Five

Devin

By the time I drive past the Southern Bypass, blue sky coaxes me to go as far as I want. I chose Karen. The neighbourhood is a straight, forty-minute drive. It's Saturday. Traffic is light, yet cars stop on the highway a mile ahead.

I flick the radio on. Even though it's only February, and the election is not until July, a news bulletin talks of a flash protest in Nairobi. Behind the voice of the reporter, I hear a hiss-scream of a whistle. The sounds of people shouting. The reporter describes placards and rivers of men with raised fists. I turn to a new station. A woman accuses the president of corruption. The story cuts to a speech made by Raila. Another interview. A woman speaks of ethnic tension. She calls for peace no matter the outcome. Next is a young man. A resident of Kibera. He's asked what will happen if Kenyatta is re-elected. He says there will be war. The reporter, with a mocking tone, asks what army will be summoned on their behalf. The young man says, "There will be machetes." The segment ends with a father, talking about leaving the city with his wife and kids in July.

Vehicles on the highway still don't move. I come to a stop. People have their engines off. I see that I'm car number umpteen in line. I get out and stand on my bumper. Heads spin in my direction with expressions of horror. "Can't see the problem," I say. Hands gesture feverishly. I return to the cool leather seats of the Land Cruiser.

I turn the radio down and flick my lighter on and off. Use its glossy surface to shine a reflection into the cabin of the truck ahead.

And I needed to get away.

December galloped headlong into a blur. Paul had me delivering seven days a week. The money piled up in my suite to the point I didn't know where to put it. It's almost March. I have more money than I'd ever have imagined. I've also had enough of the hostility from Mugbo's men. Their snarky mugs blend in memory. They insult me. Make sudden noises and laugh at my response. Bluster meant to topsy-turvy the white kid. I can take it. Along the line, fear became history. It lifted and flew away, along with the noise of Nairobi's streets, without fanfare or tears.

I catch the attention of the passengers beside me. I mouth, "What's going on?" They smile. I roll down the window. "Why we waiting?"

A teenage boy in the back seat says, "Lions." I turn the radio back up. It says two male lions are roughhousing on Langata. Traffic is jammed over a mile and counting.

"Can't someone ship them off?" I say. The woman in the front shades her eyes. With few words, I'm wearing my North Americanism all over me. "Seriously. How many people are they holding up? Where I come from, a guy tranquilizes the animal and carts it back where it belongs." They're amused at my outrage. "Thanks," I say. I roll up my window.

Reports say the lions wear smiles of blood up to their ears. Sign of a recent kill. A female voice cuts in to explain that lions roll in buffalo dung to disguise their scent.

Lily would've loved this. Funny how, in certain moments, she seems close. I can see her now, with her trademark grin she'd give when she knew I was watching.

Nice. I stood up Paul for nothing.

I slept in after ignoring Paul's call. I couldn't've explained myself without sounding weak. I need a break and crave the sleepiness of the suburbs? He'd have mocked me to death. Figured a day of pretty doldrums would fix me. I went back to sleep and dreamt of Lily.

The dream started with me. I was in bed, awake and listening to music. A crackling static replaced the tunes. I yanked the headphones off, and the static faded. I heard little footsteps in the hall, and somehow I knew it was the night of the party. Lily was just home. Someone was sobbing.

I bolted, planning to scoop her up and tell her how sorry I was. Roads of moonlight lay outside cracked bedroom doors. Lily wore her nightgown. It was torn. She walked away, dragging a chipped fingernail along the wallpaper. The crying amplified. I passed my parents' bedroom where Mom rocked beside the bed. Dad sat on the opposite side. He didn't register me as his son.

I followed Lily, careful not to startle her. She was steady as a ballerina. A pretty ghost. But then Mom's cellphone rang. The Eurythmics' "Walking on Broken Glass" echoed through the house. A tiny light vibrated across the kitchen counter. I picked the cellphone up. It was Lily on the other end, I could tell by the laughing. I needed to say I'm sorry. So I screamed it. The line disconnected. So I ran to her bedroom, and before my hand reached the knob, the door banged open, and Lily was flying at me with hands reaching for my neck.

That's how I woke, with corners of sadness folding ever inward.

I wonder what time it is in Winnipeg.

The radio announcer gets poetic about lions. Rough, dark limbs. Brooding. They walk with a sunken spine. Ruddy-blonde colour. Lordlike, deigning to linger a moment longer.

In the back seat of the car ahead there's a little girl. Sunshine from the east gives her hair a golden glow. Her cheeks are puffed out as if she's exploding from within. The dad turns, seemingly to see what she's pointing at. I'm slower to realize it. The lions are moving along the highway. I tune my ears back to the announcer. A female voice comes on. "The lions are roaming Langata. Drivers are encouraged to remain inside their vehicles."

I roll down my window. Before I speak, the teenager from next door chimes in. "They have eaten," he says. As if I haven't relaxed enough, he adds, "Enjoy." He points through vehicles. The girl in the car ahead is standing on her knees. Her father's got his lens trained at something not far from my truck.

I set my cell to video. Into my field of vision, a lion. Treading a trench in grass. Muscles flex under ribs. He stops, sits, ramrod straight. His mane lifts in the wind. He faces east like he smells something from faraway, where for him an ancient music plays. Perhaps he misses it and is considering the space between.

The other lion ambles over. Sand crusts the seams of its mouth. It's bonier than I'd expect. It shakes its head violently. The second lion walks slowly in a tightening circle, rolls and rubs its face on the pavement. The bigger one gets on top and gums the other's neck. All I think is, What did any of us do to deserve this?

A woman's voice, over my shoulder, in the car with the know-it-all teenager, narrates for me. I roll the window down another inch. Her neck's craned back for maximum volume. "They be young ones without their mother," she says.

The man with the teenager is talking to me. I cup a hand over my eyes to bring his voice into focus.

"So the mother just left them?" I ask.

Their paws resemble pounds of pie dough. Spreading and spring-loaded. Faces in vehicles are fixed in awe, as if struck by a hypnotizing soundtrack. We meditate in the same direction. Creating something new. It's like another presence. An "us."

The silence is breathless. It floats like a parachute. I want it to wrap me up too. Maybe chance says it will. I mean, what forces, mighty or magical, have shrunk time and space and brought this moment? The lions could have gone anywhere. But nature picked us.

But I'm gonna go back to being plain old me soon.

I've been too alone. I need people.

Fifteen minutes and the lions expose their bellies. People have their windows rolled all the way down. They chat about how old the lions are. The consensus is that they're teenagers.

"Does the Dad still look after them?" I say. The woman beside me gives a *you-must-be-kidding* smush face.

"She rarely hunts alone," her husband says. He seems interested in educating me, the foreigner. "She be hunting with the male. She be coming in from the side wid the tackle."

The desert could be a canola field, if the canola was cut and left to bake tinder-dry. Trees spot the terrain like boats anchored throughout a harbour.

"Mr. Bossman be waiting at the office on me," says an unseen voice that spits the air. "And dat's what he's got to do!" Laughter breaks from the cars.

The woman with the teenager calls to me. She gestures toward the lions. "I've driven this highway for eight years. Seen 'em way in the distance. Never like dis." I realize that some cars have moved on ahead. Our bit of the highway mash-up decided cyborg-style to stay. "What you say, *musungu*? Good, no?"

There's a hitch in my throat. The woman knows there's an eruption happening. This moment. It's grown big. I haven't thought about writing songs in so long. I put that dream in a box and kicked it in the corner. Lyrics are made for moments like this. To tell it to Lily, I'd say it's felt like witnessing a birth.

The lions, after considering the universe at length, too bored to comment, stand with noses pressed east. One lets off a moan. They saunter off, parting grass. Folks laugh, and a few clap. Tears fall down my cheeks. I know the woman in that car is staring at me.

Maybe that's it. What I've been missing. The best we can do with any moment. Share it.

Julia

I prefer to go deep inside. Nursing guilt takes concentration. Distractions, I've tried them. I can fight. I can screw. I can succumb to memories so dark they numb the soles of my feet. Cole, for instance, could tell me I should leave. Add to it that he doesn't care if I ever come back. This much I know. My reaction would be, "fair enough."

He's circling. It's like living near a windmill. Although he's trying to work out our marriage, his presence saps me. He knows living together is all we're doing. The epiphany of one bedroom to two wasn't lost on him. What he's doing is "helping" through reassurance. God. What would happen if he outright accused me of mental instability? It should be enough that I've kept my end up. I've been eyeing the position of the sun and following its path through meals and other marital concessions.

This morning, snow threw a coat over the lawn. Winter returns and flicks your last nerve. That's April in Winnipeg. Shovels twang on cement as neighbours scrape slush off their walks. Let me lie in the recliner, stare at a fire and think about what's left of me.

The noise in the kitchen goes still. There's a spooky lull. Cole's about to find me. I feel him thinking we should talk. He exudes pacification. Like a creepy priest, I push him away, and he comes slinking back.

He peeks around the corner. "Hey," he says, pity filtering through his voice. He shrugs. "I have nothing," he says. I take it to mean he has no good reason to annoy me. A sad smile touches his lips. "Just... we're not fighting. Some would say that's a good sign."

"It could go either way."

"I was thinking of bringing the grandfather clock back. That would start some fireworks. I know how much you love it."

"Mmm."

"I was also thinking we could get a dog."

"Fair enough."

The back door slams against the cold air. Lily has a hoodie pulled up with a ponytail hanging out one side. She shakes snow off her head.

"How was university?" I say.

"Busy," she says, her voice hoarse. "Homework."

She darts past us in sock feet. "Take care of yourself," I call after her. "You sound unwell."

She disappears upstairs, and the starburst clock ticks. I turn up the volume on the TV.

"Ah, listen," Cole says. "I wanted to give you something."

"You don't have to."

Pushing Cole away has a cheaply satiating effect. Like dosing a boil surge with an ice cube. Knowing him, though, his effort will show no signs of flagging. He walks towards me. I can't make eye contact. Eye contact is an invitation, and I'm not here.

He holds out a small envelope. It has the word "Float" on it. It's one of those plastic gift cards. "It's the new thing," he says. "Someone gave it to me at work because they couldn't use it.

Anyway, if you want it. It's like the Dead Sea. You lie buoyant in water."

Ironic. It's an isolation chamber. Isolation is all I've wanted, if only he'd allow it.

"Good enough." I kick the footrest down. I run upstairs. On the way back, I quickly listen at Lily's door. I hear quiet. I trot downstairs and throw on my jacket.

In the car, I coast through the Italian village. A young mom hustles a baby carriage through slush. At Daily, a bus stops. An old man in the last seat stares out the window, though there's nothing to see. I understand. Like everyone, he's waiting for something to end.

The spa owners stand behind the counter. They are a young couple. She has a sleeve of flower tattoos. He is slim and has blue glasses with square lenses. She asks for my address and medical information, while handing me a clipboard. The walls are coated with chalkboard paint. Clients write inspiring messages, she explains. I sit and concentrate on personal information.

I write my surname and first name in the blanks. Rush, Julia. Funny. I don't know who that woman is. I fill in the blanks for my address. I scan the list of significant medical history. This woman has none of the illnesses, conditions or skin issues. I sign indicating that I've read the warnings and that the information is true to the best of my knowledge. But I wouldn't trust myself to explain Rush, Julia, with details beyond these.

I flip through a book about healing crystals until I'm told my private float room is ready. Music plays with an undercurrent of lapping waves. I follow the male owner through a salon door to the back, where a light shines wavelike lines on the wall. He talks about showers, salt solution, temperature and the mind. I should, he says, let my thoughts and emotions go.

"It might feel like you're floating in space," he says. "Free associate. I have some of my best ideas in these. I always tell people, even if you're not stressed, it's useful."

In my chamber, there's a bench, a shower and a large, silver capsule, the length of a coffin. He explains how it works and says if blackness bothers me, there are things I can do to let in light. I laugh out loud thinking how nice it is to be young.

I shower and stand before my spaceship. I lift the hatch. It's blackness inside all right. I step in. The water is lukewarm around my ankles. I have to turn and kneel, before lying back. I then close the hatch. As I lie down, water is cool. I touch bottom. Stretch out. Hold my breath. Now. I am floating. I swish my fingers and cool funnels graze my thighs. When I stop, the water stops. Then, the water is hardly there.

Silence.

The only excitement: residual light from outside creates shapes inside my eyelids. Blobs of white light. Red stoplights. Glare off the sun. Blazing tails of fire. Explosions. My mind turns to Devin.

I feel he is alive. I focus on that feeling and try to use it like a wormhole. I aim whispers through that void. "Hey," I say. "Do you remember me?" "Do you know how angry I am?" And, "What kind of kid doesn't contact his mother? That's an attack, I'd say. Leaving me with this."

My whispers sound hollow, loud in the tank. I listen in case someone's coming to check on me.

Water. The conduit. Like a chain. It pulls thoughts into the outside. "I don't know how to explain it," I go on. "I'm not a bad person."

Suddenly, in the unsupervised area of my imagination, I see the face of Oprah Winfrey. Resplendent she is in cream, with flipped hair and winged mascara. We're on her show. On stage. I'm in a leather chair sitting opposite of her. There's an audience, well-heeled and colour-coordinated.

"Welcome back," Oprah says into one of the cameras ringing the stage. "We're hearing the story of Devin and Julia Rush." Oprah shifts in her chair to face me. "I know there will be people in the audience struggling to understand this," she says. "How do you rationalize your ambivalence toward your son?"

"As young parents," I say, "Cole and I, our conversations were dominated with two emotions. Love and fear. I'd gaze at Devin in his crib and think about how much more my life was with him in it. My heart could explode with joy, until I remembered all that would threaten him. Then I'd spend time under the spell of fear."

"That sounds like what many parents have told me," Oprah says. People in the front row nod their heads.

"Devin got older. Stronger. After he turned about fifteen, something changed. He wasn't with us anymore; he was against us. It happened like that." I snap my fingers. "And it was so hard, listening to that lack of respect. We'd tell him to do something. He'd point the line back at us. Tell us to take out our own trash. He swore. He insulted us. The harder we pushed, the harder he pushed back. We were stumped."

"You didn't expect pushback from a teenager?" People scattered in the audience chuckle. "I understand teenagers are difficult," Oprah says. "I've always said parenting is the hardest job." Thunderous clapping from the audience. "But what I'm trying to get to is the ambivalence. How does a mother get to that point?"

"I don't think you understand how bad it was. It whittles away at you. I don't know how to explain it, only that it starts with talking back, doing nothing, and you're trying to deal with that, trying to reason with a kid. But they seem so utterly angry with you, suspicious even. That you're out of tune with the world of other parents."

"Children are more intelligent than people realize," Oprah says.

"Devin lived most of the time in the basement, like a bat. He could echolocate our triggers." The audience sits transfixed. "His tone was scathing. Devin delivers sarcasm, not with a smirk, but with a slap."

"You say the behaviour was worse than the usual?"

"He tried to hurt me."

Oprah puts a finger to her lips. Her diamond ring gives off a spectacular spark. "Was that before or after you kicked him out of the house?"

"It was the moment all pleasant memories of Devin stood still."

"He hit you?"

"He would have. He pushed me. Or I fell. In my mind, each scenario has the same sharp end on it. I don't think it matters."

"So he might not have touched you."

"He touched us, alright. We had the makings of good parents."

"But the day Devin left, you stopped being parents, at least to him."

"Yes."

Oprah swivels and faces the middle camera. "For those just tuning in, Julia Rush and Cole, her husband, who wasn't able to join us, kicked their twenty-four-year-old son out of the house and sent him to Nairobi, Kenya, to teach him to be a man." She turns back.

"Why there?"

"I think Bill's wife used to give to a charity there. The only other thing I remember Bill saying was that Kenya contains the earliest signs of man."

"Do you even know if your son is alive?"

"We received a postcard about a month ago. It had a picture of the Kenyatta Convention Centre. But when we turned it over, there was no note, no signature. Cole said it was so Devin to do that."

"Let's get back to you. Julia, what I hear you saying *is* that you as a mother have a choice. And your choice is not to be a mother to your own child?"

"I'm afraid so."

"You're afraid so." Oprah turns toward the crowd with a puzzled look. Random laughs. "Let me ask this. What would have happened if your parents quit on *you*?" A cheer rises up.

"You don't understand. Our house was permanently hostile. The police were peripherally involved. Kicking him out wasn't a fun caper my husband and I dreamt up. We lived for years with a dull ache in our bones, for our former son. It was as if Devin's insides were replaced with a hard pit. We were afraid."

"Afraid," Oprah says.

"Maybe not that he'd hurt us physically. But that an eruption could begin. After Cole and Bill gave Devin the contract, things were worse. Devin was seething. He'd come in for breakfast, for instance, and I remember it so clearly, my teeth were put on edge."

"By your son's presence?"

"Kicking him out was the option Devin left us with."

"Your son held a lot of power over his parents."

"There were up times. He'd get a job for a short while, then quit. He'd be respectful for a week and then blow up. He'd adhere to a curfew for one night, then come home banging every door in the house at three in the morning. You get so tired of getting your hopes up."

"You ran out of hope. Is that where the ambivalence comes in?"

"Hope, like love, can be tapered. You see it happening to you, and soon resentment fills in the cracks." A few heads in the crowd slowly shake back and forth.

"So, to recap, tough love is punishment that makes things easier for the parents? That's what I'm hearing."

"Yes." The audience gasps. "This, right here is part of the problem."

Oprah gives a slight quiver of her head. "My interview is the problem?"

"People look at an issue like it's cause and effect. How do people struggle and hurt and yearn for help and then remain judgmental of others? What if we tried our best and all this was going to happen anyway?"

"So, you and your husband don't believe you had a hand in the upbringing of your child?"

"People don't understand how difficult it is to sort motivations. People become sick, and there's no understanding the moment when you decide, enough. I'd like to say it's thought out, proven by scientific method. But it might be based on a feeling. It might be that it's about what a parent can withstand. Which means detachment may not have to do with how many bad behaviours, or the severity of them. You reach a point. Something breaks. You're not your whole self. You're working with fragments."

"*Fragments?*"

"My marriage is a hinterland. Cole tried with Devin. It was an exercise in futility. That's a hard message for a man raised as Cole was."

"Sounds to me," Oprah says, "like your strategy is an excuse for not getting to a deeper and more compassionate understanding."

"Things were said, things happened, and then you and everyone you hold dear is on another path."

"What's at the end of that path?"

"Detachment. Anger."

"Before we go to break, you say detachment and anger are at the end of this path. It seems anger would be the opposite of detachment." A chorus of "ahhs" rise from the audience. "Can a mother feel both?"

"We kid ourselves, yes."

"So, there is hope?"

"I sometimes hope we'll see Devin again."

"Julia, I meant for you."

★

I rub my eyes and wince in pain from salt. Out of the silence, low Middle Eastern music begins. I get out. Turn on the shower. As I lather, I try seeing Devin in Nairobi, transposing environments from documentaries and movies I've watched. I see the image of a boy smeared by rapid movements. Once you've seen someone a certain way, you can't stop.

I wonder what happens, if two people separated by distance, think about each other at the same time. And if Devin is thinking of me, will he be left warm or cold? She left Dad a century ago, but I suppose I could ask what my Mom left me? Endless self-criticism. The feeling I don't deserve what I have, despite evidence to the contrary. It's been luck, she might say, that I have a husband, a big house and two kids.

And I finished high school. And university. Had jobs. What would she have done with Devin? She wouldn't have stood for his behaviour. I could see her smacking him so hard there'd be a hole in the wall the shape of his body. One way or the other, Devin would've been out, whether she kicked him out or he left of his own will.

I turban my hair and think about how flames burn yellow and red and blue, how they always point upward and other mysteries of science. Could it be said that Devin is just one of them? Maybe wondering is proof enough of my concern?

The primping area has mirrors on one side and bathroom stalls on the other. As I comb my hair, I think, What would I do if Devin ever came back?

I envision him on the sidewalk, like when we kicked him out. Only he's walking at me, up the walk to our steps, with intentions I can't read. That's as far as I get. My anxiety is too high. I can't imagine reconciliation. People talk about starting over. Has anyone done that without a lobotomy?

I slip on my blouse and pull wet hair to my chest. A young woman comes out of a bathroom stall. A moment later I hear the owners chat with her and say, "See you next time." I leave the peach tint of the primping area. A saying, hand-painted on the inside of the door, reads, "Glow. You are loved."

DEVIN

I get to Karen at about four bells. It's supposed to be going downhill, but with its two-storey homes with wide lawns and vines clinging to pure white trim, as well as a behemoth of a mall for the well-to-do in the centre of town, I don't see it. Across from the mall, I spot a brick restaurant showcasing specials on a chalkboard. Around are patios and palm trees that cast feathering shade on cool cement. Laughter riffs from inside.

A black waitress greets me and tells me I can sit where I like. I look around and see a gorgeous woman at nine o'clock, sitting near a collection of plants. She's got downy black hair and wears a big gold watch. I sit at a table between her and the window. She puts money down on the table for her bill, then looks over.

Smiles. Is she? She's coming over. I think there must be something wrong; there's no way she's interested in me.

"You are alone, mm?" she says.

"Okay."

Her chin recoils. "What do you mean '*okay*?'"

"I'm waiting for the punchline."

Her hands find her hips. She looks cute when she's pretending to be confused.

"I was going to ask if you'd like to join me."

"Oh re-ally. To do WHAT?" I ask, my signature sarcasm soaked in honey.

"I don't know." Her head warbles as if an idea rattles. "Walk?"

"I'm fine. Really. Not looking for a prostitute."

Her eyes pop open like two exploding bombs.

"Oh God! You're *not* a prostitute, are you?"

"Just a woman." She walks away.

Duh. Duh. Duh. Why am I always hitting the idiot button and doubling down? My life is exhaust and carbon poisoning and assholes. Here I've been whining about loneliness, and she just offered to hang out.

My cell buzzes. It's Paul. I jam it back in my pocket without answering. As soon as I'm outside, my legs turn into one large wheel. Breathless, I catch up to her on the sidewalk. "Hey!"

She stops.

"Sorry about that. I haven't had many conversations with women." She turns slightly so I can at least see her face. I hold up my hands, convicted felon-like. "I misread things. I'm an idiot."

"Do not worry yourself," she says.

"How 'bout that walk?" She pauses. "Unless you're not up to it now. Then, my loss."

"What is your name, mm?"

I say my name and ask hers.

"Maybe I will tell you later." She gestures towards the sidewalk, and I fall in line.

Can't let the conversation stall, so I ask what she does for a living.

"Student," she says.

"You don't look like a student."

"Mm. I study landscape architecture."

For some reason I laugh. "Doesn't nature take care of that?"

She stops near the short cement border of a garden. There's a tree and plants and flowers. "Do you know what the word 'garden' means?" she asks. "Enclosure. Here we have an area approximately twelve feet wide, the tree is about six feet tall. The bushes, closer to us, are shorter, and the flowers that soften the border are here. Balance."

"Looks good, I guess."

"Enclosure makes people feel as if the universe is safe, mm, and at the same time opens them to possibility. Happy, in other words."

We walk around the mall, past its arching entrances and white umbrellas. Beside it is a lake, spotted with lily pads. I see her in the reflection and think it's got to be a species-level change to have someone like this beside me. "The lake," she continues, "is a natural element for organization." She points across the way. "Shoreline aligns the way people move, but as importantly, how they see." She's examining my face. "You do not care, do you?"

"I don't... not like it. "

"I always understood the agenda of design." She touches my elbow. When she lets go, the skin at that spot sings. "It is opportunity. Seeing where I can lead people."

I'm not smart enough for her.

"I like the way you talk," I say.

"Are we not speaking the same language?" She talks about her father. He was born in Mombasa and studied law. He did so well, he later studied in "the United States of America." When he returned, he brought his wife. They had her and her brother. They were educated in private schools. "He lives here," she says. During the course of our conversation, we've walked to an open area by the mall where shiny people gather. "Piazza," she says.

A few clouds dim the light. Lampposts flick on, and glare reflects in the glossy-tiled fun space. "What about you?"

"Smells like rain."

"You have not mentioned anyone."

"Nothing to tell." A dad peddles a scooter, followed by his young son. They push off the pavement and glide around the piazza in circles.

"Try me."

"My family lives in Canada."

She casts her eyes forward, and we walk awhile.

"You know how odd that seems," she says, "to not speak of your relatives? We are nothing, if not for our families. You talk to any Kenyan. A person without a family is not a person."

"Dunno what you want me to say. Mom. Dad. Sister."

She stops at a bench and sits. Her skirt hugs her thighs when she crosses her legs. "If you tell me about your family, I'll tell you my name."

"C'mon."

"How else am I going to trust you?" She tilts her head. "Otherwise we can stop, mm? If this is too open for you. I think, there's not enough time to waste. Do you not agree the world is full of interesting people? If we part ways now, I think we would both be fine."

"They kicked me out."

"You must have done something heinous." Her words seem to mean she'd rather not know me. Yet, her face tells me different. "If you want to see me again, you are telling me what you did."

"I didn't *do* anything." Skepticism tightens the muscles around her mouth. "They hate me," I say.

"Every child thinks that."

I can't say it never crossed my mind. That a child version of me is on a bridge blocking the passage of the would-be adult. "Do you ever feel like no one knows you?" I say. My cell buzzes. I let the ringing die.

"My parents know me," she says. "Who else knows how far I've come?"

"You were lucky," I say. "You like design. Design is a credible career, so they supported you. What if you had dreamt of pest control?"

"Devin, does anyone really know anybody?"

I go on a tear about how sad it is people are fine with never knowing anybody. That authenticity doesn't matter. Mid-sentence, I stop, fearing I've over-shared. Geyser of relief as I watch her eyes lift from my lips. She's following. She's the kind of person who gets to the bottom of what you're saying, just as if she were in it with you.

So I continue blathering about why people don't want to really know others. How everybody accepts that copout of never knowing anyone because it's work, and no one has the time. Or, that understanding a person, knowing and feeling what they've gone through, would cause them pain and who wants that? Or maybe everyone's too self-centered. Or maybe everyone's trying to solve the puzzle of who they are, which would be all right, but what's the rush?

"Wanna know what I really think?" I say.

Her lips press out a smile. "I am almost scared to ask."

"Seems what we want from people is for people to make things easier for us."

Her hand falls on my thigh. "There is selflessness. And there is love. You are intelligent, mm, and too young to be cynical. You wear it like a shield, but it cannot protect you. It will, however, separate you from those who mean well and love easily and who have reason to hope. Those are the people I want to know." She takes in my features. "Furthermore, it does not suit you. A young man from Canada, with pearly white skin..."

"What does that have to do with anything?"

"Only a white boy can do nothing and dream of everything. If I were you, I would be taking over the world. Right now. I would be strutting around in a beautiful suit, doing important things, with powerful people. I would wish for nothing else."

I explain she's about to be disappointed. That I hate suits. Hadn't she heard of Occupy Wall Street? I riffed on corruption. Said suits are the costume of the oppressor. She laughed so hard I shifted to baby boomers like my parents, who produced fewer decent paying jobs then they will admit. I told her I'm no Big Man. In fact, the reason I came to Nairobi was to become one.

I stop short, this time knowing I'd unleashed too much. Truth be told, I wanted to tell someone. It's what the parents never understood about me. For the caged, antagonism is the only means for release. Because what else are you gonna do when no one's asking? It comes from rebel nature. What I wanted just once was to test holier-than-thou righteousness with the truth. And watch. She will run as fast as those heels can carry her.

"You are like many Kenyan men, boy."

Though I've complained, she's not rolling her eyes. She's not interrupting with counter examples. It's great. Except it's annoying too. She's all about positivity and "the world."

"I'm working," I say. "Making deliveries for a friend. Not something to dream of becoming, but it pays. It's good, I guess, to be self-sufficient. It's what my family wanted." Her hands are folded in her lap. "So you might say they were right to send me away. Yet I can't not hate them."

"You needed a push," she says. "How else does a bird learn to fly?" I almost scoff. If she's gonna walk away, let her do it on a cliché.

People in the piazza notice the clouds. They're earnest for release. She extends a hand. "My name is Mahaadi." We shake. "Now, tell me what you are really scared of."

At a loading dock, a delivery truck backfires. Men get out and contemplate the smoke. Mahaadi isn't distracted from her question. Her anticipation lingers.

"I don't want to be uninspired."

"What about school, mm?" Here's the next argument. Be like Dad. Get the graduate degree in Anthropology and work in an irrelevant office with a bunch of twats. Affect so little, remember to make a big deal of whatever small change you manage to make.

My cell buzzes. Futility clouds around her.

"I didn't do what they wanted," I say. "Okay? I didn't graduate high school. I didn't get a job. I was a jerk. End of story." Mahaadi stares at the Ngong Hills where what's left of the sun melts behind its peaks. "Music was the thing I could picture myself doing. I loved working on music. In the flow, always on the verge of an idea. Verge is where songs get written."

I hear myself talking. It sounds stupid because people who don't make music don't get it. Music is a challenge that doesn't require a permission note. An artist doesn't ask, "Mind if I try?" You do it because it's all you are. To make something original, you don't shackle yourself with advice. The greatest music was unexpected. Sometimes even difficult to hear. It's why it's the best-loved stuff.

A drop of rain spits at the arm of the bench. "I can't see myself conquering the world," I say. "I don't think I like it that much." Her eyes soften in support. "Now I have no family. But I have a job. And mostly I've thought about what things I want. Like a house."

Didn't know I wanted a house.

Mahaadi's eyes begin to shine and, for a minute, it seems a great idea just danced across the sidewalk. Instead, a man approaches with a shopping tote from the mall. His suit is beige and his leather shoes are business-cool. He stands at the edge of the cobblestone path. Mahaadi steps over to him. Their shoes only a half-foot apart. They take one another's hands.

She introduces us. He says "hello" and "so nice to meet you."

He pats the top of her hand.

The conversation is about her father and the last time the man ran into him. How he appears to be in such great health and their afternoon of golf. I can imagine them. This guy with an older, male version of Mahaadi drinking club beer and polishing balls. This guy probably has a giant house and a maid. I imagine him inviting us over, meanwhile it's one of those mansions I drove past. We'll sit on the porch with our lemonade. I'd have nothing to brag about, and Mahaadi's attention would drift exclusively to him.

★

At one in the morning, the parents' voices were funny. Dad's was a whisper, yet loud. Mom's was more of a groan.

Dad said, "I'm always gonna be second."

Bedsprings creaked when I sat up. I crept toward the kitchen. Mom. Her face was stony disappointment. Like she'd been forced to watch a movie she'd seen many times before.

"Why do you keep bringing this up?" she asked. Mom yanked the fridge door and condiments rattled. "Michael's dead, Cole," she said. "How many times do I have to say it?"

The mechanic. I'd heard Dad mention the guy one other time. Michael. I remember because of the way he said it, with his voice raised on the first syllable. He was Mom's first boyfriend. Correction, he was Mom's fiancé. He died while working under an old Mustang. The works came down on top of him. "Dead," Dad said. "But not gone."

I liked this sucky Dad. So I strolled into the kitchen like it was Sunday morning. Mom's eyes shot daggers in Dad's direction when she thought I wasn't looking. She turned to a drawer and began folding tea towels that had been tossed in. Dad was gazing out the window. I pulled Lily's Captain Crunch from the cupboard and poured a bowl.

"Uh, Devin dear," Mom said, "could you take that into your room?" I sat at the island and took a mouthful. "Did you hear us?" When I didn't answer, she slapped the counter. "Of course you did. We could all be sleeping right now."

"Know what?" Dad said. His face red. "Just go."

"I'm not going anywhere," she said.

Dad opened the screen door and swung it so hard it gyrated on its hinges. "Go already."

Mom had that holy-shit-you're-such-an-idiot face. "I'll tell you something, and I hope you get this good," she said. "If I did leave, it would be three of us going. How ridiculous is that, Cole?"

I stifled a snort. It was no use. Milk was coming out of my nose.

Dad stomped over and snared my hoodie in his hand, which was tight around my throat. As he yelled, his fist jerked, and I swivelled on the stool. He let go when my cereal smashed to the floor.

With anger drained, Dad was like a man who'd been to another dimension and seen the errors of our kind. He reached for me. I bolted to my room. I heard him coming, prattling on about how "it's cool now." I rummaged for my backpack, collected a few clothes, went through the kitchen and left. All I heard after was Mom.

"I can't talk about Michael anymore."

★

"Devin," Mahaadi's friend says, winding up his high-toned goodbyes. "I can't apologize enough for interrupting." With a slight bow, he retraces his steps back to the mall. I wanna say "Then why did you interrupt then?" Instead, I say, "Nice to meet you too."

Thunder echoes in the distance. Skies light up over the mountains. I rise, and she takes my arm. Rain comes down in sheets. She runs with me to her car. We get in the back seat together. Droplets jewel her hair. "Tell me," she says. "What would *you* have done with you?"

"So you know that guy, huh?" She watches over my shoulder as rain curtains the rear window. "Isn't it kind of cosmically unfair?" I say. "My parents are supposed to support me."

"You're in Africa talking about cosmically unfair? A nice boy, mm? But you have no clue."

The piazza is a clean slate. Friends and families snuggle under archways.

"You love your family," I say.

"Of course."

"You were a perfect child, I bet."

"I was loved."

★

As the passengers fanned themselves, the *matatu* driver glared. Mahaadi pulled out her makeup mirror and her cell and handed them to me while she scrounged for coins in her purse. The crevasses between the driver's eyes might as well have been put there with an axe, so I paid.

We sat, and Mahaadi said, "I need the plan."

It had been over a month since we met, and I'd been frenzied by lust. I'd proposed a vacation to Lamu Island. I thought our relationship was ready. She'd got her flirting down.

"I rented a moon suite," I said.

"Excuse me?" I'd booked an early flight so we'd be walking through old town before I revealed our room with the white canopy bed. "Not the whole weekend?" she asked. When I didn't answer, she said, "I am sure it is nice. But not for two nights. I am sorry."

"Why not?"

"Honest to God, it is a long bus ride. It stops for anyone on the road." I told her I booked a flight. "It's too expensive," she said.

Mahaadi was in a snit. Kenyan men say women in Nairobi only care about a few things, mainly attention and comfort. "These days, I do zero crazy," one driver said. I'd shrugged it off as macho-male shit. Yet, there I was. Spent a small fortune, and somehow she was upset.

I thought about storming off the *matatu* just to make a point. Instead, I didn't talk to Mahaadi for the rest of the ride.

When the *matatu* stopped, Mahaadi said, "I can't be away that weekend. I need to be home Sunday. I said I am sorry."

"Sorry doesn't unfuck the situation." The comment gave her a look so pitiful, I almost laughed. You've got to let them panic a little. Tip the power in your favour.

We crossed to the supermarket. Two guards flanked the entrance. I was picked out early and summoned over. As I stepped up, the guard waved an electronic wand around my head, down my waist, to my shoes. His eyes said, "We're watching you."

I found Mahaadi in the makeup aisle. I wouldn't look at her. After several minutes a hand appeared in the nook of my arm. The touch was so sweet. "I want you to go, mmm," she said. "I will cover the price of my ticket."

Teaching people a lesson requires record-setting restraint. One can't let up too fast. Or, that's the reason I'd give. The real reason is it feels better.

★

I was livid from a family scrap. I had nowhere to go, so I went in the garage and walked around Dad's precious car.

I've watched Dad many times with his rag and wax, when the garage door was open and I shot hoops. I figured the difference between me and that car was the car had potential. In Dad's eyes, it wasn't broken. It was a victim of neglect, and with support, it would come around.

The grill reminded me of a spoiled cat's smile. Headlights gleamed like they were dipped in opaque wax. Light spilled through the window and danced off the deep, red paint. A colour so ballsy, it tugged the eye.

Unlike me, the car was pent-up energy. It wasn't ready for action because Dad saved the engine to work on last. He said what interested him most was "the mechanics underneath." I'd heard that line before a few times. Leaning on the kitchen counter. Curved forward at Mom like her face was his microphone. "It's about the mechanics underneath," he said.

He'd given up on mine.

On any warm day, he'd stand with whatever neighbour passing with a dog. He'd crack jokes about how I'd probably hold a wrench wrong. How if he gave it back to me I'd probably hurt myself with it or try to unscrew a nail.

The real joke is this. We weren't family. We weren't strangers. We were something there's no word for. If it were a school project to define what we are, I'd have to make a collage. Use cut-out letters from magazines. Stick "enemy" over "disappointment." And "game" over "denial." And "rejection" over "boundaries." That's why I was in the garage, like a soldier on a bitter mission. I was combing enemy territory.

I had to admire the car's design. The bumper and the headlights, it was a seamless glide of steel that makes a person wonder how it's put together. I made my way around the garage, stepping over crates and around jugs of oil and windshield cleaner, my reflection warping in the car's curves. I would've completed the circle around his dream machine, except I saw the hammers and stopped. I picked up one from the box. The one with a fist on one end and a knob on the other. The black handle warm in my palm. I bounced it off the lid of a sour cream container of screws. *Bomp.* Off a box of sockets. Bash. A terrible idea blossomed, and the car became a rabbit crouched in a grass hollow.

I lifted a pry bar. Intriguing tool. With a U-shape at one end for lifting. With the bar over my head, I tried the tension in my bicep. Lowering it, the load shifted. It would need practice. A pry bar wants to swing.

One. The weight was surprising. I concluded it'd work better if I let the bar do the work.

Two. It's also about what part of the bar lands first. Gotta make use of the U. Plan B? I could pry up the bumper. Give the cat a lopsided grin.

Three. On the upswing, the bar hooked itself in the loops of a cross-country ski pole stored in the rafters. I tried to unsnag it, but the bar was getting heavier. I stepped out from under the bar's path and ended up yanking the ski, which skidded out, toppled backwards, bringing with it the ski poles, spikes first, onto the roof of the car.

"Couldn't do that twice if I tried," I said to the situation.

I unhitched the bar and dropped it back in the box and rubbed the scratch with spit.

The light in the door to the garage darkened, and I realized it was Dad. He stared dumbly until his gaze rose to the rafters. I braced myself, because when he saw the scratch on his baby, it would be on. Anger made me ready. If he freaked out, it was go time.

He exhaled. "None of us have skied, for how long? Lily's never been on skis. Your Mom's been after me for months to clean that stuff out." Without a whiff of sarcasm, he said, "Now it's come down on her baby's head."

He scanned my orb for injuries. "What are you doing in here anyways?"

"Looking at the car."

In a way that hadn't happened in forever, he touched my face. "Good as new." He turned to the car and shivered.

"You're not mad?" I said.

He let a knowing look fly. "You've seen your Mom upset. Once she gets going, it won't matter you're not hurt." He tapped his temple. "Where the hellfire comes from is, what *could* have happened. The scenarios I'll hear about. At least one," he smiled to himself, "will be where the sharp bit stabbed you in the jugular." His shoulders sank. "If you were me, are you gonna be more scared of *her* or a little elbow grease? We can keep this between us?"

★

The name is soft and lyrical. Half-sigh. Mahaadi. Was there ever a sexier name?

Paths curve between ancient fortresses, revealing Lamu by degrees. A Muslim prayer echoes from an amplifier that might be stuck in a mountain.

Lamu. The language is a playlist of Swahili and Arabic. Mahaadi walks with her head down and hands in her skirt pockets. She takes little notice of the shops. Even when we come to one for women's clothing, I have to coax a smile. "Couldn't hurt to look," I say. Her eyes flit between mannequin-dressed windows.

"I shouldn't," she says. She gazes up the road.

"C'mon."

We duck in. A man standing behind a table greets us to his shop. His head is covered, and he wears a type of brown robe. A white girl stands in the middle with a lace dress floating over her. Mahaadi's eyes are on her.

"Why don't you have one?" I say.

"There isn't enough time."

The shopkeeper says, "I'm afraid the lady might be right. We need at least three days after the fitting to construct a dress."

We leave and follow the smell of salt and the sound of water curling on a beach. I look out over the massive, blue marble that hems the sand in.

Resorts sit at a relaxed distance from the ocean. The high sun lights their porches. In the water, a vintage sailboat rocks. An army of tourists cheer as the bow lifts, and the boat edges faster through the blue.

Mahaadi's gone quiet. "Something the matter?" I say.

"It's just so beautiful."

"We're this way," I say. She strolls hands clasped behind her back.

I point at our hotel. Mahaadi kicks off her sandals. The balls of her feet flick sand back. She takes the stairs two at a time and, at the top deck, she waves. "It is so lovely," she says. "Infinity pool!" A Hawaiian-shirt-clad man guides me to the check-in desk, while Mahaadi lounges arms outstretched on a padded chaise.

When I return, she wants to swim in the pool, in the ocean, walk the beach. She walks seductively backwards and pulls her dress off, baring a black bikini. I pull my clothes off, baring my underwear. She laughs. I change in our suite, and soon we're swimming like pond frogs.

"Let us try the beach, mm?"

The ocean is green and purple and grey. The roar of waves is better music than any I can lift with guitar. We rush to the water's edge. Flip-flops barely stay on our feet in the bubbling white wash.

Mahaadi strides in and dives. I come up, offering myself. She lays a kiss on my mouth. Then pushes off. She swims for the deep. I paddle over and find my feet still reach bottom. Get my hands on her waist. The core of her body is close to the skin. She hops and swings her legs sidesaddle. Like a groom, I hold her in the rise and fall of waves.

I look over at the boats in the bay and the beach, where the traffic of people has tapered off. Such a place. Far from the pulsation that is Nairobi. Makes the world seem less off course. I could live here. With her breath on my neck and the smell of her salt-crystallized skin.

Sky and water fade the distinction between past and present. I think Mahaadi and the ocean are all I could ever want. Waves, the gentle push and pull, and a carpet of foam. I'd get a small apartment for us. Too small for her taste, but that'd be all right. We'd live outside in a playground painted aquamarine.

"I'd like to freeze it here," I say. "Can you do that for me?"

She shivers. I let her go, and she floats on her back, kicking her legs. Her body is an arrow pointing at our hotel. Perhaps it's not all bad that the sun drops quickly on this part of the world.

She likes the canopy bed and the shutters. We discuss dinner, and it's perfect. Mahaadi wants to stay in. I order wine and crab to eat at the pool. She treads around the room, lifting old-timey hairbrushes and silver cases.

"Personal touches," she says. "Clever." We go to the pool. Mahaadi gasps. Around the setting sun, the sky is red. Clouds slice in from the sides. "Take a picture of me." She sets herself up at the corner of the terrace. I aim. Shoot. Someone brings our wine.

"The ocean is incredible," I say. She snags my cell to see the picture. "You're not bad either."

Bauble-like lamps go on around our deck. Mahaadi smiles, maybe because we're together. Maybe because she likes wine.

The crab comes in a bucket. We talk and lick butter from our fingers. Later, we lay back with the quiet, watching a darkening purple sky. The ocean exhales through a flutter of palms. Mahaadi's neck cranes to look back at me.

"Do you miss home?" she asks.

"I used to think I'd never wanna go home. In a weird way," I say, "being with you makes me wanna go back. They'd take one look at you and know I did something right."

She crawls up the couch on hands and knees. Over my legs, to my waist. Thighs straddling my hips. I lie stiff as a surfboard. Her face is level with mine, and she lowers herself. The wind kicks up, and I move us out of the cool air, into the room. Soon, it's a patter of steady rain. Mahaadi unties her hair, and it hangs loose. She opens shutters facing the water before turning towards me. Moonlight shines on twirling palms. Water lips over the narrow channels of drainpipes. A low howl fills the room as wind vibrates through the cracked sliding doors. Mahaadi's hair is all over the pillow. She opens her eyes and rain quiets a moment, letting nature catch her breath. Then, the rain is back. It comes in from the side, seeking the open ocean.

Morning.

Mahaadi is still asleep. I reach for my clothes and step out. A strong wind ruffles collapsed sails. Fishermen stock sailboats with coolers. Waist deep, a man throws a net and drags it back to find a few wiggly fish. It'd be nice to eat breakfast from town.

About a half-mile down the beach, there's a boat with a boning-knife bow. A dozen men, muscles straining, unload fat fish by the dozens. A solo voice among the men starts to sing. The words are foreign. Now, all are singing. Their combined voices are strings strummed on a guitar. The song's bittersweet. A Swahili song, I imagine, about a man and his wife making up after their first fight. Something harmless and sweet.

I stop where the last fish are stacked. A woman nearby points at the sky. Gulls rotate above our heads. Amazing. To think you can almost miss what's right in front of you. So much worth feeling.

I spot a café, with a door like a mouth surprised to see me. Inside, the air is steeped in coffee beans. A girl grins "Hello," and waits for me to choose pastry from behind the glass.

She flicks the radio on. A reporter recounts a bloody siege between Nairobi police and suspected gangsters. The reporter interviews the mother of one of the goons. She vows vengeance. When the girl switches the channel, I realize I've been staring at her.

A weather report shifts to Parliament. A man speaks. "Last night," he says, "I witnessed the moon having turned blood red and remembered what Jesus said. 'That the end of the world will be signified by the eclipse of the moon.'"

The girl slides the glass panel aside, and I return her smile. Once you're an adult, that's it. Climate change. Corruption. Violence. All of it. It's yours.

Palm trees still sway in the storm's aftershocks. By the time the horseshoe of a beach comes back into view, the waves are bigger than yesterday. Fishermen have cleared the fish. Seagulls screech overhead in confusion.

I jog to the hotel and find Mahaadi in the room stepping into bikini bottoms. She snatches the pastry bag, and I'm chasing her until she has to give in. At our little table, I'm giddy. Sitting with her semi-naked.

"It's the best coffee I've ever had," I say.

"Mm." She sips. "How much time do we have?"

"We should leave at eleven. Airport by one." Her lips curl inward. "You said you needed to be back." I offer her a walk on the beach. She leads me to the beach chairs under hotel umbrellas, where we lay quietly for a long while.

"I started collecting records when I was seventeen," I say. "Have about maybe 300 and counting. They say the sound is better. Deeper. But it's the relationship I like."

"You mean the way music speaks to you?"

"No, the jackets. With the lyrics and pictures of the band? Some album jackets, they're special, like the producers liked the music too. Some change colour in water. Anyway, you take the record out, right? Over the years, you look at that thing maybe a thousand times. It's special."

Mahaadi shifts into a laying position. There's so much of her to discover. I don't want to rush this, but we have to go.

We head back to the room. Mahaadi drops a light dress over her head and we leave, following the beach back to town. The storm's left the fortress foundations muddy at the base. Mahaadi draws a silk scarf over her head and holds it close. What I want is to check out a music store. After all, the street isn't far away.

"Let's go this way," I say. I tilt my head toward a side alley of shops with apartments above. They lead uphill. "Just for a few minutes."

"We'll be late."

"You and agendas."

I head up the incline. At the top, the street continues. The steps of the music shop are nearby. I yell that Mahaadi will like it. She waves her hands, like I should go on alone.

The shop's dim. CDs in bins form a centre partition. A man asks if he can help. His beard is so close-shaven it looks like shoe polish.

"My girlfriend and I are about to leave," I say, "but I thought I could take a quick look."

"Of course. There are a few musicians from the Majlets." He waves me towards a sign reading, "Local." The shopkeeper pulls a CD and I think, Maybe, if I find music so great, I could look on Mom and Dad one day with forgiveness.

He clicks the CD into the player and hits play. What comes out of the speaker is a wind instrument version of a prayer. "That's the zumari," he says. "They blow into two reeds at once."

"It's not what I'd pick any other day. The low-pitched drums remind me of the ocean. The double reed thing reminds me of the sailors."

"You've had a good time in Lamu."

As the shopkeeper rings up the bill, movement outside the door catches my eye. I hear men shouting, then I see a man, with a face tangled in rage, standing halfway down the slope, shouting down the street. An older man talks with the crazy one and pans his view over to me. Something meaningful passes between us and I'm afraid. The younger man stagger-jogs down the incline.

Suddenly, I'm pushing out of the shop. Mahaadi glances around a fortress below, then disappears. I'm barreling down the hill, afraid the men might be dangerous. Ahead of me, the younger man slides, sending dust into the air. I gain speed and scream around the corner. The young guy's practically got Mahaadi pinned against the wall. The older one joins us. The young man's eyes slither off her and fall on me.

"This is why," the young man says to the older one. Then to me, "You are with her." I step between the young guy and Mahaadi. "If you knew, you would not stand by her."

Mahaadi sobs.

"Can't you see she's crying? Back off."

The younger one of the two steps back.

"Tell your boyfriend who I am," the old man says. His voice is soft and gentle. Mahaadi's pleading eyes withdraw.

I turn to Mahaadi. "You know these guys?" She's hugging herself. "If there's something to tell me, just say it," I say. "It won't matter."

The old man snorts.

"He is my daddy's relative," she says.

"Your *relative*." She'd had every opportunity to mention family in Lamu.

The older man says, "I am her husband's brother."

The word "husband" gongs in my head.

Mahaadi's face has the arrogance of a child made to look at their mess. Her hand is on my wrist, pulling. "We are going to miss the plane," she says.

I'm laughing. Cackling, even. Thoughts fly and urges spin. I could slap her. Hold her. Implode in one gaudy spasm of disgust. Maybe I've learned that sometimes you can't care anymore, and then the work is learning when to pitch a person out.

The men trudge up the slope. Mahaadi has her bag tucked under her arm. This is why I haven't seen her home. I'm forever outside the white picket fence.

"You haven't denied it," I say. I let my words drop like potholes so there's nowhere to run.

She walks ahead, tough and alone. "Airport," is all she says over her shoulder.

"You owe me the truth, don'tcha think?"

From yards away, she stops. "Owe you?" She lets off a laugh.

"How does it work?" I say. "Is your husband blind or something?"

"Most of the time, he is away."

"Because you're such a doll to live with."

"He travels for work."

"By 'travels for work,' you mean he's rich."

My brain toggles back to the beginning. We met in Karen. She lives there, no doubt. In one of those mansions. And to think I whined about not knowing what to do with my life, and she told me I was privileged.

"Really, Devin," she says. "Has it been so bad? Typically, I have a policy about dating white men. I never do. White men talk of dreams. You throw a lot of money around, and you have your fun. Then, you leave. Now that I am married, clever white boys have no upper hand." She smiles at her hand, minus the wedding ring.

"Good luck boarding the plane."

Now she's speaking again. This time through her teeth. "Why do men think there was no life before they came along? Men are the boring ones. Look at you. Any time you like, you can go home to your peaceful country and your big house while we, the little black women who pop up on your radar, are working with what we have. And getting smarter every day. Let it be known. There was never anything you could give me that I could not get or do not have already." She pulls something out of her purse. Two plane tickets spark in the sun.

"Tell me," I say. "Is anything in this country not for sale?"

Chapter Six

Lily

My best challenge was Ezra. He was handsome and playing a game I loved. I must've won over some part of him. We texted. And then, the unpredictable happened. He invited me to an art gallery gala. The idea sizzled against an otherwise pale April day. Vaulted ceilings, marble staircase. Filled with rich, educated, sophisticated people, rather than the drunk and dopily enthused. I was moving my game to a level where I might really shine.

I'd memorized a definition from an article about painting. *Pentimento*. It's an Italian word for a painter's change of heart. Apparently, old paintings are sometimes painted over to make room for better ideas. Ezra would be impressed, if conversationally, I worked it in.

I looked perfect that night. I pulled my dark purple dress down and secured a loose upsweep of hair. Mom, who lingered at my bedroom door, said I was beautiful. I was mid-ready, pulling out strands so the updo wouldn't read too tight.

"Every time I look at you," she said, "I get older." I smoothed the three-quarter length sleeves and found the dress serious, not gothic. She watched me twirl in front of the mirror.

"Art gallery," she said. "What do you know about these people?"

"They're rich, educated and sophisticated."

Then, it struck me. I didn't know anything about the art community. I was about to be buried alive. I didn't panic-text Ezra, though. At all stages, you don't show vulnerability. That's got to be contained, because once it's out, there's no getting you back.

"Is he picking you up?" Mom asked. I hadn't told her his name.

"I don't wanna get too excited about this," I said.

"You look excited to me."

"They might not like me. I'm not one of them. Art community. Art scene. What is that?"

"Snobs," Mom said. "Forget them." She brushed a tress from my eye. "You're brilliant."

"Can't we act like I'm off to the movies or something?" She left.

At ten to eight, I got out of the cab and walked in the art gallery entrance. People were inside the double doors, and beyond, through to the main hall. Lights twinkled. People were a maze of silk and suits, embroiled in conversation and backslapping platitudes.

I used my sweetest stage whisper to nudge through. A waiter with triumphant hair swooped by with a drink tray. There I was. Drinking in a social minefield. As it is with drowning, the important thing is not to panic. All you have to do is breathe, and keep your legs moving.

A few men resembled Ezra. Medium builds. Longer hair. It would take time to find him. So I wove through the crowd, flashing a smile when necessary. Patterns I'd copied from polite women in shift dresses and pearls.

I strolled, gazing at the huge canvases on the wall. The colours were bright, childish even. The shapes were exaggerated, and the lines thick. I thought it was probably *abstract*. There was playfulness in it. Vibrations too, from collisions of colour. I saw faces, deconstructed and spliced. That was what the artist intended. The faces weren't the work of my disorder. I was seeing it as it was meant to be seen.

I'd stepped a gracious ring around the exhibit. When I was done, I began to think Ezra was a no-show. To save face, I strolled to the reception booth and engaged the young woman in small talk. I told her I didn't have a ticket, and she went through great lengths explaining why I didn't need one. I asked her if she knew Ezra. She threw out two Ezras with surnames—Ginsburg and Lazar. She beamed, hoping, perhaps, for fewer points of separation.

"Lazar," I lied.

Why didn't I ask Ezra for his last name?

"He's right there." She pointed at a stout, pink man in a sea-green turtleneck. He glanced over, sporting multiple folds in his jowl.

I left in search of someone who was alone. A tactic that works wonders. People by themselves are conspicuous. So tense in their efforts to seem at ease. If I saddle up to a lonely woman, she won't care what my agenda is. She'll be all too pleased to blend in.

So I worked the long wall opposite the staircase. People stood in tight cliques of fours and fives. The only one alone was the waiter. When the hors d'oeuvres came, a niggling sensation said Ezra ditched me. A self-respecting girl can only drag a party for so long. About to give up, I took one last survey of the faces and strode towards the stairs.

A man said, "Hello." He wore a slim-fitting suit and was thirtysomething if he was a day. His tie was loose and his jacket unbuttoned. "Do I know you?"

Guys who appear casual and slightly out of tune with their environment can have wide-ranging appetites. Once liquored, they tend not to quit. It can be murder getting away.

"Don't think so," I said. His eyes roamed my body.

"I think you're right," he said. "I would've remembered." There didn't seem to be anything more to say, so I began to walk. "Wait," he said. "Lemme buy you a drink."

"They're free," I said. For maybe a century, we stood. Him squinting at me. Figuring, possibly, if I'd be worth the effort. I was immeasurably bored. Bored of humouring men who think they're humouring me. And though it was a nice party, and I didn't want to offend the wrong person, the guy in the sloppy tie pegged me an easy mark. That put me right back in the bars where I know just what to do.

"Do you have a name?" I said.

"Andrew."

"Not Andy?"

"Never." A telltale sign of family prestige. Naming kids for corporate success.

"Is that your mother talking or you?"

"Man," he said. "I'll have to remember that. Aren't you something?"

With super fine-tuned elocution, I whispered, "So, Andy." He leaned close and intimate. "Just between you and me. Do you hate women?"

A smile smacked his face. "I LOVE women." He pressed his palms together and raised them to the sky. "Please. God. Yes."

"How about rape?"

He stooped a notch. "What?"

I leaned in. "Do you like rape?"

"Whoa." He backed up. "That's... no."

"I'm only seventeen," I lied.

"Ahhh..." His head swivelled around the room. "Excuse me."

Now and then, a predator is likely to get snared in my arc, even when I'm not arcing. I almost felt sorry for him as he rushed up the stairs after another guy.

There, mid-stair, was Ezra. Black suit jacket with jeans, almost as I'd met him. He seemed young compared with most of the crowd, like an overcurious child, loitering about. Abruptly, the air was cut with feedback from a microphone.

A decadent woman in patent leather shoes gave a welcome. Followed by two men who took turns describing jubilance over the skill of the curator, the artists, the future of artistic expression and the flourishing art scene in Winnipeg.

A hand was on my back. Ezra spoke into my ear.

"What was that?"

"Someone had to take out the trash."

Presentations ended. We were free to visit the galleries. Ezra was beside me on the third floor. There were at least three, maybe four exhibits. We didn't talk much as we walked. Ezra would stand off-centre of a painting and stare into it forever, not hearing my stomach growl.

Then, he said, "A human being made that. Can you believe it?"

Sometimes I'd wander by myself. As folks clustered by the larger, stately pieces, I found a sketch of a young girl. Germanic.

Hair braided and parted in the middle. Her eyes were sad, intelligent, and I wondered how impossible it must be to impart sadness and intelligence with a pencil. Had the artist seen into the life of this girl? Did he pretend she was his memory?

As the night evolved, Ezra found me. "You really love this, don't you?"

For the rest of the night, we stood off to the side of the largest gallery, at a vantage point that allowed us to see into most of the spaces. The air was charged. Conversations were crackling. They were alive with talk of textures, inspirations and stories.

I'd been thinking of staying until the end, but I could see he'd had enough. We descended the stairs, pausing twice as he pointed out fossil prints in marble.

A cab hummed at the curb. "Are you alright for money?" Ezra asked. I gave my *I can take care of myself* glare. He glanced up at the sky. "You did alright tonight."

"How do you know?"

He laughed. "You know what you are? Something I could stand to learn."

"What?"

"Shrewd."

The night had been great. I hated to see it end. When I looked up at Ezra, I realized I'd broken the most significant rule of all. I knew his eye colour. His name held weight in my throat. I'd been thinking of him, so much so, that if I saw a piano, sculpture, child's drawing, graffiti, dresses, books, babies, a cracked teacup, it had his name on it.

There was an irrepressible fact I'd been pushing back on all night. I wanted him too much. I'd spent hours imagining us in bed. What a relief he had no idea of what we'd done or how unoriginal.

I had to calm down. Get out of my head and get back to being Lily, unmangled.

"I wonder what you'd do," Ezra said. "Lemme ask. What would feature in a Lily art show?"

"Explosions." He flinched. "I'd film it. You know that photographer who took pictures of bullets passing through fruit?" He nodded, warily. "I'd put things in a room and bomb them. Set them off with dynamite. Or throw things at active landmines until they were dust."

I walked to the cab. He latched on my elbow. We kissed. The moment was dreadful. Monumental. Like an Olympic event and someone had just fired the starting gun. Plot-wise, a total mistake.

★

I've wondered what goes on inside these buildings on Princess Street. As I creep up the dark staircase, I'm besieged by the smell of urine and bleach. All around me, pipes gush, deep in the hidden hollows of brick. I pass a man on a landing. He has an elfin body and a seven-day beard. He skips down, leaving his outdoorsman cologne to assault my nose. It's these artsy types in a place like this, smoking dope, pounding out irony, only to fall into sunken futons at night.

I knock.

Ezra answers, then moves aside with an usher's grace. Yet, the invitation comes from the room itself—paints, glosses, sheets and brushes on pallets define a path. I read lids, sniffing the impelling, intoxicating air with a sense of serenity. I feel the thrilling sense of sailing to shore, experiencing erotic tastes and disrupting a world I know nothing about. I know about abandonment, though. In here, things lay where they were tossed—paint can lids, half-finished canvases. Half-finished canvases barely set aside. Ezra, eyeing my legs, says, "Don't touch anything. You might cause a spark."

My heels clack on hardwood floors, I'm fighting the urge to be impressed. In any relationship, I'm the special one. The most ridiculous thing I could allow is convincing myself otherwise. But as I move, Lily loses ground and Ezra advances.

Hanging above a gash of exposed brick are the whites. At first, the effect is emptying. They're flat plains withdrawing from feeling. Yet, like stanzas in a poem, impact is in the detail. I see different textures. I think the word is "opalescent." Another appears blustery. Another clotted. Another pocked like the crater surface of the moon. Once my eyes adjust, deep interest settles in. Ezra was right. They aren't white. They're pink, blue, purple and orange. Lake ice. Hands held to a flame. Images appear as though through a filter. I could debate all day about the gauze we use to dab at sticky truths.

We walk on. Paint-splattered sheets led us through a path of multicoloured abstracts. After the whites, they're overbearing and gaudy.

"I don't know what they're supposed to be."

"Neither do I." He slides his arm over my shoulder.

"When people see what they want to see, is that what you call, 'safe?'"

"That's death."

There are two abstracts of earth-coloured blocks in motion—one is of a tree dropping leaves into a creek. Yet, to my pareidolia, it is a wizard, one with a long, dented nose and deep folds at the mouth. He's singing, or about to sing. It's as though he's between breaths, waiting for his cue. The other is of a woman and a white horse. I see peace in her eyes. It makes me want to witness the moment when she drops the act.

"Who is this woman?" I ask. His fingers linger at my neck. I hear him say "friend" and "Burnaby." "It's all so nice," I say into the void. Ezra presses his face against mine.

"What do you really think?"

"They're not without... depth."

He laughs and, then with an insistent face, pauses for elaboration.

"The colours," I say, "are working."

"The colours are working?" he repeats, as though rehearsing an absurd phrase.

"They... converge."

"Convergence is my middle name." He thinks a few seconds, and then adds, "I can't decide if that response is the best bullshit I've heard."

We walk the remainder of the row. I should ask questions about his inspiration and process, but I'm too involved with colours, lines and shapes.

His phone rings. He answers the call and lingers by the door.

I follow the lines of the room to the corner where Ezra keeps a ratty couch and a bike. His riding shorts are on a hook, bulging at the padded bum cheeks. There's a blanketed canvas on an easel. Ezra steps into the hall and holds the door so it doesn't shut.

I walk to the canvas, careful not to disturb a stack of brass fixtures. Ezra says from the hall, "I'd love to have her." He lets go of the door, and it shuts.

A light bulb flickers as I step around the fixtures. The sheet covering the canvas is smooth and has a slight sheen. Ezra's voice is distant. He's heated about "exposure."

I gently pull the corner of the sheet. Too easily, it comes up in the back. I check for smudges, snags. Then I pull at the other side, and the sheet slides to the floor. The painting before me is revolting—frenetic lines with colours smudgy. Mud green, mud black, sick orange and red.

I step in closer and see that the picture is composed of multicoloured honeycombs. I don't count how many. Dozens? A hundred maybe? Each showcases a picture within. I stare into the heart of the picture. Inside the honeycombs.

There are trees and mountains. Cityscapes. Deserts. But then there are forest fires. Ditches. Roadwork. Demolition. People standing in line. A street with tall buildings, and in between, an empty parking lot. The honeycombs of slashing lines are most distressing. Considering the dimensions, they dominate a lot of space. There are also fake photographs, like the ones retailers put in frames for sale. Mother and daughter. Yawning puppy. With a hypersensitive attention to detail, I step back and look again.

It's me. The honeycombs could be my facial features, with sunsets and volcano bursts to hint at hair. The fiend gazes off to the side, eyes cast beyond the frame. There is a slight profile of the nose. Cheek and ear, chin jutting out, lower lip slightly receded. A mid-reaction facial expression. A bad headshot. Tinges of blue and grey at the fringes, summoning memories of Osborne Street. My body, apparently, lost.

"Do you recognize her?" Ezra asks me. I hadn't heard him come back in. I laugh. The pitch, unshackled, rises like the squawk of a chicken when the farmer raises an axe. He says, "I'd rather have an honest opinion."

He walks over. "Your skin is bone white."

"Does it have to be so big?"

"*That's* your reaction?" His hands find his hips, and he stands like a picture hanging askew. The idiot doesn't understand what he's stumbled upon. I hadn't consented to this.

He stoops for the sheet, folds it and sets it down. I think of gratitude. How I should be flattered to be the subject. I won't thank him though. Since the Remillard party, I tend to see gratitude as a scant margin loitering between what you have a right to, and what someone's willing to give. "Can I tell you something?" he asks. "When we met, I thought you were self-centred. But then you said that thing about how there's no such thing as strangers. I thought, 'There's more to this one than I thought.' I couldn't stop thinking about the comment." He waves at the portrait. "That's when the idea for this came. Even though I don't know you, I used you as the base. As it started to take shape, I thought about metaphors for life. That's why the sections. Vulnerability and strength. You know how many eggs can hold up a car?"

"It should hang in a psychiatric hospital."

"Some of that strength, you put on, wouldn't you say? When you're pretending, you have an eyebrow that quivers. Did you know that? Your jaw tenses when you're listening. So guarded. Just when I think you're about to say something vulnerable, it's a story about how smart you are." He stops to measure my response. "You got me thinking about what it takes to get someone to that point. So much self-promotion and self-protection."

It's punishment.

I shouldn't have gone to that party. It was stupid. Reckless. Stupid reckless people deserve what they get. Those guys didn't even have to work for it. I just handed myself to them like a parting gift. When my mind swerves to that night, I see them laughing at the ease with which I became theirs. Course, that doesn't mean they had to do it. They grew up in the same neighbourhood. Their parents might've known mine. Even so. They put themselves on me and, most humiliating of all, tricked me into letting it happen.

I loathe stupid.

Ezra, dumb to my pain, seems to expect a response.

"How do you think I should react?" I ask.

"Based on the merits of the work. You're acting like it's internet porn."

"I'm without a skin."

He lets off a sigh. "You have a lot of demons. Everyone worth knowing has demons."

His arms wind around my neck. I search for what to say. I get that the painting isn't an intentional burn. It's more of a tide. Gentle and devastating.

I need to say something borderline vulnerable, yet strategic enough to get me back to steering this thing.

"You like my demons?" I ask.

Riding the back of a chuckle, he says, "Your demons are fucking voluptuous."

A flash of concern creeps across his face. He feels his rear pocket and glances around the room. Books and magazines are pushed aside as he searches.

"Is it for me?" I say.

"I might show it." His phone chimes.

"You wouldn't."

"I'm having a few guys by tomorrow."

"Who are these guys?"

"Do you want their names?" He locates his wallet and rubs his hands. "Ready?"

"Ready to know who'll be here when I die."

"You're funny." He gives me a shallow kiss before he opens the door.

"I'm serious," I say. "Would you want people to find you like that?"

Street noise slinks in. At the lip of the staircase, steps roll down and away. There is no one along our descent. Less than no one.

We duck into a sandwich place and sit at a window. I'm watching people with feet on the ground, looking forward, oblivious to the black-blue storm clouds pressing down. When the waitress asks if I need something, I scream with laughter.

The sauce on his sandwich leaks. Ezra licks his fingers and takes another bite. I wait for the clouds to burst, thinking, What happened to the face I had, before the world made it?

Devin

People meet in the weirdest ways. In April I met a guy who, after a few years working at a game reserve, became a journalist. His name is Kasim. I met him the day I was walking around Parliament and saw a gathering and a stage. People were dancing to reggae. I had no intention of joining them, but I had to know why they were sprayed with pink and orange paint. A banner stretched across the stage that read, "Peace." Soon a middle-aged woman was trying to draw me in. She took my hands and made them sway while she nodded at my feet. She sent a high-pitched staccato scream up, and people, they were whopping, and I was in a circle of swaying bodies.

I backed into him and said, "Whoops!" Kasim had his camera aimed at a street child, a girl, who had walked into the field and was tugging on a man's pants. She wore dirty suspender jeans with an oversized soccer jersey underneath. The man kept dancing. So she kept tugging. Kasim twisted his long lens and took her picture. The shutter clicked several times and, when he finished, he turned to me.

He had the clean-shaven face of a boy. I thought, Probably studying to be a doctor.

I was right.

He spends off-time interviewing people downtown or in the slums. I could see this in him even on the first day. Had an unwavering way of looking at a person and not being bothered about it.

I apologized. Said I was curious about the event, that's all.

He asked, "Are you voting for Kenyatta?"

I backed up a step. "I don't live here."

He put his hands on his hips. "Do you use the Commercial Bank of Africa?"

"No."

"Do you stay at a Heritage Hotel?"

"Eh?"

His voice got louder. "Do you consume Brookside Dairy?"

"Maybe I should leave you to your pictures."

His hands went up to his head. Fingers jutting out like sticks of dynamite. "Buying from Kenyatta is voting for Kenyatta. Voting for conflict of interest and crimes against humanity."

"Okay," I said.

"Him and his friends. One shows the plunder, while the other hides the thief."

"I'm not buying anything Kenyatta's got to sell. Let's leave it at that."

"See?" Kasim said to anyone within a quarter mile. "A *musungu* gets it." I didn't, really. He stretched his arms out. "Kenyatta expands his empire while Nairobi rots in traffic. While we ration water. While families live on the street. He is one billion strong and getting stronger." People shifted away to dance elsewhere, except one belligerently happy woman.

"Peace," she said and danced away.

"Not to be rude," I said, "but I don't wanna be your prop." I headed toward University Way. Kasim called after me.

"Please," he said. "I am done making my point." His tone was apologetic. "Though I must say the look on your face was priceless. *Jambo*," he held out his hand, "I am Kasim Karega Otieno."

"Can I call you Casey?"

"No."

I liked him right away. He didn't put me on a pedestal. In Kenya, whites are treated too well. We're patronized, flattered. Put into gilded cages, which makes it impossible to really know a local. Kasim, however, wasn't gonna call me "boss," or "sir." "I know I frustrate people," he said, "but there are Kenyans like me who know peace cannot exist without justice."

"I'm no stranger to the idea of hypocrisy," I said. He asked how long I'd been in Kenya. Why I was alone.

I said, "Would you believe I'm a refugee?"

He laughed and said, "Do you take coffee?"

It happened that easily. My adoption. We walked off the field together, and he introduced his theory of football, a sport I knew nothing about. "How much is one?" he asked.

"The distance between zero and one?"

"Playing on a team makes a person one *plus*. According to your response, it makes a person one-and-a-half people long." He shook orange powder from his hair. I asked if he thought Kenyans were a team. His expression turned. "There's divisiveness. Walls so big people cannot see around them."

"Like the folks in the slums?" I said. "They've been left to fend for themselves. I think it's wrong to underestimate them. Maybe they feel rejected?"

"Ah, yes," he said. "It does not help that Kenya is under constant guard from terrorists who would make a violent statement. Why? Fundamentalism is rejection borne in rejection."

I didn't know what Kasim meant, so I said, "Nothing's real. Except baggage."

Kasim gave me a short nod that said he'd consider that.

The next day, Kasim invited me to a *harambee*. I asked what it was. He simply said, "Birthday party." I protested, saying I wouldn't fit in. He laughed without maliciousness and told me when and where to meet him.

We bused it to Kangemi, a quiet neighbourhood where gates and high fences broadcast safety. When Kasim entered the house, the crowd shifted, fragmenting into clusters. People made their way over to greet him. I saw why. It's hard not to be impressed at the way Kasim keeps a conversation going. How he makes people open up. I could see the journalist in him. He's an expert at interviewing because he has a genuine ear for people. "How is your mother? How far now, into your studies are you?" His hands pressed hands as he listened. There's no rushing him. Doesn't matter how long it's been, how tired he is or if he has tickets to a concert starting in thirteen minutes. Kasim has to make sure people are doing well and their loved ones are doing well too.

"Who are these people?" I asked him.

"My friends and family," he said. As in who else would they be? "*Jambo*," he shouted to the room, and the hugging began.

The buffet spanned three tables pushed together, draped with red-checkered cloth and piled high with Cellophane-wrapped goodies. The crowd was decked in their church duds. No one had a head bowed toward a cellphone, not even a teenager. There was no kids' table either.

I spent much of the *harambee* trying to figure out what it is about Kasim that makes him so special. I came to the conclusion that he's a true believer in himself and other people. When I told him, in an off-to-the-side comment by the gift table, that the music I liked is anti-folk, he didn't scoff. "I should take a listen. Where do you perform? Do you have a style I would recognize?" And finally, "Where can I buy your music?"

I told him I didn't have a record out, because it was a process, and I didn't even know if it would lead anywhere. I couldn't tell him that the world's's rigged against us, that we labour on a table that's tipped, or that motivation is hard to come by when only a few can count on luck. I couldn't say it to *them*, who worked and studied every day in a country with a government that was apparently as corrupt as one could be, and was finding it more difficult to say it to myself. I mean, without family, what did I have to rail against? I'd actually been feeling pretty good. In the faces of Kasim's family and neighbours, I saw a question pressing. Where did I want to go from here?

A scratchy afghan on the couch grated against my arms. Kasim's parents came over to chat. His mom slid in beside me, riding the sofa sidesaddle. She had long, shiny nails and cherry red lips. Her sister, with round hips and cat eye glasses, scanned my body, yanked my t-shirt and said I was too thin. More grinning women came. They discussed my appearance, and whether I needed more fat. I was asked to stand. Kasim's aunt asked where my wife was and what she was feeding me. I told them I wasn't married, and that I didn't have a girlfriend. That pushed me further out into open water.

"My dear boy," Kasim's mother said, "WHAT ARE YOU DO-ING?"

We went into the tidy kitchen, and Kasim poured himself water. He said the party was for a college girlfriend. They had dated once and were still good friends. I saw a dainty presence by the gift table, standing with her parents. When we walked over, the girl took my hand in spite of a shy smile.

Kasim said, "This is my friend, Mary."

Mary had the face of a studious girl about to cakewalk into her future. She asked me questions, recognizing, I think, that family was a taboo topic.

As people began to say their farewells, Mary hung back with me. Her arm hooked through mine. Turning toward the gifts, I said, "You did well."

"*Asante.*"

Months passed from warm to cool. As Kasim and I hung out more often, I thought he'd befriended all of Kenya. When he walked through his neighbourhood, people came to the sidewalk. *Matatu, boda boda* drivers. Street kids. He treated them like he'd treat himself.

In May, Kasim said his grandmother had been ill, and now that she'd recovered, he'd like me to meet her. We visited one afternoon in her small, clean house. The living room was dark and cool. She was sitting with Kasim's cousin and his wife. The television was tuned to an outdoor church service. She wore her short grey hair back from her face. Even though she didn't speak English, the light-pink paint gave the place warmth. His grandmother's hands rested in the fold between her thighs, and as Kasim spoke, they rose as a way of welcoming me.

Kasim brought crepe-like bread and tea to us, which he arranged in front of her just so. I noticed his grandmother seemed to rest with eyes shut, as if saying grace. Kasim's cousin leaned towards me. He said, "Swahili you get, you get it, no problem." I shook my head. I didn't get it.

I'd heard Swahili for months. Picked up a few words and phrases. That day, it was like hearing it for the first time. Rhythm. Pitch. Refrain. Their conversation had the rocking motion of a lullaby. I listened like a sleepy child holding his cup with both hands.

It was a short visit. Just enough to drink half my tea. After Kasim said our goodbyes, we walked to my vehicle and I asked about his dad.

"My parents lived in Gatundu, Kiambu County," he said. "It is a small community, maybe eighteen thousand people. Some farms and villages are settled on the lands below. On a good day, it smells like cardamom and orange peels. On a bad day, it smells like chemicals from the mortuary." I laughed in horror. "When I was a child, my father couldn't find employment, so he went to other towns where he sometimes got work, sometimes not. He was away so often we started to think of him as an uncle. One day, when I was six, the rainy season fell, and the roads became impassable. He did not return home. Not that night, nor the next."

"But didn't I meet him at the *harambee*?"

"When I was a teenage boy, I asked my mother about him. For weeks, she refused to answer. I remember those days. Everywhere, veils. Bedsheets hanging, her skirt twisting away. Then one afternoon, as I was fixing a bicycle chain, Mother came up and asked me what I thought of Father. I said I only remembered that he was untidy. Finally, she said our father was an unpredictable man who had no idea about money."

"He didn't deserve you guys," I said. "He left. You can't let someone get away with that."

"Then," Kasim said, "almost three years ago, he came back." His eyes cast out over nearby buildings. "He was poor as ever. When I saw him standing outside our mother's house, it was sad and beautiful. He wanted to come home. Just. He did not know how. As Mother walked to him, his face changed. She kissed his palms. I know because we watched through the window.

"Something was happening to us as well. We huddled together, arms around each other. We knew that he had been close all that time, hearing about us through relatives, aware of our whereabouts. To see him on the other side of a few concrete slabs? Incredible. When he kissed Mother, we ran out."

I couldn't believe what I was hearing. "How did everyone else react?"

"They threw a party, of course."

A man with an orange cart at the roadside waved. Kasim gave him a salute.

"For the poor and unemployed," Kasim said, "there is little feeling of contribution. You live to die another day. It is dehumanizing. It divorces people from themselves and from their loved ones. So when a man finds that he has lost his influence, he leaves to find it elsewhere. It was not easy when he returned. We had to relearn ourselves. But, as my mother used to say, 'If the moon loves you, why worry about the stars?'" A *boda boda* driver pulled up beside us. A little girl clamped herself to the back of what might have been her brother. Kasim gave her the Queen of England wave. "You know, Devin," he said, "I shudder to think where any of us would be if we received what we deserve."

While idling in traffic, I asked Kasim about his grandmother's eyes. He said she'd taken the bus to work every day for years. One day, in two-thousand-and-something, two men attempted to bomb the US Embassy. They couldn't get past the gate and panicked first and threw grenades. The sound brought people in neighbouring buildings to the windows. The explosives in their truck blew. The blast took down the office building next door and sent window shards from the bus into his grandmother's eyes.

Kasim's voice quaked a little in the retelling, especially about her being buried in the fallout, alone, taken to hospital, not knowing where she was for three days.

"Let's change the subject," he said.

He asked about my process for writing music. I said I didn't really have one. His eyes waited. I said, "Strumming chords, humming melodies. I kind of get lost. Much of it seems accidental."

He was bouncing. "Music is meant to share," he said. "Sing one for me."

"If I do, you have to tell me what you really think. You have to be brutally honest."

He looked at me strangely. "I would see your music as a gift. Tell me, why would I be brutal?"

With Kasim, I was comfortable exploring Nairobi's music scene. In May, I found a venue called Carnivore Grounds. Kasim and I went one night. I expected him to know the place, but he was rubbernecking like me. Heaped on the stage, mounds of blinking audio equipment. Tables and chairs scattered in an arc like a cathedral. We took a table next to a guy with long braids pulled back in a ponytail. He wore sunglasses even though it was dark, and he had a glass of dark beer in front of him. His arms were on the table, hands flat, like he was holding the table down.

The place was filling up. Glasses clinked. Voices rose.

"Puh. Puh. Puh," a man on stage spat into the microphone. Another tweaked buttons on a synth. Then the lights narrowed to a spotlight on the stage. The crowd fell silent. "This is gonna be good," I whispered. A woman walked into the light. Her hair, a Medusa mop of copper curls. Red leather pants up to her armpits. She raised one arm, brought it down, bam!

A seven-piece band. Convulsive percussion jabbing into the bottom part of lung where I rarely draw breath. Electrifying wall-to-wall beats. The singer sidestepped across the stage, dragging the microphone stand. Her hair whipped, and her lips opened like drum cymbals. The wall behind the band lit up, and images from Nairobi played on a screen—slum shots. Downtown core. Poverty contrasted with mansions. Designed to stir an audience. But it was her voice that really did it. Pure power. She could pull off a high-octane glissando and drop back into a chorus like nothing happened.

It was like a feast. I didn't know which shade of cool to savour first.

I swiveled around to see Kasim, ready to say, "They're ripping up this set." Lights from the stage lit his face. He had a strange glare in his eye. I knew he was thinking about politics. I wanted to get his attention and say, "Look at this." Just once, couldn't he slough off the layers of virtue and get back to fun? I turned away as the guitarist ran his fingers in rapture along the neck of a guitar.

In the months after, Kasim would get more serious more often. He was always lecturing about the free press. Saying if Kenya didn't have fair reporting, if it weren't for the army of reporters beating the streets, the country might implode. He said, "While the rich interpose, the poor debate. But to tell the truth, to tell a story in goodly time, that is the basis of democracy. Kenya must at all costs pay attention to the truth."

He almost always had a newspaper. I called it his axe. If we went anywhere, he'd fan it out on a table and point at this story or that. When I said something ignorant, he'd hit me with it.

On a rainy Saturday, the kind made for watching YouTube, Kasim dragged me to a political rally. It was the last thing I wanted to do. But how do you let someone down whose shown only enthusiasm for *your* stuff?

The crowd was large and mostly made up of young men. I thought, Aren't there risks when that many people clump up? Kasim led me to the centre. From that vantage point, deep inside the crowd, I was relieved to see police watching over us.

I saw Raila Odinga, Kenyatta's opponent, up close. Middle-aged and dressed like an office worker on a casual Friday, he was standing on a stage with bright banners propped up behind. The speech was in Swahili, but I got the picture. He held the microphone with one hand and, with the other, painted the nation's future.

Kasim yelled in my ear. He said whatever problem in Kenya, underdevelopment, blah, blah, blah, corruption was at its heart. "When Obama came," Kasim said, "he told us, 'every shilling that's a bribe could be put in the pockets of someone doing an honest day's work.' That was a tough message delivered with love. Once corruption gets into the structure, it's nearly impossible to get out."

"Raila is the first to oppose Kenyatta?" I asked.

"Kenyatta does not have opponents," Kasim said. "Opponents are exhausted, silenced, fattened or killed."

Kasim was running at the mouth. He shouted about a corrupt judiciary. About corrupt police. Heads turned. Faces were angry. Men shouted. Kasim shouted back. The crowd began to sway like some pent-up force had been released.

A fight broke out a few yards away—football-player types throwing their weight around, causing a whirlpool of arms and fists. I stood my ground, even as the shouting around us grew. I latched onto a conviction I didn't know I had. I wasn't gonna let Kasim down.

Raila warned about people getting hurt near the stage. The fight quieted, but faces didn't relax.

"They seem to hate you," I said. Kasim explained that the men weren't attacking him. They were arguing with him. Others were agreeing. "Sometimes," he said, "men incite violence simply because they are hungry."

"How does that work?"

"They can loot vendors or markets."

"When they do that," I said, "they prove that they don't deserve democracy yet. That's acting like children. The message they send is they can't handle the responsibility."

"No, Devin. The message is that their government has let them starve."

That's when Kasim read my face. I'd had enough disagreeing and agreeing for one day. So we left, but even so, Kasim couldn't let it go. "Protest has meaning for me," he said. "It is a real thing that we can do." Then he turned inward, keeping the rest of his thoughts to himself.

We walked past the curve of University Way, past yappy hucksters and Muslim men drinking coffee. Away from the rally, I hoped Kasim and I could enjoy the city and its characters, like the leather-clad drivers and the men in oversized suits. His friendship had shed a new light on the city. I could see it changing before my eyes. I wanted to taste it. So I suggested we stop and get something to drink. Maybe do some people watching.

We walked down the middle of the choked street, carving a disappearing line through the throng. I commented on *matatu* graffiti, popular culture icons, and I had to admit, pretty punk rock.

On all sides, drivers confronted billboards about lotto.

A city of chance.

I deserved this. After suffering alone, I deserved to enjoy Nairobi with Kasim.

We wound up in a market where Kasim extended his political banter. He talked to women selling Styrofoam containers of roast beef layered with green vegetables.

By spring, I'd spent so much time with Kasim, I came to see him as the family I should've had. We took turns suggesting things to do with each other, yet one thing he never compromised was family. Usually there was a cousin or nephew to bring with. I saw them as family too.

One Friday, he was going to watch his cousin, Matthew, play soccer. He was considered a star at his school. I could hardly say no.

In the bleachers, Kasim took out his newspaper and a book by Paulo Freire.

"Don't worry about politics," I said. The centre on the opposing team had a breakaway. He sprinted and tapped the ball lightly to keep it in front. Two opponents raced after, almost falling over their own momentum. "I mean, isn't the game always this jerk versus that jerk? Sorry if that's insensitive, but you get it." The kid with the breakaway torqued left, then right, ran off on an angle, then scored. Kasim glared at me like I was the problem in this world.

"Imagine what we could do if man believed in itself?" He watched the game with his elbows on his knees. Then, out of nowhere, he asked, "What's it like to live so close to America?"

Matthew and another player slid for the ball in front of Matthew's net. They collided, and Matthew lay in the field. The other player picked himself up. Matthew didn't. One leg was up as a fellow player felt the tissue around the ankle. The coach, a squat man, knelt as players stood in a group.

"You have to adjust," Kasim said, "to the notion that you have power to change things."

The coach pulled Matthew to his feet. The crowd gave a polite golf clap of respect.

There was a substitution. Kasim stood. The opposition swamped the new kid from both sides. When he ran closer to the net, he snapped his body right and swung his left leg back for a kick. The ball soared high, arcing over the goalkeeper's head, hitting the top of the goal post. The post shattered into dust. Kasim moaned and sat back down. "Termites," he said. "They take down anything."

★

"Are you in a car?"

"Eh?" says Paul, his voice garbled in a tunnel of wind. "Nuh. How long?"

"What?"

"This friend."

"Couple months. Going to the National Park, though I'm not hot on caged animals."

"Sounds like you got something very special."

I tell him my plans aren't compatible with his Saturday delivery. His beard grates across the receiver.

I meet Kasim at his cousin Noella's house. I see a girl sitting in the window. She appears to be holding a doll. Her father bends to see who's arrived. He waves.

Kasim comes out. He's wearing a t-shirt that reads, "Who knew I could make 50 look this good?" Behind him is a thin girl with a high forehead. "This is Elizabeth," Kasim says. "One of life's miracles. She goes to Moi Secondary School." Elizabeth says she's heard all about me. The front door bursts open again. A little guy comes running and hugs Kasim's hip.

"Devin, this is Patrick, my nephew. We call him *Mtu Mdogo*. It means 'Little Man.'"

There's a trace of Kasim's positivity that lives in Little Man's way of rising onto the balls of his feet. Kasim opens the back door of the car for him, and he scrambles in. As I drive, I see his reflection in the rear-view. His eyes hungrily follow people and cars on the street. "She is a good egg," Kasim says of Elizabeth. "I said good things about you." I admit I'm curious what he'd say to Elizabeth, but I don't want to grill him. "You made friends at the *harambee*," he says.

I did?

He drums a rhythm out on his thighs. Little Man smiles, and I see myself smiling back. He claps his puffy hands. Kasim says, "That's it," to Little Man. "You should play the drums," Kasim says to me. "You can take it with you anywhere." He drums again. Little Man imitates. "You can make up a whole song by the time you are ready to walk back out into the sun."

"There's a song lyric in there somewhere," I say.

"I'll help you. We'll write it together. But it must be hip hop." He drums, head nodding to a melody only he can hear.

"Let's try it," I say.

"Oh, yeah?"

"We'll do a rhyming death match. I'll start." I clear my throat. "Yo…"

"No 'yo.'" Both Kasim's hands bat that idea away. "No, to 'yo.'"

"How about… be telling 'bout the way I am."

"Try it again," says Kasim. I repeat the line. Kasim drums.

"No," I say. "You come up with a line too." I repeat the line again and sing, "Be saying I don't give a damn." His chin's grooving. I lay down some percussion for him to jump in on.

"While mammas wash the baby's pram."

"Mammas what?" Kasim laughs so hard his body shakes. "We have a baby?"

Little Man giggles himself into a sneeze. He says, "You are going to hell. Burn. Burn…"

"No one's going to hell, Little Man," Kasim says, "except Devin. He is the white man." The two laugh, and I laugh with them.

Kasim turns on the radio, and bits of chatter and music spew nonsensically as he toggles through the stations. "Up ahead," he says. It's a black iron gate off Langata I'm looking for. I turn and creep toward the ticket taker. The woman at the gate takes my money, and I throw three tickets on the dash. Kasim points at where to park.

A path leads to the animal enclosures beneath leaves of low-hanging branches. A large chain-link fence skirts the edge. Little Man's arm is high as Kasim holds his hand. Monkeys scamper in branches above. Kasim calls to them. They tiptoe along the top of a fence.

We walk to a cage with a brightly-furred animal. It is half-hidden and seems to be sleeping, and I think this is what the visit will be, us watching animals lying sedate. Kasim rattles the cage.

"You're way too close," I say.

A tail flickers from behind brush. It's a young cheetah, so light on its feet that when it walks, its paws seem to absorb sound. "This guy," Kasim says, "is here forever."

Little Man wants me to lift him. His weight fills my arms.

"He is too young," Kasim says.

"Little Man?"

"The cheetah. He did not learn to fight for himself. Now he cannot be rehabilitated like the other animals here."

The cheetah sniffs the fence. A black tear-like line runs from his eyes to nose. The purr reminds me of a lawn mower. The cheetah presses his forehead against the chain fence, and the three of us are taking turns scratching it. His purring gets louder. He turns and shows us the back of his neck. Fifteen fingers reach out to scratch it.

"In every way a cheetah," Kasim says, "except for what cheetahs are supposed to do."

I take in the logs, rocks and trees within the cheetah's enclosure. "It's safe," I say.

"Safe," Kasim says, as if it were a terrible shame.

Does the cheetah miss running ragged for food? Does he miss defending himself against predators? If given a choice, wouldn't he pick this?

An animal keeper in a green jumpsuit carries two plastic buckets. He and Kasim speak in Swahili. The keeper looks at Little Man and me, then scoops a chunk of raw meat from Bucket A. He pushes it through a hole in the chain-link fence. The cheetah sticks his tongue through and gobbles the chunk down.

The next sign reads, "Hyena." I'd read that they can chomp through a man's thigh. I'd have expected the killing machine to rifle at us, but his body's a rolled up doormat.

"It is rehabilitation for this guy," Kasim says. Little Man yawns.

"He hasn't forgotten how to hunt like the other one?" I ask.

"The hyena is not so young. He will not forget."

Little Man totters to an enclosure with a low fence. The sunlight sparkles in the ripples of a water feature. I can't see what animal it's supposed to be. Then, it's right in front of me. The colour of putty. An alligator.

Little Man runs around benches on the other side of the path. He stops to look at a female lion asleep on her side. We join him and the keeper rattles the cage the same way Kasim did. The lioness doesn't move. He rattles again, harder, and the fence screams from all corners. Her tail ripples. The keeper whistles.

"Maybe we should leave her alone," I say.

The lioness has slits for eyes, as if four sweaty guys don't tantalize her. Eventually, her legs gather beneath her. She saunters towards us. As the lioness paces, I'm told to take her picture, and I'll know when. The keeper holds the pail out to Kasim. He takes a chunk of meat and presses it high up against the fence. A low rumble babbles from her throat. "Hurry up," Kasim screams. I tap the camera icon, thinking, Goodbye, Kasim's hand. She's going for it. Her body stretches, making her taller than us. Then, her tongue snakes through the chain-link, shifting the meat closer to a hole. I take a picture.

Kasim holds the pail out to me. "Now it is your turn."

I'm half-laughing, half-backing away, when a voice stops me.

"I didn't authorize this!" We turn.

It's Paul, looking at me. "Hi, honey," he says. I'm suddenly cold. "Ah, right," he says. "After the call, I thought, come on. The park's on my way. I could say a quick, 'Hi.'"

I introduce Paul to Kasim and Little Man.

"You mind if I try?" Paul says to the keeper. Kasim hands the pail to Paul. "Just because they're in a cage," he says, "doesn't mean they shouldn't work for it." He steps up. "Take a picture of this, kid." Paul lifts a chunk high above his head as Kasim did. The lioness lunges. I snap a picture just when Paul turns towards me with his high-voltage smile. The lioness's arced body, teeth bared. Her wide jaw level with his scalp.

Our group, bigger by one, moves forward. Kasim walks beside me. "It's a tourist trap," Paul says. He's looking around. "You don't see tourists flooding to Kenya for the people." Like that, I'm tired of Paul. The same guy I'd been chasing for months to hang out with. The same guy who gave me a job and so much more. Compared to Kasim, he's sarcastic. Tedious. "It's a comment," Paul says. "Not an insult."

Twittering birds fill the void. In the light of dusk, the male lion appears made of gold. He pads towards us with shoulder and hip muscles pumping. I'm thinking, Why should *he* need a break from the world?

The last enclosure is a fence of stacked logs. The gate is short enough to see over. The sign reads, "Maximilian." Inside is a rhino. His cement-coloured hide walks past the gate. He circles to the opposite side and returns back to me. Maximilian, with his armoured presence, circles aimlessly in this enclosure.

"He blind," the keeper says from behind. "He no fend for hisself. Deh moder gone leave." With each step, the rhino's head nods along with the keeper's story. I think, He's probably old enough to remember. Young enough to want more. Could one say the rhino is lost?

"What happens if people stop coming?" I ask the keeper.

"Dat never happen," the keeper says.

"Say something happened," I say. "Some worldwide thing and people stopped coming. Would the animals die?"

Kasim has a screwed-up smile. "You must not worry about that. You see this place. You saw the keepers." His tone is genuine. But he's wrong. There are things to worry about. Reasons big enough for many young people where I come from to not plan to have kids. Even here. It's like he's forgotten the live-bullet police killings.

I have an image of a post-apocalyptic world, where mushroom clouds peal beyond the timberline, and the keepers scatter. There's a blast. Not a shrill scream like footage of an atomic bomb. A sound so heavy, it falls in on itself, like a muted hollowing of the earth. Animals lick their noses in confusion and jostle nervously in their cages.

Kasim puts Little Man down. He's watching my face.

"If everyone had to evacuate," I say, "even if they released the doors first, the rhino and the cheetah wouldn't have a chance."

The hippo stops at the gate. His whiskery head bobs.

"He's looking at you," Kasim says to me. He has a big grin.

"Boo," Paul says. Maximilian raises his head, sniffs and circles in the opposite direction.

Palm trees and fan-like leaves. Sunlight sprays the grass in swirls. A woman in red flats and a blue-flowered dress walks with her hand on her daughter's head. The little girl is more certain of her talents than Little Man. She waves. "Girl," says Little Man. He rakes one shoe in the dirt creating a moat.

Kasim touches my arm. "So we can go now? Are you ready?" The trouble is I don't want to leave. "I am glad you came to Nairobi," he says.

"I'm glad too."

As soon it was said, I felt ridiculous. Not a single pure, generous thought can pass through Paul's vortex without being attacked.

"That's sweet," Paul says. His sarcasm spreads like so much uncollected garbage. Kasim walks ahead with Little Man. The boy wouldn't go. Kasim, on bent knee, asks Little Man what's up. Little Man is staring at Paul.

"What's this bloke's problem?" Paul asks.

"He's not normally rude," Kasim says. He takes Little Man's hand and wiggles it, as in "Wake up, little dude." The boy is locked on Paul.

"Dragon," Little Man says. His finger comes up to his nostril. We swivel our heads in Paul's direction. He has on his cargo pants and beige wind shirt. He is beige on brown with blond, a dragon if I'd ever seen one.

Kasim announces it's time for Little Man's washroom break. He takes Little Man and backtracks to where rustic shack-like restrooms sit. Little Man glances back at Paul, until Kasim lifts him off the ground for a second. His little runners land in dirt and pick up the pace. He runs up the ramp, and Kasim closes the door.

Paul horks a loogie. "Where'd you dig him up?"

"We met at a peace rally."

"You're going to peace rallies?"

"Kasim's super political."

Paul stares at me as if he's watching a slow-moving catastrophe.

"He's always going on about corrupt police, the police shooting kids in the slums and corruption. He wants a peaceful Kenya."

Suddenly, Paul strides to the bathroom.

The keeper taps me on the shoulder. "You enjoy?"

"Oh, yes."

I think, maybe, Kasim will take me to Maasai Mara. We'll see the free animals. The Big Five. And we should write a song for kicks.

The wood door opens and Paul skip-steps down the ramp. He says. "I think your friend's a wee sick."

Kasim comes out of the restroom missing his smile. Little Man runs down the ramp. Fearing he'll spill cockeyed off the side, I extend my hand to him. Kasim screams, "No!"

"I thought he might fall." Kasim's eyes vanish behind a self-involved glaze.

We walk. I wait for Kasim to say something. But like the skip of a turntable's needle, something's off.

I fall back and let Kasim catch up. I give him a playful shove. Instead of responding in kind, he veers away. I jog in front and turn around, walking backwards. Kasim glances. Little Man makes a circle with his pointy finger and thumb and looks as though through a microscope.

"Hey," I say to Kasim. "Great idea, coming here. Been thinking about our song." I put my fingers out, framing the future. "Song writing duo. I mean it. I used to think about songs all the time, but I haven't for months. Guess I thought that part of me was over. Or, I don't know. Is that a weird thing to say?" A glottal sound clicks in Kasim's throat.

I slow even more. Kasim halts to avoid running into me. I lower my voice. "Here," I hand Kasim my lucky lighter. "I want you to have this. You've been a friend. This was my grandfather's. We didn't have the best relationship. It's for you. For today."

"I could not," Kasim says.

He slips the lighter into my shirt pocket, and Paul sucks on a cigarette and exhales a pillow of smoke. If only I could get Kasim and Little Man in the truck, away from Paul, I could clear this up.

"I'll take you home," I say. Little Man clings to Kasim's leg. "Maybe Elizabeth can introduce me to her father this time."

"Her father will be at church," Kasim says. "He is a good man, and you should not disturb his devotion."

"Okay. Just *thought*. Another time."

I can't understand how he got so cold. He looks like I spit in his grandmother's eye. And after everything we've done together. He's my best friend. He knows I've never experienced real tragedy, so when I say or do stupid things, he forgives me.

I move close so Paul won't overhear. "I'm sorry he showed up," I say. "He's not my friend. He's just a guy I met. I don't know what he's doing here. It's weird for me too, okay?"

"You know," Kasim says, "There is an animal here that you would like." His eyes, now barbed fishing hooks, meet mine. "The chameleon."

Kasim marches toward the park gate. Until they disappear, Little Man's legs switch back to keep pace.

Violet clouds slump in a sky of ash. Paul slaps me on the shoulder. "Looks like you can make that delivery today. Good thing I caught up with you."

Julia

I agree to drop magic mushrooms at the cottage, on the eve of my forty-sixth birthday. I'm no virgin to drugs but Cole, until recently, was monolithically against them. When he proposed the idea, he was wearing his dad's purple-swirl sweater and said,

"The constant tension is preventing release," followed by, "Sometimes not being yourself is the point."

His recent purchase, a surprise pug, scampers past my feet as I open the door. It's Winston's first time at the cottage. His claws scrape hardwood until he reaches carpet. In the living room, he wheezes in circles, then bolts upstairs, where I hear his bowling ball body bound through the bedrooms. Cole comes in hoisting two bags. At the sound of his voice, Winston runs backs down and sits at Cole's feet.

I walk around the place, touching the wood's open grain. I stack books right-side-up. Pull the drapes open. Though the cottage has been my refuge, our pretty place overlooking an island, it doesn't feel that way. Forget old age. It's routine that rusts the joints. Still, it's better than dragging Cole to summer festivals and parking on blistering downtown streets.

Cole is talking to Winston. "Such a good boy!" The pug's tail wags. "Do you wanna go for a swim?" He comes over and leans into me. I coerce a smile. Then Cole resumes putting things away, and I'm grateful that's the extent of the romance.

I take a load off in the living room. Cole lands on the couch beside me with the Ziploc bag of mushrooms.

"What did you say Lily was doing?" I ask.

"Staying at a friend's."

"I can't remember the last time the three of us were together."

He looks at me as if all I've done is think of things to worry about. "It's alright," he says. "We'll do something with her next week. For now, we've got the weekend to ourselves." He presents the wormlike shafts. Their brittle shells quiver on the coffee table. "At your weight," he says, "you should have half or less." His share of worms rests in his palm. He tosses them back with childlike zeal. I eat a quarter and sweep the rest back.

Cole turns on the television and settles on a show where couples bid on a storage shed. Forty minutes in and I think maybe Cole was right. Devin gave up the right to be sympathized with. But I miss defiance. I miss the surge that comes with realness. How exhausting performance is.

I miss those early days of marriage when you have lust to look forward to. The way a man sees what's impressive about you. When, in that charged way, he narrows his eyes, and I can see the possibility of a new life. A new self.

I could go back to acting. Community club stuff. I could move near Waterfront Drive, where all the divorcees rent. Get a small place and decorate it midcentury modern. Meet interesting people, frequent little eateries and debate politics at corner tables.

I miss excitement. I miss verve.

Verve.

Vee.

Vee is a crack in the moulding,
  The head of a viper.
 A toddler-stroked
  arrow
   pointing to hell
    VERVE
     is
     the
     virid
      quake in your voice,
 As you shrug off old skin.
    Air
   crackles with
   spirited sparks
   of fancy
    Standing
   each
   hair
   on

"Do you feel anything?" asks Cole. His face is magenta. He thinks something's funny.

The neighbour's Labrador Retriever lumbers onto our yard. She sniffs along the water's edge, running back and forth along the rocks. When she stops, her head hangs toward the opposite shore, where a chainsaw's whiny scream pierces the distance.

Voices. Men. They call to one another. The dog's barks rebound off the opposite shore and she sits there barking at her echo.

Can't be bothered to pretend to give a care about whatever. Except adventure. At the centre of a good adventure is a question. Should I leave right now? The thought sets up a tingling behind my jaw. So I test-drive a scene: Me. I get up as though I'm going to the bathroom. Disappear to the bedroom. Noiselessly pack a light bag. Creep downstairs, through the mudroom. Crack the door. By the time Cole hears the engine turn over, I'm in third gear.

Here's the hitch, though. If I do it, I can't turn back. It has to be *it*.

Cole's studying me. I realize what's happened. I've exhaled like an old train.

"We in this together?" he asks.

"I ate the 'shrooms, didn't I?"

Nature should hold clues for what I ought to do. After all, it lies under the atmosphere, receiving. But it's a humid, windless afternoon. Just washed-out sky under workaday sun. Only a beaver fishtails along the surface. Otherwise, the lake lacks the hustle to heave.

"Let's go for a walk," Cole says. He's up and pulling a ball cap from a shelf. "Leave the dog. What? We're not going to lose our minds."

Pine cones crack underfoot. A creature bolts through the underbrush. A deer. Our eyes meet. Hers are blank and beautiful. We take a few more steps and it leaps away, its white fluff of tail disappearing into the thick. Then solitude. And an earthy scent that brings me into the moment. Everything is eating, sleeping, fucking or dying.

We come to the sleepy highway, a low-to-medium-sized vein that connects to our part. Cole gestures towards a side road that'll skirt us past a row of cottages, with long driveways that obliterate the buildings from view.

A simple Jack pine grows in the ditch. Perfect, this little one. One day, her branches will curve with music. Doing what they were meant to. With roots so fragile, they can't transplant.

God. Nature is everything.

A screwlike line forms between Cole's brows. Suddenly, I've lost a piece of the puzzle.

"Where are we?" I ask.

"We're here, fire road nine."

What is "here?" To the astronaut, the view from here is the earth. For a baby turtle, the view from here is the ocean's ledge. Here, to the scientist, is a plop of water on a slide. To a baby birthing, here is a canal pointing at a glowing slice of light.

"Come on," Cole says. As he tromps ahead, I hum the wedding march. He stops a few yards out. "You're feeling it," he says. "You never smile like that."

We circle back. A woodpecker nails a tree. Cloud shadows glide over the lake. I feel the earth turning beneath my feet. As Cole mounts the cottage steps, Winston barks.

Sitting at the picnic table on the deck, I think of sleeping with the window open and loons with a birdsong that's blue. I think of parent loons swimming in the glossy wake of a crescent moon. With their baby by their side. Learning to dive. To seek out food from seaweed's grasping fingers. They call over the lake as the shoreline shimmers.

Suddenly, emotion has grown wings and bursts from the treetops. Cole's *Cat in the Hat* smile curls to his temples. He says something, and I explode in laughter again. "Let's get some food into you," he says. "How 'bout Maui ribs?"

What is this thing, "mealtime?" A punishment, surely. I don't know what the question is, but it has something to do with a white flag planted on scorched earth.

He fetches a log. "It's too warm for that," I say.

"I'd like a fire tonight," he says with a love-you, love-me-back tone.

He smashes newspaper into balls and throws them in the fireplace. He covers the balls with wood. A match is struck.

He sits in a chair by the window. His head is a pumpkin. He seems a relaxed and cheerful pumpkin. But, I say, the pumpkin is a front. Inside, he's a hurtling rocket. Everything outside his shell zooms by so fast, it's a blur. He can't keep up with us. When he thinks he's caught up, we go faster. We change direction.

I lean back and put my feet on the coffee table. Over Cole's shoulder, the sun rolls under the horizon. He looks at my bent knees and says, "Are you gonna pop a kid?" I realize my knees look as though I'm in stirrups. He slides off his chair and laughs like three unrelated men.

His attention switches back to television. Somehow the picture's gone and he can't breathe if something doesn't work. He walks to the mudroom and returns with a flashlight.

"Why do that now?"

"Because, Julia. I fix things."

That's rich.

He says something about cables before diving behind the television cabinet. The television screen zaps, and pixels come together into a fuzzy rerun of *The A-Team*.

He pulls himself out of the corner and swings onto his feet. The man can't stop moving. He's in the kitchen. I hear a frying pan sizzle over an element. I walk back to the deck. In the moonlight, grass blades glisten. The air is sweet, as if the trees wear crowns of fruit.

An eagle is high in her nest. She is learning, too. As the loon parents dive, she soars, for she knows they will dive deep, but baby won't. A baby bobs. When the parents surface, their baby is missing. Their spine-chilling song cries past a sleeve of cottages. I swear I hear them every night.

"Dinner's ready," Cole calls. He comes outside and says, "Whoa!" I follow his eyes. My arms are wrapped around the railing, allowing my feet to suspend in mid-air. I put my feet down and unravel myself from my perch. I'm exhausted. The intensity of what I don't feel is too much.

"When's it over?" I ask.

Cole puts a hand on my back. "Without you, my life would be a blank hole on a map."

"That's nice." I can't eat so I leave the kitchen and lay flat on the living room carpet, with my arms stretched overhead, testing gravity's pull. A salve-like feeling climbs over me. Love for the world and my enemies. All can be solved with a change of heart. What is greater than love? Who among us doesn't possess the power to push aside the clouds? What problem is too big?

I roll on my side. Beside my head is a basket of dog toys. How did they arrive without me noticing? Kitties and rabbits and trolls. But new toys have been inserted into the ripped bowels of old ones from home. White foam covers the carpet. The pug is shredding them. He's gnawing the eyes off a chicken right now. I reach, and my hand lands on a wiener dog jammed into the back of a tropical bird. It's cutely sinister. Like an ex-Soviet playground.

"Here," says Cole. He holds out his hand. I reach up, but my head barely clears the floor. I push myself up and stalk him, walking with the gait of a mature elephant. Arms swing low and long, and feet stamp the floorboards. In the kitchen, I collapse on a stool.

"You have to end it," I say.

"How about a bonfire?"

"What's with you and fire?"

He hands me a bag of ketchup chips. "Eat something."

Cole slips outside. Through the window, I see him walk to the shed. I move to the big window and watch as he soaks firewood with gas and drops in a flame.

I linger at the window with a ketchup chip in my fingers. Winston's reflection is in the glass and there's something else. Between the moonlight outside, and the lamp's glow within, I see fissures in the window. No. A web. A hairy-legged spider the size of a cashew is between the double panes.

"What are you doing?" says Cole.

"Inside." I point with the chip. "The spider is *inside the glass*."

He looks. "Let's get you some air."

He wraps me in layers, and we go down to the lake. He helps me into an Adirondack chair set back from the fire.

"And peace onto you, my friend," I say.

Dear world. If I could put everyone I've known in a theatre and show them my life as a play, show them the "everything" of it and the why, they'd understand.

Sparks send ashes into the night air. I track the passage of two caught in a sudden breeze. The ashes rise and wobble, swirl and couple on their way down in ever-slackening spirals, like mating dragonflies.

Chapter Seven

Devin

With Kasim, without Kasim, in Nairobi something always happens next. I'm in the Toi Market, this time carrying the delivery on my back. I'm conscious of its bulk as I pass idling vendors to the mouth of west Kibera.

It's Saturday. The Kenyan flag flies red, black and green. Entertainment radiates. The mood is joy. Soccer reports blast on every radio as women shop and chat in queues that wind past barred shop windows. There's a row of dwellings with darkened entranceways. Behind one door, I hear a crowd cheering. Inside is a large room with rows of church pews and a sign that reads "twenty shillings." Dozens of young, male soccer fans are glued to a big screen TV. A team scores, and the room overflows with cheers, laughs and high-fives.

Back outside, a cluster of boys asks me how I am. I say to the children, "*Habari yako?*" One child takes my hand and tries to pull off my ring. I snap my hand closed, and his fingers retract. He laughs. I open my hand again. The sneak is sliding the ring slowly down my finger. I snap my hand closed, and he laughs again. Suddenly, he holds his arms up, showing that he'd like to be picked up. His mother doesn't seem to mind, so I lift him. His little sandals clamp onto my sides. He is what kids are supposed to be—fearless.

A store with soda and candies is a few steps away. I tell the vendor the boy around my neck can pick anything he wants. She translates this into Swahili, and the boy's eyes become sparklers. Chocolate bars. Potato chips. He points to the small fridge on the side. The woman brings out a plastic cup with a lid. The bottom is yogurt. The top is cornflakes. I put him down, and he dips in his plastic spoon and runs back to his mother.

I miss Kasim and Little Man.

After our visit to the park, I went to Kasim's house. The inside door opened, and there stood a man. From the shadows, he addressed me by my name. It was Kasim's father. He opened the screen door, but remained inside.

"I'd like to see Kasim."

"Mmm," he said, like a robot scanning for human form.

I heard a squeal. Little shoes on flooring. I tried to see over the old man's shoulder. Little Man was home. A chase was going on.

"Could I please talk to him?" Kasim's dad watched my mouth move. "I'm not a chameleon, like he said."

I searched for Kasim's judgment of character in his father's face—a generosity required for humanity. What I got was a shell. Something in his expression told me what I already feared.

"I will tell him you visited," Kasim's dad said and closed the door.

After that, I was depressed. I left Paul clumsy messages saying I needed time. He didn't call back for a month. Yesterday, I told his answering machine I was ready to work. He called back sounding like his brutal self and roped me into this delivery. Then he hinted we'd get together afterwards.

Twenty-two degrees in the city, but Kibera boils like only something sealed off can. I stop near the public washroom, a stone tower. My watch says it's been half an hour. Nearby is a wood crate of a pharmacy, with a sign advertising a plant that will cure illnesses, everything from cancer to erectile dysfunction.

A man wearing a white shirt cuts toward me. A cigarette droops from his mouth. He lights it midstride. In the gap between his vest and pants, I see the handgrip of a pistol.

When our eyes connect, there's that recognition between people who have to meet. I'm tired of these guys. No matter what his greying hair and gentlemanly looks, I know he's going to give me a rough time. He'll make jokes at my expense. Share a laugh with a minion. But Paul tells me that he needs what I've got.

The ash on his cigarette turns red. "I'm guessing you're with me," I say.

"You're not Paul."

"I'm not Ringo either." I shoulder off the bag and stick my hand out. "Devo." He exhales smoke and stoops to lift the bag.

"Where is Paul?"

"Wish I could tell you."

His brows, barbecue bristles sewn in skin, catch the sun. "You wish?" A sparkle of amusement flares. "We have a discrepancy to discuss."

"If you're expecting Paul, how did you know me?"

He smiles. "He told me about you." He blows smoke over my head. "Proceed."

Above our heads, brittle cracks of daylight illuminate the narrow passages between squat hovels. It's the man behind me people see, and my feet fall beside the water trench with a little more room. Sideways, I get a look at another store sign. It reads, "Chill and stay a life tailoring."

We're walking faster than usual. The slum grows quieter. Gone are the playoff hoots of soccer fans and the bartering of market vendors. Impossible as it seems, the dwellings get shabbier. Bars jut out of frayed roofs and a smaller dwelling up a ways wears a tire on its roof.

Greying One leads me onto an even tighter path between huts where there's room for one at a time.

We reach another road. I sidestep a half-ton truck and dodge a boy carrying empty plastic cartons on a bike. Rudolf High School. We might be heading east. Greying One rolls up his sleeves, and we walk toward a path hooded with sheets. When we resurface, I track back in my mind the journey between where we are and where we started. I've lost the thread. Greying One steps beside me and says, "You look like you have seen Saint Teresa of Ávila. Saint Teresa spoke comforting words. Allayed many worries for Catholics. She also gave the most detailed description of hell. 'The entrance seemed to be by a long narrow pass, like a furnace, very low, dark, and close. The ground seemed to be saturated with water, mere mud, exceedingly foul, sending forth pestilential odours. At the end was a hollow place in the wall, like a closet, and in that I saw myself confined.'"

The landscape has opened up ahead. Scattered shacks spaced far apart dot the scene like upended coffins.

"Are those outhouses?"

Greying One smiles, and I get it. We're at the end of the world, where people live in dwellings with space enough to hang a goat.

"Here," Greying One says, suggesting we've arrived. It's a piecrust of mud. Then, in come the minions. Two guys. Mid-twenties. One is short and hoists a long, bulky bag. He wears a corporate t-shirt that reads, "upload your image here." His mouth is open, as if locked on gape. The second is tall, and walks with one arm swinging pendulum-style, while his other arm hangs in a sling made of a woman's scarf tied around his neck.

The one with the swinging arm walks up to Greying One. "We haven't been paid."

"Not sure what to tell you," I say. "I'm just the delivery guy." The men look at one another. "I mind my own business." Johnny Pendulum seems unimpressed.

"So you have no money with you?" Johnny Lockjaw says.

"I understand Paul not being here is a problem," I say. I gesture at the bag I've put on the ground. "I wasn't given money. Not for whatever you've got here."

The men bowl over in hysterics. Except Greying One. Leaders prefer to study.

"Whatever we've got here?" Johnny Lockjaw says, mimicking my accent. "You've come with no clue what you trade?"

"Paul's the brains."

A shoulder bumps into mine. I think, Another hit and the world turns. Let the intimidation commence. "Paul is your friend, yah?" Johnny Pendulum says. "Well, your friend is trading up." Johnny Lockjaw doesn't join his chuckling. He's got his eye on something else.

"Do you want to see it?" Johnny Lockjaw asks.

"Have a look," says Johnny Pendulum.

There's a sudden urgency to definitely not open the bag. I've spent over a year diligently not opening the bag, of not messing around in the trunk, and convincing myself that what was in the trunk was helping people. That knowing for sure wouldn't change things. Now, I'm all dread—primitive, gazelles-sprinting-into-the-hills, dread.

Johnny Lockjaw unzips the bag. The contents are wrapped in tarp. He unravels it. Once around. Twice. "Hold it." Johnny Lockjaw shoves it against my chest so hard my fingers spring open.

It's cool. Oily. What a real mistake feels like.

"The M-16," says Greying One. "American steel, alloy and plastic. Feel its weight." My biceps flex as my hands dip and rise. "Look at the grip." I tilt my head down, but all I see are orphans. "Look down the chamber." I look over the machine to find the viewfinder. Greying One jams it up close to my face. I look down the barrel. "Headshot out 300 metres," he says. "Imagine the sound bullets make as they fragment on impact." He makes a popping sound with his lips. "There are many objects a person can use to defend themselves. The filleting knife. The baseball bat. Police badge. But," his hands glide over it like a dishrag, "this darling is made for one reason only."

"Devo, my man," Johnny Lockjaw says. "This weapon is first-rate." He takes the gun and holds it out. Greying One flips it. "Like new." He puts it back in my hands. "But this be not what I asked for."

Greying One pulls me close. "What he say, Devo, is where is my Russian?"

"Your..."

"AK-47."

I must look lost.

"Not everyone agrees with my friend here." He points at Johnny Lockjaw. "He thinks the M-16 is best. Sight radius, more rounds, has the protective shell for when things get hot. But look." He turns the rifle upside down. "The magazine feed, there? Weak. The ammo does not go in evenly. Tell me, what good is a rifle if it won't load?"

"So we're okay here or what?" I ask.

The guys laugh.

"I do not think so." Greying One leans in. "Though the gun, she be nice," he says, "without the proper item we cannot complete the transaction."

"Gentlemen," I say. "I'm sorry. This hasn't happened before. I don't have an explanation. So I'm gonna go back to Paul and tell him there's a screw up. I'm sure he'll get right back to you." Greying One smirks at the others. "I have the truck. Which I'll leave in your good hands 'til we straighten this out."

Greying One grips my shoulder, and we begin walking again. "We cannot let you go, just like that," he says softly. "We are beginning to think you and Paul are cheating us." His head lists back when a military helicopter flies overhead.

"Trust me," I say. "Let me fix it. Who am I gonna go to? The police?"

"See?" Greying One says. "The problem in Kenya. No one trusts the police."

Johnny Pendulum takes my arm. Flanked, I'm led down an uneven path. Fear fills my legs with lead. Lost footings, shouts and screams. I fall and Johnny Pendulum goes down on his bandaged arm and yelps on impact. Johnny Lockjaw pulls at my t-shirt. I let my body go dead-heavy. Greying One has me by the belt. I'm airlifted until my feet find ground. I'm hurried toward one of the stand-alone shacks. When we halt, Johnny Lockjaw sucker-punches me and tosses me in.

Stifling air. In the feeble light, I see a single nail that holds a dust-coated shirt. The axis of somebody's world. The door swings shut. One of them is tearing something. They've got my arms behind my back. They're manacling my wrists.

"Paul's coming," I say. "Right? Call Paul. Then this'll be over." I see Paul as I once did. Knights, squires, steeds.

Johnny Lockjaw's eyes are orbs of mirth. He steps toward me as a child does toward a new toy. He wrenches my arms behind my back and pulls up. I imagine muscles tearing. Unable to stuff the pain inside, I cry out.

"Here," Johnny Pendulum says. He signs to Johnny Lockjaw that he should get me on my feet. Johnny Lockjaw clamps his fingers under my pits and lifts. I'm hovering. He lowers me onto my knees. Johnny Pendulum undoes my belt and slides it out. Johnny Lockjaw holds the belt up and yanks it hard on both ends.

They scrounge through the confined space, even feeling along the walls. Johnny Lockjaw has found a rusted nail. Johnny Pendulum, on the other hand, has been out and back and carries a medium-sized rock. As Johnny Lockjaw spreads the belt on the ground, Johnny Pendulum raises the rock. The nail goes over the belt, and the rock comes down.

Chink. Chink.

Chink. Chink.

Johnny Pendulum winds the belt around my neck, grabs the protruding end, tightens it around my throat and pushes the belt's prong through the new hole. The long end of the belt is my leash. Johnny Lockjaw pulls, and my head comes up. They cheer. I'm coughing as they drag me to the door.

Outside, a hand takes my chin. Greying One looks down. He unfastens the belt. The Johnnies protest, but eventually fall silent. He offers me the belt. It hangs in his palm like a wilted stem. I take it and slide it back through the loops.

His calmness is terrifying.

"Go," he says, like a lone shot in the sky. Around us, the wide open sleeps under a skullcap moon. "Now be the moment. *Bonne chance.*"

Steel sheet roofs twinkle in the *film noir* light. A tiny beam of a flashlight zigzags the earth. I consider running. Maybe the curve of my back indicates intent. Greying One's got his hands on me. He has jawbreaker knuckles. I cower in anticipation of a blow. He's pushing me back into the shack as the Johnnies "whoot." Then they dogpile me. I'm half-nelsoned, unable to suck in a folded laundry bag's worth of air. Tears sting my cheeks, but this might be a good way to die. Slowly going numb. After leading a life where little was lived.

Johnny Pendulum. I see him most clearly. His withered arm is held back and away from the pain. I feel for his withered arm. It stands for every time I tried to reach for something.

Bored, they get off. My ears tune in to the noises outside. There's nothing, not even the overpass. Which is worse? To die alone, or to die with people near?

The door is unhinged. It bangs for about half an hour.

Some part of me floats. My mind surveys the beaten wreck of my body and checks its functions. Throat is dry. Chest, tight, but breathing. Shoulders ache, but can move in their sockets. Dying to pee.

I am alone. The shack is dark and the minutes lie down back to back. What other punishments await? My mind clings to Paul and the hope that there's a code of loyalty between murderers. 'Til then, there's nothing to do but remember.

The moon is a yellow coin split by slats of wood, lighting up a path with all the people I know on it. I see Mom, as she might've been when she was acting, because then we might've seen eye to eye. I see Dad in his den, looking over the street like someone plotting an escape. I stand in his door. Tell him not to bother turning around. That I'm sorry. That the only thing we really fought about was his opinion of me, which is why I've been unmaking everything he ever tried to sell me.

And worst of all. Lily.

I go back to the night of the party, to when those guys hand her that drink. I kick the shit out of everyone there. Things break because I'm just throwing punches and spin kicking, Bruce Lee-style. Lily stands there confused and I hand her a yellow coin of regret, and it's reflection gleams off the shattered surfaces. I tell her, No one here loves you. That's okay. Because we could be friends again like we used to. She doesn't say anything, but a hand reaches for mine. She lets me lead her out.

That's the image I could wink out on. But Lily's not mine to keep. So I put her back with the rest of them, in a past lit by starlight, and send them mental messages that they are loved.

Padded footsteps. The door opens. There's a stranger in here. A bent shadow puppet. I hear a match being struck and see the flame bobbing in a hand with weathered fingers. I'm looking into the face of an ancient woman. She speaks Swahili in a hushed way, as if soothing a missing child. She lights a candle and reaches for something in a dark corner, a crate she must have brought herself. She brings out a small bowl and a bottle of water. She dips a rag into the bowl and squeezes it over my face. She rubs it around, and when the rag dips back in the bowl, it leaves a black slick.

I hadn't noticed I was caked in mud. I don't remember how it got there. What I remember is the feel of the gun. Solid and electric.

Outside, the wind comes up. The candle's flame strengthens as she dabs down the sides of my nose. I raise my chin so she can clean my neck. The old woman hums. It's not the '70s classics Mom used to play, but I can see her. Rinsing dishes in the sink while gazing out at her garden.

The old woman inspects her work. Our eyes meet, and I want to hold her there to say that I'm human. That I'm decent, and I don't belong in whatever mess this is.

She rotates my face one way, then the other, and then wiggles her rag in my ears. These gentle movements keep me from hysterics. I search the folds in her skin for a clue to my future. But she has no answers for me. She's too peaceful. All I see in her eyes is my own reflection.

She moves around the hut in a space-hobbled position, using her arms and legs to crab her way around. She lights a cauldron of coals. Flames crawl until it's a cooktop. She dollops oil from a plastic jug into a pot, then drops meat in. Another pot for corn flour. With water added, she taps it over the coals. The liquid hisses, and slowly cornmeal becomes bread-like. My hunger jumps. She plunges three fingers into the cornmeal and offers it to my lips.

I've seen Kenyans eat with their fingers. I suck the paste without contact. More cornmeal falls than what goes in my mouth. So I take the next lump with the tang of her fingers. She introduces tiny cuts of meat and blots my mouth after I swallow.

There's a noise outside. Greying One bows in. His eyes slowly track from the woman to me, then he finds a bare patch of dirt and kneels. Three humans made small. Our knees are touching.

What does it mean that he isn't looking at me?

Greying One is angry. He wraps my ankles in tape. In response, the old woman spits. Her voice is surprising. It's big as air strikes. As they argue, Greying One looks wounded. He talks in weak barks and sullenly scrapes his bowl.

Johnny Pendulum holds the door and levers himself in. He has space to stand against the wall. He whispers to Greying One and is hushed by the woman. She takes the M-16 and sits with it to provide more room. I hope she's defending my life. I've triggered this issue before. What to do about Devin? Keep him, or...?

Memory traces back over the many deliveries I've made. It flips through all that I'd read and learned from Kasim about Kenya. Good people, a proud nation, weakened by violence, corruption and greed. Then I imagine selling guns to fatherless boys.

The men glance at me.

"I need to lie down," I say. The woman crawls over with a knife. My tied arms wag, and my back aches. The woman pauses, then with a rough sawing motion, sets my arms free. She leads my head safely to the earth. I roll on my back and let the cool ground heal the pins and needles shooting up my arms.

Then, as gentle as you please, the old woman is moving. There's something slithery about it. I open my eyes. She has a sack. It's cut into a kind of hood. Her eyes are business. "No," I say. She cradles my head and slips it over. Little fibres get into my nose but I don't fight. Maybe, on some level, my body has agreed to this. Then I think, With hands untied, I could yank it off. But living means focusing on what's practical. I've got to keep my head.

Focus.

Breathe.

Listen to the sound of my breath.

I've been asleep. Don't know if it's been a few seconds or days. Tiny spikes of light pierce the sack and turn into pink, yellow and orange balls. It's morning, I think. The sounds of people. Plucky greetings. A drunk screams into the void. The earth is warm under my back. There's something over my chest.

I don't trust my ears. They're filled with the sound of my heart. Turn my head. They'll do something if they think I'm awake. Nothing stirs.

My hands are still free. I slither one hand up over my chest, slowly, like it might be an accident of sleeping.

Silence.

I lift the hood. Everyone is gone. I've been covered with the crusty shirt that hung on the nail. My feet are yellowish white around the tape. I push myself up. Outside, wheels turn in the muck. There's a faint chop of wood.

The next phase would be just this. Let me think I can escape. Meanwhile, they're out there with their M-16. When I run, they'll track me in their crosshairs.

Through a space between boards, I see in the distance, a wide-hipped woman carries a tub of soapy water. Boys and girls run past her.

I could go for it. Problem is, my feet are shackled. I walk the dirt floor with my hands, inching my lower body along like a mermaid's tail, toward where the woman's cooking pit used to be. I see a water bottle. The empty shell cracks in my hand. I find the paring knife and, with elbow grease apply it to the tape until the rust-stained edge breaks through. Can I allow myself to believe the woman left the knife to help me? I put it back and consider what of mine I could leave for her. I press my handprint in the dirt.

On maps, Kibera is darkness. Storm clouds shadowing a lake. Now, it's yards of earth, stretching into miles. The scene appears to be clear. Just dirt and grass and tombs floating in the mist. I spring to my feet and knock my head on a wooden beam.

I suck the pain in. The future is past this moment. Take the fear. Run.

My knees could crumble under my weight. Drawing on core fuel, they keep pedalling. I try to watch for Greying One and the Johnnies, but I can't see everywhere in full gallop. I see only the ground as it humps and sags. After a wild sprint, I take a sharp turn and stop behind a shack.

While pissing, I consider the half-a-soccer-field distance I have to cross. I zip up and book it. Yet, there's this thought about hopelessness. Eyes will get me. Tens of thousands of eyes. Greying One and his minions will get word. The M-16 will cut me in half.

I'm keeping arms tight to my body. A quarterback drilling the yards. Rows between the homes will provide privacy. I bound in and catch my breath. People go about their routines. Paths are perfectly crammed. I feel submerged. I skirt the opposite row of hovels. A child about five years old jogs after me. He's calling to his friends who chirp from all corners.

The bypass is still far; yet it's right there. I sprint to a cluster of short palm trees, and my feet stagger to a stop beside the wall of a butcher shop, where someone has spray-painted, "Crickets are the new kale." Along the road, a boy rides a bike, standing as he pedals. On the back of the bike are several sacks tied down with rope. I remember what Paul said—many vendors come from Kibera. The men are gonna expect me to take the shortest distance out. That's too predictable. This kid may lead me out a different way.

I follow from a distance, staying close to walls, the few trees around, barrels and posts. The boy gets off the bike and walks it through a trail of water. He struggles as the weight causes it to swerve. Slowly, he progresses. Slow is better.

A shout rises up. It's the bluster of cocky young men. In the small crowd, I see a familiar head of hair and a hand dipping into a shirt pocket. Paul. It's about time.

I could laugh; the relief is that enormous. I'll tell Paul what they did, and he'll end them. That's how the world works. Punishment fits the crime.

He doesn't hide that he's holding cash. I want to yell out, "I'm right here!" Something tells me to stay invisible. Paul pats Johnny Lockjaw on the arm. Does he have to be so civil? Did you ask about me? Your buddy Devo is missing. Where's the off-the-rails panic? Their meeting ends. Paul isn't following them back to my cell. He's vanished down a different path, in the opposite direction.

The boy with the bike is far away now, visible only because of his cargo. I can follow him as planned. I know where he'll end up. Or, I can follow Paul. Paul it is. He's walking fast. In the distance, police sirens whine. Paul speeds up. I check the bypass for signs of an accident, but traffic is normal. Paul breaks into a sprint and vanishes into the mouth of the Toi Market. I bolt with knees bending against the tide. By the time I reach the strip mall, uniforms have swarmed him.

Lights circle from four police cars. People watch as they cuff the white guy. Even though I hate him, I feel empty watching them put him into the back seat of the cruiser. He was a stranger. Then a friend. Now he might be the enemy. And then, I see that click-on smile. I see him for who he is. He's not even bothering to look for a friend.

Lily

I met the girls at the Golden Nugget. It was the new haunt for hockey players. Even more appealing to the masses, a girl's recent stag party had gotten out of hand there. Mindy had heard different versions of the story, but in all of them the soon-to-be bride stumbled out minus pants. Once that was known, everyone wanted to go. I'd been waiting in line, expecting the girls for twenty-five minutes, with nothing to do but inhale cologne wafting off some Saudi guys. Finally, when I was four people from the front of the line, Jade's Daddy's Audi swooped in and dropped Mindy and Bianca at the curb.

The line lengthened behind us. Huddles of men brought up the rear. Cars honked at girls in heels shifting foot to foot. We paid and drifted inside.

Bar tops, cocktail tables, stage area, dance floor, pinwheeling red lights. A funhouse for cowboys, jocks and pretty little things. Ground zero for gonorrhea.

I offered to buy the first round before Jade got back. As the bartender filled glasses and foam spilled down the sides, my reflection haunted the glass behind liquor bottles. "Random Bar

Girl" is what it said. I wore the same uniform, even though I'd never been a joiner. But my reflection didn't lie.

I could hunt men, but I'd lost taste for the grift. Then I realized I wasn't ecstatic to be *anywhere*. I'd felt distancing within myself. I blame it on Ezra's painting. I blamed *Her* for losing form, though I couldn't articulate why. The mirror behind the liquor confirmed. I'd gone gaunt.

I'd also become irritable. By irritable, I mean a thinly-blanketed terror. Mom used the term "rageaholic." I told her I couldn't help it because I'd become impatient with stupid. I didn't mean Mom was stupid, but the force with which I delivered the line made it impossible to retract. So in the next breath I blurted "Sorry" in the same way someone would say, "Screw you." It was as though I'd inherited a late-onset disability, one where I had to point at fools.

The bartender popped a bottle of champagne. There was a giddy cheer. How fun it used to be, I thought. Bursts of confetti. Electronic bracelets. The soft-focus eroticism of low lighting. That night it was irritating. I needed real conversation. So I leaned to the bartender and said, "Could overpopulation of a species ever land them on the endangered list? I know it's counterintuitive. But think about it. So many of the same means no adaptation. No adaptation means death. Know what I mean?" The bartender squinted his eyes as though he'd heard me through a translator.

Jade joined us, and we found a table at the edge of the dance floor. I didn't care about the band and planned to ignore the dishevelled masses. I wanted to talk with these girls.

"Let's play a game," I said. Mindy's eyes lit up. "Picture yourself at your ugliest. Hard night. Haggard morning. No makeup. Who's happy to see you?"

Mindy laughed richly and said, "Probably no one."

Bianca said, "Why would I let them in the room? Oh-my-gah-DUH."

Jade snapped her colourless eyelashes and said, "Why's everything about looks with you?" I asked her to explain herself. "You're so wrapped up in your appearance, it's sad." Mindy said

Jade didn't mean anything by it. That observation only heartened Jade. "Instead of testing everyone, maybe you should have a good look at *yourself*."

Mindy and Bianca said Jade needed a drink and dragged her off. "No worries," I called. "It only hurts when I laugh."

I thought of Ezra. We'd been texting for months, ever since the *Her* reveal. I'd been hoping to reconnect, but Ezra had, since meeting me, caught fire. Paintings were spewing onto canvas, he said. I commented on being his muse, a word that kept me energized. He texted me that I was, "in many ways what nature and society had already imagined," which sounded like a compliment of the highest order. The disturbing part came later, when after days of zero contact, Ezra wrote, "Showing it to some interested parties."

By the time I read through the trail of Ezra and Me dialogue again, a crowd thirsty for cover tunes had gathered. Mindy, Bianca and Jade were on their way back. A roving spotlight hit Jade's face. She'd been chastened into submission, which was a rare opportunity.

"Jade," I said. Her glance was hostile. "Did you want to sit here? It's a better view." Mindy seemed as though she could've applauded me to the skies. "Seems like you need me to do something nice for you."

Even Jade couldn't concoct a reason not to accept my offer. We traded places. Once settled, the band's singer spoke to the audience. He referred to the previous New Democratic Party government with an insult. The drummer hit the snare. A cheer rose up from the masses. Already, I could hear AC/DC, the Stones and Van Halen. And so it began with Van Halen's "Jump." A line of straw-sipping fems bobbed like it was the first time they'd heard it. The music was absurdly loud. My manhunting diva appeared to be permanently vanished.

I became restless. Haunted by the image of *Her*, hoping to feel less broken, I tried a new topic. "Say you find a dish at a rummage sale," I said. Their eyes bounced between my lips and bodies on the dance floor. "On the way home, as it rolls and rubs around in your back seat, a genie pops out. But instead of granting three wishes, it says with an echoing voice, 'The years to come are a waste of time.' What do you do?"

Mindy said, "Uh-huh."

Jade pretended not to hear me.

Bianca said, "So weird."

The singer, drunk presumably from trance-inducing power chords, straggled across the stage. I was entranced too. By panic. When cymbals crashed, I jumped.

I tried to trace the panic's source. All I could feel was Devin.

I threw my focus to Jade who yawned so wide that if I leaned that way I might've kissed her. Then there was Mindy. I wondered what it must be like for her, being cozy and warm in her thoughts, even out here, in the world of women and men.

The audience whooped as the guitarist whipped his thinning hair. Three guys wedged between our table and the dance floor, and it crossed my mind to entice the old Lily back. But there wasn't enough alcohol anywhere to get the old Lily back. Old Lily receded someplace where she spoke a language without words.

The three guys turned on us. Jade crossed her arms, and Mindy wore a look of invitation. One of the guys asked if we'd seen this band before, how much the girl in charge of the Smirnoff line was charging, if we wanted anything. As he spoke, his eyes bounced between us four, yet always slithered back to Mindy, confirming one of my time-tested theories—the alpha male, primed by ego, needs conquest. Having an idea of what he likes, he sees the woman who meets his preferences, he gazes into her eyes, capturing the female gaze in return. In that space, he plants a flag. It reads, "mine."

Mindy, confident in the alpha's gaze, opened like lilies after the rain. She showed leg. Was funnier. Her face, simply put, was apple pie. The leftover people, assuming we weren't picked up, would get repositioned as baggage to be dispensed with or otherwise stowed by the end of the night.

A stubbier version of the alpha, wearing a t-shirt he was too chest-hairy to pull off, moved in. He engaged, in an obvious bid for heterosexual optics, in a fit of wrestlemania-style play slapping with the third guy.

Spilled beer in my lap was the climax of quaint coercions. I swore, as Mindy lurched with a tiny, beer-branded napkin. Sasquatch apologized as if it was funny. As if he was the best I could do. After all, I'd been picked over by the alpha.

"Can you please fuck off?" I said.

"Whoa," the alpha-Mindy worshipper said. "We've got a live one."

"It's called tough love," I said.

"Ewww," the Missing Link said. "Are you gonna teach us a lesson?"

I ignored their innuendo, lifted my drink to my chin and said, "There's not enough time in the world to teach people like you a lesson."

Mindy gasped. Jade wore a grin the size of Québec.

That's when the third guy in the group stepped forward. His big beak gave him a hatchet face. "I wonder how tough our baby would be," he said, "if she were sitting in Syria right now."

"Heeheehee-yah," the alpha said, with special menace. "Or Saudi Arabia."

The Gorilla said, "Afghanistan!"

If I'd turned around, I would've seen oversized, threatening grins cast in the smothering role of bro humour. I let off a mirthless laugh, and the guys took their time shoving off, muttering "don't need this shit" and "slut."

"What's your problem?" Mindy said. Her apple pie face had gone tart. "Look," she pointed from her lap, "they're telling people." A vortex formed around Sasquatch and friends. Drunks eager for a joke closed in. A finger came out, and faces turned. "Tough love," she said. "Who..." she stammered, "Who's tough loving at the bar?"

The singer wound down the set. Indistinguishable, vile hollering echoed.

Thinking it over at top speed, I leaned in. The girls watched me as though I was a werewolf under a solstice moon. "Ever get in the line they make us wait in," I said, "and wish you said to the ones pushing from behind, 'Don't bother holding my place. I'm getting a life.'"

Bianca, through a pinched lens of insight, said, "What?"

Jade held her jaw in a way that spoke to respect.

Mindy shook her head.

It was time to leave. There was no turning back.

Dimly lit strangers were swamp reeds in the spaces where a mere hour ago I'd coasted through. My field of vision had narrowed as if I saw with antennae eyes. People snaked arms around friends' shoulders, hissed into ears. I shouldered through the crowd, gaining ground in fits and starts. Screaming, "Excuse me!" A woman snarled with a witchy voice.

Sasquatch and friends were tipping back shooters. When I barrelled through, they bayed from the bar and I remembered why I hate attacks of emotion. They lead to distortion, which turns red flecks into explosions. I felt a closing in behind me—a teaming up and a division of duties. In movies, people see a monster and have to kill it. Assemble. Gather your guns. Once that notion hit, full-blown fantasy began. I felt the masses unite and coil like razor wire.

The front door, framed by the bright lights outside, cast the bouncer as a bulky, dark silhouette. He saw me coming and caught me in a bear hug. I heard a cheer. He held me so close I could taste his sweat.

God. If there ever was a time I needed some luck. A fire, for instance, just to be safe. I pushed back on the thug's chest, legs kicking.

"You don't know what I'm capable of," I said. "Lemme down."

He let go, having, apparently, overestimated the fun.

I sprinted out and snapped a heel on uneven cement.

Limping, I crossed Portage Avenue aware that I wasn't in the Exchange District anymore, where people stream in and out of bars and restaurants at that time of night. In the downtown core, sounds aren't of music and laughter. It's wind and shadows. And me. Seeing with new distinction, the dark.

I spotted a bench and called a cab. Then, I thought, What kind of art collector buys a broken life? I summoned Ezra's *Her*. She was me, after all—everyday, with a face less certain.

I played a game to pass the time. To see how long I could hold my breath. My first attempt was eighteen seconds. Next, I held it for twenty-five. When I exhaled, air gushed out of my lungs, and my abdomen seemed to split. I dragged in another ton of air. Again, I held my breath and thought of *Her*. I told myself I was blowing up those honeycombs. Holding in air for the both of us. At thirty-two seconds, a cab pulled over.

The driver was a middle-aged woman with frizzy hair. I gave my home address. She U-turned, and headlights illuminated my face.

As Portage Avenue rolled into the Wolseley neighbourhood, I had that feeling I'd had in the bar, of wishing to get caught up with the wind. The shame I'd carried, how I kept paying for my mistakes, and I thought, What's my future? Love or punishment?

"What's the problem with authenticity?" I asked the driver.

Furrowed brows traversed the length of the rear-view mirror. "What mean you by that?" Her voice was deep and salty. I imagined her owning a lizard called Vlad.

"You know the expression, 'being yourself'?" Her head tilted back so she could see me through her bifocals. "The 'real' you. What's the problem with being yourself?"

She scoffed in such robust fashion I expected spit. "What is this, *being yourself*? Who should any of us be? You, Barbie. I, Rockefeller."

My driver's window was open. Street lamps took turns spotlighting the coarse fabric in her sweater. It was just after eleven, and though the thought of home appealed, fears revolving around *Her* wouldn't subside.

The driver turned down Academy. "Another two or so miles," I said. We coasted through the neighbourhood. Elms slumped on boulevards. Their leafy branches, thick and twisted, shielded dark and sober homes. My house was dark too, except in the living room. Big and timidly inviting.

The driver pulled to the curb and fiddled with the meter. "Eighteen," she said. She pulled out a cigarette and, when it tipped from her lips, she brought close a flame. She was about to light it when she said, "Sometime tonight."

"I changed my mind," I said. I was rife with fearful excitement. "I want to go somewhere else." She gazed at my house, as though someone should come and answer for my foolishness.

She lit the cigarette and exhaled out her open window, blowing long, luxurious clouds. Each time she inhaled, soft crackles ignited as the cigarette shrivelled. To my surprise, it only took her a few huffs to finish it.

"You pay for this much?" She pointed to the meter. "Then, we go." I paid. "Good," she said. "Now I kill you in peace. Joke!" We pulled away. "Ask me this, Miss Philosopher," she said. "Love, when do you have it?"

"You mean, how do you know if someone loves you?"

"No!" she said. "When do you know if you have it?"

"I dunno."

"Come on, you. You with the big questions. You have an opinion!"

"I guess, you know. When you're bored with yourself."

She was silent for the length of a bridge and a red light. As the meter clicked eleven dollars, she said, "I don't understand."

"When you're bored with yourself, you might as well be bored with someone else."

She cackled. "You," she said. Her hard red lips drawn into an upswept arc. "I like you."

Main Street to Bannatyne. Yawning brick buildings of decades past, each reminding me of art, toxins and severed nerves.

"This is me," I said. The corner of Bannatyne and Princess was ahead. People crossed between entertainments.

The driver parked. I paid up, and she went to hand some change back.

"Keep it, for your tip," I said. I put my feet on pavement and remembered my broken heel. When the driver saw my foot, her smile dried up. I stripped off my shoes and dropped them into her passenger seat.

"Throw them away for me." I turned my back to her cab, and she pulled away.

As I moved toward Ezra's building, an old Aboriginal woman approached. She held out her hand as though she wanted money. "Sorry," I lied. She peered at me. Anyone could see I had money. She said, "Your eyes are sad."

She had a soft-spoken, priestly presence. I stammered until I found what to say. "What else do you see?" Her eyes shut and her chest rose like the ocean. "You are a trickster," she said. "Half-human, half-spirit. Who is your one beyond?" she asked.

"Does that mean who died? My Gramps. Other than him, no one since I was a kid." I caught the reverberation in my voice. The old woman smiled at it.

"Connection," she said. "Talk to her." She began walking away.

"Her?" I cried out. "Don't you wanna know what I'm about to do?" She flapped an arm, as in "Enough, move along," and evaporated like exhaust.

The staircase was concrete, cold and dirty. I breathed easier when the motion light came on. Life was all around me. Live guitar music, loud discussions. And walls without windows to see in.

Near the fourth floor, my foot landed on what felt like glass. I sat midstairs, peeling off a plastic shard. Noise came from Ezra's studio. I inched up with my bum, one step at a time, until the noise became voices. I squirrelled up against the wall, listening.

"How did this happen," Ezra asked, "that you popped into my life? You never seemed to pay attention before."

"Your leaving," a woman said.

My mind flipped through months of texts. No mention of him going anywhere.

"You know *Madison*," another female voice said. "She's too busy with her art magazine to notice artists." I heard what sounded like a kiss. "Alright," the same voice said. "Get a room. I have somewhere to be."

"You could throw your support behind it," Ezra said. "Put it on your website or a write-up in your magazine."

"She's a lot," Madison said.

"I haven't named a price."

"She's a lot to take in."

I whispered to myself, "A lot to take in?"

"There's so much going on."

There was a pause. Ezra said, "She's a lot to meet."

"She's *real*?" Madison said, as if it were unthinkable.

"If you took a girl and dragged her through the worst of what society offers, and her natural developments succumbed in order for more tragic means to survive, what do you have? I consider this my best work."

I almost laughed. *His* best work.

I heard heels on hardwood, pausing, and stepping slowly again.

"I'm trying to imagine buyers," Madison said. "It's not a corporate asset."

"An individual?"

"I hate to say it."

"Hurry and get it over with then."

"Her premise," Madison said, "is lucid. But I think it's a clumsy way of making a point. The colours that dominate… It's actually pulsating. She's trying to be deep. But she's a caricature. I say cut your losses. Paint something else on top."

"Caricature?" Of all I could be angry about—Ezra's leaving, his thing with this woman. She didn't know what I'd been through. She didn't understand how shame shapes a life.

Suddenly, the sounds of goodbye. I slithered down the flight of stairs. Outside, I ran off-kilter, past glossy event posters, down a quarter block. I stopped at a back alley, stepped around the corner into its shadows and then peeked back. I wanted to see who rejected the most genuine part of me.

Finally, a woman, thirtyish, the kind of woman who sleeps between scented sheets emerged. She glanced at her watch. A cab drove up, and she got in. She could have been anyone.

Ever since I'd seen *Her*, I'd had a terrible, wonderful feeling that I'd forgotten something monumental, only to rediscover it just before its collapse. Like I'd owned a century-old, 2,000 square-foot house, but due to neglect, it had become dilapidated. Picture it. Driving up to this mansion, seeing it from afar, you'd wonder what everyone wondered. "Who owns that?" Closer up, you remember that it's *yours*. You enter and you see that everything is crowded in the middle of every room, as if it was abandoned. All you know is it can't be dismissed, because with immense work it could be great.

Someone walked into my alley from the other end. I swivelled towards the dark. Adrenalin lit a prairie fire in my veins. I could've killed a grizzly bear bare-handed. Yet, I sensed kinship with this stranger.

I said into the mouth of the alley, "It's not that I deserved to be raped. It's that I was undeserving of love."

People walking out of a café stopped. I spot-checked myself and found trails of dirt. I padded across the street, where a cab had just dropped people outside a house. Once in the cab, I sat cross-legged so I could tuck my hurt foot under my thigh.

The journey home revealed a new anxiety. Seeing my house ahead made the feeling swell. I sped into the basement, threw my dress on the floor and let a steaming shower pelt my skin until it was tight. I broached the stairs to my bedroom. Mom had left on the little lamp by the bed. I sat at my vanity and said, "What if the monster is you?"

I summoned "Her." But she didn't come. So I had to move into *Her*.

Eyeshadows, blushes, glosses and creams, my vanity was a treasure trove for birds of paradise. I tapped out some Hawaiian Romance eyeshadow, and Teak His Interest bronzer, and mixed them into burnt orange. With a sponge, I applied it to the right side of my forehead. It went on in partial squares. I scrounged for green shadow, found a brownish shade in an Exotic Nights palette and ground the green in. I used the edge of my sponge to define veinlike lines spreading out towards my hairline.

I found mascara and dug the wand into the ink, scraping the side for larger globs. It became the base of my new colour. I added petroleum jelly to it. It came out cloud-black. With my finger, I dotted it in the wells under both eyes and swiped back and forth, blending it into dark pools. It gave my eyes a bulging, animal-eyed appearance.

I was beginning to look organic.

"This is me," I whispered.

A click blurted from the parents' bedroom. I turned off my lamp. Slippers paused outside my door. I froze. I knew there was no universal explanation for the thing I was creating. I was unbecoming what I was, but had not yet become someone else.

I hurried with the last bits of cheek, left forehead and lips. I needed my greenish-brown. I went back to the eyeshadow palettes and blushes and found that if you add any rainbow of colour together with a cream, eventually you get mud. I piled it on my skin by the layer.

The mascara-Vaseline had gelled into a type of shell. The skin beneath pulled. Barely existent lines, underneath, and at the corners of my eyes, deepened. In less than thirty minutes. It was terrifyingly simple.

Her.

Only one task remained. Ask *Her*, did she speak to loss or reclamation? She had to be tested. I snapped a selfie, and with tainted fingers attached it to my Instagram feed and tapped "Post."

Chapter Eight

JULIA

"By that I mean he couldn't face it."

"Here Lies Bill Geoffrey Rush," reads the tombstone. I touch the note in my pocket and sigh one of my audible sighs, the kind referring to unpleasant tasks ahead. It would help if other people were here. I could kill for a grandma right now or another mother-daughter set. Someone to take the burden off.

Lily scans the cemetery with its slopes and valleys, the walkways and dogwood bushes.

"I miss Gramps too," she says.

Clouds hang flat with edges busted at the fringes. There's a snake of air swelling, sending strands of hair into Lily's face to be drawn back behind an ear.

"I brought you here for a reason," I say. My voice seems to fly away on a string.

"I know," she says. She wipes her nose. "To pay my respects."

"Do you miss him a lot?"

"Yeah," she says.

I sigh another of my sighs. One about secrets that root in the forest floor and swell into tangled underbrush.

*

The morning after the post, I went to Lily's bedroom door, inwardly rehearsing what to say. I knocked. Waited. My mind raced with what she might've been expecting. Perhaps she saw a lecture coming and had chosen to hide. "I can shut up and listen," I said.

I listened for a hand on the doorknob. What I heard instead was plastic things colliding and something that sounded like pellets dropping. Finally, a click. Almost imperceptively, the door opened, like a slit in plastic. I oozed into the room, careful not to upset anything.

Lily was in bed with her knees drawn up. Her hair hung down her chest. She was far away in thought, adrift on dark seas. I wanted to lie in bed with her, but the intensity on her face kept me back. Her pain was insistent enough. I chose not to provoke it.

On the vanity was a picture of her taken at the Red River Exhibition. It was a close-up of one side of her face, eye and cheek, which I'd taken during a ride on the Tidal Wave, a pretend boat that rocks ever higher, until you scream because you're not sure you can hold on. Lines around her eye show she's laughing. There's a tress of hair sailing away. Her eye is skyward, determined to see things through.

The sun was big and pushy. I traced its shaft to the wastebasket. In it, powder, rouge and cream containers. The surface of her desk had been wiped clean. I peeked under her bed. I saw something and snuck a hand under to retrieve it. One of Devin's records, of course. I crouched to see what else lurked there and saw an old book. I turned it over. Kafka's *Metamorphosis*.

I surveyed her closet and a heap of clothes and heard the pug panting at the door. He came sniffing upward toward the bed. Usually, he'd vault on her and paw the covers, hoping to snuggle. This time, he hesitated. I whispered, "Come on." I patted the carpet. He scratched an ear with a hind leg and waddled out.

I sat on the foot of the bed. "I saw your post," I said. She didn't respond. "May I see your face?"

Her skin appeared sand-scrubbed. It must've taken some elbow grease getting the layers of makeup off. I searched the bathroom for ointment, and when I returned, I dabbed pinky fingerfuls of salve on her cheeks. She quivered. I stroked her hair and thought she was going to cry, but her mouth was a seam of rocks.

"I got killed," she said.

"Okay."

"I got killed and could only come back while a guy was inside me."

"I see."

"I thought I was in control. I thought pretending would rework the world so I'd be in charge."

"You're the kind of person who should be in charge," I said.

She glared at me with a crooked eye. "Don't compliment me," she said. "I won't believe you."

The photo she'd posted flashed through my mind.

"The picture scared us," I said.

"It's me when the lights are on."

"That picture is all of us," I said. "It's Dad thinking of where things went wrong. It's me when I think *I've* somehow done this to you."

Here, I thought. The road from hell. Even if all we can see is what's right in front of us, eventually, we'll make it all the way out.

Later that day, I gave Cole the gist of Lily's story.

"You ever notice that one thing can change everything?" he asked. "Lily used to be our little girl. Now we're living with a stranger."

"Maybe strangers are what we need."

"What are you suggesting?"

"You're gonna be my wingman."

I invited Cole onto the patio, where we spoke about a multipronged effort. Therapy. Positivity. I told him what I thought being a good wingman entailed. Instead of talking to Lily about *Her* or how she felt about herself, Cole would become the one with a smoothie ready when she came home. He'd know where the cookies were in the freezer. He'd rap on her door before going to bed and tell her his worst puns. He'd have travel stories he'd read on the internet about gazelles fending off hyenas.

When I finished, Cole sat for a long while.

"I'm ready," he said.

Lily finished her third year of university. It was a feat of immeasurable courage. Cole threw a beach party. He laid parchment paper over the picnic table, an old fishing net over that, and

Dollarama seashells around the edges to the hold the works down. When he looked up and saw me watching, he pulled up his golf shirt to show his pecs. Then, he found a bucket of sand we used to coat ice patches in winter. He put out the bucket and stabbed a few of my toothpick umbrellas in it. By the time five o'clock came, our patio looked like it'd been dipped in glue and dragged through a Hawaiian souvenir shop.

When Lily arrived, we yelled "Surprise!" She looked around and asked, "Where's Mom's grass skirt?"

I think what got to Lily was Cole's smile, which said hope you like it. Hope you don't mind. Hope it isn't pushy. Or dopey. Hope it helps.

We spent the evening listening to seventies classics and sipping carbonated fruit juice. Cole told stories about growing up; how the kids on his block played games of hide-and-seek.

"Once," Cole said, "this kid Garvie hid in a garbage can. The owner came out. A mid-thirties guy with no time. When he ran after us, Garvie became the Roadrunner. After dinner, we met up at Kenny's because he was the only kid with Super Nintendo. We didn't know the irate owner recognized Kenny and talked to his dad. So there we were, spread around the television with our consoles, and Kenny's dad came in with a broom. Kenny's dad said, 'Time to clean the deck.' When that broom swung, we scattered. Kenny got a blow on the shoulder, but we managed to peel upstairs. It was every man for himself."

"Gramps would've loved that guy," Lily said.

Cole's chin rose. "I wonder sometimes," he said, "if we're not all children inadvertently fulfilling our worst fears."

The story stayed with me. I was convinced Bill was still hurting us as long as Lily didn't know the truth. "She has to know why Devin left," I said to Cole later that night. He looked terrified. "Think it through," I said. "What if Devin comes home? Do you want it to come out like that?"

"I'll be a babbling mess."

"She seems a bit better," I said. "Once in a blue moon, we get a smile."

Cole sat at the desk and wrote for half an hour. I wondered if Lily would understand how a letter meant well. If I put myself in her place, I'd think it rung cheap. When I suggested taking her to Bill's grave, he asked, "Is that wise? It's twice as upsetting."

"Or maybe it's perfect."

★

Over the graveyard, clouds of feathered umbra are unbroken by blue. Lily takes the crook of my arm. Seeing her by Bill's graveside, she's eerily mature. "There's something I have to tell you," I say. "It's about Devin." She half recoils. I pull out the note. "Dad wrote this for you. It was important to him that he write something. He thought if he was here, he'd go off course."

She tosses her hair back and jams her hands deep in her pockets. I unfold the paper. The top waves in the breeze.

"Dear Lily."

"Why's he got to be so correct about everything?" she says, her eyes focused on the highway, where construction crews set out pylons and tape. I read:

> Dear Lily,
> All my life, I've thought I've known what's best. But we adults are not necessarily better at this than you. Life has a way of blurring the lines between right and wrong, to the point where there is no right or wrong, only action or inaction. So many times I've responded to someone with a differing point of view, saying, "If only it was that easy." Now it's I who has stumbled into a hard line of thinking.
> Hopefully, your father hasn't seen the truth too late. The mistake I made was an omission of truth about why Devin left. I let you think he left as he always did. I let you believe it was his choice, because he was a rebel kid. In truth, your grandfather, worried about Devin's

future, drove him to the airport and gave him a ticket to far away.

You might be thinking Devin didn't have to leave. Only he knows why he got on that plane. In case you're wondering why Devin hasn't come home, it's because we've had little contact. Your mom called everyone to find Devin. We've received a single postcard from Nairobi, sent, we think, to say he's alive. There's no way to locate him or send a message. If you're wondering if we've been worried, look at your mom.

All this is to say, I'm still a man, unfinished. I'm sorry that it's so. Humans are born into an organism we call family. Parents worry and, in my case, end up trying to control the story. That's not an excuse. The organism is us, we're in it too, and as parents we're supposed to know what to do with it.

Dad

Lily snapped the letter away and reread it from the middle. "It says Gramps sent Devin away."

"I'm guilty too," I said. "Maybe that's the point of the letter. When Gramps was over and Dad said Devin was gone, I didn't say anything. I knew his leaving hurt you."

"I lost my place in the world."

A wrinkle has taken root, where her lips turn down.

"Then that is our saddest regret."

She folded Cole's letter and then knelt at the tombstone. A twig had fallen over the print. She brushed it away, and I crouched beside her. The stone had no letters, other than Bill's name. In the right-hand corner, there was the embossed outline of a lily. In the left corner, a musical note. Lily stroked the Braille-like stone.

"Did Dad do that?"

"Maybe."

"Did Gramps *ever* like Devin?"

"I'll never forget," I said. "He once said of Devin, in that voice of his, *'He seems to get everything I'm saying.'*"

Lily snorts.

"He'd sit him on his lap like a ventriloquist's puppet and get Devin talking. He knew Devin had brains. I think for him that was the hardest part."

"It wasn't Dee's fault," she says, "about the party."

"I know."

"I created a world around him," she said. "When I was small, I'd wait in his closet sometimes, until he put on his earphones. He'd lie down all the time, and I'd sneak up and put my stuffed animals around him. I'd put Barbie and Ken dolls on the shelves over his head and make up stories about why everyone was on this distant planet. Once, I hid *after* the set up. Can you guess his reaction?" I shook my head. "He looked at the stuff with this cheesy grin. Pulled out a garbage bag and swept all of it in, and then put it inside my bedroom door. Never said anything about it at dinner or anything."

"You understood him best."

Lily hugged me. The woman in the funeral home looked on with a phone to her ear.

"His fucking records," she said.

"Yeah."

"Such an asshole," she said.

"Which one?"

When the embrace ended, she rooted around in her pocket and brought out a ragged Troll Doll. It had surprised eyes and a tuft of yellow hair shooting off its head. She lay it at the end of Bill's name. An exclamation point, rigid with perpetual astonishment.

Devin

It's a queasy Sunday morning. Candy wrappers stick to cement. Signs of a street party are familiar on River Road, the location of my former home and Paul's hotel. After he was hauled to prison, my suite was robbed. Clothes, records and strobe lights were thrown on the bed. The new paint job I gave the place was stained with coffee and something fusty and green. Keepsakes from the markets were smashed, and a stash of shillings, thousands, was missing. But not all of it was. I'd wrapped big notes inside shampoo and conditioner caps. Put more inside rolls of toilet paper, inside drilled bars of soup, inside the lids of ball caps, even under the labels of soft drinks. As for the larger stack behind the ventilation grate, it was there. I didn't stick around to count it, but safe to say there were tens of thousands. I took the money and vanished out the back.

I've been in a basement suite on Munyu Road ever since. With nothing to do, nothing to look forward to, I stayed in bed for nearly a week and, while the TV was on, I don't think I watched it. I kept thinking about the life I would've had if I'd met Kasim, not Paul. I saw myself being the best man at Kasim's wedding, falling in love with Elizabeth and playing with Little Man. Pseudomemories of all that never was.

Regret divided night from day, and Gramps kept time with me like an apparition. With wetted lips, he recounted my failures, my atrocities, emphasizing my pride and naïveté. Not only him. Mr. Canada came back, holding a paper bag. Both keep me raw-boned as I whiled away hours in a jackknifed position. I was scared too. Were the guys who gutted my suite still looking for me? But then, I was too outraged to care.

I played back the scene where Paul and I met. How I escaped the prison of home only to rebuild a new one in Nairobi. And how, without Paul, I may have found something legitimate. Paul cost me everything. Kasim. Little Man. Company now is a keyhole of light, a hole in light, which passes through closed curtains.

I wonder if Kasim's heard about Paul's capture. A newspaper article about a thirty-two-year-old arms smuggler mentioned a Paul Ferguson. I wonder if Kasim thought I was there when it happened, helping murder people in the streets. When you think so well of a person, it bottoms you to know how far, for them, your worth may have fallen.

Kasim would have to applaud the police for pinching Paul. What Kasim couldn't know is that Paul is out. I know because I almost ran into him near the train station. I was at the arrivals and departures schedule. I didn't see his face, but I heard someone shout his name. I thought, nah, but then I heard Paul's voice. I don't know why he's out. I just know what Kasim would say about corruption. That Nairobi is a mall, and if a man needs to hide, the easiest way is to spend money.

The cell Paul gave me shut down. That's when I knew that I hadn't imagined hearing Paul that day. When I got my own, I went on social media. I looked up my old friends, Mom and finally, after a particularly awful night, Lily.

Like me, she had abandoned social media after the party. Her posts were years old, except one. A close-up I might not have recognized if it hadn't been her account. Something bad has happened. That thought cranked a wild motor that I calm by reminding myself that I'll see her before too long. But first, Paul needs to know he can't hurt people and dance away.

Outside, a fog of misting rain has sent churchgoers under awnings. Though parked cars are an obstruction, I see the entrance to Paul's hotel. If he thinks I'm dead, he'll walk around in his life, psychotically unfazed, thinking how clever he was to set me up. I treat it like a job. I've been coming here every day for nearly three weeks. I sit for hours in the same corner with blinds dropped to shield my face, keeping an eye out for him. I eat budget jerk chicken from a cardboard box. The waitresses have come around to ignoring me perfectly.

My senses are awake and recording. It's as though I can detect the slightest environmental disturbance. It's this adrenalin-perception that pushes me forward. I'm waiting for the door on Paul's hotel to open with him in it.

Memories of Paul compact into chapters in a how-to-con video. Befriend the target. Save him a little. Give him options, yet make inconvenient choices sound risky. When the target picks you, massage his ego. Lead him a little. Make him feel good about himself in the way you know he needs most. Then be yourself and let him rationalize every lousy red flag. You'd be amazed how far some chumps can go on so little.

It's depressing, yet this dream of confronting him lifts me out of myself. I could plan the confrontation. But you can't script a showdown. You have to leave room for improvisation. That's what motivates me, imagining how, in that gleeful moment, I'll let emotion win.

Not that this is about revenge.

The hotel deskman smokes on the sidewalk. Backpackers duck in, and he follows them. It's enough for today. The waitress receives my tip and doesn't bother saying goodbye.

Outside, the bedlam of the city is dampened by rain. I turn onto Accra Road. At the corner, a stork feasts on roadkill. I know I'm doing it again. Choosing a direction because of the past, but I don't know how not to. Yesterday isn't over, yet every day that goes by I'm further behind.

Taxis are double-parked outside the Hilton. I forgot about the technology conference. It's cruel that on a Sunday, the city's bogged. From around the world, people pull an overpopulated, underdeveloped city closer to mayhem.

There's a white face in the mix. It can't be him, though I've been waiting. This creature is turtle backed. Paul's always got his eyes on the horizon.

Yet, my chest is a livid bruise. The air is charged, and I'm on the balls of my feet, trying to track him. I pick up the pace. There's intensity coming off me. People seem to feel me coming. Their directions veer, their feet step aside. It's my *this-is-the-moment* moment. I'm poised and ready to expose the criminal for what he is. I slide past traders hawking CDs. Glide past Sunday school children. I'm playing fast and slow, to keep pace with him, careful not to reveal myself. He's babying one leg. How easily I could pick him off.

Intersection. I hide in a crowd of men with light-coloured caps and robes. I shoulder my way to their centre. They are arguing. One is red-hot. The other is laughing. The man with a dispute steps around me and faces off with the other. I need a way to cross the street.

A crew is ready to move. Heads turn towards the onslaught of cars. One of them steps towards the median, and the rest follow. I draw behind their curtain of suitcases and skirts. I swerve around a cart of fruit.

"Mr. Land Cruiser. *Mon ami.*" A familiar face shines in amazement. The Somali vendor wags his handless arm. "Just one look." He holds out a slice of mango. He cries, "She be what you like."

The white guy glances over his shoulder. He scans faces until his eyes pin me on the spot. Paul's cheekbone is a split shell over mincemeat.

He breaks into a clumsy sprint. He seems puny. Like a field mouse. I'm the snap trap closing in. He clears the next curb, only to be slowed by a singing, bouncing throng. There's some kind of gathering taking place. He pushes through as if crossing a field of sunflowers. A hollow trail follows him, and soon, a hole forms. People bend towards it. He's tripped. "I'm alright," he says. By the time I squeeze through, he's left pedestrians standing around.

He's ahead, but I've got a lock on him a few yards back. He checks over his shoulder. I let myself gain. Soon I'm on his heels. People recoil as I grab Paul by the back and ragdoll him around the corner of a building.

He stumbles into the blind alley. When he gathers himself, I see it's one plum of an eye he's got. Green and black bruises lace flesh. Where's his seen-everything confidence now?

"Nice face," I say. "Did you get it caught in a bumper?"

A wincing smile deepens cracks around the plum. "I think the plastic surgeons did a good job." His gaze is even.

People with placards surge in the streets. Portraits of President Kenyatta with an "X" over his face bounce. A Swahili voice on a megaphone blares. The election is just days away. In the chaos, Paul steals off to the main street. I'm not ready to be dismissed. I run after him with a sense of licence that gives me strength. I close in easily. If he had a tail, I could snatch it.

"Hey," I say. My fingers claw at the back of his shirt. "What do you call a guy who leaves his friend to die?" He half-turns. Finally, the crowd is too thick. He staggers to a stop.

He tries to shrug me off, but he's in too much pain. I drag him into a blue-tinted parking lot and the woof of decaying fish. I shoulder-bulldoze him. On the backwards wobble, his shoe finds a loose brick, and he lands backwards with a whump. I kneel at his side, about to say, Are you all right? when a snicker parts his lips.

"I saw you in Kibera," I say. "You gave those freaks money."

Paul registers the comment. But his brain doesn't seem to be scraping for an excuse. He just raises his fingers to the back of his head. "What were they gonna do?" He touches the sore spot and scowls at the pain. "I was dead, wasn't I?" He tries to roll on his side. I cage his shoulder under my palm and roll him back.

"Did you think I was dead all this time?" His response is a sad clown face. I get up and hoof him in the ribs. He rocks on his side, hugging himself. I hear myself say, "Not so fun now, is it?" I wrench on his shirt, and his head lifts from the ground. The pain is getting to him, but I think he could hurt a bit more. As I consider the possibilities, his mouth pops open.

"Go home, Devin," he says.

"*You* go home."

"Good idea, that."

"Did you leave me to die?"

"I hung some shit on you. Seems they found you to be zero threat."

"A lie would have been smarter." My fist winds up for a punch, and my knuckles sheer off his chin. He kneads his jaw as I massage the tendons in my hand.

"After everything, there it is," he says. "Your spine. You come to Nairobi with barf on your chin and shit in your drawers. Rapt by the first bloke to show interest." His voice mimics mine. "'Wanna go for a drink? Hey, Paul. I don't wanna work, but I like your money.' What else was supposed to happen?"

"You used me. I was your sneeze shield."

A laugh snags in his throat. "That's pretty good." He fumbles a cigarette he's yanked from his shirt pocket. He sticks it in his mouth and feels around for a light. "Here's the thing. You became difficult, Lamb Chop. You lost me business."

I throw my lucky lighter at him. "Wouldn't want to slow down your murder racket."

Paul finds his own lighter. "While your head's up your arse? The US, Russia, China? They've dumped heaps of weapons in this region. Enough to outfit armies. Ever since the Cold War. Ammo is everywhere. You honestly think I'm the only one?"

"So hypocritical. Pretending you provide a service."

"Kenyans have no means to produce defence. The US isn't gonna police the world anymore. They're in a bind, mate. Is it so impossible to imagine the bang of a gun is someone trying to live longer?"

"You're selling rifles to gangbangers."

"That was here before I was." He stands. "You can point at me if you like, but even Winnipeg. Did you know you manufacture assault rifles?" He shines his smile at me. "Ah, no worries. You did all right by it. Can I go now, yeah?"

I push him. He stumbles into a brick wall. "Now you have Stevo," I say.

I clamp my hands around his neck. In a squeezed voice, he says, "Let go."

My periphery senses another presence. On the main street, a woman has separated herself from the pack. She sees that I have my hands on Paul's throat. My thumbs want to shut him down. The woman signals. It's a rotating motion, meaning come to her? Come around?

I wasn't always like this. When you're a kid, you never think about what people can be. How fear and self-criticism narrow your vision. The woman speaks in a beckoning voice. I think she's saying something like, "without dreams, how will we live another day?"

Paul's eyes ping-pong between the woman and me. My hands release. He's thinking he can leave. Yet, I can't let go. I can't get to the heart of what I want. What's the principle of the matter? When there's no way to say it, throw a punch. I clock him. His hands leap to his face.

The voice on the megaphone speaks rapid-fire. In our little alley, blood streams into Paul's mouth. His eyes take on a predatory look. He rallies. Rears up like a cobra. I lick my lips and let my mitts drop. A punch in the face would feel good right now. He strikes me above the liver. I double over.

A helicopter hovers overhead. Rotor wash pounds the air. I scream, "We could've been friends!" Our hair flies around. "I should've checked the trunk!"

"Would'na done no good, mate! My lorries have hidden compartments!" He hobbles away. The protest absorbs him, and I'm left with the puzzle we've trod in dirt. I tremble with justification. I charge toward the protesters. I Zamboni Paul to the ground. I could cry with delight at my physical prowess. His pants are torn and bloody at the knee. "Jesus-fucking-Christ, you're full on. Should'a listened to Mugbo. The bastard before, he became a pain. Wanna know what happened to him?" He stands and bats dust from his pants.

I don't understand myself. As I watch him lumber away, I wipe scalding tears. I'm crazy. I hate Paul. When I think of what he did, I wanna kill him. Yet, goodbye hadn't occurred to me. I could tackle Paul for the rest of my life and keep retelling our story from the beginning.

My armpits are sweat-soaked. The showdown should be done. I should let him walk away. What was I expecting? Him to disintegrate? Soon he'll edge into the crowd and get away with murder. Where is his shame?

My legs ache to chase him yet I'm stopped before the urge becomes action. The protest is an expanding rim, six and more people deep, overtaking a bunker of cars. Men yell in the direction of City Hall. One sets fire to a tire, and a cheer volleys. Black smoke chuffs, until it chokes the sun into a strawberry moon.

Across the way, a staircase leads inside a multi-floor building. There are hundreds of windows. I slither from the mob, mount the staircase two at a time, and after two flights, find a window overlooking the street. The protest is two blocks long. Some drivers, who mistakenly decided to take this route, have abandoned their vehicles.

Then, a rumbling.

A fire truck has rolled to the end of the second block. Correction. It's the water cannon. I can make out the front half of its smooth, green shell.

The ground shudders. Protesters begin receding. Water shoots from the cannon and floods the street. The deluge turns the street into a river. Protestors slide and fall. They get up and run and topple over others. Water surges into every corner of my periphery as rubber reeks from a smouldering tire. The protest has been capsized. In window reflections all around, rays leap, as though we're on the surface of the sun.

I see agonized faces. There's shouting. Police in riot gear are an advancing steel line. In their path, bodies, like fish wiggling free of an ocean net, squirm away. A block the other way, Paul jogs with his jacket over his head.

Gunshot. There's a joint scream. Two children are scooped under their arms and flee like ghosts. It's tear gas. A cop behind the moving wall carries the launcher-like assault rifle. He trains it at the mob's centre and shoots again. Despite the sound of the jostling crowd, the fading chants and the helicopter gone high, I swear I can hear the spinning rattle of an infant's toy.

Gas fizzes. There's a metallic tang on my tongue. I stretch a sleeve and hold it to my mouth. The massive truck sits at the top of the street, as though deciding what to do.

Another canister is fired. People are on hands and knees. Then, as if a movie reel slipped, the green rig rolls back. The line of police is a quarter way—helmets up, rifles down.

Want to know where nowhere is? Debris from what was, falling into the shadows of what could have been.

JULIA

The funeral bagpiped in a new era for Cole. It was little things at first. His insults lost their footing. His sarcasm lost its punch. His cross-grained disposition mellowed into a disarming stammer. Over months, he helped me with cooking, raking the garden clean, pulling dead annuals, while his vintage Mustang crusted over with dust.

The veranda screens are closed. Though it's summer, a dip in the temperature chilled the air. Birds twitter and I have a fur blanket over my legs. Cole wears a long-sleeved shirt. He's brought an Albert Camus novel with him, and he sits with his reading glasses low on his nose.

Winston scuttles into our sanctuary, panting through his upturned mouth, and heaves his absurdly dense mass into Cole's lap. "That's my boy," Cole says. He pats its back and its bulging eyes narrow. Just when I thought it was rude of Cole to love the thing in front of me, he says to the pug, "You should go see your mom. Where's your mom?" Perplexed, the pug glances back at Cole, who points at me. The pug hoists its bulk onto its matchstick legs and barks its body into convulsions. Cole shushes it.

I return to my knitting, a hobby I've taken up for distraction. I have a basic knowledge from my grandmother and, if I purchase chunky wool and huge needles, mistakes can be camouflaged with knots. My fingers have already become accustomed to the motion, and my eyes wander. Sure enough, Cole lifts the pug up at the front legs, so I can see the white streak running down its chest. Cole takes one of the pug's paws and points it at me. "That's my mom." The dog's head gazes up and then back to lick Cole's lips. Cole points the paw at me again. "I love my mom," he says. I feel a tinge of remorse for not participating in the bizarre game. I wave. The thing barely registers the motion. Cole carries on. Pointing Winston's paw, swirling it. "I've got the best mom in the world."

The sharpness of Cole's U-turn seems like the most unlikely event. I've taken Cole's hook many times and found it baited. I was front row to the increments of marital collapse and am suspicious of sudden shifts.

I've fallen to studying his every word. Analyzing for signs of progress, as if I have binoculars and can zoom in from a distant outpost. Now he's the quiet one. There's a "sorry" in every word he says. I sense a lightness. I just think better of him and wonder, is Cole open to conceding his part in what happened?

That question evokes a revelation, like a searing light has been shone in my face. What I've really wanted all this time was confession. I needed somewhere to park blame.

Living with Mr. High Intellect hasn't been easy. Over the years, banter locked me into a strenuous position, always filtering for contradictions and irony. Being wrong in this house, even about the most inconsequential thing, meant being shunted to the periphery.

It often made me wonder why Cole wanted to marry at all. Of course, that question was never better articulated than it was through the tension with Bill. Cole should've known that being agreeable with Bill would've meant knocking myself down. He knowingly put me at the disadvantage of having to choose family over dignity. He could've said something to take the pressure off; instead, he let me live in a spot with so little territory to manoeuvre. That left me a seething mad, molten-hot version of the original.

Funny thing, wrath, when the hurt lessens and what remains. Relief can be an awkward friend, but Bill did the right thing by dying.

Cole has gotten up. A few moments later, the dog's leash jangles, and the door closes. I put the knitting down and look at the time. The takeout will arrive any minute. That's how long I have to formulate a plan to get Cole talking. Which means preparing myself to peel guardedness back. A man accused deserves an opportunity to defend himself. So I pick tonight: an unsung Wednesday in summer.

By the time they return, the food has arrived. The spittle-head charges, clawing up the hardwoods. Winston then settles into his bed with a treat, and Cole turns to me.

"What's for dinner?"

"Chinese."

Without the busyness of food preparation, the kitchen is awkward. I divvy the Chinese food on plates. Cole's talking about sauces and smells. I pour the red wine realizing red wasn't the right choice for Asian flavours. It's something Cole would normally get high-hat about. Instead, he attacks the food and talks about the irreplaceable taste of MSG.

Dinner is devoured. Cole finishes the last of his wine and carries our plates to the sink. I tell him to leave the rest and he pauses for a moment, until the silence creates a syrupy tension. Then, he takes the newspaper to the living room.

I pour another glass of wine. Tannins gather in the dustbins of my throat. When I go in the living room, Cole's behind the paper. It lowers.

"Thank you for dinner," he says.

The weirdness of having not much to say is too much. I click on the television. The weather station comes on, a series of amateur photographs sent in from viewers: sunset over a golden lake in British Columbia. Angry prairie sky darkens a lonely Saskatchewan house. In Manitoba, cars are backed up as a family of geese crosses a highway. Five minutes in, Cole gets up. Climbs the stairs. I hear the shower curtain rattle, and the bathtub faucet gush. Now is my chance. We're going to talk. Unscripted. While all but his person is submerged.

I slip into the bedroom and pull a blouse from a hanger. The blouse's sheen gives me hope. Cole bought it for me near the State Opera House in Vienna. It was unseasonably warm that April, and the city wasn't wasting it. Everyone was drinking beer from tall glasses or oozing in and out of storefronts. The boutique where we bought the blouse had glittering costume jewellery. I asked how much the blouse was in dollars. Cole laughed and passed the girl his credit card.

The faucet turns. Water shrinks to a drip. Two splashes. Cole's butt skids the bottom of the tub. Breathe, I tell myself as I push on the bathroom door.

Cole's eyes are closed, and his chest hair parts down the middle. His sun-starved legs are pink from the heat and slightly spread. Rivulets swirl between his arms and waist. I haven't seen him naked in months. His body is a monument to grief. If he loses any more weight, he'll be nothing but cock and rib.

I step to the toilet like I'm on a lunar mission. Cole opens his eyes and jumps. He grabs the rim of the tub for support. "Sorry," I say. Tub water shifts, creating hollows and dells. He has my soap in his hand. The air is steeped in jasmine and ginger root, and I have to come up with something to say.

"It's like a bomb went off in here."

He lifts a leg and bongs his heel on the far edge of the tub. His face is the picture of exhaustion. Clay sliding into rock. I'd been reliving what he'd done to me. I hadn't questioned his purchase of the pug. I assumed it was a desperate ploy to bond over. The pug and he have many routines, from walking to training to feeding. It sleeps with Cole at night, on top of the covers, tucked up against Cole's back. Winston was, is, his way of coping. Coping because I've been too self-involved to see it.

Silence strengthens as I gaze at his mound of pubic hair.

"I know you know this already," he says in a phone voice. "I really thought it would work, sending the kid up the plank." He gathers water in his hands and splashes his face. "You always talk about feelings. When we kicked him out, he *was supposed to* be angry. He *was supposed to* rise up amongst men and tell me off, beat me up, through better living."

"I know."

"Dad used to talk about the Cold War. How the Americans and Russians were in an arms race, and the Americans needed to make a show of force. They needed to make the Russians *feel* it. Cause according to Dad, that's all people respond to, really, is the feeling of a thing. So America, in the late '50s, was planning to nuke the moon."

"Now Devin's gone."

"There's something else you don't know." Our eyes lock, and I endure the outright intimacy. "When I go out, sometimes people come up to me. The parents of Devin's old friends. They ask about Devin. That's not the hard part. The hard part is what they tell me. I ran into one of his teachers, English, I think."

"Ms. Dunbar."

"She gushed over Devin's use of words. How expressive he is. The woman actually said that skill is one she admired. That our kid 'walks to the beat of a different drum,' and how she looks forward to hearing what Devin will achieve, because 'certainly, it'll be really something.' Like we had this unusually observant child. That's not all. She said Devin reminded her of Ziggy Stardust."

"Bowie?"

"She saw a movie about alienation called, *The Man Who Fell to Earth*. It hurt that she had pegged him as a musician."

Bowie's "Station to Station" worms its way into my brain. "The return of the Thin White Duke / Throwing darts in lovers' eyes." Cole rolls his head towards me. "She talked about how, in this society, in this time of polarity, we have to preserve artists. Maybe, I was too busy trying not to encourage wrong directions to pay attention. Think about it. If you *think* someone's going to do something bad, you can rationalize shutting them down forever."

I uncross my arms as Cole explores the fields of his inadequacy. "If that wasn't enough," he goes on, "his teacher talked about a poetry assignment. They had to find lyrics and talk about figures of speech." His chest balloons as he inhales. "Well, our boy, apparently bored with the idea, made an anthology with lyrics that spoke to theme. Ms. Dunbar was stumped by the *insight*. And how *unfortunate*—her emphasis—that he had to fail because it didn't fit her rubric."

Cole exudes guilt. It's as if cops have pulled up to the house, cherries flashing. I have to stop letting him off the hook, though it's a pretense of mine. It wasn't that he was wrong. It was that he was bullheadedly wrong.

"Always said Devin was sensitive," I say.

Cole blinks water from his eyelashes. "I saw you hating me, which I didn't think would last. I look at Lily, and I wonder if she'll ever come around. Then I think, okay. At least I have a job. But even that's untenable. I can't do it anymore."

"You want a divorce?"

"All my life," his voice shakes, "I've sought to be strong. But can a man be self-sustaining if he's alone?" I shift around on the toilet seat. "And right. Work," he says. "I dogged my way through job postings, wishing and waiting, suffering through the slog. I *hate* what I do. I'm middle management and pushing fifty. It's what Devin was trying to tell me. He thought he could do better, he just didn't know what to do." He's crying. "It's the cheat of youth," he says. "You want the house, the car. Life becomes a mortgage and gas receipts. I don't recognize myself."

"I thought you were happy."

He judders his butt back into sitting position. "Why?" His expression is riotously quizzical, as if he's painstakingly left no proof of happiness anywhere.

We sit in companionable silence, dwelling in our thoughts. I think about how the portrait of a family comes apart.

"I don't think you've ever talked like this," I say. "It'll be alright."

"You shouldn't cushion me," he says. "I've got to face the truth no matter how it hurts." Then he says, "In anthropology, they teach us that cultures develop with ecology. I didn't know what Devin's absence would do to the family unit. But it's like the world lost its tilt, and the seasons haven't changed." Cole laves up his chest and slops water over the suds. "I saw you," he continues, "when Dad died. I knew you were holding back." He watches to see where that pronouncement lands.

"What did I ever hold back?"

"Your victory lap." A smile flickers at the corner of his lips. His penis drifts like wreckage from a float plane. "I know people think I'm a know-it-all," he says. "But I'm not bull riding past this mess. I've decided something. Arrogance is thinking you know someone."

Downstairs, a heavy door shuts. "Hello?" Lily calls.

Cole stands in the tub, I pass him a towel and he pats himself dry. I think about crimes and punishment. So much attention spent on retribution. When the biggest cop, the one that gets to you, is in your head.

Chapter Nine

Devin

Safe to assume the old man will be there. He'll wanna see the result of his experiment. What'll I say? I can't depend on the truth. The more I explain, the more he'll twist it. I should've thought of a good one-liner, a custom zinger for his *can't-wait-to-hear-how-you-screwed-it-up* mug. The gas station coffee will kick in any second. When he lights up, I'll be scorching.

I park the rental near billets of wood. Over the lake, blue sky is coated in powder-hot haze, and the air is capable of drying up thought. Parched grass, prickly with needles fallen from firs, cracks under my shoes.

High-pitched barking comes from the cottage. A string figure stands in the window. The side door opens. Dad gestures that I should come up to the deck. So I follow him under the ferocious sun.

He opens his arms. Hugging seems artificial after everything. His fingers press into my back. "Is this really you?" he asks. He pulls back, and his fingers grip my biceps. From there, his eyes survey my torso, my legs. Maybe he's looking for clues to who I am. But what does his body tell me? Skinny. Under the afternoon sun, his features are as carved as faces on a totem pole.

The dog barks again. "Well," he says. "Let's not keep your mom waiting." When the door opens, a blond pug plows at my shins, snarling at this intruder. "My boy," Dad says. He picks up the menace and cradles it in his arms. "Isn't that right?" he says to the pug. The dog whines between growls. "This is Winston." Winston wets my wrist with his nose.

I've been ready for awkward, but the moment I expected is pushed aside by roast beef. The smell is more than gravy. It's nearly finished snowmen. Abandoned hide-and-seek games.

I edge in deeper and find Mom in the kitchen, holding a half-finished glass of wine. She dons the expression of packed ice. "You're driving now," she says.

She hugs me, and I breathe in the floral scent of her hair and remember a Hindu woman in Nairobi's Eastleigh laying down a wreath. "Are you just off the plane?" I stare at her winched smile. "You must be exhausted. Cole, help me."

Everyone tears off in opposite directions, strung out on instant-release hysteria—fetching salty snacks because they fear my electrolytes are low; stirring lemon water to aid my metabolism; hunting down Aspirin for the headache I might have. Then rummaging through clothes from my old room, trying to find a spare toothbrush. And would I like to sample the garlic-smashed potatoes?

"What about Slick?" I ask.

Mom gears down and turns toward the bookshelf. She's reaching for the cage and hoists it over to the coffee table in the living room. I'm relieved to hear Slick bolting through his mulch.

"He took a bad turn months ago," she says.

Dad holds the toothbrush out to me. "Mycoplasma pulmonis," he says. Awe hijacks his face. "Can't believe I know that."

"It means his coordination isn't so good," Mom says.

Hinges squeak as I lower my hand. Some pellets and, little by little, Slick stands in my palm. I lift him to eye level. He whiskers my chin.

"See?" I say to him. "I didn't give up on you."

"Put him on your shoulder," Mom says. "Like you used to."

I prop him up there just when laughter peals from upstairs. It's just a laugh track from the TV. Still. My heart blows open.

"Lily's here?"

Winston suddenly smells Slick and barks himself hoarse.

"Is she coming down?"

"Tell you what," Mom says. "Before she comes down... I mean, if we're going to stumble through this, let's do it with drinks." Mom goes in the kitchen and returns with her glass refilled and two more for Dad and I. I put Slick away, and we toast my return, though I've never liked wine. Mom says it's good to have me back. Dad agrees, asking how many months it's been. Then, silence swells with the strain of concentration. We're on our best behaviour and don't know what to say.

I circle the main floor. The hutch has the same dust-crusted rings under champagne flutes, yet there are two lounge areas now, each with a TV. The clock that separated kitchen from dining room is gone, but the couch has the same indent where I used to play Xbox.

With front paws on the windowsill, Winston barks at something outside. It's nothing. It's a lake so serene it's begging to be jumped into. We stay in formation anyway, under the warm downdraft of the ceiling fan.

Feet beat softly down stairs. Lily! Dad strolls over and takes her hand. "I trust you remember each other?"

Lily's fragile grin is about to break. Her body is thin, yet she looks something like herself. Her hair is as red as I remember it. But she says nothing and leaves to get herself some wine.

"The water is lower than I've ever seen it," Dad says. His eyes point at flaking, lichen-coated rocks.

"Lily's had a bit of a rough time," Mom whispers.

Lily returns and flops into a chair by the window. She sips her wine and sends me a simmering grin. "If you wanted to leave so badly, I'd have told you sex is the best way to get the hell out."

"Lily," Dad says.

I stare in silence.

"How can you even stand to *be* here?" she asks. Her voice is sulphur-tipped. "After what they *did*?"

"Gramps did," Mom says.

Lily lets off a gravedigger's laugh, and I'm back in Nairobi where everyone knows what's happening but me. "Hey," Lily whispers. "Do you even *know*?"

"Alright," Dad says. "Let's slow down."

Lily stands and targets something on the wall behind me. "Remember the bullfighter's wedding?" She totters over to inspect. Mom recedes into the kitchen.

"Just realized... there!" Lily points, just over my head. "The dark knot. See below it? The lines are waves like a lake. The knot looks like a moon suddenly exploding out of the sky."

"Mom!" Lily calls into the kitchen. "You know what Ezra would do with us?" A cupboard door shuts. "He'd sketch us on a cardboard box, shred it in a log splitter, and then string the bits against the side of an old barn. Just leave us in the wide open to figure ourselves out."

"Let's not talk of that now!" Mom calls.

"Doesn't matter," Lily says to herself as much as anyone. "It was never about him."

There's zero trace of Lily's goofy charm. Just a not-here-any-more glaze.

Dad turns on the television. He scans through the channels and settles on CNN.

"Thought for *sure* Gramps would be here," I say.

"About that," Dad sits. "Gramps had a heart attack months after you left."

"Gramps *died*?"

All eyes divert as I compute this thing. There are strict rules of privacy when there's a loss. What they don't know is what I actually feel—the warmth of summer and the soft drumbeat of ducks at the water's edge. The thought of Gramps tricking me or being dead doesn't have the claws a betrayal like that should have. I'm not torn. Not anything. The ghost I came in with has lost his reach.

Mom leans on the frame where the kitchen ends and the living room begins. I pull my lucky lighter out and toss it to Dad. A crooked smile springs forth as he rolls it over. "I told 'im you wouldn't steal it," he says. He reflects a few moments. "The lost can come back."

Winston jumps in Dad's lap and does a full-body shake. "It's probably time to tell you," Dad says to me. "That day, at the airport. Gramps gave you the flight without us knowing."

"And there was no way to reach you," Mom says.

Lily lip farts. The rip punches sideways. I can't guess why. I just know with Gramps dead and everyone else innocent as can be, there's no one to pay for what happened.

"Aren't you mad?" Lily asks. Her eyebrow's twitching.

"I thought Gramps spoke for all of you," I said. "I thought you wanted me gone." Lily's eyebrow stops. "Now here we are talking about it like its just another thing that happened. I guess things cool down after fourteen months of not hating people more."

Three pontoon boats link on the water making a mega party raft. Rowdy teens crank heavy metal rock gods of old. At the outer limit of the lake, a fishing boat putters. We hear the stove opening and utensils clanging. Mom comes into view gripping forks.

"I just want to get it set," Mom says. "Go outside. It's too nice a day to waste."

Dad leaves. Lily and I follow.

"Besides," Lily says. "It's time Dee tells his story."

We tread to the water. A squirrel hopscotches over rocks. It's a one of a kind day. Sun and blue sky forever. On the dock, captain's chairs gather. They're cushy, yet no one sits there. Dad. Lily. They act like tourists who've lost their guide.

I hadn't given thought to how I'd tell them. I just knew it'd be the double-barrelled truth. The parents can do what they want with it. Let them be alone with it and wrestle with its purpose. Then we'll see. That's the beauty of the outdoors. Exits on all sides.

"All done!" Mom slow jogs downhill, then stops and looks at us.

"Dee was just gonna tell us," Lily says.

I adopt a flat-toned, reporting style. Starting with the flight and Paul. Lily sits cross-legged, and Mom sits with her. Dad watches the fisherman who wears a utility vest so blood red that even from this distance, we can see him. His boat slowly disappears behind the peninsula.

I spare them no detail of my hotel, downtown Nairobi or Kibera. I tell them about the Land Cruiser, driving for the first time, the Somali vendor. Carnivore. Paul offering me a job, because of what he said he saw in me. I tell them about the men at the end of deliveries, and Mom turns her gaze toward the bush as if she'd rather relocate to the oblivious side of that line.

Seagulls soar and with a kind of peripheral hearing, I listen to my story too. It's not a straightforward tell. Poverty and violence have history, and I know, almost as well as Lily, that misrepresentation is snake oil. So I backtrack to what Kasim taught me. How colonialism robs a place. How corruption gets into the bones of a country. I don't know much, and context is a struggle. I'm hopping time periods. Jumping borders. Because Kenya isn't one story, Kibera isn't one story. I could be stuck in their roundabouts 'til dawn.

Glitter on the water breaks, and the screech of heavy metal has disappeared. So far, they haven't asked me a single question.

I pick up the plot near Somalia. The purple desert. Dad's hand goes to his face as I describe the Towering One. Mom shivers when I describe Mahaadi's body, the trip to Lamu. For some reason, I enjoy telling this part.

Kasim, Little Man, the *harambee*. And, yeah! How people talked about my music without ridicule. I set up my second trip to Kibera. The kid I carried around, that momentary joy. How people smile and laugh and cook and love in what seems the most impossible of places. Dad squats and picks at blades of grass, occasionally tossing them at the lake.

Carefully, I launch the description of Greying One and the Johnnies.

"Do you smell something?" Mom asks. Dad turns and his eyes explode. Our heads swivel back to the cottage. Smoke's billowing out like the tar blur of lit gasoline. Mom races uphill, crying, "My God!"

Sootlike smoke spumes inside. The parents mount the stairs. Dad yells about the fire extinguisher. From outside, we hear it spray, and Dad shouting, "Stand back!"

"Should we call the fire chief?" Lily asks.

Mom winds the windows open, coughing into her sleeve. Escaping smoke rises up the side of the cottage, where it meets the breeze, loses grit and gives way. Mom yells, "Under control!" Then coughs so hard she has to step outside. Dad fans smoke with magazines.

After an era, the smoke filters to light grey. We hike up. Mom leans over the railing.

"I charred a tea towel."

"Stovetop!" Dad shouts from inside, "Curtains! And the side of the cupboard!"

"Don't know what's got into me." She sips some more wine and Dad talks about how quickly flames overtake a house. How people die from smoke inhalation.

Foam splatter coats the countertop and stove. We step into the unfamiliar chemical smell. I get garbage bags, and Dad pushes slop in. He whispers reassurances to Mom. But its not until it's clean that Mom comes around to the idea that not all is lost. She snaps back into cooking position. Soon, vapour rises over a saucepan.

In the west, the sky is pink with an orange centre. I miss the ocean and salt on the air. Driving country roads that stretch so far, life has room to end and start again. I miss the genuineness of most of the people I met. Especially their long hellos, as if wherever they happen to be, people belong.

Mom announces dinner's ready. Lily sits beside Dad. Soon we tuck in, carnivores all.

Peering over her wine glass, far, far away, Lily spots something outside. Her face collapses. Mom asks her what it is. "Summer goes by so fast. Then, the leaves change." She's always hated the end of summer. But this time, her eyes well up. "Every years it's the same." Mom reaches for her hand. "Summer's lost to fall. And I think, if fall's a loss, how will winter ever be enough?"

Mom rubs Lily's hand as the room braces for the impact of women's tears. Then, Dad winces and rubs his calf. Mom asks if his legs are acting up.

A CNN report rattles from the TV. A reporter talks about the Kenyan election to be held tomorrow. There's shouting, shots blasting. Eyes rise to meet mine. A new report starts. The US President promises North Korea "fire and fury" over a nuclear threat.

Smoke lingers in the house, and I see that burning tire in Nairobi and the rose-coloured smog on the soft morning of my departure. I couldn't decipher Kibera's shadow from among the skyscrapers.

I think of my other family. Kasim and Little Man. Kasim's grandmother. Samirah and Mercy, the Somali vendor. The ancient woman. And the old man who hums Bach. Mahaadi even. Their images take shape. Maybe if I picture myself holding them, they'll be all right.

"You seem different," Lily says to me.

"Let's be thankful he's alive," Mom says. Now *she's* watching me. "You're familiar as my kitchen after a reno. You've lost your baby fat."

"Even his profile," Lily says, scanning the outline of my face. "Besides the five o'clock shadow, it's, I don't know..."

"Broader," Mom says.

"A different energy's coming off of you," Lily says.

Mom finds her fork and stabs her meat. "We want to hear the rest of your story," she says to me. "Just not now. Can't take any more."

Mom. She was always a mixture of love and regret, yet not enough of either.

I don't argue. The story untold is the part of me that Mom won't be able to imagine. Or maybe it'll fit her just fine. When it comes out though, I won't riffle past how I helped kill people.

I scoop mashed potatoes with my fingers. Lily says, "Ew." As I eat, Dad examines me. He's been spec'ing me from afar all night. Winston begs at his knee, but Dad's oblivious, like he's been receiving ambient messages from the future.

Mom throws down her napkin. "My mom," she says, "used to call this dessert 'sex in a pan.'" She gets it from the counter and carries it to the table. It's chocolate sludge. With heaping piles of sex on our plates, Mom spoons it into her mouth and moans as if she hasn't had dessert in a decade.

Dad stares into an abyss, and I feel oddly close to him. Society teaches us that people get what they deserve. So when someone's not turning their life around, it's tempting to tilt power in your favour. In the alley, I could've hugged Paul or killed him. Even now, I thirst for the blood spilling at his knee.

The yard has an otherworldly feel. It's glowingly alive with tiny flies buzzing in clouds. The full moon is off to the left, signalling the beginning of night. Mom's eyes find Dad with an untouched dessert and his mental springs cranked tight, and she says, "You don't like it."

"Earth to Dad," Lily says. "Earth to Major Tom."

It's like we're no more than a door jamb to his thinking.

"Is something the matter?" Mom asks.

"Yeah, Dad," Lily says.

Finally, he picks a face to talk to. Mine. "Man," he says, "is the only creature who refuses to be what he is."

Mom and Lily exchange looks.

"Wow." Lily laughs. "That's deep, Dad."

Mom's mouth curls up at the sides. "Maybe your dad's getting deep because he has a big birthday coming up." Her eyebrows hover.

Dad's dessert is carted away. Water rushes into the sink, and fresh tea towels are put in our hands. Mom says she's brought a photo album she thought I'd enjoy. She doesn't wait until my chores are done. She's in the living room crowing at old Brownie uniforms, bad haircuts, and babies' bare bums. "Cole and I," Mom says. "Skip those."

When the last dish is stacked, Lily and I are alone. "Hey," I say. "There were times I wished you were there. I uh... I met good people. Had fun too. It's great, you know, especially in the countryside. Could have been better with someone, though." Lily's face seems small. "If there was anyone who deserved to experience that, it's you." A couple of beats later. "Okay, you won't believe this. Know what I saw?"

"It's not your fault," she says, "about the party."

There's a glow in her eyes. The fire isn't out. It's just gone soft like a pearl. And, like that, I'm part of the human race again. Home.

Winston whines. Lily opens the door and stands outside, keeping an eye out as he pees, and smiling back at me every so often.

"Come and see this!" Mom calls out. The full moon's over the lake. Mom tells us to turn off all the lights so we can see it better. It's huge in the picture window. Planetary. It lights up the lake. The world is quiet, finally; only the wind whispers while winking fireflies orbit. Slithering sounds interrupt the soft murmur of insects from the surrounding bush. Silky sounds. Winston whines. Mom pops on the table lamp.

There, as if by some sleight of hand, Dad appears at the door. He has his shoes on. Has a backpack. He's sliding on his windbreaker. He bends down and scratches Winston under the chin, then pushes the door open. Lily asks where he's going, but the storm door swings closed behind him.

"Where could he be going at this hour?" Mom asks. Shrugs all around. She stands, surveys the contents of the room like she's mislaid today's date. The engine of my rental starts. Soon, we're all up. Mom rushes out. Winston leaps past her feet. Lily and I watch from the kitchen window. Dad reverses the car and stops at the foot of the property. "Where on earth are you going?" Mom shouts.

Dad's eyes roam to the window where Lily and I watch. "I'll decide at the airport."

The rental coasts over the gravel. Mom's black silhouette stalks it to the end of the driveway. She screams, "Perfect!"

High beams disappear. Winston begins to run after the car, but Mom grabs him and treks back with him kicking in her arms. I have a feeling of knowing something before I should, like when a gift is half-opened and there's a wink in the giver's eye. Dad is me. The part that's ripe for being taken apart.

"What's with Dad?" Lily asks.

"Maybe he's seen the mechanics underneath."

Mom comes in and shakes off a shiver.

"I wanna study painting," Lily says.

Mom does a double take. "Your Dad's gone God-knows where. It's no time for jokes."

"I've figured it out. I'm meant to be an artist."

"Lily, dear," Mom says. "You're smart. You could do anything. But art isn't a career. Besides, Dad's paid for four years of psychology. You're almost *done*."

"Why do people say they're listening if they don't plan to change?" Mom's face goes blank. "This is me," Lily says.

"Faces?" Mom's eyes slip to me for translation. "It's why I got with Ezra. It's why, even with therapy, nightmares don't control their laughter."

"You're serious." Mom says. "I can't believe I'm hearing this from you."

"I'm going in the wrong direction."

"See how much Devin's grown? It's not from strumming that guitar of his."

Lily looks at me. "It's probably hard, Dee," she says. "You put everything into music. It's all you guys fought about. Now I'm saying I wanna try *my* dream."

"I'm embarrassed by it," I say.

"What?"

"I wasn't very good."

Mom looks like she just won the Powerball.

"I'd hoped," she says to me, "you'd return just like this. To be the man we need around here." She takes a breath. "To think you hated me," she continues. "No contact for well over a year?" Her jaw is hard and her eyes burn. "Dad's gone. You're free to say it."

"Your lyrics were good," Lily says.

"Just admit it. It's just us."

I've hated Mom, but I won't say it to please her.

"Why," I say, "am I doing all the admitting?"

Mom's arms fling out to the side. "I *should've* been an actress! So you'd know poverty and think twice about throwing your lives away."

Suddenly, I get it. I did it. I became an adult. Worse than any hypocritical, suitcase-toting felon I was ever repulsed by, I picked a lane, locked doubt in the trunk and called it manhood.

Mom goes on about the life she would've had, the people she would have known. If there's one thing I've learned, it's that people can't learn while on defence. Time alone would help her.

"Hey," I say to Lily. "I'll pay."

"What do you mean *you'll pay*?" Mom asks. "What're you doing?"

Maybe music's it, maybe not, but right now standing up for Lily is a job I can get into. "I've got money." Mom's lips open.

"I can rent us a place and pay for your classes. Whah-do-yah-say?"

Mom's anxious eyes go raw. "No-no-no-no-no." She scream-laughs. "No way." She peers at Lily, who is quiet. "Lily?" Lily doesn't answer. "You're not gonna leave home?" She pinches fluff out from Lily's hair.

"No conditions," I say.

Lily's eyes bounce between Mom and me and then settle on Winston. "*Seems* like a decent idea," she says. Mom gasps. "We'd be on our own. It's what you wanted, right? Mom?"

"Amazing," Mom says to me. "You're back, what? Two seconds? And BAM! Like the old Devin. Poison. With no respect for what I do. You didn't mention, do you even know where you're going with your life? No. See? After everything, you have no clue."

"Luckily," I say, softly, "I'm not auditioning for you." Mom's throat clicks. I look at Lily. "Our dreams should be the least forgettable thing about us." She beams with applauding eyes. "Play to the audience who gets you."

Acknowledgments

To my husband, Grant Ganczar, for being glass-half-full from the beginning,

To our Kenyan friends, Hannah Mzee and John Njihia Chege, who took my husband and I around to the sites in Nairobi that I needed to see,

To Kenya itself for being a beautiful and inspiring place,

To the city of Winnipeg for being my home,

To writers in residence at the Millennium Library and at the University of Manitoba, who commented on pages from *Bombing the Moon*. Patricia Robertson. Christine Fellows. John K. Samson. Jennifer Still. David Bergen. Jordan Wheeler.

To my writing group. Kim McCrae. Donna Janke. Joan Marshall.

To friends and family who provided feedback, though I had nothing to offer in return. Susan Holiday, Joanne Rush, Erin Daniels, Ron Mark, Joan Birell Bertrand. Gord MacKay.

To my copy editor, Melva McLean,

To my family,

To my friends,

To the "strangers" near and far who I've met and remembered,

Thank you.